OUTFOXED

AN INSPECTOR WILLIAM FOX SERIES

PETER THOMAS PONTSA

Iconic Scribes Press Inc.

Reviews

That was an ambush. A distraction. And we fell for it! – A sizzling new series opens!

Grady Hart, Independent Book Reviewe

Thrilling, heart-pumping, and entertaining, author Peter Thomas Pontsa's "Outfoxed: An Inspector William Fox Adventure" is a must-read international mystery and suspense thriller filled with action, adventure, and romance. The twists and turns will keep the reader hanging onto the author's every word, and the author does a wonderful job of leaving just enough breadcrumbs or loose ends to allow room for more adventures for fans of the next great international action hero in the literary world. If you haven't yet, be sure to grab your copy today! Rating: 10/10

Anthony Avina is an author, a journalist, and a blogger

The premise of the story is fascinating. The age-old search for treasure is sure to catch the attention of many readers. Yet this book isn't just about seeking treasure. It's also a police procedural and political thriller. Each of these three genres can be difficult to write. The storylines must be interesting, and the characters, descriptions, and facts portrayed in the stories must be realistic. This is difficult to maintain for each of these genres separately, but combined, this becomes much more difficult. Peter Thomas Pontsa does an admirable job in this novel.

Andrea Martin

As a person of Chinese heritage, it was very exciting for me to read a book that spotlights Chinese history, an area I'm fairly familiar with. The novel's meticulous inclusion of elements from my culture resonated with my appreciation for the significance of Chinese history. Zheng He's portrayal, in particular, really stood out to me because of how his groundbreaking sea discoveries and historical importance are often sidelined in discussions due to cultural biases. Witnessing his prominence in the narrative was not only gratifying but also a poignant reminder of the importance of inclusive representation. The entire time I was reading the book (especially in the more action-dense parts), it reminded me of one of those Jackie Chan espionage action adventure Hollywood blockbusters. While Outfoxed was by no means written like a screenplay, the constant switching between third POVs from different characters and sides exudes a dynamic akin to what we often encounter in movies. It definitely created more tension, which is perfect considering the type of story Outfoxed is telling. The impression I got from reading Outfoxed was that if hypothetically it were to be adapted to a screenplay, it would definitely be easier to adapt than other books purely because of its writing style and storyline.

Anne Clarence, The Reading Life

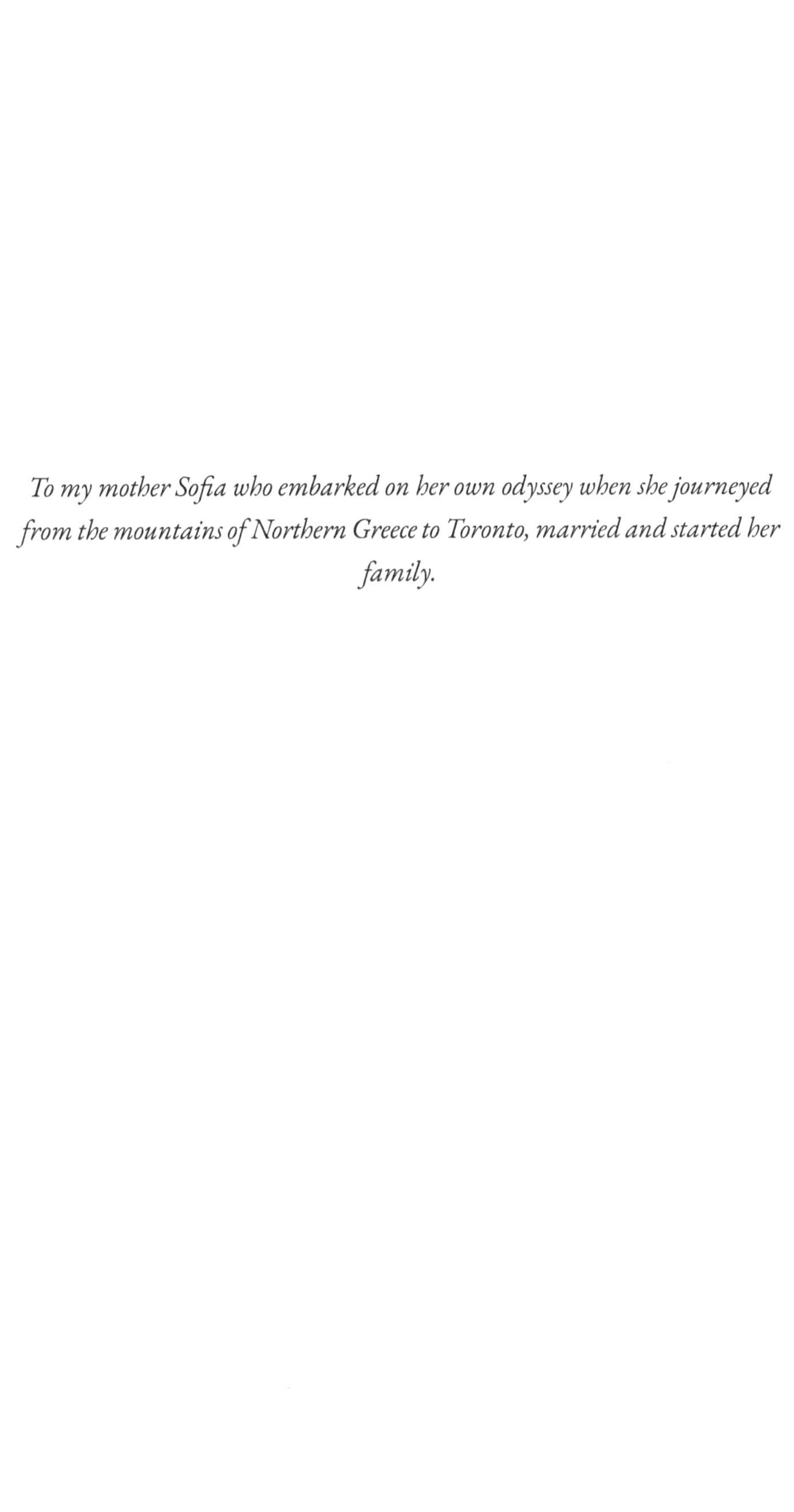

To my mother Sofia who embarked on her own odyssey when she journeyed from the mountains of Northern Greece to Toronto, married and started her family.

Greet what arrives, escort what leaves and rush in upon loss of contact.

Yip Man

Contents

One

The Midnight Fox

INSPECTOR WILLIAM FOX sauntered into René Bouchard's office with the morning paper, placing it front-page up on the well-organized desk. The headline in the *Montreal Gazette* for November 20, 2018, read: "Montreal Begins Controversial Sewage Dump into St. Lawrence."

"I believe your text message was about this," said William, as he leaned his lanky frame over the desk.

William was thirty-two years old and handsome in a rugged way with balanced features, brown hair, and eyes that unmasked an inner calm and intelligence. He stood in front of the desk, prepared for anything. William's yellow RCMP jacket fell open over his black jeans exposing his standard-issue Smith & Wesson sidearm.

"That's what I like about you, direct and to the point," said René Bouchard, the RCMP superintendent at C Division, affectionately known as the Frenchman. His forehead wrinkled as he looked up from the paper, his hazel eyes somehow showing his years of experience and wisdom.

René was fifth-generation French-Canadian and his bespoke suit mirrored his passion about law and order. He was forty-two years old. René's cheekbones were chiseled, and his lips were firm and pronounced.

"I'm concerned about the public, the environmentalists, and the media," said René. "This is exactly the type of situation that could become confrontational." He added, "We need you to partner up with Philip White and patrol the river."

"Sure, I could use a change of pace."

"We have a slight problem though," René said. "We don't have enough patrol boats available," his voice trailed off. "Would you mind using your own boat?"

"Okay, but can I count on the department to cover my expenses?"

"Of course. We really appreciate your help," said René.

"Where is Philip?"

"He should be at the marina by the time you get there."

William made his way to the RCMP carpool, commandeered a late model unmarked black SUV, and proceeded from C Division headquarters to the Port on Rue de la Commune Est. He thought René was presumptuous sending Philip to the marina before asking to borrow the boat. He parked in the lot at the Yacht Club de Montreal. His powerboat was berthed there because it had the closest waterway access from his office.

Stepping out of the SUV at the marina, the heady scent of diesel and fish greeted William. Waves caressed the boats, iridescent in the cool November sunlight. The river meandered like a pewter snake as it slithered over the rapids.

In 1535, Jacques Cartier discovered the gulf on St. Lawrence's feast day and named the river after the patron Saint. The grand river moved freely, beginning at Lake Ontario, flowing past the colonial city of Kingston, past the Gulf of St. Lawrence, then spilling into the Atlantic Ocean. The aquatic ribbon sustained the lives of migratory birds, striped bass, and endangered beluga whales.

But in the next few days, the City of Montreal would yet again violate the river by dumping billions of liters of untreated sewage. Both city and impartial experts had concluded that there was no other option than to shut down the southeast sewage system for repair. The unwarranted discharge provoked indignation from people in towns and cities downstream.

Politicians and New York advocacy group Save The River were worried about the city's decision. The media crowd already named the fiasco "Flush-Gate." Worried about possible altercations on the water, Inspector William Fox and Constable Philip White would be patrolling the river.

William searched for Philip and gazed along the walkways between masts and cabins. His eyes were drawn to the Sailors' Memorial Clock Tower that dominated the pier across the basin. The structure, a memorial to mariners who had lost their lives in WWI was a comforting sight along the waterway, still functioning as a lighthouse and a timepiece. The mechanism was a replica of London's Big Ben without the clarions' melodic chiming that make that landmark so famous. William often thought the clock tower could be Big Ben's silent little brother.

Midnight Fox, William's cigarette boat, was moored meters away. Trudging along the wharf, William wished he could be somewhere else. He found Philip sitting on the dock with his feet dangling over the edge, like some kid, daydreaming. *How did I get myself into this shit patrol?*

They nodded at each other. "Come on board and put on your life jacket," said William. "Attach the RCMP banner to the flagpole," he added.

"Done. Where are we patrolling?" asked Philip.

"We will head along the southeast sewage line, toward Jacques Cartier Bridge. Stay alert for disturbances."

William switched on the power and started the twin Mercury Racing engines. He moved the throttle forward and piloted the boat out of its slip and into the channel, not creating a wake that would disturb the shore or other moored boats. As soon as he reached the clock tower and left the basin, he accelerated to a cruising pace.

Philip turned his head toward William, looked forward, and then aft, and yelled over the rumble of the Borla exhaust note.

"On a cop's salary, how the hell can you afford this boat?"

William shouted back over the blare of the mufflers. "This boat was confiscated for drug smuggling and after the trial was put up for auction. I just managed to outbid the few people who knew about it."

"Nice going, she's a beaut!"

"Yeah, we need to get further downriver. I would like to see how the city workers are managing to control the waste in the containment booms."

The smell of raw sewage filled the moist air around them.

In the distance, a luxury cruise ship, the *Gulf Mist*, was headed upriver toward the old port, where it usually docked to offload vacationers into old Montreal. The cobblestone streets and colonial buildings were a national treasure, rife with stylish shops and trendy restaurants.

William pulled back on the throttle and turned into the center of the river to avoid getting in the ship's wake. Philip raised the binoculars to his eyes and monitored the river's edge around the southeast shore. "I see some protesters on a cabin cruiser with placards saying Down with Flush-Gate! They are near the sewage system," said Philip.

The sound of an approaching helicopter echoed through the air. Philip zoomed in. "Media," he said. "Headed for the protesters' boat."

The marine radio crackled, "This is Griswold from the US Coast Guard Auxiliary asking for immediate assistance. Over."

"This is William Fox, RCMP marine patrol. What is your location and status? Over."

"On our routine patrol we came across a dozen boats protesting the sewage dump. They are lined up and blocking the southern entrance to the international St. Lawrence Seaway, and we have a few large container ships that are being prevented from getting through. Over."

"Will respond immediately to your location, also notifying emergency response teams. Out."

William turned to Philip and said, "We've got big trouble on the other side of the waterway. Take the radio and get our response team from the marine division over to the seaway ASAP."

William depressed both throttles and braced his deck shoes into the billet footrests. He aimed the powerful cigarette boat toward the southern tip of Île Sainte-Hélène, his body moving naturally with the boat's action as it pitched and rolled under wide-open throttle. The whine of the engines was unsettling, and the propellers raised a colossal geyser that followed the boat. The boat covered the distance rapidly and redlined as it rounded the island, the container ships now in view.

The *Midnight Fox* approached the seaway locks on the south side of the river near Longueuil. William stopped in front of the line of boats spread across the seaway's opening, then picked up the bullhorn and switched it on.

"This is William Fox, RCMP. All captains and owners hear this. You are contravening maritime law by refusing free passage in an international waterway. I am politely asking you all to disband. If you resist, you will be arrested, and your boats will be confiscated. I am giving you five minutes to leave; police officers have been summoned."

Infuriated outburst resounded like a high-voltage charge.

Far from the middle of the assembled boats, William saw a figure raise a bullhorn.

"Everyone, this is Paul Henderson, chair of Save the River. It looks like we made our position clear." He looked up and pointed at the media helicopter hovering above the flotilla. "Let's go home before we get arrested."

Motors came to life and boats maneuvered, a few bouncing off each other before proceeding into the St. Lawrence River. A powerboat called Sea Grace did not move off with the other boats and bobbed gently in the water.

The radio came to life, and the US Coast Guard Auxiliary thanked the RCMP officers. William watched them wave goodbye as they took off to continue their river patrol.

"Ahoy!" yelled William. The Sea Grace was eerie and silent.

Philip turned to William his head tilted and a quizzical expression in his eyes. "Should we look?"

William was equally perplexed. Only minutes ago, the cacophony of angry voices from the protesters was overwhelming. The silence equally so. *Where is the crew? Why is the boat in the middle of the international seaway?*

William and Philip turned toward the whine of another speedboat as it pounded over the water toward them. Jarred by the waves, a man struggled to aim his machine gun accurately. Seconds later, the buzzsaw staccato caused geysers and plumes of white water to explode upward, drenching William's boat.

Successive bullets missed the *Midnight Fox* and hit *Sea Grace* around the transom, igniting the fuel tank near the engines with a boom. The cabin cruiser flew upward before being consumed in a massive fireball. The blast threw both William and Philip onto the floor of the cockpit. Debris and boat fragments rained down on them and the surrounding area.

Philip was holding his ears as he sat up.

"What the bloody hell?" said William.

"You okay?" asked Philip.

"Yes, just barely. I hope there was no one on board."

Both officers bounded back into their chairs. William depressed the throttles all the way forward to gain some distance. The twin Mercury engines bit into the river, catapulting the cigarette boat up the seaway and away from her pursuers.

"Bait," William shouted over the engines' whine. "That was an ambush. A distraction. And we fell for it."

"Who'd be gunning for us?" asked Philip.

"We put a lot of bad people away over the years," said William. "It could be anybody. But this is going to a lot of trouble."

William maneuvered the boat in a zigzag pattern to avoid incoming rounds and kept the speed at just under the redline. How long this evasive action would last was uppermost on their minds. The pursuing powerboat was making gains and was now launching rocket-propelled grenades. William felt the violent jolt beside the boat.

"Philip, get down!" he shouted as he ducked under the control panel and steered the boat blind. Another plume and concussion and then another. The pursuers were closing the gap even further.

Machine gun fire erupted again, bullets whirring over their heads and penetrating the deck, tearing fiberglass pieces off the cockpit.

"Holy shit!" shouted Philip.

William raised his head and peered over the windshield. "There's a cargo ship just turning into this stretch of the seaway canal. I'll head for it." He took a quick look over his shoulder to ascertain the situation and pushed the throttles to the end of the gate. They started making distance at once, leaving the speed boat behind. The container ship was mid-channel and heading south toward the Atlantic.

William decided to slide along the portside of the mammoth container ship, slip around its stern, and hide.

"How long is it?" said Philip.

"Long enough to maneuver around it and pull these bastards into a trap of our own." William steered the *Midnight Fox* in close to hug the side of the *Canadian Ranger*.

The captain was frustrated that pleasure boats would be racing up the seaway in what looked like an unsanctioned race. It was irresponsible, and it was creating a marine hazard. He deployed the foghorn, expressing his displeasure with the race boats. Three blasts rang out, scattering cormorants and gulls along the shore. Then he picked up his microphone and yelled into it.

"Get away from my ship!" His exasperation could be heard across the river reaching downtown Montreal.

"The captain's not happy with us," said William.

"To hell with him," said Philip.

William piloted his boat around the *Canadian Ranger's* stern and bounced across the backwash to eventually come around to the starboard side. He turned his cigarette boat around and reversed the engines, giving enough throttle to pace the large ship about midway from its churning propellers.

"Now we wait," William said as he pulled out his Smith & Wesson.

Philip followed suit, both hands aiming his gun in the direction of the stern.

"I have an idea. Philip, open the storage box and hand me the flare gun," shouted William. "They will be here soon; get ready and give me cover fire!"

Philip sprang into action, handing the flare gun to William and resumed his wide-footed stance as the boat rocked in the slipstream beside the big ship. The pursuing speedboat followed them to the rudder of the *Canadian Ranger* and cautiously rounded the stern.

Both William and Philip immediately started shooting at the speedboat, riddling the cockpit with rounds. The two men dove below the windshield for protection. William pushed the throttles forward, and the *Midnight Fox* surged ahead, easily reaching the other speed boat. Just as it came alongside, William fired the flare gun into the cockpit. The flare started burning the plastic seats and carpet, then burst into flames, engulfing both men's clothing and the entire cockpit.

The dazed and confused men stumbled over the transom and leapt into the river.

The *Canadian Ranger* was already moving away slowly toward the Atlantic. The unmanned speedboat was darting haphazardly in circles. William decided it would be too dangerous to board. The immediate priority was to save the men in the water before they drowned. The speedboat would eventually burn and blow up. The thought of explaining this calamity to his superiors was of secondary importance.

William reduced his speed, came within proximity of the sodden assassins, and tossed them a rope with a lifesaver attached to it. Philip watched over them with his Smith & Wesson, leaving the men no options but to surrender. The two Asian men were dressed in black, of medium build and could have passed for twins. William noticed matching tattoos on their forearms as he handcuffed and shoved them into the rear seats.

Two container ships were already plying their way up the seaway in single file. William maneuvered the *Midnight Fox* away from the seaway and toward the river, and set a course to the marina at medium speed. The *Midnight Fox* had been shot up significantly, but the instruments and transom were undamaged.

When William had agreed to loan the boat to the department this morning, he hadn't expected the ambush and subsequent gunfight. Let alone the sinking of two pleasure boats, interference with marine transportation, and numerous other infractions—too many to think about.

"If you guys move, you're done," said Philip.

On hearing Philip warn the prisoners, William leaned over and said, "You know Phil, looking back, there probably has not been a significant event here since 1959 when Queen Elizabeth II and Eisenhower christened the St. Lawrence Seaway as they sailed through on the *Britannia*."

"Well, I think this morning's mess is a significant event—a real political shit storm. The cameraman on the CTV News helicopter filmed everything. Including our little fiasco," replied Philip.

"You're bloody well right. I believe we upstaged Eisenhower and the queen," said William.

William's smirk lasted a few seconds. "Let's get these guys locked up."

He turned forward and resumed steering toward the marina. As they arrived mid-river, an RCMP patrol boat was coming their way

"Here comes our rescue, a bit late," said Philip.

"Whatever the outcome, we did the right thing."

"We are still alive. But facing the Frenchman won't be a picnic."

Two

The Admiral's Seven Voyages

TRACY JORDAN WALKED into the auditorium at Nanjing University, searching her surroundings for a suitable seat while surveying her classmates to get a feel for the group. A few male students were also scrutinizing her. Tracy was thirty-one and stood mid-height in comfortable flats. Back in the US, her blonde hair and steel-blue eyes were considered attractive, but not unusual. Stepping into the lecture room, the college men became infatuated with her flaxen hair and Western looks. Tracy could have been Scarlett Johansson's stunt double.

Raised in California, she earned a Ph.D. in Chinese archaeology at Stanford University. The program offered fieldwork research and an internship, so she came to China. She chose Nanjing University's School of Liberal Arts to study classic Chinese literature, classical documents and ancient Chinese history. Tracy was interested in doing secret research on the famous Admiral Zheng He, who had made seven epic voyages on behalf of the Yongle emperor during the Ming dynasty.

This morning found her in the sparsely filled lecture hall.

"Good morning," said Professor Peng Lixin. "You are perhaps our overseas student, Tracy Jordan?"

"Yes," she responded.

"Please sit down here toward the front where we can exchange dialogue much better."

"Yes, yes," she stammered as she composed herself and got her legs to move. When she sat down, he started the class and discussed ancient literature from the Ming and Qing dynasties. One of the students asked impulsively, "Professor Peng can you list a few fictional works?"

"Surely both Ming and Qing dynasties have experienced enormous triumphs in the creation of fiction. The distinguishing works are *Romance of the Three Kingdoms, Outlaws of the Marsh, Journey to the West, A Dream of the Red Mansions*, and some ghost fiction, *Strange Tales of Liao Zhai*. These novels and short stories are revered throughout the world and should be on your reading list," he said. "This is also the end of this session. See you next class."

Peng Lixin was proficient in ancient Chinese culture and had become a professor at Nanjing after his mentor passed. He approached midlife philosophically. His shiny dark hair was graying slightly at the temples, and he had learned to deal with stress through meditation and his love of Buddhism.

"Tracy, please follow me to my office as I'd like to speak with you," said Peng Lixin. Before Tracy could follow the professor, a few male students surrounded her clamoring to speak with her. Professor Peng scattered them.

***

Leaving the lecture auditorium, they settled into his organized and modest office.

"Tracy, would you like some green tea?" asked Lixin.

"Yes, I'd love some."

Lixin poured the steamy green liquid into two tall ivory teacups embossed with blue stylized orchids. Tracy raised the teacup gently to her quivering lips, hoping the hot tea would not scald her.

"Wonderful aroma," she said at last, "and greatly beneficial as well."

"This tea is prepared for me by my friend, an herbalist here at the university. Our traditional Chinese medicine program is the oldest in China," said Lixin. "This reassures me that our herbalists only use best practices to prepare this ancient recipe. If you like, I can introduce you to him."

"If it's no trouble," Tracy said.

"No trouble Tracy, none at all."

"Thank you."

"Before you go to your next class, I am curious about your enrolment in my course."

Tracy's right hand nervously brushed her blonde hair behind her ear. "You are aware of my Ph.D. and my tenure as an assistant professor at Stanford. It should come as no surprise that upon completion of this course, I will become a full-time professor."

"Yes, I have read your curriculum vitae. From your research and investigations about our history, I suspect you also have another reason for enrolling at Nanjing. You published a controversial paper on the *Seven Voyages of Admiral Zheng He in the 15th Century.* You mention in your paper the admiral may have sailed to North America. Yet you have no definitive proof," said Lixin.

Does he know what I'm looking for? Tracy wondered. She felt Professor Peng was going beyond simple conversation and was confrontational. He had just cross-examined her with the thing she wanted kept secret, especially from the Chinese government— that she and her father, Jeffrey Jordan, were convinced there were missing documents that would explain the North American connection. She needed to steer the dialogue away from this subject and get Lixin to move on. Tracy put the teacup down gently on the table and rotated the cup around to see the orchid.

"Professor, I can see that it might be obvious to someone with your educational background to ascertain that I still harbor those interests. From an early age, I was influenced by my father's opinion about Admiral Zheng He. Please forgive me if I have caused you concern because of my past articles. I am simply here to further my education. I hope that answer reassures you that I am sincere." Tracy looked down at her wristwatch and then looked back at Lixin with an encouraging smile. "Professor, I'll be late for my next class. Thanks for the tea. It was an interesting talk. Bye."

She got up and left before Lixin could react. She knew he was not finished with her on this issue and felt remorse for lying to him. Now with the professor off her mind for the moment, she prepared to initiate her master plan. Her research, with the help of her father, could now be put in place.

***

With classes over until Monday, Tracy packed her carry-on and made sure her asthma medication was in her handbag. She hailed a cab in front of her apartment and slid into the back seat. She knew that international students could not travel within China without permission and to avoid being labeled a foreign dissident or, worse, a spy, she took precautions against being followed.

"I have an ex-boyfriend who is stalking me. Can you lose him? I need to get to the Nanjing Lukou Airport," she said to the driver in Mandarin. Her emotions were on high alert since Professor Peng called her into his office to question her.

"Some guys are messed up," said the cabbie in English. "Please put on your seat belt and hold on."

Tracy felt the seat belt tighten as the car's tires squealed and the cabbie cut into traffic, sending pedestrians in all directions. "Wow! That was close!" she exclaimed.

"Maybe you should close your eyes; this could be quite dangerous," he said. "What color is your ex-boyfriend's car?"

"I'm not sure. He could be driving anything."

"Well, there is a blue Audi sedan keeping up with us. Your boyfriend is very persistent. I know a leveled parking lot that is just the place to leave him behind."

***

Tang Dao, a member of the Foo Dog Triad, could feel his muscles tensing, his heart beating faster, and the sunlight torturing his eyes. He tried relieving his tension by clutching and unclutching the steering wheel repeatedly. *How could I fall for such an amateurish trick?*

Engaging the handsfree feature on his car, he called up Ru Fa Zhong, the leader of the Foo Dog Triad.

"Do you have good news?" asked Ru.

"Yes and no," said Dao. "She must know someone is following her movements."

"How do you figure?"

"The cabbie undertook some clever driving skills in crowded streets to elude me."

Ru responded, "Brother, I will allow you only this one transgression against our honor. I will send enforcers to the train and bus stations. You head over to the airport and find out her destination. If you can't find her, wait for her to come back. We can pick her up later if we need to."

***

Tracy settled into her seat on the plane, destined for Kunyang. She was following a lead she and her father had uncovered. She recalled that during the Ming dynasty, Emperor Zhu Di sent the admiral to explore foreign lands and collect tribute from the barbarians. How far he traveled remains debatable.

When the fleet returned in 1423, a new emperor was in place, and his vision didn't include expensive expeditions. His isolation policy left the ships to rot at their moorings. Confucian scholars from the court burned the maps and logbooks of the admiral's starfleet. Although documents of the journeys were destroyed, some may have been saved. The stories survived over the centuries because crewmembers had refused to acquiesce and had related their adventures to their families. If still in existence, Zheng He's ancient records and maps might reveal if he did indeed discover the Americas.

Tracy and her father's research revealed that the admiral had four sisters, and through a genealogy search, they found a descendant in Kunyang, Zheng He's hometown. It was Tracy's only lead, and she hoped she could get information that could lead her to these lost records.

Tracy arrived at 489 Tan Street and knocked on the door, and a short elderly woman opened it. Her silver hair was in a neat bun, her dark brown eyes were slightly sunken, and her wrinkled skin showed lines of an austere existence. Her narrow mouth parted slightly as she said, "Yes?"

"Miss Kwan," Tracy said in Mandarin. "My name is Tracy Jordan, and I am studying Chinese Literature and History at Nanjing University. I've come to visit you and speak to you about your ancestor, Zheng He. Do you think you could help me?"

"I am surprised that anyone would be interested." Curiosity overcoming her cautious nature, she said, "Please come in, Miss Jordan, and call me Jiang."

"And please call me Tracy."

"Let me make us some green tea."

Jiang returned to the small living room and placed the teapot on the black lacquered table. She poured the steaming liquid into the porcelain cups glazed with motifs of flying cranes.

"I find your interest unusual for a westerner."

"I have always been fascinated by the travels of Zheng He."

Jiang was wary. "There is not much to tell, just stories..." She was reluctant to reveal too much to a stranger.

Tracy sensed Jiang's discomfort, and said, "It is important that the true story of Zheng He should be told."

"Our family has carried the burden of this secret for centuries." Jiang's eyes met Tracy's and saw sincerity.

"What can you tell me about Admiral Zheng He?"

"Only what my grandfather told me about his exploits."

"Do you by any chance have or know of any records of his voyages?"

"My yeye, grandfather, mentioned that Zheng He didn't return from his last voyage. When Zheng He's deputy envoy found out that the city officials were destroying the official records of the voyages, he hid his own diary. My grandfather said it contained firsthand accounts of travel to the Americas. The contents contained illustrations, inscriptions, and maps. Official records say the deputy envoy's name was Wang Jinghong and that the admiral died at sea. The unofficial truth is Wang Jinghong disappeared with his diary, changed his name, and moved away. Admiral Zheng He remained in the Americas."

"It's interesting that he got away with the diary. But where did he hide it?" asked Tracy.

"Previous generations have passed down a story that Zheng He's deputy envoy hid the diary in Yangzhou, where the Tomb of Puhaddin is located. Puhaddin is believed to be the sixteenth-generation descendent of Muhammad. Next to the tomb is a mosque, which houses a collection of valuable manuscripts and records of Chinese–Muslim relationships. As you probably know, Zheng He and Wang Jinghong were devout Muslims. Our family believes that the diary is hidden in these archives."

"Dear Jiang, you have been a great help."

Tracy gracefully gave a slight nod with her head and shoulders to show her respect.

"You have given me hope that Admiral Zheng He's story can be told. The world should know the truth about who arrived in the Americas first."

Three

That Was Dicey

AFTER ARRIVING BACK at the Blue Gulf Marina, William and Philip escorted the two Asian prisoners to C Division for interrogation.

Sitting in the car, Philip said, "That was rather dicey out there on the river."

"It was. But I recognize these guys from an earlier case," replied William.

"Just who are they, and why were they trying to kill us?"

"Not you. They were after me. I figured out who they are."

"What gives?"

"It's a bit of a story," said William. "It started six years ago when a ten-story office building collapsed in on itself, killing multiple residents."

"That's tough."

"Entire families were devastated."

"Should never have happened."

"The investigators felt that way too. It goes further than poor building upkeep," said William. "The rebar was fabricated from cheap Chinese steel."

He stopped the SUV for a red light. "The cement was analyzed and was found to be inferior. The chemical matrix showed that the standards of practice were not met."

The light turned green, and William eased into downtown traffic.

"The Montreal police located Wu Sunfay, who owned Sunfay Engineering and Construction. The Anti-Corruption Squad ultimately raided his home and offices. These searches were related to the awarding of municipal contracts. Sunfay's company did the work on the Place Ville-Leveque."

Philip turned around to check on the suspects. Both men looked crestfallen and defeated.

William continued, "After some preliminary inquiries, C Division found out some of the engineers were adept at manipulating construction contracts. They did it to inflate the final price tag awarded to companies that had given them kickbacks. Construction engineers hid the phony expenses behind legitimate but unexpected costs riddled throughout the projects."

"It's obvious there was collusion between the planners and the engineers," said Philip.

"At the time, the LaFond Commission was the task force exposing corruption in the construction industry in Quebec. So, they subpoenaed all the financial accounts from Sunfay Engineering and Construction," said William. "The task force turned them over to us at C Division. My assignment was to find hidden money and payoffs."

"I heard about it at the time. René told me you received an MBA at McGill, picked up a diploma in forensic accounting, and that the RCMP recruited you to help root out money laundering and insider trading," replied Philip.

A young girl ran across the front of the SUV. William jumped on the brakes.

"Lucky kid," said Philip.

"Somehow Sunfay got wind of my involvement in the investigation, and before I could get started, two gangsters forced their way into my house around three in the morning. They had me at gunpoint and took me back to C Division to retrieve the case files. No files, no evidence, no jail time."

"What did you do?" asked Philip.

"I waited until we were beside the file boxes. One of them told me to pick up a box and carry it out. I threw it at him, knocking the gun aside. The distraction allowed me to overpower and arrest them."

William spared Philip the details but saw it play out in his mind as if it was yesterday.

He had delivered a roundhouse kick to the closest man and hit him solidly in the kidney. He half-turned and back-fisted the other gangster in the temple; he dropped like a bag of cement. William immediately turned back to the other man, double punched him in the stomach, and put all his weight into a palm thrust to the chin. He went down as well.

"Are these the two guys?" said Philip.

"Yeah, they're the same guys."

William turned the black SUV into the underground garage and parked. They escorted the prisoners to the detention center.

"So, this Wu Sunfay is the guy who wants to knock you off?" asked Philip.

"Yes, it's him. We had enough evidence to convict him for tax, fraud, bid rigging, and manslaughter. He is serving hard time at Archambault Institution."

***

René Bouchard came around to the detention area, carrying a cup of coffee.

"You two have had an interesting day. Are you all right?"

"We're fine," William replied. "These are Wu Sunfay's guys."

"Let's get to the bottom of this," said René.

"It was an attempted hit. Sunfay wants payback because I put him away."

"Probably, but we need solid answers."

"I'm worried about my family. Sunfay could get to my father to punish me. Can we get the local police up to his chalet to keep an eye on him?" asked William.

René pointed at Philip. "Get on the phone and get a car out to the house right away."

Philip nodded.

"I'll take excellent care of these two assholes," said René. "You go be with your father."

"Thanks René." William paused. "The *Midnight Fox* got shot up. She's at the marina. They'll be sending you the bill."

René rolled his eyes. "Of course, they will." He called an officer over to help move both prisoners into the holding cells. As he shoved the last one in, he said, "Enjoy your stay, *connards stupides.*"

William took the elevator to the underground parking, saying nothing to the other officers. He was thinking of stopping Sunfay before he tried again. William felt that familiar satisfaction of formulating a plan.

Downstairs, William sauntered to his Triumph Rocket 3 TFC motorcycle, put on his helmet, and engaged the starter. He felt that reassuring vibration throughout the bike as the exhaust note revved up. He eased into first gear, let out the clutch, and rumbled out of the underground and onto the street. Within twenty minutes, he was out of Montreal and on Highway 117, headed for the Laurentian Highlands.

William was born north of Ville-de-Sainte-Agathe-des-Monts, where his father had a chalet on Lac des Sables. In an hour, he would be there, probably just in time for dinner.

He passed a group of overweight middle-aged bikers all driving Harleys, trying to recapture their youth. They gave him the thumbs-up gesture all bikers give each other, verification they were all from the same fraternity.

William thumbed back at them, cranked open the throttle and sped by them with the wind in his face, appreciating he was following his own path.

***

René pulled out the crime sheets on the two suspects, using their fingerprint data. Both had a long history of criminal activity in China and Canada. They called their lawyers, but the courts denied the pair bail as they were being charged with the attempted murder of two police officers. The way the whole thing was stacking up, it looked like these two Triad gangsters were going to be guests of the Canadian government for a long time.

Four

The Foo Dog Triad

THE FOYER WAS OVERFLOWING with people who burst into unanimous applause as Minister of Culture Chu Bojing cut the red ribbon and opened a new public library in the Beijing suburb of Tongzhou.

Bojing smiled at the response. He was a noted poet, teacher, and national hero even though his mentor had been exiled for criticizing the communist party.

He walked up to the podium to give the opening address. His physique was slender, and he used the comb over technique to hide his bald spot. His thoughtful eyes peered at the crowd, his nose was small and flat, while his face was rounded with high cheekbones.

The minister shuffled his notes and focused on the crowd with benevolence, then looked at the media with annoyance. He expected the newspapers and television factions to use the event to pose embarrassing questions.

Bojing put his hands on the podium and began to speak. "Ladies and gentlemen, our government is pleased to present this modern library to the people of Tongzhou. This location was selected because of its proximity to key schools in the neighborhood. Students will have access to all forms of media and an excellent selection of books and periodicals. All citizens are encouraged to enjoy this new facility. Finally, as your minister of culture, and with government direction, I will oversee that our traditions survive through books, plays, films, paintings, and antiquities. Please enjoy the pastries and tea."

There was raucous applause, then Bojing nodded and walked away with his protective detail, avoiding the media.

Representatives from all the major television stations and newspapers started to complain about the lack of accessibility to the culture minister. One journalist shouted out, "Minister Chu, what are you doing to get our antiquities reappropriated?"

Bojing kept walking as his detail directed him out of the building and into his waiting limousine. He slumped into the lush cowhide of the rear seat. He was pleased to have escaped the event with only one question regarding antiquities stolen from China. Still, it was a question that concerned him.

A few days earlier, his old friend Professor Peng Lixin told him that Tracy Jordan, a new student from America, was attending his class. Bojing's interest was piqued when Lixin explained that the young lady had published a paper on Admiral Zheng He's travels to the Americas. Based on her credentials, Lixin believed there was some truth to it. Her father, Jeffrey Jordan, had an international reputation as a gifted archaeologist and had written many papers on the subject.

Bojing's common sense suggested the notion of Admiral Zheng He's sailing to the Americas was absurd. *The taking of tribute and sharing gifts among the uncultured during the voyages was expected during the Ming dynasty. How far did he travel to achieve his goals?* These two thoughts jolted his mind and sent him speculating. *What if it were true? Would it be possible to retrieve the antiquities? Would this discovery elevate me to a higher status in the Party and make me rich?* Bojing couldn't second guess himself now; he had already set his plan in motion. On his orders, associates from the Foo Dog Triad were watching and following Tracy Jordan. It was time to get a progress report.

"Driver, take me to my office."

"Yes, sir."

Bojing reached into his suit pocket and took out his cellphone. He pressed his thumb on the fingerprint sensor of his phone, found the favorites list, chose one, and waited.

****

The incense wafted upward and filled the room with the musky fragrance of sandalwood. Ru was sitting in the lotus position, his body still. A ring tone permeated his sedate meditation. The piece of music was the High Plains Drifter theme from the movie, The Good, the Bad and the Ugly. It was a dark and moody melody.

Ru was in a leadership role in the Foo Dog Triad. He was an ambitious, sadistic criminal determined to become even more powerful. The music was a reminder the dark side had beckoned him, and he had followed. He unfolded his legs, sprang up onto his feet, disconnected his phone from the charger, and picked up.

"Ru speaking."

"This is Bojing. Are you free to talk?"

"Better we meet in person."

"King Parkview Hotel in Beijing tomorrow at 10:00 a.m.," said Bojing.

"See you then."

Ru Fa Zhong was a handsome Eurasian of thirty-two years, with hair black as coal, a narrow forehead, square-jawed and penetrating eyes. He was a meticulous dresser, often wearing dark striped suits and handmade shoes together with a Bvlgari Chronograph, popular with pop musicians and rappers. He was a professionally trained assassin and notorious for kidnapping wealthy businesspeople for ransom. He also ran drugs, prostitutes, and gambling clubs and was known for dealing out harsh punishments. He'd chopped off a gambler's hand for cheating on his ship and threw him overboard.

Chu Bojing was cultured, a poet laureate, and had risen through the ranks in the Communist Party to become the culture minister. Even so, he embraced his collaboration with Ru and the Foo Dog Triad. Bojing was very powerful, but he still kept a cautious vigil because Ru was dangerous and unpredictable.

***

Ru drove to Hong Kong International Airport and boarded an Air China flight to Beijing. He checked into the King Parkview Hotel and prepared for his meeting with Chu Bojing. Ru selected the same floor as Bojing's so he could slip over in secret. His actions were a precaution since being on Mainland China meant not benefiting from Hong Kong police protection. The communists' surveillance of the internet and cellphones made those systems vulnerable to cyber-infiltration, which is why the clandestine meetings were necessary. Plus, Ru knew the one-on-one sessions meant he could observe his collaborator's body language. For the moment, he felt comfortable playing the lesser role as he watched for non-verbal cues.

Five

Could This Be The Diary?

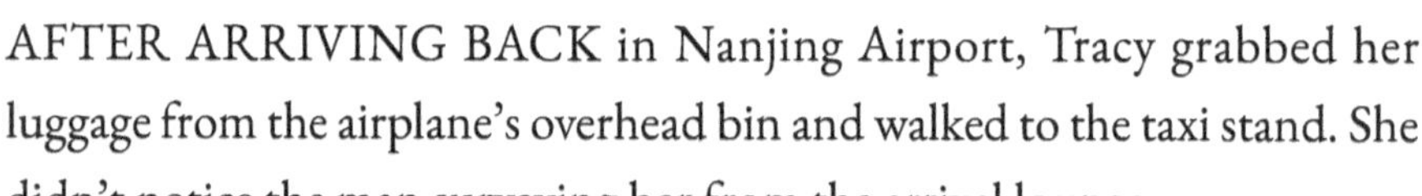

AFTER ARRIVING BACK in Nanjing Airport, Tracy grabbed her luggage from the airplane's overhead bin and walked to the taxi stand. She didn't notice the man surveying her from the arrival lounge.

Tang Dao was waiting in the airport parking lot in the blue Audi when he received the text. *She's coming out now.*

He called Ru Fa Zhong, using the hands-free function.

"She just arrived," said Dao.

"Where was she?" asked Ru.

"I tried to find out, but the airline agents were not cooperating."

"Okay, you have her now. Don't let her get away again."

"When should we grab her?"

"We will let her do all the research and grab her afterward. You are on borrowed time if you fail again," said Ru. "For now, just follow her."

"I'll do what has to be done," Dao said. He put the car in gear and followed the cab.

***

Tracy was in the university library searching for architectural drawings of the Crane Mosque in Yangzhou. Hours later, she found what she needed on the internet.

The information she sourced explained the ancient mosque was built in 1275 to serve the needs of Arab traders. Nearly eight hundred years ago, the area was also planted with pine and ginkgo trees. The main entrance looked like the head of a crane, the walls on either side the eyes, the left-hand path the neck, the prayer hall the body, the north and south walls, the wings and archive room.

***

Back in her apartment, Tracy peered out her window and saw the blue Audi. Concerned, she waited up late to compensate for the time difference between China Standard Time and California and called her father's office at Stanford. On the third ring, Jeffrey Jordan picked up.

"This is Professor Jordan."

"Hi Dad."

"Hi Tracy. Is everything okay?" His voice was full of concern.

"Dad, I need your advice. Someone has been following me. I don't know who they are, and I am worried."

"Is it about your research?"

"I think so. I discovered there was a diary kept by Admiral Zheng's deputy envoy, and it could be hidden at the Crane Mosque in Yangzhou," she said. "I'm going there on the weekend to see about retrieving it or copying it. Whichever is the least risky."

"Please be careful."

"Someone may have figured out why we are looking for the diary."

"Okay, let's consider a plan where you can slip away."

"What do you suggest?"

"Go shopping, act normally. Buy a wig, a cane, and baggy old clothes. Then dress up as an older woman, walk for a few blocks, and slip into the subway. After a few stops, hail a cab and go to the airport. Get a locker, hide your disguise, and fly out to Yangzhou. Please call me when you get back."

Tracy spent the week in and out of classes, maintaining her cover as an international student. She avoided Professor Peng as much as possible, smiling and moving along before she could be summoned.

On Friday night, she went shopping as her father had suggested. Dao was watching Tracy from the blue Audi. After a brief walk toward the campus, Tracy suddenly ran into the subway station and took the train south to Xinjiekou, the central business district of Nanjing where she could get the supplies she needed for her escape.

Dao immediately reacted, opening his car door and darting down the street after her. The last subway car had disappeared into the darkness when he arrived at the platform.

"Shit!"

Dao went back to the car to wait for her. Since she had no luggage, he presumed that she would return. Later that night, Tracy returned, carrying two shopping bags.

Dao eyed the names on the bags. *Probably just some lingerie or fashion accessories.*

***

Tracy showered on Saturday morning, followed by dim sum and jasmine tea for breakfast. Refreshed and feeling confident, she donned her wig, baggy clothes, and extended the collapsible cane. She stooped over and stepped forward slowly like an elderly woman as she walked out of her apartment building.

Dao had been replaced with another triad thug, and he did not take notice of the elderly woman as she labored along the sidewalk. Tracy managed to complete her task and hailed a cab to the airport to catch her flight to Yangzhou. She was confident that no one had followed her. The taxi dropped her off at the Crane Mosque. Tracy was now wearing a gray floral hijab.

The Crane Mosque was made of brick, and its solid gray steel doors were opened straight to the epicenter, which was shaped like a flame. Two stylized kneeling rams were on either side of the doorway, protecting it. The architecture was a combination of Persian and Chinese.

She stepped through the doorway into the courtyard and garden. The fragrance of the pine and ginkgo trees enhanced the beauty of the old place as she stepped forward on her way to the front door of the mosque.

When she entered, Tracy whispered, *"As-salamu alaikum."*

An imam stood before her, and replied, *"Wa alaikum as-salaam."* And upon you be peace.

"Are you here to pray? There is no area here for women to pray. Besides, it's a museum filled with historical and cultural literature," he said.

"Please forgive the intrusion. I'm not here to pray but ask permission to research the archives," replied Tracy in Mandarin.

The imam's serious nature was reflected in his brown eyes. His nose was hawkish and narrow and his face angular. His smile, if you could call it that, showed worn and stained teeth. He was wearing a flowing thobe, and a taqiyah cap. He stood in the doorway like a physical wall of faith separating her from her goal.

"The materials in the library are made available at my discretion. Some of this information is not accessible to external researchers. What type of research are you conducting?" he asked.

"Here is my student card from Nanjing University. My studies include ancient Chinese history, classical literature, and documents."

"The manuscripts and records are primarily of Chinese and Muslim relationships. How does this support your studies?"

"The information I'm looking for are constitutional government records of the late Ming dynasty."

"You are American?"

"Yes, I am an international student. I've been studying at Stanford University and am preparing a paper on the historical politics between Persian and Chinese Muslims during the 15th century. I would be grateful for your cooperation."

The imam stroked his chin for a moment while considering her request. "I will allow you access to that area. The way you presented yourself in the traditional hijab is a sign of respect for the Muslim faith, which is a significant factor in my decision," he said. "As a condition when you present your paper, I expect you to mention our mosque as a reference."

"You have my promise," answered Tracy. She touched her notepad as a sign of reassurance.

"Please take off your shoes and follow me to the library. Try to finish as soon as possible."

They entered the dust-laden room with shelves crammed with manuscripts, books, and records of every description. There was a plain simple desk and chair in the center. The utilitarian and practical room was large and accommodating.

"Everything from the Ming dynasty should be on the west wall," he said as he left the room.

Tracy stared at the shelves and wondered how it was categorized. Hopefully, the earliest imam had created an organized designation, allowing for proper sorting, by year, month, and day. After looking for an hour, she decided there must be some other method of searching since she wasn't finding anything remotely close to her objective.

Looking more closely around the room, she discovered a worn tapestry hanging from floor to ceiling. Inquisitive, she walked over and lifted it away from the wall. Shelves of books and manuscripts were hidden from view. Tracy's eyes began drifting down and from left to right, as she read the spines. Donning soft cotton gloves to protect the ancient manuscripts from the moisture and oils in her hands, she pulled out some bound papers and looked for the titles. Occasionally dust would float up into her nostrils, causing an immediate sneeze.

She continued her search and noticed a more significant book, which when translated read Tobacco: Black Poison from the Barbarian Lands 1420. This did not fit into the contemporary historical model since Christopher Columbus had discovered tobacco in the Americas in 1492.

This book title and date must be out of synchronization, Tracy thought. It was believed that tobacco had arrived in China from the Philippines during the Ming dynasty between 1522 and 1566. *So how does this fit? It doesn't. How can a book be written over a century earlier about tobacco in China? Could this be a clue hidden by Zheng He's deputy envoy?* Tracy's hands started trembling. She carefully took it down from the shelf. She released the binding string and opened the cover, revealing another book hidden in the hollowed-out area. *Could this be the diary?*

She removed it from the recess to examine it. The light brown parchment paper was bound at the right side, with a thin double silk cord threaded through four holes. It had two vertical columns of ancient Chinese script on the front, establishing it as a personal log. An oblong circle with the traditional red seal of the officer in its center indicated this memoir belonged to the deputy envoy Wang Jinghong.

Tracy's face flushed with excitement as she vigilantly looked around to see if the imam or anyone else noticed what she was doing. Confirming she was alone, she placed the personal log on the table with great care. Opening the first page revealed the initial entry in the logbook:

April 2nd, 1420 at Nanjing Harbor

The ship's name is Lin Yao, registered Nanjing China

Master Admiral Zheng He

Language Chinese

Looking further into the deputy envoy's account, Tracy could read the ship's speed and heading, wind direction, weather conditions, details of course changes, time of arrival, berthing or anchoring, descriptions of places visited, and a myriad of administrative duties recorded.

From the ancient record, it should be possible to reconstruct the course followed during the ship's passage at sea, enabling a navigator to calculate dead reckoning and estimated positions.

Tracy pulled out her cellphone and started photographing every page of the log, all two years of it. After her final photo, she turned the last page, repackaged everything, and placed it how she found it, exclusive of the dust. She left the library and entered the prayer room to meet the imam.

"Have you concluded your research?"

"Yes, I have, and thank you for access to the manuscripts."

"May I ask if you have had a good experience here in our mosque?"

"Yes, it was. It's the first mosque I have ever visited."

"Islam is a peaceful religion not unlike Christianity and Judaism. Sadly, in parts of the world, it is taught by way of rape and rifle."

Tracy felt a heavy heart at the thought of those poor abused girls and women she saw on the televised news. They were sold from one fighter to the next. "I have read the Quran during my studies, and the difficulty is not with the passages, but with the context. If the women of Islam can be equal in the eyes of Allah, why can't they be as equal in the eyes of men?"

"I believe there are reformists of Islamic doctrine, even here. Only compassion will make itself felt." He smiled at her and pointed to her shoes resting on the floor.

"It's been very enlightening," Tracy said.

She bowed her head slightly, stooped to the ground and put her street shoes on. Tracy slipped her purse strap over her right shoulder and patted the side in a satisfied gesture. As she walked out the front door of the mosque, the scent of pine and ginkgo trees embraced her again.

Six

Flights of Fancy Best Left Alone

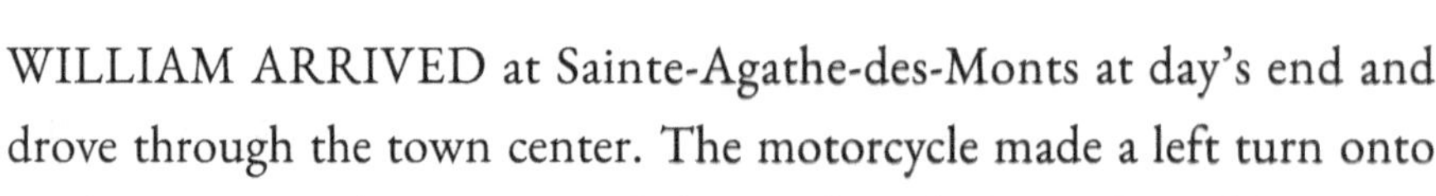

WILLIAM ARRIVED at Sainte-Agathe-des-Monts at day's end and drove through the town center. The motorcycle made a left turn onto Highway 329 and went around the south end of Lac-des-Sables as the orange orb scattered golden-brown beams across the lake's surface.

He maneuvered up the driveway and saw that a police cruiser was in position in front of the chalet with a vigilant-looking officer sitting behind the wheel. He parked his Triumph beside the cruiser and instinctively pulled his leather badge holder out and held it up toward the car's window. The power window opened like a glass screen and moved downward with an electric hum.

"Bonjour, je m'appelle William Fox."

"Je suis l'officier Charles Bodoin. Aucun problème à signaler," replied the officer.

"I'm glad to meet you, Charles. That's good. Let's hope it stays that way."

The chalet was an A-frame structure encased in natural cedar planks with a peaked gazebo attached to it. There were terraced flower gardens leading to the back deck, which faced the lake.

William walked the few short steps and entered the chalet.

"Dad, it's William. Where are you?"

The sound of a pocket door sliding open made William turn in that direction.

"Dad, I missed you."

"You, too. My God, boy, you're shaken. What's happened?"

"My partner Philip and I almost got killed today."

"What the hell! Tell me what's going on!"

"Got any single malt?"

"Sure. In the study."

James poured liberal amounts of The Macallan 18-year-old, and they sat down opposite each other, William in the high-back chair and James on the leather couch.

James was an older version of William. He was very tall and lanky, with a slight paunch, his gray hair was full and neatly cut, black-rimmed glasses gave him a stern but friendly look, while his brown eyes, long nose, and jowled chin highlighted the intelligent and experienced politician.

William described the life-threatening ordeal, making himself relive every fateful moment. "That's it, Dad. I needed to settle myself down. I'm okay now. Can we talk about something else?"

"Yes, sure. It's all right. Just relax," James said. "I'll make dinner reservations at Maison's for 7:30. Be ready at 7:00. I have a few things to do first."

James left the room, leaving William with his thoughts. William poured another Scotch and sat back in the high-back chair. He began staring at the picture of Michelangelo's *The Creation of Adam* on the study's wall. He had seen the original when he had visited the Sistine Chapel on a visit to the Vatican during his college years.

He couldn't stop thinking about his near-miss on the river and became transfixed with the picture. His eyes focused on the narrow space between where God and Adam's fingers nearly touch, surrounded by his angels floating in the ether.

The Vatican's masterpiece was mesmerizing William. Michelangelo had painted Adam's head remarkably like a youthful twenty-year-old. The features were smaller and tilted back, perhaps to accommodate the Sistine Chapel's curved ceiling.

As he was called in Sumerian text, "the Adam" was depicted with a lighter skin tone on his left side and appeared younger, his bent leg showing a muscular, solid thigh. His right side was shaded in shadow, looking older, encompassed in a layer of fine hair. His flaccid, uncircumcised penis was flopped over his right thigh, small like a child's, not proportional to a grown man, certainly not large enough to satisfy Eve's yearning.

Did church politics decide how large the penis should be? Adam's abdominals looked like he had once been an athlete, but now there was a roll over his waist, which revealed a man in midlife who had moved on from youth and enjoyed the bounties of life. Could Michelangelo be trying to convey to us his years of painting had taken his youth from him, or maybe God nearly touching Adam's fingertip meant his youth could be restored?

William sipped more Scotch then decided the drink and, his drifting mind were flights of fancy best left alone. Resolute, his eyes moved away from the picture. He tried to focus on what he could do to make his apprehensive feelings disappear.

He realized he had buried a survival instinct, which his upbringing had prevented from surfacing; one must become the hunter, not the hunted. He decided that he would go to Archambault Institution and visit an old friend. In the meantime, he got cleaned up and dressed for dinner.

James Fox arrived back from his chores and entered the chalet. He found William in the kitchen.

"Why are you eating?" asked James. "We're going out for dinner!"

William put down the cheese and cracker, brushed the crumbs from his sport coat, and took a quick sip of coffee.

"I missed lunch and then had a couple of drinks. I need to be clear-headed."

"I'll tell you what. Let's take the convertible. The cool air should help alleviate that foggy head of yours."

"Really? It's bloody November!"

"You drove up here on your motorcycle."

"Yeah, but that was during the daytime and it's much colder at night."

"Come on, it will pick you up better than anything I know," James insisted.

"All right, it's not that far. I want to drive."

"No, son. You have too much to lose if you get caught driving impaired."

They removed the cover from the Rolls-Royce Corniche and climbed into the 1987 classic. The exterior was Old English White, and its leather upholstery felt soft and elegant. Creased and milky white with blue piping, it flattered your presence. The dash was burl walnut, and it encompassed all the instruments in grand fashion. James turned the ignition key to start the engine, engaged the button to lower the top, put the transmission into drive, and pulled out of the garage.

"This is an experience to appreciate," said William, settling into the comfortable Connolly leather.

"I'll put on the heater to keep us warm," said James.

The cool November air swept around their heads, tugging their hair one way, then another.

"I'm feeling better already," said William. "I've always loved this car. I remember the day you got it on auction at Barrett-Jackson."

"It's already been fourteen years. Just after we moved back from Seoul."

"Mom said you were one of the best ambassadors Canada has ever had and the Prime Minister's Office knew it."

"Look, son, I'm glad to be retired. Being a diplomat was a life ambition. What happened to you and your brother Jamey will be a spot on my career."

"You know it shouldn't. It was out of your hands. My brother will have to be in a wheelchair his entire life because of my ineptitude."

Both men were quiet, immersed in their own thoughts as they watched the landscape unfold around them. Finally, James spoke.

"Son, we will both have to come to grips with these feelings eventually."

They arrived in downtown Ville-de-Sainte-Agathe-des-Monts and parked down the street from Maison's Bistro. James let the Rolls-Royce Corniche come to a gentle stop in the parking lot. Its hydraulics slowly descended like a ballerina, coming down from her toes, onto the stage with graceful finality.

The two walked up the steps under the entrance canopy and into the foyer. A young woman escorted them to their table and gave them each a menu. She explained that André would be their waiter.

As they sat, William stared at the embroidered tablecloth, the crystal wine glasses, and the meticulously arranged silverware. There was even a potted succulent, placed to the side, for decoration.

The waiter arrived with his pad and pen. He pushed his black rim glasses back over his forehead to where a full head of hair should have been. The ceiling light was reflecting on his shiny dome. "My name is André, and I will be your waiter this evening." He then lit the candle with the stick lighter.

James ordered a bottle of Château Cantenac Brown 2009. Both men ordered tenderloin au poivre with seasonal greens.

They were amused as the reflection on André's head shimmered with every nod of their order. Over dinner, William and James began reminiscing about their days in South Korea.

"Here's to good days to come," expounded William.

"Here, here," said James.

They clinked their glasses together, and the distinctive sound of crystal filled the air. The men sipped their Bordeaux and beamed with appreciation.

"Do you still practice taekwondo with Mr. Kim?" asked James.

"Yes, we still see each other at his studio and sometimes for beers and dinner."

"At least you have a skill set and mentor out of that tragedy."

William remembered it like yesterday. Sue Lee, his nanny, had taken him, his brother Jamey, and Tracy Jordan to the open market in Seoul. They had traveled by car from the Canadian embassy to the city center.

The group walked through the stalls buying groceries and other incidentals. It was busy and the children became separated from their nanny and entered an empty alley by mistake. William was sixteen, Jamey ten, and Tracy fifteen. The children were too inexperienced to be on their own. They turned around to go back the way they came in but were trapped by four Korean teenagers.

The young thugs demanded everyone's wallets and watches. All were scared and handed over the items. One of the juveniles demanded Jamey's running shoes, which he refused to give up because they were a gift from his mother.

The kid lunged at Jamey, executing punishing blows, swift and brutal, like an expert. He punched and kicked Jamey, then spun around and side-kicked Jamey in the lower back.

Everyone heard the snapping sound as Jamey fell to the ground.

They called for help. People entered the alley only to be pushed aside by a short, stalky man in a police uniform.

He shouted, "Stop! You are under arrest!" in Korean. The teenage gangsters ran away. Two bulky men who appeared to be their leaders ran into the alley and tried to dissuade the police officer from pursuing and arresting the young gang, telling him that this was their turf and he had no business here.

One of them reached over with a folded bundle of Korean won and tucked it into the policeman's pocket, patted him on his shoulder, and asked him to disperse the crowd.

The police officer didn't waste any time discussing who was in charge and stepped toward them and told them they were under arrest for bribing an officer. One of the heavy-set men arched his arm into his waistband and produced a gun. He was hurled over the police officer's hip and slammed to the ground. While the other gangster threw a punch, the officer sliced by and brought a back fist to his temple, then grabbed his neck, and connected his knee to the gangster's head. To further subdue the assailant, he slipped his leg behind the gangster's leg and flipped him on his back. With equal speed, he turned him over and handcuffed him. It all happened in a matter of seconds.

William had never seen anyone move so fast. Jamey was rushed to the hospital. Later, William's father came to get Sue Lee, William, and Tracy from the police station, after an officer took their statements.

The survivors were grateful. Mr. Kim from the Seoul Metropolitan Police Agency stood close by. They thanked him profusely. William asked his father for permission to learn taekwondo, the discipline at which Mr. Kim was proficient. Considering what had occurred, William's father agreed, and Mr. Kim encouraged him to attend the world-renowned Kukkiwon Academy in Seoul.

When Mr. Kim's wife passed away from breast cancer, he wanted a new start and immigrated to Canada. He started his dojang in Montreal to be close to his protégé.

Over time, the discipline improved William physically and mentally. He became an instructor with a sixth-degree black belt.

"Son, is everything all right?" asked James. "You seem pensive."

William moved his hand away from his forehead and focused his damp eyes back on his father.

"I'm fine. I was just living it over again." He paused, "It's my fault Mom left with Jamey and moved to Toronto."

"You were too young to know, but your mom and I already had our problems."

"We should get out of here and go home," said William.

Seven

Nice Suit. Are You Going to a Funeral?

THE MORNING SUN came over the lake, warmed up the bedroom, and penetrated William's eyelids, with a soft amber light. He took a shower, got dressed in his motorcycle gear and went down for breakfast. During his meal of Greek yogurt, topped with pistachios and honey, he made mental notes of his upcoming visit to Archambault Institution. Comfortable with his plans for the morning, he left a note for his father. It was great to catch up with you. Talk soon. W.

He nodded to the officer on duty, mounted the Triumph, started it up, and drove out of the chalet's driveway toward Archambault Institution. The trip would take about fifty-five minutes, mainly on Highway 117. William reached Sainte-Anne-des-Plaines and drove through the town to the prison.

He walked through the entrance to the glass-enclosed booth and presented himself on arrival.

"I'm Inspector William Fox with the RCMP, here for a professional visit."

He passed his badge and photo ID through the slot to the correctional officer. William took stock of the heavyset man. He was balding and had narrowly formed eyes with a tattoo on his forearm, suggesting a military background. His name tag read Logan.

"Who did you want to see?" he asked.

"Walter Smith."

"What do you want with that dirty cop?"

"Police business," replied William.

"Please sign the visitor's log," said Logan. "If you're carrying, you need to hand over your firearm."

"I'm not carrying."

"Now, if you don't mind, step through the metal detector."

William did. He was led through a security door into the visitor's area, where several other people were visiting and talking. A few looked over at the new arrival.

"Sit there," said the correctional officer. He pointed to a stool and a table that was bolted to the floor. Ten minutes later, Walter was brought in and sat across from William.

"You don't look too bad considering," said William.

"If you think a broken nose and bruised ribs are okay," replied Walter.

"Hell, man! Look, I know you have it tough in here. I'm pushing the prosecutor to reopen your case."

"I don't need any sympathetic bullshit from you."

"It's not bullshit. You need help, and I need a favor," said William. "I would like you to do some dirty work, hypothetically."

"I will if it gets me out. What do you need?"

William looked around to see where the correctional officer was situated. He was at the other side of the room.

"Have you seen Wu Sunfay around?"

"He's here, and his entourage always follows him."

"Hypothetically, if he were to be laid up in the infirmary for a long time... You do understand what I'm asking?"

"Consider it done."

"I'll pressure the prosecutor and get back to you soon."

William felt no remorse with this request. Compromising Wu Sunfay would make it easier to scatter his henchmen.

Nodding goodbye, William got up and went to the doorway. The guard let him out, and he headed back to Montreal.

***

The sound of the motorcycle reverberated off the high concrete walls. William had entered Autoroute Décarie, where it dips below the regular city streets into the southbound underpass heading into the downtown core. The lunch hour rush was making his progress slow. His cellphone vibrated.

He hadn't talked to René, his supervisor, in twenty-four hours, and speculating on who the caller could be was a waste of time. Trying to reach the phone while traveling in hectic traffic was virtually impossible. So, he accelerated and started darting in between the uncooperating maze, making a quick left turn on Ville Marie. He reached the city's heart and was on his way to C Division.

He liked living in Montreal and enjoyed the vibrant nightlife as it reminded him of Paris but driving in Montreal was just as challenging as that famous city. Minutes later, he parked the Triumph in the underground parking and checked his phone for messages. One missed call and a text from René: *Get here ASAP.*

William rushed through the building up to René's office and stood in front of his supervisor's desk, unsure of what to expect.

René turned away from the window and faced William. He was wearing one of his bespoke black pinstripe suits with a light gray striped tie and matching puff. His posture was one of agitation and menace, his forehead was frowned, and his mouth turned down.

"Nice suit. Are you going to a funeral?" asked William.

"As far as I'm concerned, it could be your funeral. I was called in late last night because of the fallout from your escapades yesterday," said René.

René passed William the *Montreal Gazette*. Splashed across the front page under the banner was the headline, "Gun Fight on the River." The subtitle read "RCMP shoots it up with notorious gangsters on the St. Lawrence River."

"The mayor, the commissioner, and the chief are right up my proverbial. The mayor wants someone to take accountability so he can explain to the citizens of Montreal we are not vigilantes shooting at anything that moves," said René. "We need someone to take responsibility for this disaster."

"Philip is not taking the fall for this," said William.

"No. But you are. Starting now, you are on administrative leave until further notice. The gun and badge, please, on the desk. Now!" René's voice boomed in his sternest French.

William was incensed. "That better be the end of this harassment," he said. "We were just doing our duty, fighting for our lives!"

"Look, I empathize with you, but the media have video footage of the entire episode. Two pleasure craft sunk and a near collision with a freighter, not to mention the environmental impact of both sunken vessels."

William was shocked and said nothing.

"Just go home. Our public relations people will take care of the situation. Comprends?"

"Oui, Patron."

William called Philip while he was still in the underground parking lot.

"Hey man," Philip answered. "What's up?"

"We've got a serious situation with the higher-ups. The mayor, the commissioner, and the chief are coming down on René about the gunfight on the river. Have you seen the newspaper?"

"Yes, that's why I didn't show up at the station. I am at the marina following up with the repairs on your boat."

"Thanks. Meet me at the MVP Sports Bar on Rue Sainte-Catherine's in an hour."

***

The bar was filled with university students clustered around various TV screens. They watched Major League Baseball on one screen, UEFA soccer, the NHL, and the NBA on others. The aroma of pizza, wings, and beer drifted across the room, as did the chatter of young people's voices, cheering for their respective teams. Five video games were also buzzing, whirling, and flashing, engrossing both winners and losers while they bounced in their seats. The bar was popular and noisy, a great place to be unobserved and not overheard.

It was late afternoon when William and Philip slipped into the vinyl seats of a booth located furthest from the crowd.

The waitress dropped off a Budweiser and poutine for Philip and jalapeno poppers and a Sleemans for William.

"I take it René gave you a time out?" asked Philip.

"Yes, and he's happy with just my suspension. If I were you, I'd play it safe for the next few days," said William.

"Fine, I'll do that, but what are you going to do?"

"I'm still trying to help Walter Smith with the Crown prosecutor. I'm hopeful Wu Sunfay will finally admit to perjury, and we get Walter out of prison soon."

"How do you propose to get Sunfay to confess while he's in jail and protected?"

"I've convinced Walter and associates to admit Sunfay into the infirmary without his consent," said William with a wry smile.

"René hasn't found out you visited Archambault?"

"No, but add that to all the other trouble, and it could get worse. Much worse. Not just for me but for Walter if that bastard Sunfay talks to the warden about my visit..." He trailed off for a few seconds, thinking. "There's a good chance he got Walter's message and is talking to the Crown about his involvement in implicating Walter," he added.

"Leaving the city about now is probably a good idea. So where to?"

"Until I get reinstated, it's best we part company. I won't tell you where I'm going. If René asks you about me, tell him the truth. René has a good bullshit meter, and this would make it difficult for you, despite our friendship."

"Okay, brother."

"I'll be in touch."

William slid along the seat, stood up, removed his wallet, and placed a few bills on the tabletop. He smiled and nodded at Philip as he strolled away.

Eight

The Dolphin Earring

——◆○◆——

TRACY KNEW GOING back to Nanjing could be dangerous. She was frightened to the point that she did not want to return to her apartment and needed to distance herself from whoever was following her. Tracy had all the information she needed from the mosque and decided that she could pick up clothing and toiletries at the hotel before flying back home. She bought a ticket on Cathay Dragon Airlines to Hong Kong International Airport with a connection to New York City.

Arriving in Hong Kong late at night, Tracy had to wait until the following evening to catch her American Airlines flight to New York. She was bustled along, surrounded by many busy people heading for the arrival lounge, and finally made it to the taxi stand. Waiting in line, she realized the enormity of the place. At last, it was her turn for a taxi to take her to the nearest hotel.

Tracy found herself losing her footing and floating in the air. Two men dressed in black had picked her up under her arms as if she was a pillow.

Tracy screamed, "Let me go! Help!" and struggled against the two men, as they moved her along the sidewalk with little concern shown by the staring and indifferent public. One of the men lifted his sport jacket to show his gun to the taxi attendant. He acknowledged, quickly turning toward his next customer, and waved over the waiting cab.

The men forced Tracy into the back of a waiting black Range Rover, slipping zip ties around her wrists and duct tape over her mouth. She struggled, her flaying legs trying to gain traction on the back of the driver's seat. Frustrated, she collapsed at the futility of her efforts and became still when she realized a hard object was pushed against her side.

Tang Dao had his favorite gun, the .45-caliber Norinco, shoved up against Tracy's ribs. It was a Chinese knock-off of the Tokarev. He favored this gun because it was easy to shoot, reliable, and astonishingly accurate.

All these unique qualities were lost on Tracy as she shivered in fear. She was defenseless and at the mercy of her abductors. She had to match their viciousness with her tenacity and strength to survive.

One of Dao's men slipped off Tracy's shoulder bag, removed her cellphone and handed it to him.

Dao looked at Tracy and roughly grabbed her thumb to unlock the device. After scrolling through it, he said, "Is Deputy Envoy Wang Jinghong's personal log on here?"

Tracy nodded.

"Let's move it!" Dao shouted to the driver.

Dao turned over the phone. "We need a paper clip or a toothpick."

"Nobody has anything like that," said his driver.

Dao's mouth opened in frustration. He took a deep breath, looked around, and reached over to Tracy's ear. He grabbed the hooked earring, shaped like a dolphin, and with a sudden jerk, pulled it free.

Tracy's scream was muffled under the duct tape. Her weeping was silent, and the tears went unnoticed by her captors. She raised her bound hands and wiped away her grief.

Dao straightened the earring's hook and pressed it into the pin hole on the side of the phone, removed the SIM card, and threw it out the window. With a glimmer of relief in his eyes, he pocketed the phone.

Tracy's breathing became distressed and labored. Her asthma, usually mild and easily controlled by puffers, flared up due to the stress and the gag across her mouth, restricting her breathing.

Dao realized Tracy was having a severe asthma attack. "Give me her purse," he shouted. He ripped off the duct tape and held up the puffer to Tracy's mouth. Her breathing normalized.

Maneuvering around the main airport terminal, Dao and his crew used the connecting South Perimeter Road to the Hong Kong Business Aviation Centre on the other side of the airport.

At gunpoint, they forced Tracy onto a Harbin HC 120 helicopter. The triad crew flew themselves across Hong Kong to the middle of Kowloon Bay.

Their destination was the landing pad at the stern of the *Lucky Star*, Ru's gambling ship. Under Ru's guidance and leadership, the Foo Dog Triad had invested their illicit finances into the profitable casino ship, making him and his band of gangsters very rich.

Hong Kong gambling is restricted to football, horses, and lottery betting. The serious gamblers take the ferry or drive to Macau an hour away or spend the night aboard a casino ship like the *Lucky Star*.

Ru's cruise ship was the length of a football field, single-decked, and capable of carrying four hundred passengers with a crew of sixty. A karaoke club, massage room, hairdresser, mahjong room, slot machine area, and gym were available to patrons should they tire of gambling.

The *Lucky Star* was registered in St. Lucia and was about to sail two hours from Kai Tak Cruise Terminal into international waters, where gambling was free from government intervention.

Macau casinos paid a hefty tax to the government, whereas the gambling ships paid none, furthering the Triad's profits. The unregulated wagering revenue would fund other criminal activities like loan sharking, money laundering, extortion, and blackmail

The ship was also used for high-level triad security meetings and drug deals. Even Communist Party officials quietly slipped on board for clandestine meetings, where bribes could be exchanged. The *Lucky Star* was a refuge for the upper and lower echelons of Hong Kong's contemptuous and corrupt. Now it would be home to Tracy. An innocent woman caught up in her own crusade.

Gangsters forced Tracy into the dreary stateroom and duct-taped her to a wooden chair. Confused and in pain, she could hear the lock being turned shut. Then the ship's propellers started to rumble, and the vessel was underway.

Dao stood beside the captain, gripped by the vibrant city lights, as the *Lucky Star* left Kowloon Bay. He was pleased that they would be in international waters soon.

Nine

You Would Starve Your Master?

WILLIAM ENTERED THE room quietly to avoid making any noise. He bent over and pulled off his motorcycle boots.

"Kihap," someone shouted. William heard a whisper of fabric, a crack, and the sound of wood hitting the floor. Clapping echoed throughout the dojang. William moved forward two steps and bowed before entering. The taekwondo class came to a stop as the unexpected figure presented himself.

"William, glad that you can join us," said Mr. Kim.

William gazed around the room and saw a board-breaking demonstration taking place. Two junior black belts were in the act of picking up broken pieces of pine. The twenty or so students were sitting lotus-style, surrounding the mat laid out in the center of the room. All eyes stared at William as he bowed to his sensei, Mr. Kim, who politely bowed back.

"Students, this evening, we have Master Fox visiting our humble dojang," said Mr. Kim. "He is an old friend and a student of mine. Before starting our class, shall we persuade Master Fox for a demonstration?"

The room resounded in a tumultuous "Yes!"

Mr. Kim stepped onto the middle of the mat carrying a yellow plastic gun and pointed the barrel near William's forehead. "Now, Mr. Fox, your wallet and your watch," he demanded.

"Students, in this situation, it is best to do what the assailant demands," said William. "If, and I say if, you sense after you have handed over your possessions, you still will be shot, then you must protect yourself and any person you are with. A good approach is to engage your assailant in conversation like, 'What can I do for you and what do you need?'"

"The gunman will insist you shut up and repeat that he wants your wallet," said Mr. Kim, as he moved ever menacingly closer to William.

"Sure," said William, as he reached into his back pocket to remove his wallet and extended it in his right hand toward Mr. Kim.

Kim removed his left hand from the gun, with only his right hand now holding the weapon pointed at William. Kim reached for the wallet. William released the wallet and moved his head left, out of the way of the gun sightline. He grabbed the gun barrel with his left hand and the handgrip of the weapon in his right and stepped into Kim, pulled the barrel and his wrist back to break the trigger finger. A "kick" to Kim's groin and William wrestled the gun away, pointing it at his opponent. Kim threw up both arms in mock surrender.

"Remember to take definitive action—distract, deflect, disarm, and defend," said William.

"Well done, Mr. Fox," said Mr. Kim. William bowed as the students clapped in appreciation.

"Black belts, please start the class."

Mr. Kim turned and headed to the office, followed by William.

After entering the dojang office, Mr. Kim closed the door and sat down on the sofa. William sat in the opposite chair.

"You're in trouble, aren't you?" said Mr. Kim, as he opened the window and lit up a cigarette.

"Why is it you assume I've got problems every time I see you?"

"Well, since you joined the RCMP, you hardly show up at the club anymore."

"But this time, you're right, sort of," replied William. "I didn't come here to talk about it but to go out for drinks, food, and catch up."

"Well, William, I think we should do that right after class," he said as he took another puff and blew it out the window.

***

The Seoul Chaco Korean Restaurant was a short walk from Mr. Kim's Taekwondo Academy. Despite Mr. Kim's age, his pace was brisk. He had power to spare. William was impressed with his mentor; he was a man out of the ordinary and still a remarkable athlete.

Rue Sainte-Catherine was busy as they weaved through the pedestrians and arrived at the restaurant at 9 p.m. A few couples were enjoying a late-night dinner. William and Mr. Kim were seated by a young, tattooed girl with pink highlights in her hair and a ring through her nose. Pleasant girl, but far too removed from Mr. Kim's sensibilities. He made a shrug with his shoulders to indicate his confusion. William looked back at him and gave him an understanding smile.

The waitress arrived to start the grill and placed two Sapporo beers in front of them.

"What will you have?" she asked.

"I will have bulgogi and vegetable rice," said Mr. Kim.

"Chicken and vegetables for me, and we will share the kimchi."

After a few sips of beer, he asked, "So, tell me what's bothering you."

"It's hard to explain, but I have these feelings, you know, about how Jamey got hurt."

"You know you were just a kid."

"I know that's what my dad says, too."

"How about Tracy? Have you stayed in touch with her?"

"Tracy and I haven't talked for a long time," he replied. "We were in love then, but that was a long time ago."

The food arrived and they placed the meat on the grill. They ate the kimchi, while the chicken and beef were sizzling and sputtering.

During dinner, William spoke of the ordeal, and his time at the Kukkiwon World Taekwondo Academy and how he missed his mom and brother.

"Do you still stay in contact with your old academy friends?" asked Mr. Kim.

"Not for some while. They have moved on and become masters of their own dojangs," replied William.

"You should keep in touch. A man in your line of work needs friends like those."

One last piece of kimchi remained on the dish. The masters thrust out their respective chopsticks. There was a blur of motion, as both pairs of sticks seized the pickled cabbage. They looked into each other's eyes with astonishment. William was quick to retrieve the kimchi, but before placing it in his mouth, Mr. Kim grabbed his forearm.

"You would starve your master, my young protégé?" asked Mr. Kim, his eyes glowing with the patience of a doyen. "Here is some advice from your old friend: share, and perhaps that guilt you have may disappear."

He grabbed the kimchi with his chopsticks and placed it in his mouth before William could absorb his wise words.

"You should pay as well," said Mr. Kim as he got up and headed out of the restaurant into the cold evening.

William wondered about Mr. Kim's advice and abrupt departure. Had he just screwed up their friendship?

Ten

The Situation is Serious

WILLIAM WAS PAYING the bill after Mr. Kim had left abruptly. The waitress with the pink highlighted hair thanked him and told him to have a great evening. When his cellphone beeped, indicating a text had arrived, he waited until the waitress was gone before entering his password and reading his message.

Imperative that you return to C Division immediately. René.

William was annoyed. It was only twenty-four hours since his suspension. His first thought was, Why give a shit? How dare he send such a demanding order? William gave René's command serious consideration and decided to be a good cop and returned the text message.

I'll be there soon. W.

William arrived within the half-hour and made his way to the third floor and René's office.

"You look tired. These late nights have got to hurt," said William.

"I see you are as witty as ever," replied René.

"This text you sent me sounds important. Am I back on the force?"

"Yes and no. The deputy minister of defense asked for you specifically. You are proceeding to the Department of National Defence in Ottawa, where he will brief you on a specific assignment."

"Why me? Why now?"

"How would I know? Just do as you're told." René was still displeased. "There will be a military helicopter to pick you up on our roof in approximately one hour."

While waiting on the roof, William started to deliberate. *What could the ministry want? I'm just a cop. A good one, I think, but just a cop.*

***

The flight from Montreal to Ottawa took about an hour through a cloudless night. Small talk with the pilot was about the Montreal Canadiens; he was betting the team would make it to the Stanley Cup finals this season. The pilot recommended a seafood place near the Department of National Defence building at 101 Colonel By Drive. William intended to try the restaurant if he had time.

When William landed on top of the DND building, he said goodbye to his new friend. As soon as he leaped off the helicopter, he was encircled by two military guards. They searched him methodically and confirmed he was unarmed.

He was led down a flight of stairs to the sixteenth floor and into the deputy minister of defense's office, overlooking the Rideau Canal.

The man behind the desk stood up. "Please be seated, Mr. Fox," said the deputy minister. "My name is John Abbott, and I apologize for bringing you here at such an indecent hour."

William was swift in his appraisal of the deputy minister. He was approaching his mid-forties, tall, heavyset, and dressed in a striped, gray suit with a checked blue tie. A red maple leaf pin adorned his lapel.

As John Abbott sat, he adjusted his rimless glasses above his tired blue eyes and reached for his coffee cup.

"Would you like something to drink?"

William shook his head.

"The reason you are here is a bit complicated."

"How complicated?"

"Let's start with your father. His mission as ambassador in South Korea was a crucial success for Canada. As such, he has many friends in our government and around the world."

"Is there something that the DND needs my expertise for?" William interjected.

"This is where you come in because there is some proficiency and expertise, we require from you. There is a situation, and we'd like to ask you how to approach it."

John Abbott removed his glasses and looked resolutely at William.

"Candidly, the situation is serious. Tracy Jordan is missing and believed kidnapped. Possibly by the triad."

"I can't believe it. Do you know what happened?"

"Not exactly, but this is what we have learned from Tracy's father Jeffrey Jordan. She went to China on a secret mission to discover whether an ancient admiral named Zheng He had landed in a remote part of Canada in the fifteenth century. She and her father believe there may be a fortune in artifacts buried on the East Coast."

"So, she did follow in her father's footsteps."

"Yes, she did. Jeffrey is presently a professor of Chinese archaeology at Stanford University, and they are working together. Tracy sent her research to her father via the cloud and was booked to fly out of Hong Kong to New York." Abbott paused, "When she didn't arrive back in the US, Jeffrey called the FBI and then your father. That was thirty-six hours ago."

"How can I help? You must know I haven't seen her in many years."

"Well, your father and Professor Jeffrey Jordan kept in contact with each other. Jeffrey thought you and your father might be able to help because of your past relationship with Tracy. It's why I requested you. Jeffrey says you are the only person she ever trusted besides him."

"She is an American citizen. Shouldn't the FBI be investigating this?"

"They've arranged a legal attaché from the Consulate General of the United States in Hong Kong to meet with you there."

"What could Tracy be caught up in?"

"We don't know, but you need to find out."

"I don't have experience in that part of the world, except with Wu Sunfay, a triad member currently incarcerated at Archambault because of my efforts. However, gangsters approach their organizations pretty much the same all over the globe. That kind of dirty business I'm very familiar with," said William. "I'll do whatever it takes to get her home safely."

John nodded and said, "We have outlined a plan where you and FBI agent Patrick Reilly will work with the Hong Kong police and Interpol. You two are to find Tracy and bring her home safely. Consequently, establish which criminal organization is involved," said John.

"Do I have time to get a change of clothes?"

"No time. Expense everything." The desk phone rang.

"John Abbott." He listened and then said, "Thank you, René."

Smiling, John turned to William and said, "I have some good news. Sunfay recanted his false testimony. Walter Smith is being released. Now that his pension with the department has been restored, there is word he'll be taking early retirement."

"Walter deserves some peace after what he's been through," said William.

Deputy Minister Abbott looked at him quizzically. "I was told Sunfay is in the infirmary. A bit banged up before he confessed."

"Minister, all I know about prison life is that it can be pretty tough going."

John got up, handed William a large envelope and said, "The helicopter is waiting for you."

William headed to the roof. When he was seated in the helicopter, he opened the envelope. It contained a satellite phone, a new passport, and an American Express Platinum card. William threw his head back in relief. As he settled in for the flight to the airport, he wondered how Tracy would feel about him after all these years. That is, if he could find her alive.

Eleven

The Irishman

HONG KONG IN December was cool but not cold, and the lack of humidity made it comfortable. The blue sky looked exceptionally serene to William as he stepped outside The Pottinger hotel in central Hong Kong.

William got off the phone with Patrick Reilly, his new partner and legal attaché from the FBI. John Abbott seemed to be thrilled about being part of a united defense team. William was hoping his new partner was up to the task. He wondered if he was a seasoned professional or a newly minted graduate from the academy.

William stepped around a crowd of shoppers in the road as he made his way toward his rendezvous at the Gecko Lounge and Wine Bar. As he entered Erza's Lane, mellow sounds of bongos echoed between the walls and vibrated right through him, drawing him closer to his destination.

Midway through the narrow bar, he passed a couple dancing and spotted the Irishman sipping a drink and surveying his surroundings. William thought he was not hard to make out with the short red hair, somewhat curly on top with gelled peaks. He looked thirtyish, had the frame of a middle-weight boxer, and wore a three-button blue blazer and gray slacks. As he got closer, William noticed his light blue eyes. His forehead was developing a severe furrow, and high cheeks tapered toward a chin with a prominent cleft. He was handsome, likely a ladies' man, but he also had the demeanor of a field-experienced officer.

"Hi, you must be Inspector Fox," blurted out Patrick. He stood and extended his hand. William took it and gripped hard. Patrick seized back firmly.

"I'm looking forward to working together," said William.

"Likewise. Sit. What will you have to drink? I'm buying."

"I'd like a Connoisseurs Choice neat."

"And I'll have another one of the same." The waiter removed Patrick's empty glass and left.

William sat on the red leatherette stool across from Patrick and assessed him further. When the waiter returned, he placed William's drink in front of him. Then the waiter placed a glass containing a pale green liquid on the table. Next, he positioned an elongated slotted spoon over the glass and arranged a sugar cube on top.

William leaned forward with curiosity fascinated at the waiter's actions. Then the waiter used a cold-water drip to dissolve the sugar cube into the contents of the glass. The pale green liquid slowly transformed from clear to milky, releasing an aroma of anise and fennel.

"Patrick, what are you drinking?"

"Absinthe. This is the only place in Hong Kong you can get the real deal."

William smiled in friendly acknowledgment.

"So that you understand, there were a lot of nineteenth-century avant-garde writers and artists who drank it. The likes of Ernest Hemingway, Pablo Picasso, and others," Patrick elaborated.

"I've never met a bohemian from the FBI before. So, are you just being adventurous or tempting the devil?" teased William.

Patrick scrutinized William and calmly addressed his question.

"Absinthe is also called la fée verte, "the green fairy" Being Irish, I grew up with leprechauns. I am just hoping to get my wish granted so we can find Tracy Jordan," replied Patrick nonchalantly.

"Now there's some blarney if I ever heard it."

"You may think it's blarney, but this bohemian is going to explain the finer points of absinthe. The intoxicating result produces a state of alertness, which improves sensory perception and enhances creative forces, therefore making me a better detective," explained Patrick. "You know, like Sherlock Holmes."

William could not tell if Patrick was drunk or playing him for a fool. Frustrated with the idle banter, he became firm. "That sounds like nonsense passing as intellect. We have much ground to cover, and we need to play this out to a positive conclusion. People's lives are counting on it."

The musicians stopped playing, and the couple dancing sat down at the bar. The place was quiet enough for a more somber conversation.

The absinthe was affecting Patrick's perception, and he let the rest of his feelings be known.

"William, I have some concerns about you. My colleagues at the consulate gave me a heads up about you. They say you are good with martial arts and weapons, but you often go off script—like the fiasco on the St. Lawrence River just recently."

"My partner Philip and I have a sacred trust that we protect each other. Both of us were targets to be assassinated by a mobster I put away. So, we sank a few boats and pissed off some officials. At least we're still alive."

Patrick took another sip of his drink and stared at William.

"The point I'm making is my partner and I survived because we trusted each other. That's what I'm prepared to do with you to get Tracy Jordan back. If we can get past this bullshit interview you are conducting!"

Patrick started to smile. He realized William was no pushover.

"You have some guts, not what I expected. Some of us Quantico veterans were under the impression the RCMP dressed in red suits and paraded around on horses."

"For your information, we are on top of cutting-edge technology, and we have been putting away the bad guys long before the FBI got on the scene. The amusing thing is some of us get to wear pointy hats and flashy red suits."

Patrick was grinning from ear to ear, and he knew despite getting off to a weak start, the two of them were going to be moving ahead from here.

As the night progressed, the mists of the testosterone-infused conversation drifted away, leaving mutual respect to develop.

As William helped Patrick through the front door of the hotel, he said, "See you in the morning."

Twelve

There is No Retreat

THE GENERAL'S EYES were cold and empty. His still body hung over the balcony's edge, suspended by a taut nylon rope. Wei Lei, president of the People's Republic of China, had relieved him of his command of the Strategic Support Force, an elite arm of the People's Liberation Army. The new leader had decided to investigate and remove anyone suspected of engaging in bribery and corruption. The People's Republic of China was a communist regime, and doctrine did not tolerate the bribes and the favors of the few. Those in powerful positions who appeared immune to the policy line were now open for prosecution, or perhaps they would disappear.

Under house arrest, General Po had had time to plan how to appease the Communist Party, while leaving his family to their accustomed wealth and privilege. His goal was to avert an embarrassing trial, leaving the president's reformation plan to go in another direction.

As a result of his arrest, he had a complete loss of face. General Po felt like an exile, especially from his men in the Strategic Support Force. These men whom he had led and who respected him would eventually find out. Sequestered in his home, waiting for an unpredictable outcome, his moment of truth had inspired him. His shame became increasingly futile, and he realized only action could correct his misdeeds.

Inspired by others who had written a poem instead of a suicide note before taking their own lives, General Po sat at his elaborately ornate desk and dipped his pen into the ink. The calligraphy began to appear on the parchment in perfectly even strokes.

The path taken to secure our treasure

Forced entrapment, darkness, confinement

My roaming mind seeks approval for deeds done

Here, there are sins in the kinship

Voices that rumbled stand silent

There is no retreat, only paralysis

Descendants lie to redeem themselves

Is there deliverance for a fallen disciple?

Perhaps toward the limitless boundary

There lies the forbidden truth.

General Po set his pen down, satisfied with his poem, he was ready for the next step. His captors had removed all weapons from the house, leaving him few options. The nylon rope was readily available in the garden shed. Earlier, he had removed it and slipped it by the guards while pretending to maintain his meticulous garden. He looped one end of the rope around his neck and tied off the other end to the balcony's railing and hurled himself off the second-floor.

***

The shrill of the military whistle bounced off the courtyard walls. Soon the stomping boots of six members of the People's Liberation Army stopped, and they all looked up toward the lifeless remains of their commander.

"General Po is dead," said Captain Yuan Shao.

"What should we do?" asked his corporal.

There were whispers among the men.

"Quiet, everyone quiet," said Captain Yuan. "Haven't you seen a dead man before?"

He pointed at his men and said, "Get him down now."

They responded, moving as a well-trained unit. The general was down and on the ground in less than a minute.

"Just look at that fucking bastard. What a shameful way to end his own life," said the corporal.

"General Po was one of the country's finest officers. What he did was an extremely offensive act," replied Captain Yuan.

"Corporal, radio the major at HQ and relay our circumstances. Ask him to send medics to take care of the body," said Captain Yuan.

"Yes, sir."

The death of a prominent officer in the Strategic Support Force was an exceptional occurrence. The report of his suicide rapidly made its way up the succession of power until the news reached Chu Bojing's office.

***

Ru's cellphone dinged. He picked it up and looked at the text message from Bojing.

Po is dead. Meet at my hotel suite.

***

Knocking at the door aroused Bojing from his pensive state and he went to open it.

Ru entered the room, quickly moved to the cabinet, and started preparing a drink. Looking over his shoulder, he said, "Would you like one?"

"You could at least give me a proper greeting," said Bojing.

"Forgive me for being blunt but let us get down to the business at hand," answered Ru.

Ru put three ice cubes in his glass, followed by Belvedere vodka, and turned to face him.

"With General Po dead, we need to modify our plans. It also means we must discuss Tracy Jordan," said Ru. He took a long sip of the cold vodka and gave Bojing a challenging look.

"We are in this together and will get through this together as well," reassured Bojing.

"We just lost our covert operative to imprudent and greedy circumstances."

"Unfortunately, General Po got caught up in President Wei Lei's corruption crackdown or political purge. Whatever you want to call it."

"His watchdogs are relentless and everywhere. One thing is for certain, he died shielding his family, including us," said Ru.

The ice cubes hit Ru's teeth with a light ding as he gulped the last of the vodka. "What do you know about Po's involvement with this bribery charge?" he asked.

"General Po was fortunate to take his own life; by doing this he spared himself and his family from torture."

Ru was at the cabinet fixing himself another Belvedere and ice. He turned around, transfixing his eyes on Bojing.

"I don't care about these mainland communists and their misguided principles. General Po probably saw it coming."

"Ru, I'm trying to explain something to you, so just listen," said Bojing. "General Po was working with us because I bribed him, and I was threatening him for his cooperation."

The second drink relaxed Ru, and he finally sat down on the replica Ming armchair across from Bojing. "As a communist, I thought General Po was a very cautious man."

"Like all men, he had a weakness. Calligraphy, specifically the type handwritten by Emperor Qianlong of the Qing dynasty," said Bojing. "I found him a set of four that Qianlong had written in 1773 while he ascended the White Dagoba Hill on a pilgrimage. Our government is always looking for signs of bribery, however if a gift is recorded as having very little value, how can that be considered a bribe?"

"How did you find your way around the real value for such priceless ancient scrolls?"

"You must be familiar with Polly Auctions, a huge auction house in Hong Kong. My connections allowed me to present the scrolls for valuation. The house estimated the value to five million US dollars. General Po was rich now, but someone talked."

"Too bad," said Ru.

"As you know, our arrangement with General Po helped us track Tracy Jordan because he was in charge of satellite surveillance, electronic warfare and cyber infiltration."

"Thanks to that intel, we have Tracy now. Dao has confirmed that her cellphone contains Wang Jinghong's diary."

"Yes, but there's more. The young professor outwitted General Po and his team. She used her cellphone to hide the information on the cloud so her father could download it."

"How did she outsmart them?" asked Ru.

"She kept the final coordinates to herself," said Bojing.

"Now that we have Tracy, we'll get the coordinates from her one way or another."

"We need to move cautiously since the Strategic Support Force that General Po oversaw will be looking into his personal affairs to see if their operations were compromised. The suicide poem he left behind is ominous."

"We better act quickly and remove any trace of our relationship with him."

Thirteen

Hanging on a Slim Probability

THE SWEET SMELL of dim sum and green tea infused the teahouse. William and Patrick were taking breakfast early. They had an appointment with the Hong Kong police at 8:30 a.m. sharp.

The red urban taxi arrived at the central station and dropped the men off at the front steps. Both were texting their immediate superiors on the day's plans while Patrick fought a foggy brain.

A corporal escorted them into the office of Whang Yang, senior superintendent of the Interpol Liaison Bureau Hong Kong Office.

"Good morning, gentlemen," said Yang. "Please make yourselves comfortable."

William and Patrick introduced themselves and sat opposite Yang who was wedged between stacks of files.

"We understand Interpol has some information regarding our investigation about Tracy Jordan," said William.

"Yes, we started a few days ago as soon as the FBI informed us," replied Yang.

"What can you share with us?" asked Patrick.

"This is what we know. The FBI forwarded a picture of Tracy Jordan to the Interpol network. We also spoke with her university professor Peng Lixin who had no pertinent information. We traced her cellphone signature to a Ms. Kwan Jiang in Kunyang. Did you know she is a distant ancestor of Admirals Zheng He? Ms. Kwan suggested that Ms. Jordan go to the city of Yangzhou to the Crane Mosque at the Tomb of Puhaddin. Our investigating officers questioned Hassam, the imam. He said she visited the mosque and spent time researching government records of the Ming dynasty—"

"She was gathering information on the Zheng He's starfleet," interrupted Patrick.

Yang nodded. "Let me continue."

William and Patrick briefly looked at each other and then back at Yang.

"Ms. Jordan flew directly to Hong Kong and didn't go back to her apartment in Nanjing," said Yang. "Instead, she bought a ticket to New York."

"That is peculiar," said William. "Perhaps Tracy became suspicious that someone was on to her," he added.

"Her last GPS location was at the Hong Kong International Airport when her cellphone signal was lost," said Yang.

William said, "Let's make some assumptions about the information you just gave us."

Patrick gazed at William, becoming perplexed and agitated. "The Quantico training manual explains why assumptions are not productive."

Yang was amused at both Westerners. He shifted his weight back in his chair and waited to see the outcome.

"We know she was using her studies as a pretense, and we know she was researching the archives in the mosque. She found Ms. Kwan an ancestor of Admiral Zheng He. She could be close to finding the hidden antiquities, they'd be worth a great deal," said William.

"Yeah, that's right, but there are a few missing and unproven scenarios," said Patrick.

"Okay, let's stay focused. Our investigators searched her apartment and found her luggage, and clothes, meaning she left in a hurry," said Yang.

"Her cellphone signature may indicate where she was last," said William.

"Assume the SIM card was removed and whoever they are kept the phone. That could be why she is off the grid," said Patrick.

"At this point, we can't exclude even that possibility," said William.

"We have methods to track the cellphone without the SIM card," said Yang.

"Then we can locate the phone and Tracy," said William.

"I am not comfortable that our investigation is hanging on such a slim probability," said Patrick.

Yang looked up at his corporal tapping on the glass of the office door. His next meeting was due. He stood up. "You two grab a coffee and work on a plan we can put into play. We will talk in an hour."

***

William looked at his Rolex Submariner and realized that an hour and twenty minutes had passed, and the plan was not coming together. There was a knock at the door, and it swung open.

"The superintendent will see you now," said his corporal.

William and Patrick brought their notes to Yang's office. Patrick started shuffling his papers, and before he could say anything Yang took control.

"Whatever you two have worked out is redundant. Hong Kong police have fresh evidence that changes everything we know. Using CCTV surveillance and facial scanning high-tech glasses, police officers identified Tang Dao as one of the men who kidnapped Tracy Jordan at the Hong Kong airport. He is a known lieutenant of the Foo Dog Triad. His immediate superior is Ru Fa Zhong and is as dangerous as they come," said Yang. "No doubt the one behind the kidnapping. A taxi stand attendant we interviewed said Dao was one of the men who grabbed her, and they drove off in a black Range Rover," he added.

"The technology of those glasses is impressive," said Patrick.

"L.L. Vision Technology is manufacturing the glasses here in China. The technology can recognize a multitude of faces and do it in milliseconds. That's how we identified Tang Dao."

"What do we know about the Foo Dog Triad?" asked William, as he shifted in his chair.

"The gang is notorious for gambling, kidnapping, prostitution, and drugs," replied Yang.

"Can we expect a ransom demand?" asked William.

"It's a possibility, but we are scanning through CCTV surveillance footage to catch a lead on the Range Rover. We have the situation under control. You two should wait until we can verify the location."

William looked at Patrick and raised an eyebrow. "We should report back to our people about what we've learned," he said.

They excused themselves and met out in front of the police station.

"What is all this report back to our people shit?" asked Patrick.

"Can't you see? Yang is freezing us out of our investigation. He has a pretty good idea where they are and is not telling us. Let's get your office at the consulate to find Tang Dao and Ru Fa Zhong. I'd like to get on top of this and stop wasting time with Superintendent Yang and his political aspirations."

"Okay, I'll call a car from the consulate to pick us up."

William looked past Patrick's shoulder and saw Yang's corporal standing beside a police car a few feet away. Seeing William's expression, Patrick slowly turned to see the corporal disappear through the station's door.

"Do you think he heard us?" asked Patrick.

"Not sure, but it shouldn't matter. We know the game."

Fourteen

The Two Billion Dollar Submarine

FLYING OVER the submarine moored at the Royal Hong Kong Yacht
Club, the engineer pointed out its exterior features to billionaire Qi Ping,
such as two surface tenders, jet skis, and several underwater vehicles. The
aft deck included lounge areas, sunbeds, a bar, a saltwater pool, and a
helicopter hanger. Ping stepped out of his Augusta Westland helicopter
onto the pristine surface of the helipad. His vision of success reinforced
with every stride he took toward the conning tower of his submarine.

Educated at Peking University, Ping created the China Evergreen Group,
a Hong Kong real estate development company, trading on the Hong
Kong Stock Exchange. He managed to become one of China's exclusive
billionaires.

Ping had mistakenly thought his affiliation with the National People's
Congress would protect him from predatory action by prosecutors.
He learned from his contacts that party loyal industrialists had been
discredited and their assets seized. Others disappeared only to reappear and
regain some losses. Others fled overseas to escape the tyranny. What was
emerging was a Communist Party that frowned on personal connections
and considerations with no concerns for the rules as they could change at
any time.

Beijing demoralized the affluent and led many to hide their capital
underground or out of sight. These politics and unwritten policies
motivated Ping to protect his interests. He built his submarine so he

could disappear with some of his accumulated wealth. He also initiated investigations into the deaths and the disappearance of some of his close friends, executives, and public figures.

After five years at the shipyards, the submarine was ready. Ping felt satisfied he could exact true justice by exposing his friends' killers. It was time to act and escape where the authority of rule could not reach him and consider his next move.

The breeze off the bay ruffled Ping's hair as he ducked down into the conning tower. This morning, preparing for final inspection and handover, he wore simple deck shoes without socks, a cashmere crewneck, a white Moncler Benoit windbreaker, and Zegna blue jeans.

Ping had allocated two billion dollars to the project and was impressed with the results. The engineer unveiled the bedroom suites, the gaming room, the cinema, the wine cellar, and the gourmet kitchen.

Transferring responsibilities to the captain, the engineer left the submarine, and the supporting team took over. The captain had been recruited from the Chinese Navy and was a former submarine officer. The crew was also ex-Navy. Ping felt relaxed and secure he was in the hands of a capable mariner and his team.

Captain Ho Chan introduced himself and saluted Ping. "Let me introduce your crew and give you some specifications of your submarine," he said, as he presented the officers, staff, and chef.

"The submarine mirrors the design of the US Navy's Zumwalt class destroyer. It is fast, maneuverable, and capable of defending itself," the captain explained.

"And the cloaking technology I requested?"

"Yes, the new material acts as an underwater acoustic shield. Somewhat like the stealth bombers."

"Excellent. And the munitions?"

"Our crew is well versed in military combat, and as you requested, the arms locker is well stocked. Enough to start a small revolution." The captain grinned.

"It won't be necessary to storm a small country to prove a point, but I feel safer," said Ping. "Thank you, Captain. It's been a long day. Have someone escort me to my suite."

***

Ping sat on the edge of the sumptuous bed, removed his shoes, and started to knead one foot at a time. He fell back onto the bed, satisfied, and placed his hands behind his head, feeling the best he had in years. His carefree mood changed abruptly when he heard the click of a key in the lock in the door. Ping jumped up, ran to the door, and engaged the levered handle. The door slammed against his chest, and he fell backward like an unbalanced toddler stumbling from a tricycle.

Captain Ho Chan stepped inside the suite with a Tokarev pistol and pointed it at Ping. He waved the gun at him. "I'll take the cellphone. Move over to the chair and sit down."

Ping was angry and annoyed as he back crawled over to the chair.

"Whoever you are, you are not going to get away with this. How dare you treat me this way? Do you know the power I wield? You're going to pay for this with your life," said Ping.

"Shut up, you pompous ass. You think your power scares me?" replied Chan.

As Ping took the seat, Captain Ho Chan strode with a seaman's gait across the room and brought the gun butt across Ping's temple. He slumped over unconscious. Chan placed duct tape over his mouth and used the rest of the roll to wrap up his hands and his legs together on the chair. Chan moved out and locked the suite. Then he walked away along the submarine's corridor toward the bridge. *That is what you get for stepping in my way.*

***

After meeting with Bojing about Po's suicide, Ru flew his helicopter back to the *Lucky Star* to prepare for the next phase of his plan. Keeping the communist regime away from his affairs was paramount. Bojing's men had eliminated any traces of their involvement with General Po. Executed efficiently, the Strategic Support Force and the Chinese government would never find out about their complicity, but if it did, Bojing's brilliant plan of coercing General Po to spy on Tracy would be their downfall.

Ru and Dao talked at length about their direction before really bearing down on Tracy. So far, they were being cautious because they had found out from an informant that the police knew the Foo Dog Triad was involved in the kidnapping.

Later that day, Bojing tried to contact Ru. When he could not reach him, he got in touch with Dao instead.

"Where's Ru?" asked Bojing.

"He's gone to Toronto to buy a suit at Garrison Bespoke," said Dao.

"Why did he fly all that way there, when we have such fine tailors and fabrics in Hong Kong?"

"He's getting a custom suit that could save his life."

"I'm listening," replied Bojing.

"Nanotechnology. Ru hates being in conflict situations wearing a bulky bulletproof vest. The suit is lightweight, and underneath the fabric are several layers of carbon nanotubes stronger than steel and fifty percent lighter than Kevlar. It stops 9mm rounds."

"Impressive. When is he expected back?"

"I'm not sure. Soon."

"Have Ru contact me as soon as he is back in Hong Kong."

Dao realized he was caught in a trap between two uncompromising and powerful men. A position of indefensible consequences if either of them should get angry. A good reason to stay vigilant.

Fifteen

The Lucky Star

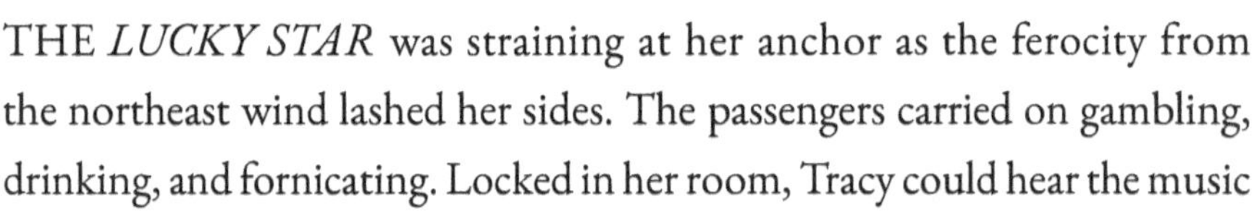

THE *LUCKY STAR* was straining at her anchor as the ferocity from the northeast wind lashed her sides. The passengers carried on gambling, drinking, and fornicating. Locked in her room, Tracy could hear the music and the boisterous talking and laughing.

Her hands throbbed from her previous struggle to tear apart the duct tape that had her paralyzed to the chair. The sharp pain in her earlobe had subsided somewhat and she wondered what kind of damage had been sustained.

Tracy's asthma medication was on the table, out of reach. In her mind, she recited the chants she had learned in yoga *nidra* class to keep her breathing calm and steady. Unsure of how much time had passed, she hoped her father was looking for her. Her inner strength was all she had now to keep her sane.

***

Ru and Dao were on the bridge commiserating as thieves often do.

"Are you going to tell me about your recent trip to Toronto?" asked Dao.

"Toronto in December sucks. I could not get back here fast enough," replied Ru.

"So, did you get fitted for your bulletproof suit?"

"I did. The tailor custom-fitted me to a tee."

"Business or casual?"

"I picked a navy blue pinstriping. It gives you a commanding presence without feeling overpowering."

"Cool. By the way, Bojing was asking about you. He expects you to call him back to discuss the project."

"I'll get back to him shortly. I'm going to pay a visit to our special guest. Care to join me?" Ru asked him jovially. Dao beamed like he had received a select invitation.

***

Tracy flinched as the stateroom door opened and the cool night air touched her face. Ru and Dao entered the room. Their swagger and arrogance were intimidating. Dao was clutching a rubber hose in one hand, beating it softly into the other. Tracy's response was immediate as the adrenaline intensified her fear.

Ru placed the doctor's bag on the nightstand. "How are you, my dear?" asked Ru, as he removed the duct tape from her mouth.

"What do you want?" she squeaked, averting her eyes away from him.

"My name is Ru and let me introduce my associate Dao."

"I... I didn't do anything." She was barely audible, her hands trembling and damp.

"Do you need your puffer? Are you thirsty or hungry?" Ru asked.

"Just the puffer. What do you want?"

"You can have your puffer after you've answered my questions," Ru said.

Tracy resisted being frightened and willed herself to be calm.

"I apologize for your damaged ear. A nurse can look at it if you like," said Ru.

"Okay, I'd like that."

"They are stunning earrings. I especially like dolphins. Where did you get them?"

"My father gave them to me," she said reluctantly. She was wriggling her hands, the tape firmly holding them to the arms of the chair.

Dao placed the hose on the bureau. Ru lit a cigarette and blew smoke in her face.

"Professor Jeffrey Jordan is your father, is he not?" asked Ru as he flicked cigarette ash into a paper coffee cup.

"How do you know that?" asked Tracy, feeling guilty that she may have betrayed her father.

"We have been following you since your admission to the university. We know why you are researching Admiral Zheng He and his voyages. So, I advise you to cooperate."

"I can't tell you anything!" exclaimed Tracy as she tried to regain some dignity.

"Your answer comes with dire consequences."

Dao picked up the hose again to reinforce Ru's threat. Tracy's body jolted, blood rushing to her head, ears flaming red, ears pounding in anticipation, breath getting short.

"We have the diary from Admiral Zheng's deputy envoy," Ru said.

"We need the coordinates that you decided to leave out of the file on the cloud. If you don't cooperate you can join the whores on board," said Ru.

Tracy looked away from his cold black eyes, the pit of her stomach fomenting the taste of vinegar.

Dao stepped forward and lifted her chin with the rubber hose. With a swift movement, he brought the hose down hard on her thigh.

Her sharp cry pierced the room. Stinging pain took over. She didn't know how much longer she could hold off the asthma attack.

"That was a warning," said Dao. A sadistic smile crossed his face. "Ru gave you a chance, and you refused. I can do several things to persuade you. Like, hunt down and kill your father. He would suffer as we are well known for our torture methods—"

Ru interrupted, "Get to the point."

Dao opened the doctor's bag and removed a syringe.

"There are sex workers on board servicing men all night. Heroin can make fucking those pigs more bearable and less painful. Our whores use it until they can't live without it. We will shoot you up until you are hooked. Do you want to waste your youth this way? Do you want that? Your life has more meaning than becoming a whore," Ru said.

Tracy thought about her father she loved and the work she wanted to finish. She knew heroin wasted good women. One minute life has meaning until it's interrupted by the drug that consumes you, replaced by euphoria and a sense of safety and warmth. Then the men repeatedly come and go, filling the night. Good women, wasted remnants of their former selves, like empty vessels fallen with depraved apathy. Tracy envisioned her future vanishing and a new terrible one beginning. She nodded her head up and down in submission.

Ru accepted her surrender as his hand touched her shoulder. "What are the coordinates?"

"I don't know yet. I was still working on them when you abducted me."

"What I need is your cooperation to get us to the treasure. Do I have it?"

"Yes."

Ru removed the commando dagger from its ankle sheath and cut away the duct tape freeing Tracy from the chair. He handed her the inhaler.

"Dao, get food and water. Bring the nurse, too," said Ru. He left the stateroom, pulled out his cellphone, and dialed a mainland phone number.

Bojing would be glad to hear this good news.

Sixteen

Unsavory Business

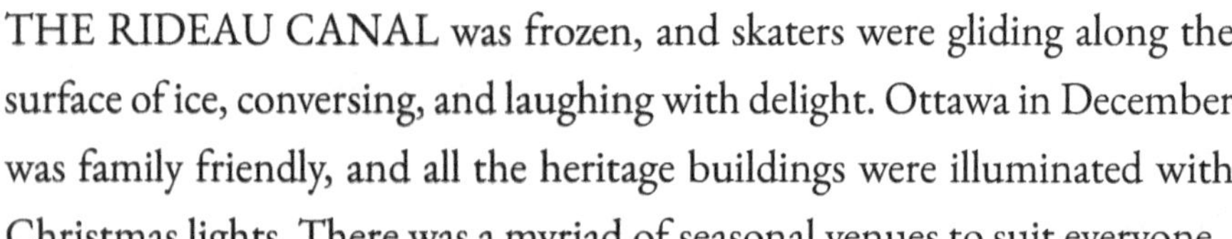

THE RIDEAU CANAL was frozen, and skaters were gliding along the surface of ice, conversing, and laughing with delight. Ottawa in December was family friendly, and all the heritage buildings were illuminated with Christmas lights. There was a myriad of seasonal venues to suit everyone.

For John Abbott, it was a brisk cold walk to the office after a boring lunch with an opposition party member. The Department of Defence Building was two blocks from the restaurant across the canal. The elevator trip was uneventful. He nodded at his receptionist as he removed his cashmere overcoat and hung it neatly in the closet. He circled his desk and pulled out the pale brown leather chair. It rolled easily along the beige carpet. The chair was not plush but was functional with chrome armrests, as it was a government office, not a corporate one. The deputy defense minister was appointed and not elected, so a lack of luxury was expected.

Accordingly, he didn't answer to constituents but made friends on the way to his position. A position worth preserving because men like him did the heavy lifting in the background while politicians paraded around the world stage. He sat down and rolled the chair closer to his desk. The folder was still there. He avoided opening it and instead looked around the room at pictures of F-18 fighter jets and navy destroyers on the walls. The chair shifted again, and his eyes rested on the promontory overlooking the Ottawa River. He admired the Parliament Buildings situated there and the Gothic Revival architecture. It was across the way that he had heard distant pops of gunfire where a Canadian Forces member posted by the memorial of the Unknown Soldier had been shot and killed. There had been two attacks in less than a week, and it was right at the heart of Canadian sovereignty. That period was a sad time for all Canadians. He gazed at the top of the Peace Tower. The Canadian flag was rippling southbound at the mercy of the wind. He looked at the folder again and realized the wind was not blowing his way either. His intercom buzzed.

"James Fox is here for your 1:30 p.m. appointment," said the receptionist.

"Give me two minutes and then send him in."

He opened the file and re-read it again. Handling bad news is never pleasant.

William Fox's father James walked steadfastly into John's office and extended his hand. "It's been a long time. Thanks for setting up this conference call."

John reciprocated with a firm grip. "I must warn you that this is very unsavory business. Take a seat."

James unbuttoned his tweed sport coat and pulled the leather chair closer to the desk. He folded his hands in his lap and stared toward the screen on the wall above John's credenza.

"How is he?" asked James.

"I don't know. But we'll find out in a minute," replied John.

The conference call started with Jeffrey Jordan sitting in front of his camera. John and James saw a sad parent who was looking for answers. His steel-blue eyes looked heavy. Dark patches underneath them revealed sleepless nights. A ponytail of unkempt gray hair fell over his left shoulder. He was dressed in a blue polo shirt, wrinkled from days of wear. Jeffrey Jordan was a desperate man.

"We feel your pain," said John. James waved to the screen.

"It's nice of you to keep me up to date on Tracy's situation. The FBI hasn't told me much yet," said Jeffrey.

"We have heard from William," said John. He opened the file and began to review the report with them. "William and Patrick Reilly from the FBI have been cooperating with the Chinese Interpol liaison. There isn't any good news. She is still missing, but they are focusing on someone identified in surveillance footage. He is a well-known gangster. William and Patrick are working with the Hong Kong police to locate him," said John. "That's all we have now. Perhaps the FBI will contact you with more information." He closed the file and pushed it away to distance it from his disappointment.

"Thanks for this," said Jeffrey.

"Stay strong and get some rest," urged John, even though he knew it was no use trying to console someone so distraught.

"Keep in touch," added James sympathetically.

"Will do, and thanks to both of you," said Jeffrey, as he did his best to keep up a good front.

The screen went blank.

"What does your experience tell you?" asked James.

"Your son may be Tracy's only chance."

***

The building housing the Consulate General of the United States of America in Hong Kong was located on Hong Kong Island. The complex housed federal agencies with a large staff of US citizens who worked in support of the American Chinese bilateral relationship.

William and Patrick arrived at the entrance where US Marine security guards checked them into the compound. They stepped out of the black van and entered the consular building's plush foyer. The guards passed them through the metal detectors, and they descended the elevators to the lower level.

William measured his pace behind Patrick's leonine strides as he proceeded to the FBI agency intelligence section. A single cherry wood door defended the soundproofed room. Patrick fingered the scanner pad, which relayed a message to click the door open.

Patrick led William across the threshold into the room. The video wall comprised fourteen monitors. Analysts enmeshed in various tasks faced their computer screens.

William focused on the CCTV monitor feeds from various locations around the consulate and surrounding streets. The ticking of an electronic digital clock caught his attention. It was 10 a.m. Tracy had been missing for three days. A twinge of remorse made him waver for an instant, realizing the technology in the situation room and good police work would be required to get Tracy back to her father.

Two analysts turned around and greeted Patrick.

"Hi, boss," they said in unison.

Betty and Frank were seated at their respective workstations.

"Let me introduce you to William Fox, an RCMP officer with whom we are coordinating our efforts to locate Tracy Jordan, a US citizen," said Patrick.

"She is an old friend as well," said William.

"I'm going to show William how our systems operate. While I do that, you two start a search for a fugitive named Tang Dao," said Patrick.

"Include in your search Ru Fa Zhong," added William. "We'll need images of both men."

The computer keys started tapping a rhythmic beat while the images on the video wall monitor changed from screen to screen.

"We have miles of telephone and fiber-optic cables and hundreds of computer terminals. This room is connected to four networks, the internet and various FBI databases, and a classified intranet. That means no outside access, especially from Chinese government hackers.

We also have secure video and computer connectivity with the FBI Strategic Information Operations Center in Washington, DC. The facility is open around the clock and manages classified intelligence that we can access."

Betty was downloading data on organized crime in Hong Kong. She was wearing a V-neck blouse and a gray skirt. Her brown hair hung back over the white jacket draped across the steno chair.

Patrick turned to the young analyst. "How are we doing?"

Betty answered, "Sir, there are a lot of Tangs in our search network."

"Okay, let's focus on his digital trail. He's probably on social media. Look for him on China's leading social networks."

Betty turned back to her keyboard with renewed enthusiasm.

Patrick asked Frank to find CCTV footage at the airport when Tracy Jordan disappeared. Patrick remembered Superintendent Whang had noted it before, and Frank was looking for the triad's SUV leaving the scene.

Patrick picked up the office phone, called the mess hall, and ordered a pot of coffee. When it arrived, he poured out two cups and handed one to William.

"So now we wait," said William.

"Our analysts are quite good. I expect something to break shortly. Let's enjoy our coffee. I believe we are going to be very busy soon."

Seventeen

Has She Capitulated?

THE CHINESE CULTURE Minister paced toward the mural of white lotus flowers. When Bojing reached the fresco, he leaned in, and lightly ran his fingers over the wood lattice frame of delicate leaves. He straightened his shoulders and with new resolve walked toward a cherry wood bench. Despite the diminutive size of the 18th century bench, Bojing cradled himself in it, a big child somehow seeking comfort.

Bojing's apartment had been decorated according to the teachings of Feng Shui. Red wallpaper dominated the room and radiated strength, power and influence like Mao's Little Red Book. While its style exuded harmony and bliss, it was a place for contemplation and strategic planning. A classical melody alerted him to a phone call.

He answered his smartphone. "Has she capitulated?"

"We forced her into a compromising position. Kill her father or turn her into a whore. She had no choice really and is cooperating fully now," replied Ru.

"Before we assign any more resources, have we some approximation of the value of this treasure?"

"Before we get to that, let me explain what I have learned from Tracy. As you know, Zheng He's fleet was enormous, and it included sixty-two treasure ships. We are currently examining the diary from Wang Jinghong, who was Zheng He's deputy envoy.

"In 1477, there was a proposal for another tribute voyage. The vice president of the Ministry of War confiscated Zheng He's records and maps from the archives and destroyed them. His reasoning was that the voyages were deceitful exaggerations that wasted money and were of little benefit. When Wang learned his master's life work was ruined, he disappeared and hid his diary to save himself and preserve the truth. The diary suggests the fleet sailed to destinations in the Americas, including Eastern Canada where we believe the collected tribute remains."

"The sooner you have an indication of value, the sooner we can develop a more specific plan."

"We will persuade Tracy to estimate the value of the treasure and plot a course to its destination."

"That's excellent. Let me know when you have the information."

Bojing tapped the phone and disengaged the call. He walked over to the black lacquered bar and poured a glass of baijiu. The drink had a rich and complex nuance. It was satisfying, not dissimilar to the excellent news Ru had just conveyed.

He sat down on the hand-carved cherry wood bench. He was enchanted with the turn of events. *Was it the liquor or the feng shui that was the cause?* Bojing's shoulders declined an inch, his body leaned back into the bench, certain good fortune was coming his way.

***

The sun's morning rays penetrated the gray cauliflower-shaped clouds. Ru grabbed the handrail and strode up the slippery steps to the bridge.

Captain Li stepped away from the ship's control panel, surprised at the abrupt opening of the steel door.

Ru stepped in and ran his open fingers through his hair, combing it back to straighten It.

"Captain, it's time to take the ship back to Hong Kong," he said.

"Sir, the passengers are still gambling," replied Captain Li.

"Tell them there is an emergency and offer them $100 casino chips each as a consolation."

"It will take an hour to get the engines online."

"Get my ship moving immediately, or you will be swimming back," snapped Ru.

Captain Li yielded to Ru's demands. Being adversarial with a triad leader was tantamount to a death sentence. It wasn't his money, or his ship, and it didn't take a genius to figure out Ru was a smart toumu, an arrogant, clever, and deadly ringleader. Li slid back, using his hands on the armrest to guide himself into the commander's chair. Intimidated, he sat down abruptly. He took a cursory look around the bridge, swirled the chair around to face the forward windows, and examined the white caps on the horizon.

"Bring main engines online, check the most recent forecast and navigational warnings, update all charts, set course to Hong Kong and do it now," he bellowed.

Satisfied, Ru made an about-face, stepped off the bridge, and trod down the stairway.

***

The porthole in Tracy's stateroom became flooded with light. It stirred her awake to a new day of trepidation and despair. She got up, entered the cramped shower, and began to bathe her battered body, hopeful she would eventually be rescued.

Ru unlocked the stateroom door, entered, and heard the shower, and smelled the shampoo and soap. Lavender panties and bra, pastel blue blouse, and white slacks lay on the bed. He maneuvered the chair beside the bed, pulled up his pant cuff, sat, and crossed one leg over the other. He remained there waiting for his new collaborator to make her appearance.

Tracy stepped out of the shower, wrapped in a white towel. She let her wet hair fall behind her neck with a swift swoop of her head. Her awareness of someone in the room became evident as the last remnants of steam dissipated through the open door.

Seeing Ru's leering face infuriated her. "Don't you have any common decency?"

"On my ship, I do as I wish, without interference. As a matter of fact, you should be grateful it's not one of my men sitting here."

Tracy was surprised at her sudden fierceness. Something inside her was fighting back. "If you want me to cooperate, I need some privacy. Now get out of my room!"

Ru stood, feeling the wrath of a confident woman in a moment of fearlessness. He realized her help was going to cost him some humility. So be it, he thought. So be it—within reason.

"When you are dressed, meet me in the mess hall." He left the room pissed off and slammed the door in disgust.

Eighteen

The Minister of State

OVER THE MAIN gate, the flag of the People's Republic of China was partly unfurled, as the breeze had just settled down to a slight murmur. A group of disillusioned tourists marched around the red walls of Zhongnanhai, formerly an imperial garden. A devious guide had told the group it was open to the public. This couldn't have been further from the truth. The group from Spain had just visited the Forbidden City to the east, where they met the guide who managed to relieve them of some easy cash. Now armed guards dressed in uniform at the front of Xinhua Gate told the group to move aside. The public was kept away for security reasons because the Communist Party Headquarters was in the garden.

Due to its proximity to Tiananmen Square and because of the deadly response to the protest in 1989, Zhongnanhai had vastly increased its security with strategically positioned state-of-the-art surveillance cameras, ensuring the garden and compound were secure.

The buildings in the compound were synonymous with the White House in Washington, DC. From here, the Chinese president and the government staff carried out their day-to-day duties.

President Wei Lei was sixty years old, tall, slightly portly, with eyes that were close together. He had a flattish nose that predominated his features. His hair was a burst of black, short along the sides of his head. Lei's mannerisms were bold and humble, often bowing from the neck with his hands at his sides. Reminiscent of a giant panda, friendly and kind on the outside, devious and ruthless inside. He was a man to be wary of under any circumstances.

His father was one of the founders of the Communist Party and was purged in 1963 before the Cultural Revolution. At fifteen, Lei was sent to the rural countryside for re-education and hard labor. Through persistence, he graduated from Peking University with a degree in chemical engineering. After joining the Party, Lei became a consummate chess player with a strong man image. He rapidly consolidated power within the party and became president. He had become the most authoritarian leader since Chairman Mao.

His policies pumped billions of dollars into Asian and African investments while influencing and dominating the South Seas. He had pursued the great rejuvenation of the Chinese nation with the "China Dream Vision" and launched a crackdown on corruption and dissidence.

Lei's viewpoints were accepted and became a fundamental part of Chinese law. Any challenge to his analytical thinking was considered a threat to the Communist Party rule.

Lei commuted from his home in Jade Spring Hill to the compound every day. He always felt a twinge of passion entering the gates of the garden. Bright red banners on either side reiterated his belief in the Communist Party Manifesto. On the left, *Long Live the Communist Party.* On the right, *Long Live the Invincible Mao Zedong Thought.*

His car was a black limousine with bullet-proof windows and armor-plated doors, its large grille and red flag ornament evoked classic luxury. As the car bounced over the speed bump the limo phone rang. His personal attaché picked it up and handed it to him.

"It's the minister of state security."

Lei retrieved the phone from the attaché, listened for a moment, and handed back the phone.

"Postpone my eight a.m. appointment. Driver, speed it up," said Lei.

When they arrived, his security team escorted him directly to his office, where Guan Yin, the minister of state security, handed Lei a classified folder.

Ms. Guan became the first female of the Ministry of State Security because she had navigated around China's male-dominated, heavy drinking political culture. Not playing by these rules notably held back most aspiring women. A steady, rational, and shrewd person who came top in most of her courses, she was recognized for capability over political maneuvering.

She became a single mother by choice after reporting her husband's dissension regarding China's invasion of Nepal. He was a devout Buddhist who would have ruined her career with his rage. The communist Politburo relocated him to a re-education camp.

Guan Yin, an elegant woman in her early forties, rarely wore makeup and was regarded as one of the most beautiful women in government. She became a role model for ambitious young women following in her footsteps.

"Minister, sit down while I look at the file. There may be questions," said Lei.

His eyes scanned the single page rapidly, and a pensive expression emerged.

"Why was General Po allowed access to this rope?"

"He was permitted to enter the garden shed and use the tools," Yin sighed with frustration. "Our security detail has been reprimanded," she added.

"General Po left a suicide poem. Is there some message in it he was trying to imply?"

"We have had language experts, literary scholars, and poets trying to figure out if there was any significant meaning."

"Well, is there?"

"Our security experts think it's a relatively simple narrative poem. However, it doesn't really shed light on how he became compromised in the first place."

"My task force had a tip and found out he was rich beyond his means. It is a good indication he was corrupt. My reformation policies were going to make him another example, to be prosecuted in the courts."

"The Ministry of State Security will look into the matter more closely."

"Since the poem is a dead end, perhaps you should find out how he had scrolls worth five million US dollars in value."

"I have an agent who is quite capable of the task."

"Have him report to me. Give him my private cell number and send me his file," said Lei.

Yin stood up and walked toward the door. She turned around to face the president.

"Sir, we will find out who was responsible for compromising General Po."

"Thank you, Ms. Guan. Keep this affair out of the media."

Yin realized the importance the president had emphasized on his operation. She intended to fulfill her duties to the party and find the individuals responsible for General Po's death. An air of urgency compelled her to immediately send her specialist's file to Wei Lei.

When the agent's file arrived, the president wasted no time in going through it. As he read the profile, it became apparent this agent could not only find out General Po's influencer but could be utilized to perform a secret task for him. One that had been plaguing him for many years.

He took a sip of water and leaned back in the leather office chair. A sudden coldness tingled the skin on his backbone as the memories flooded in.

In 1985, Lei led a delegation to Paris to attend a scientific conference. At the time, he was a mid-level county functionary in his early thirties. This trip made an indelible impression and shook his image of the CIA's covert operations and the US intelligence community.

At the Second International Conference of Environmental Chemistry and Engineering, he met his nemesis.

His best friend from university, Chen Hao, and a delegate had been approached to have dinner with another noteworthy scientist who had published many renowned papers. Hao, along with Lei, had received their masters in material physics and chemistry from the Peking University of Technology and, along with a few other scientists, represented China's emerging chemical industry.

Dr. Chen Hao, as with others in the group, was chaperoned by two Secret Service men from the Consulate of China. Unfortunately, both became ill and were struck down with vomiting and diarrhea. Their absence presented an unexpected opening for an approach by a covert operative.

As the delegation leader, Lei was dismayed that his friend was missing from the festivities. Busy milling about at a dinner reception, Lei searched for Hao in the crowded banquet hall. Hundreds of international delegates made the search virtually impossible. After locating one of the sick intelligence agents and explaining his friend's disappearance, the agent used the shortwave radio to contact a surveillance van operated by Chinese security. The agent implored them to help locate Dr. Chen.

The Chinese agents had placed a tracking device on Dr. Chen earlier and located him in a small regional airport on the outskirts of Paris. He was found with a scientist and two other men who were reportedly CIA intelligence officers. The Chinese agents approached with sidearms drawn and surprised the CIA agents who realized their compromised position and allowed Dr. Chen to leave without incident.

Whisked away to the Chinese Embassy, his friend was interrogated without mercy. Lei tried to come to his rescue, citing his friend's past loyalty to the Communist Party and excellent work done for his country. It was to no avail, as this was neither insubordination nor a misguided step. No, this was downright treason, and as such, the head of security sent him home for punishment under the ambassador's orders.

Lei felt responsible for his friend's demise. Hao, his good friend, had suffered the consequences of his actions. *But why had he betrayed his country? How was he deceived? How did the guards both get sick?* Although his friend was lost, Lei was praised for his swift actions.

As he made further strides and became more powerful in the Communist Party, he swore to find the CIA agents who recruited his friend to defect. One day, he promised himself, *I will get my chance.*

Over the years, he had compiled a file folder of information regarding the CIA and its complicit behavior. A primary concern was the CIA spent millions of dollars to stage scientific conferences worldwide to lure scientists and delegates to foreign countries where they would be accessible. Their intelligence agents, under the guise of genuine meetings, would approach individuals and coerce them to defect. The researchers and delegates had no idea that they were set up, and a supposed legitimate professional educational venue was a scheme manipulated by the CIA.

Lei also found from security channels that there were throngs of FBI at these events. Future targets were identified by the US National Security Agency, and dossiers of personal, often revealing information were compiled on them to leverage their cooperation.

The CIA methodology suggested there was no substitute for getting together with peers, networking for jobs, checking out the latest technology, and delivering papers that would be published in professional journals. Lei noted that US and foreign intelligence officers flocked to these venues as vast arenas for recruitment.

There was one individual that Lei was interested in finding, and he didn't know whether he was a well-versed CIA intelligence officer or a rare academic involved with recruiting Chinese delegates.

The premise of the whole operation was to tap intellectual and academic wisdom. Lei finally pieced together evidence that in 1985, his friend Hao was being poached. Agents from the CIA enlisted the kitchen staff at the Paris Convention Centre to poison the Chinese guards so that Hao could be whisked away.

Foreign spy agencies would effectively use their massive organization to coordinate necessary visas and flight documents to convey recruits, wives, and children to the US mainland. Promises of a better life away from repressive regimes was the familiar narrative the foreign agents used to sway them.

Looking through the file, the minister of state security had sent, made him realize this particular agent, this instrument, this man named Ren Bo, would be able to track down the individual responsible for General Po's downfall.

***

The minister of state's private line rang. "Minister Guan speaking." She hid her surprise when she recognized the president's voice.

"The agent you suggested will be perfect. I also have another very private assignment for him," Lei paused, "I will courier you the file."

Nineteen

Keep Your Opinions to Yourself

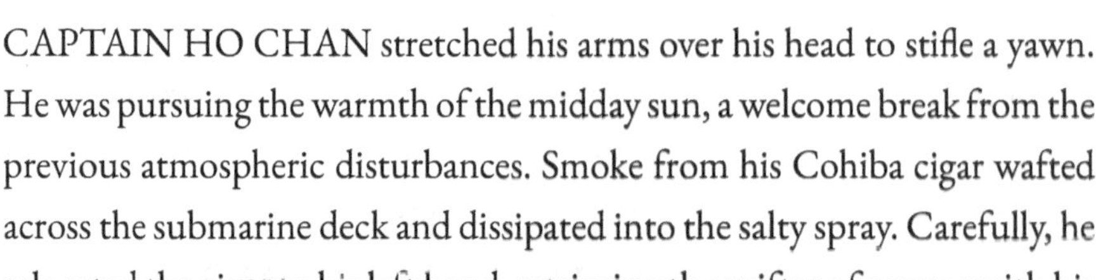

CAPTAIN HO CHAN stretched his arms over his head to stifle a yawn. He was pursuing the warmth of the midday sun, a welcome break from the previous atmospheric disturbances. Smoke from his Cohiba cigar wafted across the submarine deck and dissipated into the salty spray. Carefully, he relocated the cigar to his left hand, retrieving the snifter of cognac with his right. The movement caused the lounge chair to groan from his weight, his gluttony, the downside of his lavishness.

He was a former submarine commander in the Chinese Navy. After twenty-five years of saluting incompetent men, he denounced communism and embraced life's many pleasures. A brown-eyed, black-haired, barrel-chested man, a master tactician, he was an expert navigator.

When the submarine moved unexpectedly, the result of a sizable wave, the ash at the end of his cigar fell onto his Hawaiian shirt. Reacting quickly, he thrust the end of the cigar into his mouth and swiped at the ash, which he managed to smear throughout the red hibiscus patterned apparel. "Oh shit," he said.

The calamity managed to disrupt his fantasies. The mishap interrupted his thoughts about what he would do with his portion of the ransom for kidnapping Qi Ping, the billionaire who owned the submarine.

Chan and his crew had received word of the money transfer and left Qi Ping on a deserted island in Kowloon Bay. The equivalency of fifty-two million in bitcoin from the Evergreen Group was transferred to Ru's bitcoin address on the darknet. Then, the gangsters gave the CFO of Evergreen Group the island's coordinates to rescue the billionaire.

The captain reveled that neither the Hong Kong authorities nor Qi Ping's vast empire could retrieve the money or even find them.

When the bitcoin arrived in Ru's account, he used a contact in India who specialized in black market money to convert the bitcoin into actual cash. Each Foo Dog Triad brother was collecting a bonus for their involvement in the kidnapping.

Some of the fraudulent money was sponsoring the expedition as a ship and provisions would be required to accomplish the mission.

Chan heard soft pacing of rubber soles behind him. Turning around on the lounge, he positioned his feet on the decking and faced the crew member. The man stood in front of him shirtless, one shoulder was tattooed with a dragon and the other with a phoenix, mythical animals, stained with indelible colors on a canvas of skin.

"Sir, the *Lucky Star* has docked at Victoria Harbour and is moored beside the Kai Tak Terminal. Ru passed on an order to keep our position until further notice."

"Okay, inform Ru I understand. Tell the first mate to breakout the baijiu and the chef to organize a quick meal. It is time to celebrate before our next job," replied Chan.

***

The Harbin HC 120 on the stern of the *Lucky Star* prepared for liftoff. Ru, Tracy, and Dao made their way toward the cockpit door. They huddled down, waddling like ducks in a windstorm. Ru stepped into the small cabin while Tracy, hands bound with zip ties, was pushed inside. Dao was close behind her. He closed the door and locked it shut. Everyone strapped in and positioned the headphones over their ears. "Doors shut. We're ready to go," said Dao.

"Where to?" asked the pilot.

"Take us to runway thirteen at the old airport. Our warehouse is the blue one midway down the spit," said Ru.

Tracy looked over, bewildered that Dao had brought his doctor's bag. She was cooperating with them to the best of her ability. Dao's menacing presence and his past cruelty concerned her.

"Are you all right?" asked Ru.

"Yeah, um, yes; just thinking about my father," she said.

"You will see him as soon as you're done," he replied.

The chopper landed near the warehouse, surrounded by various construction projects.

"Locating us will be difficult since I kept the chopper below the radar scan," said the pilot.

"I am impressed with your flying. Any closer, and we could have gone fishing," said Ru.

"No problem with this chopper," said the pilot.

Everyone unbelted and stepped out of the helicopter and hurried to the warehouse.

"What's going on here?" asked Tracy. She surveyed the construction site and heavy equipment.

"Our group is part of a consortium on the revitalization of the old airport. We are going to build a five-hundred-suite hotel over there," said Ru.

He pointed to an excavated depression in the distance.

"We also are building low-cost apartments closer to the highway," he added.

"Don't tell me you guys are developers," replied Tracy.

"Tracy, don't be so cynical. We do good things occasionally."

"You are just hiding illicit revenue in legitimate real estate. I'd say that's money laundering."

"Listen here, we don't care what you think. You are here to help us. Keep your opinions to yourself, and maybe you'll live," said Dao.

Tracy stumbled as Dao pushed her forward toward the warehouse door. The building was prefabricated for easy assembly. It was made of aluminum siding and had overhead doors on either end, with an entrance door Dao had unlocked. A collection of construction equipment crowded the dirt floor. In contrast, a well-equipped office with a cement floor was positioned off to the right side. The three of them settled into the chairs around the desk.

Ru opened the laptop and slid it over to Tracy. "Now get to work on a feasibility plan," he said.

"I'll need to access my cloud account," said Tracy.

"You have access to the internet, but don't even think of trying to contact your father or the authorities."

"Fine." Tracy hid her disappointment.

"Would water or tea make this happen faster?" asked Ru.

"Yes, tea. Jasmine tea if you have it."

The dim fluorescent lighting on the warehouse ceiling generated shadows from the construction equipment, affecting Tracy's concentration. While her fingers moved the cursor across the screen, she looked through the office window, envisioning a specter in the gloom. Decisively, the cursor stopped, and she started evaluating the first pages of the ancient diary. Two years of information to shift through would be a lengthy undertaking. Scrolling to the second year brought her to the information she needed. Unwisely or not, she prepared a strategy despite her better judgment. It took a constructive approach that even Ru could appreciate.

Dao entered the office with the aroma of vegetables and fried rice wafting behind him.

Ru placed his gun cautiously on the coffee table as he rose from the couch. "Before we eat, I would like to see your plan," he said.

Dao placed the takeout bags beside the gun and stood firm beside Ru. Tracy turned the laptop around with the screen facing both.

"This is a condensed manifest of the cargo and treasure that was listed in the diary," said Tracy.

Ru stepped forward and adjusted the computer screen to reduce the glare. "You say this is a summary of the fleet's treasure?"

"Yes, Wang Jinghong's diary is not an official record of treasure and cargo but an observation. Because the treasury was so vast, it would have been impossible for him to record every detail. The fleet landed in dozens of ports on its journey, its ambassadors dispensing gifts and receiving other riches in return," said Tracy. "A summary is all we have."

"Still, this looks very promising," said Ru.

"Can I have a look?" asked Dao.

Ru repositioned the computer screen so Dao could see as well. "Embroidered silks, carved lacquerware, imperial blue and white porcelain plates and vases—there are thousands of them."

He stopped for an instant to look at Ru and Tracy. His bewilderment amused Ru.

"I took the ancient weight system and converted them to a modern version so you can appreciate the enormity of the goods," explained Tracy.

"Gold figures, gold hairpins encrusted with jewels, gold bowls, cups, gold coins, swords, muskets, and embossed boxes for jewelry." Dao stopped.

Ru placed his hand on Dao's shoulder.

"Tracy, would you say this is the tip of the iceberg?" asked Ru.

"Yes, it is. Let me explain some finer points. Historical records indicate Zheng He was captured and partially castrated at the age of ten and was put into service as a eunuch for the Prince of Yan, who later became the Yongle Emperor.

"The diary revealed some startling entries. The admiral didn't die at sea. On his final voyage to what is now known as Canada, he met a medicine woman who discovered the burden he carried. She created a potion that restored his manhood using local plants and tree barks. After a while, they became romantically involved. Pure of heart, they pledged themselves to each other. He decided to stay and keep a cargo ship and a treasure ship. He sent the starfleet to finish their voyage and head home with a new commander."

"What about the history books that state he was buried at sea?" asked Ru.

"Wang Jinghong wrote that after a few months at sea; his death was staged," said Tracy.

"So that would suggest he lived and died there with the Indigenous peoples and that his treasure may be undisturbed," said Dao.

"Could you estimate the value of his property?" asked Ru.

"Just the imperial porcelain alone could be worth billions, never mind the rest. Then there is the historical value to consider," said Tracy.

"I appreciate your summary, but now we have to get there before anyone knows our plans," said Ru.

"The lengthy exercise of examining all the starfleets' headings, wind directions, weather conditions, course changes, and places visited was a challenge. I used the locations and reconstructed a direct plotline to the final North American landing. A program called Navi Planner was quite helpful."

"Do you have the coordinates?" asked Ru.

"Yes." Tracy nervously shifted the cursor across the computer screen and tapped a new image. She redirected the laptop to Ru.

He smiled and pulled out his cellphone. *Buddha has smiled on us and changed everything,* he thought. He positioned his cellphone over the computer screen and snapped a picture of the island and the GPS coordinates.

Twenty

They Just Vanished?

THE FBI INTELLIGENCE center in the lower level of the consulate was still, like a mortuary at night. As early morning broke, the CCTV monitors in the surrounding street showed chaotic crowds of people commuting to work. The analysts had arrived early, seated themselves, and returned to their tasks from the day before.

The harried public procession outside contrasted with the methodical progress that Betty was making with her investigation. Exhaustive research on Tang's social media footsteps revealed photos posted by a young woman.

William and Patrick were sleeping in their chairs; they had spent the night at the center after a draining evening. Clicking computer keyboards and the hum of electronics permeated the room.

"Sir," said Betty.

William and Patrick were rousted from their sleep.

"What do you have for us?" asked Patrick.

"Found something on Tang Dao on social but nothing on Ru Fa Zhong. There are billions of people in China and the surname Tang is used by ten percent of the population. Millions of individuals are on the internet in Hong Kong, and more than half of those people have mobile phones."

"Would you get to the good part?" asked William.

Frank interrupted. "Can I break in here for a few minutes?" I have something from the airport cameras."

"Make it quick," said Patrick.

Frank was in his early thirties, brilliant and making a name for himself in the analytical theater. Before his transfer to Hong Kong for more international experience, he had helped the FBI capture a terrorist in New York.

"The CCTV at the Hong Kong International Airport corroborated Interpol's footage from the cameras. Tang Dao was one of the two men who took part in Tracy's abduction. Facial recognition, cross-referenced with police mug shots, proves it was him. We have footage from the Private Aviation Centre cameras that Tracy, Dao, and his crew flew off in a helicopter."

"Any idea where they went?" asked Patrick.

"We checked flight plans. They didn't submit one," replied Frank.

"They just vanished somewhere over the harbor?" asked William.

"Seems like that lead is gone for the moment," said Patrick.

"What about the social media approach?" asked William.

"We confirmed several pictures posted with a woman and Tang Dao. Her name is Susan Yu. Her profile on social media posted her employment as a jewelry store owner with phone number and business address on Queens Road at the New World Tower," said Betty.

"Thanks for that," said Patrick. "Let's use Susan Yu's phone number to get the phone records and see if Dao has recently called her. Then we can ping his location."

"Right on it, sir!" said the brunette.

Patrick and William looked at Betty, amused by her enthusiasm.

Minutes later, the information arrived on her screen.

"I've got his number, sir, and I'm triangulating a cellphone position. He is at the old Hong Kong International Airport," said Betty. "Satellite imaging is showing a warehouse. Sending the coordinates to your phone now."

"Do you have any agents close by?" asked William.

"Yes, we do. Lynn is in the area."

"Send her there to keep an eye on them and have her contact us if they leave suddenly," said Patrick.

Patrick turned to Frank, "Have Agents Fielding and Emmett been brought up to speed on this assignment?"

"Yes, sir."

"Tell them to meet us at the motor pool."

"Done. Go get 'em boss! said Frank.

"Shall we saddle our horses, partner?" asked Patrick, turning toward William.

"Very funny. Doing the Mountie jokes again?"

"You Canadians are too sensitive."

"Says the man who drinks absinthe."

"Touché. Let's get going."

William and Patrick made their way into the motor pool, their black van fueled and ready. Patrick slipped into the driver's seat and William sat beside him. FBI agents Aaron Fielding and Randall Emmett slid into the backseats.

Patrick drove the team from Hong Kong Island over the bridge and into the city's business core. He navigated the busy roads toward the former international airport which extended into Kowloon Bay.

"We should be there in another twenty minutes or so," said Patrick.

"Hopefully we can catch them unprepared," said William.

Twenty-One
A Possible Plaything, Perhaps

GUAN YIN'S SECURITY team escorted her to the Ministry of State Security Building across the compound. Her purple blouse rustled beneath the sky-blue jacket she wore. Her bejeweled Versace flats crunched on the gravel footpath. The designer shoes were a reward she allowed herself after succeeding in two prominent regional posts.

Headquartered in Beijing, the Ministry of State Security with which she was entrusted could be compared to a combination of the CIA and the FBI. With two years in her current position, her mandate had broad powers, which allowed her to conduct all types of espionage, both domestically and internationally. Her primary goal was to maintain a hard line on counter-revolutionary activities designed to sabotage or overthrow the Chinese communist system. Her authority included maximum effective countermeasures against agents of foreign nationals.

She decided that Ren Bo would be the best agent to fulfill President Wei Lei's mission. He had been recruited from the Strategic Support Force, a group of highly trained specialists. His responsibilities, while there, were for intelligence gathering analysis and establishing a support team in the criminal world. His latest assignment was in Northern Africa, where he was instrumental in thwarting a rigged competition for an internet system. A French telephone company was bribing officials to gain a lucrative contract to the detriment of Chinese G5 technology. Ren Bo and his team succeeded in exposing the criminal activity. This resulted in the Chinese corporation securing the contract to develop the G5 wireless system.

Ren Bo stood in front of Guan Yin with his feet apart, firm shoulders, back straight, ready to report. A fine specimen, she thought. *Mid-twenties and handsome. A possible plaything, perhaps.*

"Good to see you're back," said Yin.

"Nice to be home," he replied. "The African dust and the heat were barely tolerable."

"Excellent work on the last assignment. Your next one is closer to home."

The minister passed the file on General Po over to Ren Bo.

"Please sit down and take a minute to read the file because it can't leave the room," said Yin.

"Yes, Minister," he said, his eyes fixed on her firmly.

He read the classified document, interpreting the line-by-line description of events.

While he was occupied with General Po's file, Yin reopened Ren Bo's personnel file and started rereading it.

Born in the city of Caidain, in Hubei Province. Schooled at the Chinese Military Academy. His last position was colonel in the Strategic Support Force, a specialist in communication planning and executing intelligence-gathering operations. Also, an expert in probable courses of action. Instrumental in establishing a competent support team in the criminal underworld. Additional languages: expert in English, Korean, and Russian.

Yin closed Ren Bo's file, reassured he was the right choice for this assignment.

Ren Bo closed the secret file he had just read and handed it back.

"President Wei Lei approached me with another assignment of a sensitive nature," said Yin. She slid him the dossier the president had couriered over to her earlier.

Ren Bo opened the file and read the contents. "A tragic ending to what could have been a stellar career," he said. "I will do everything I can to apprehend the CIA agent involved in recruiting Dr. Chen."

"It's of utmost importance that both assignments are limited to you, President Wei Lei, and me," said Yin. "In fact, the president will require reports from you on a consistent schedule. I have added his encrypted cell number to your phone."

"Yes, Minister."

"We can arrange for you to join General Po's old unit as an advisor. You can start there," said Yin.

"Minister, I would appreciate some latitude. To get the best results, a more clandestine approach would be better," said Ren Bo. "For both cases."

"All right. Use your discretion."

"You're giving me complete freedom of authority to act for the Ministry of State Security?"

Ren Bo had reiterated her statement because he wanted to be sure that no bureaucracy stood in his way.

"You heard me, now get started."

***

William flipped through the satellite images of the warehouse where Dao was holding Tracy. The uneven road shaking the van was distracting his attention. His focus on rescuing his childhood sweetheart was averted momentarily.

"William, how is your strategy coming along?" asked Patrick.

"It is iffy at best. First, we don't know how many men Dao has and even if Ru is there," said William. "Second, we don't have a five-man SWAT team to breach and clear the building."

"You said Superintendent Whang Yang was excluding us from the investigation. I recall, you said we should get back to 'our people.' As far as I am concerned, we are 'our people,' and we are on our own," said Patrick.

"If you feel that way, we could ask Yang's team to join us. You know they will bring SWAT and breach the building. They won't be subtle. Not the best idea for a safe hostage extraction," said William.

"We start off covertly?" asked Patrick.

"Yes. First, we do a field assessment. Then we'll decide. Plan A will be a rear and frontal attack."

"What's Plan B?"

"We could follow Ru and Dao and wait for a better opportunity."

"Not ideal. Time is running out."

William's cellphone rang. The name John Abbott flashed across the screen.

"You gonna answer that?" said Patrick.

"Not yet." William shifted in his seat and lifted the satellite images out of the way. "What plan should I tell him we are taking?"

"Tell him we are coordinating an action plan with Superintendent Whang Yang of Interpol."

William was incredulous. "You can be a duplicitous bastard."

He hit redial and said, "John, what a pleasure to hear from you."

"Cut the crap, William. I've had to go to the FBI in Washington to find you. You need to bring me up to pace on your progress."

"We have met with Whang Yang, superintendent of the Interpol Liaison Bureau. They have identified the kidnappers as members of the Foo Dog

Triad. We think Tang Dao kidnapped Tracy on the orders of Ru Fa Zhong, the gang leader. We have located them in the warehouse on Hong Kong's old Airport Runway number thirteen. Right now, we are en route to rendezvous with Interpol and enter negotiations with the kidnappers."

"This sounds promising. I'll inform Tracy's father."

"Patrick will update the Washington FBI office."

"I'm looking forward to a positive resolution. In other words, bring Tracy back alive."

"That's always been my intention."

"If it's money they want, Dr. Jordan is preparing financial backing for a ransom."

"We'll keep you updated."

William disconnected the call. He swiped his sweaty right hand along his heavy black canvas pants and leaned back in his seat.

"We are close to the warehouse now. Look for a good rendezvous point," said Patrick.

A few minutes later, William said, "There's a good spot!" He pointed to the patch just north of Shing Fang Road Bridge. Patrick glided the van gracefully onto the abandoned site. Dusk elapsed into night, and darkness soon embraced them.

"Any word from Lynn at the stakeout?" William said.

"They are still in the warehouse."

The team exited the vehicle, and Patrick removed a rugged shipping case from the rear of the van.

"What have we here?" asked William.

"That's what we call our Jack in the Box. It's waterproof and airtight." Patrick unfastened the metal clasps and exposed the contents. "Let's see: two .40-caliber Glock 22s, two boxes of ammunition, two Motorola APX 7000 radios, one Rock River Arms rifle LAR 15, one thermographic camera, six stun grenades, one Remington 870 shotgun, ammunition, and gas masks. It's all here," pronounced Patrick.

"You brought tactical vests and folding knives?" asked William.

"Yes. We've got everything we need."

"Excellent."

"I think you should take point."

"All right then. Mountie's upfront," William said. "Okay team. Stay off the walls, keep your balance, move in and control the situation. Make your shots accurate and discriminating."

A flashlight illuminated the satellite photo that indicated an excavated hollow a short distance away from the building. William motioned for Patrick and the other two FBI agents, Aaron and Randall, to follow. Each man moved tactically and silently through the rubble and brush of the former airport. The equipment in the Jack-in-the-Box was distributed between them all. William took the lead, using hand movements to motion them over and forward. The team crawled behind William as he edged toward the hole. He put his hand up from his bent elbow and the group formed a single file as they trundled through the broken brick. Patrick and William landed in the hole. Dust erupted around their tactical boots creating a dense haze. Aaron and Randall slid in behind them, one armed with the Glock, the other with the LAR-15 rifle.

William aimed the thermographic camera toward the warehouse.

"The infrared camera is picking up five bodies inside. Two in the heavy equipment area and three in the office," said William. "I see another image on the other side of the warehouse."

"That'll be Lynn," said Patrick.

William looked at Patrick. "Plan A or plan B?"

"You'll have to explain to John if we get crushed," said Patrick.

"Plan A. We go in first."

"Lynn will radio Yang at Interpol and tell him to get his SWAT team here the moment we breach the warehouse."

Twenty-Two

The Chopper of Hong Kong

RU MADE TWO cell calls from behind an excavator in the far corner of the warehouse. The first was to Bojing to inform him of Tracy's efforts and strategy. On the next call, he ordered Chan to covertly sail the submarine to the old airport docks and wait for him and his accomplices.

Ru re-entered the office. He wore his bespoke bulletproof attire, and his muscles rippled beneath the dark blue fabric. Roaming between the desks, his arms swayed with each stride. His bearing exhibited courage and fearlessness as a warrior and leader of the Foo Dog Triad.

Tracy had overheard his men call him "The Chopper of Hong Kong." Watching him enter the office reinforced that reputation.

"Listen up. Chan is bringing the submarine here. We should all catch some sleep. We will need to rest for the long journey."

"How can we leave when you haven't organized a research vessel for us?" asked Tracy.

"We can't wait here. Interpol is looking for you, and I need your expertise for this task."

"This mission needs equipment and manpower!" replied Tracy.

"We are well aware of the logistics," said Dao.

"You should let me reorganize this mission. It could take weeks to sort out the details."

"We don't have that extravagance. We need the submarine to get us out of here," replied Ru.

"I've thought of an entirely new cover story for the mission."

"You better not be stalling for more time, hoping to get rescued. In fact, we will be starting in a few hours. Chan is sailing the submarine here now. So get some rest."

"You too." He pointed at Dao, then settled himself into the office chair, and lay his feet lightly on the desk.

The old airport was still. Construction crews were at home relaxing with family. Many of the workers were drinking and having fun in the local bars. City lights glimmered faintly in the distance. Junks and dragon boats were furrowing through the bay, churning white froth behind their sterns as they made their way to their destinations.

***

A single light shone over the doorway to the warehouse, making a covert approach almost unfeasible, but not impossible.

"Where is everyone now?" asked Patrick.

"I only have heat signatures for three hostiles. They are all stationary," said William.

"Probably sleeping."

"I can't see the other two. It must be the glass. These infrared cameras can't penetrate the anti-reflection coating."

"The other two must be in the equipment area, probably armed."

"Best scenario, send Aaron and Randall to the back door to provide a distraction. Their task is to pick the lock on the rear door, get inside and pitch a couple of stun grenades and take down the two enforcers in the equipment area," said Patrick.

"We break down the front door, pitch stun grenades into the office, isolate Tracy, and shoot our way out, if necessary," added William.

A jet airliner screeched in the distance as it raced across the city, giving the two men a moment to ponder the next move.

William whispered, "Tracy is our primary concern. They won't hurt her. She is more valuable alive to them. Let's get the magnitude and timing of this action just right. If we move and get the direction or timing wrong, we're all dead.

An unnerving stillness settled around them. William motioned for the team to move on to the warehouse. They split up. William and Patrick taciturnly deployed to the front of the building and the other FBI agents to the rear.

Lynn stood guard on the other side of the building with her cellphone in hand, ready to call Interpol when the teams entered the warehouse.

William glided around the steel-framed barriers, over a mound of excavated soil, and paused to listen. Patrick stopped behind William and tensed up.

"What's wrong?" asked Patrick.

"Nothing. Thought I heard something," he said. "Let's move around to the scaffolds and over to the bulldozer. We should be at the door in a few steps."

***

The intense flash permeated the space beneath the doorjamb. The stun grenade explosions ripped through the building.

"That's our cue. Let's go!" said William.

Patrick placed the Remington shotgun at a forty-five-degree angle between the lock and the doorframe. Boom, boom! Splinters of wood and metal burst and smashed out the locking mechanism. William drove his right boot into the door, hoping there were no deadbolts. It gave way.

Shots were fired as William and Patrick arrived at the office door inside the warehouse. The other team kept the two gangsters pinned down in between the construction equipment. Then there was deathly silence.

William and Patrick gave each other determined looks before putting on their respirators. Their mindset was of complete domination of their surroundings. William tossed in two stun grenades, one into the warehouse and the other into the office.

Tracy, Ru, and Dao were disoriented, confused, blind, and unable to hear.

William found Tracy and gripped her hand, pulling her through the damaged front door into the cool night. Her determination returned with every step she took. The flash-bang grenade had ignited loose papers. Flames erupted, and smoke filled the office.

Tracy's eyes stung from the burning smoke. "Is that you, William?"

"Yes, it's me," he said. "Get away from the building as fast as you can."

William had re-entered the warehouse to help. Patrick prepared to handcuff Dao as the thug shook off the effects of the stun grenade. Ru stepped in to intervene, landing a sidekick to William's solar plexus. He buckled over, his peripheral nervous system screaming from the intense pain.

Ru's ears rang like he had been at a rock concert. He lost his balance and smoke burned his eyes. Somehow, he found the stamina to hurl a head punch at William and dislodged his gas mask, but William quickly repositioned it. Sucking in fresh air, William felt adrenaline overcoming his pain, and the professional training pushed him into action. He blocked and kicked high, connecting with Ru's chin, knocking him out flat on the floor.

Dao also adapted to his surroundings and leaped midair toward the coffee table for the gun.

William instinctively realized he didn't have time to reach his holstered Glock and hurled himself out of the office door.

Two .45-caliber bullets whirled over Patrick's head, accompanied by equally loud discharges. Patrick dove and rolled behind the backhoe just in time to feel the rounds glance off the front loader. William slipped in between the back wheels and the backhoe arm. By now, the smoke was dissipating, and he could clearly see the office.

William felt the wetness on his left shoulder. "Damn ricochet," he muttered, squelching the blood flow with his right hand.

Aaron and Randall moved between the backhoe and the office. Aaron started firing his Glock at the office, providing cover. Randall shouldered the LAR-15 rifle pulling it tight against his shoulder, his eyes focused on the office. He started laying down rapid-fire. Spent brass cartridges were flipping away from the scorching barrel. The smell of gunpowder infused the air.

Ru and Dao took shelter behind the office desk as the rounds saturated the air in a perilous conflagration. An inferno was crackling behind them, and the heat was excruciating.

William ignored the pain in his arm as he and Patrick moved swiftly out of the warehouse and into the darkness of the night. Randall rapidly changed the magazine, Ru stood up, firing back. He took two rounds and was thrown backward off his feet. Randall continued his onslaught and Aaron kept up a burst of bullets as they backed out of the rear door. Ru managed to shake off the punishing salvo. Nothing he could do about the bruising and the damaged fabric, but the suit had saved his life.

Tracy saw William, ran toward him, and threw her arms around him. He grimaced, then smiled at her.

The reverberation of the helicopter's approach reassured everyone that help from Interpol would soon arrive.

***

Captain Ho Chan was docking the submarine along the western side of the spit when he saw a succession of flashes and heard multiple explosions. He rallied his men who rushed toward the warehouse armed with AK-47s. Their orders were to extract Ru and Dao, get Tracy safely to the submarine, and salvage the mission. Chan and the gangsters entered the warehouse, each man stepping between the equipment and searching for safe passage to the office. Ru and Dao were racing toward them, their faces tucked into their arms, coughing and gasping.

***

The Avicopter AC352 carrying the Interpol team landed near the FBI van. Superintendent Whang and a crack force of the Hong Kong SWAT team surged toward the warehouse. The Foo Dog Triad guarded Ru and Dao as they made their escape to the submarine. The Hong Kong police team split into two groups. Yang led one team toward William and Tracy and the other squad ran after the escaping triad members. As the police reached the dock, only the submarine conning tower was visible descending into the dark, murky water of the inlet. In frustration, they fired anyway.

Tracy looked into William's eyes. "You are a life saver. Thank you. But what are you doing here?" she said with apprehension.

William prepared to answer when the flames shot higher. Everyone stepped back. His response was lost for now. Explosions rocked the warehouse as fragments of Bobcats, cranes, and backhoes were tossed everywhere before plummeting to the ground.

Two paramedics approached Tracy and William. One pried Tracy away from his arms and escorted her to the ambulance while the other patched up William's arm. Tracy waved to William just before the rear doors closed with a thud.

***

"Dive, dive, dive!" Chan shouted, as thuds of machine-gun bullets hit the submarine conning tower.

Ru and Dao stayed cool as they jumped down every other step into the control room. Eighteen crew members ran to their respective stations, having trained for an emergency dive just like this.

Dao landed with a solid thump, his face turned beet red, and his body shook intensely. "We were lucky this time," he said.

Ru was catching his breath. "It feels like I have a cracked rib. That suit was worth the money." He placed Tracy's smoldering laptop on the map table and examined his hand.

"You need the medic," said Dao.

"What I need is a stiff drink."

Restless, he started pacing around the observation hall. He stopped and looked through the pressure-resistant glass. Old tires and cans littered the seabed.

Concerned for the men, Ru turned around. "They almost had us. Thanks to Chan and the crew, we got out just in time, but we lost two good men. If those cops interfere again, they will die."

"The extraction team was efficient at getting Tracy out. They destroyed a valuable warehouse," said Chan.

"What's the plan now that we have lost Tracy Jordan? She was the single most important part of recovering the antiquities," said Dao.

"We do have the laptop and the GPS location, so we know where we're going next," said Ru.

"That's good, but the Hong Kong police are looking for us," said Dao.

"Let's not worry about the Hong Kong police or Interpol. They have the girl, and it is not worth it for them to follow."

"They may be trying to find the submarine we stole," said Chan.

"We are leaving China. Interpol has to find us first," said Ru.

"What about the *Lucky Star?*" asked Dao.

"Contact the captain and tell him that it's business as usual. If the police ask for us, he can tell them we are on a well-deserved vacation," said Ru.

A few of the crewmembers started laughing and cajoling at the mention of time off.

"Taking a vacation would be good after what we just went through," said Dao.

"Believe me, where we are headed will be much less dangerous, and you might just enjoy yourself," said Ru.

"Captain, have the helmsman plot a course to Macau," said Ru, amid the cheers of the crewmen.

"Aye, aye," responded the captain.

***

Ru had decided to celebrate and returned from the submarine's wine cellar carrying a 2009 Château Pape Clement Blanc. As he arrived in the observation hall, Dao swiveled the computer around to show the new agenda.

"Is this a good time for you to discuss a strategy with us?" he asked.

"In a moment, but first we should have a toast," said Ru.

He poured liberal amounts into three wine glasses. The straw color of the wine gleamed like gold. Ru moved the glass under his nose, capturing its essence as the wine rose up the sides.

"The fact that we are safe is a favorable omen. 'For in the midst of chaos, there is also opportunity,'" said Ru.

"From the *Art of War,* a great quote from Sun Tzu," said Chan.

The three men touched their glasses together. The bohemian crystal echoed across the room, and the bond was forged.

"One of the first issues to discuss is a cover story. So, we can explore the area without any fear from authorities," said Dao.

"Leave that with me," replied Ru.

"Where are we headed after Macau?" asked Chan.

"I am going to New York. I'll be able to tell you much more once I arrive. But chances are exceedingly high that Tracy and her father may be organizing their own expedition. So, let me investigate that angle first," said Ru.

The submarine voyage to Macau was uneventful but lavish. They arrived during a tropical rainfall. The harbor was frothy as the crew was brought to shore by water taxis. Ru selected a hotel within proximity of the port and submarine.

After getting comfortable, Ru messaged Bojing about the attack on the warehouse and their escape. He used a private, encrypted instant messaging app that neither hackers nor the government could penetrate. His message read:

This is to inform you we are safe. Going forward without the girl.
Purchasing ship and equipment. Relics are a top priority.
Will keep you updated. Ru.

Ru set the self-destruct timer on the telegram message and pressed send. Bojing had less than five minutes to read the message before it would disappear into the ether.

Bojing replied:

William Fox of the RCMP and Patrick Reilly of the FBI rescued the girl. Interpol on your trail; watch your exposure. Bojing.

Ru responded:

Flying to New York to set up a new strategy. Ru.

Ru leaned back in his chair and thought, *William Fox? The guy who cost us millions when he went after Wu Sunfay in Montreal? That Fox?*

Twenty-Three

This Nightmare Really Got to Her

YANG AND WILLIAM sat in the waiting room of Kowloon Hospital, sipping coffee and waiting good-naturedly. Tracy was showing signs of trauma brought on by her ordeal. Doctors explained it was essential for a thorough physical and mental examination before her release. Although the pain from the burns and bullet wound that William suffered were tolerable, doctors strongly advised him to take desk duty for a few months. He was more concerned about Tracy's outcome than his own. His promises to John Abbott were nagging him as his head began to pound. His cooperation with the Hong Kong division of Interpol had been less than stellar. He wished he had some of his father's diplomatic finesse, it could have helped him here.

The Interpol team and fire department were still on the scene. Interpol was stalled by the cold trail left by Ru and Dao's departure. The firemen were dousing embers and flare-ups. The explosion and fire were headlines in the morning newspapers and were featured on the internet and television stations worldwide.

William stood up.

"Where are you going?" asked Yang.

"I need a private area to inform Deputy Minister Abbott about Tracy's rescue," replied William.

William breezed along the sterile pink corridor, avoiding a nurse pushing a patient in a wheelchair. He found a bench in front of a memorial plaque, sat down, and dialed the secure line to Canada.

John's encrypted phone chimed. He picked up the cell, walked to the office door, and shut it. "How is she?" he asked.

"She is dazed but holding up. The doctors are with her now. This nightmare really got to her."

"How are you?"

"I'm okay, just exhausted from the gunfight," said William, neglecting to mention his injury.

"I am relieved that you and the team got her out alive, but you should have followed protocol."

"Patrick already reported to FBI headquarters enlightening them about this predicament with Interpol."

"As Canada's deputy of national defense, my position wields some influence in certain circles. But this time, I must confer with my boss, the external affairs minister, with the US State Department, and the FBI to reconcile with the Hong Kong government."

"You should know that Superintendent Whang Yang was not happy we did not consult him, but he was impressed with the team moving in with the rescue. Patrick, the team, and I were invaluable in saving Tracy—and he knows it. By calling Interpol at the last minute, we handed him a political feather in his cap, so to speak. We will be escorted to the airport with the proviso that we do not return. Sort of a voluntary deportation. Yang wants a report about our involvement, and that sums it up," said William.

"The director of the FBI in Washington informed us that Yang has been in touch with him regarding your departure. As soon as Tracy is released from hospital, the bureau is flying all of you to the United States. They will reunite her with her father, and the Washington FBI field office will debrief you all. I will notify your father you're all right, then inform René Bouchard at RCMP C Division you'll be reporting back in a week."

"Thanks; I owe you one," responded William.

"You don't owe us anything. If I were you, I would make up for lost time with Tracy. She deserves a proper explanation," said John.

"You know about that?"

"Your father told me."

"Tracy and I do need to talk."

Twenty-Four

Listen We Should Talk

WILLIAM SPENT THE morning at FBI headquarters with Tracy and Patrick, being debriefed on the Hong Kong mission. Both Canadian and American enforcement agencies managed to avoid a diplomatic fallout. However, neither agent would be allowed back to Hong Kong. Diplomatic immunity or not, a multinational enforcement operation not approved by the ambassador or local authorities jeopardized the working relationship between nations.

When the debriefing was over, the FBI agents in charge agreed that despite the danger of causing an international incident, there had been a clear goal from the onset: get Tracy Jordan back alive. And they did it. Ru's gang was on the run, and the Hong Kong branch of Interpol had received credit for the termination of two gangsters.

Even though the team had not adhered to proper procedural protocol, the operation was a success under extraordinary circumstances. William Fox, Patrick Reilly, Aaron Fielding, and Randall Emmett would be receiving the Shield of Bravery medals. For national security reasons, the ceremony would be private and scheduled for late March when the FBI director, along with the president, would present the medals in the East Room of the White House.

***

William followed Tracy out of the building and hailed a cab to the hotel they were both staying at. He was anxious to speak with her. On the trip over from Hong Kong, he had tried to talk to Tracy, but she had kept her distance. The jet was small, and privacy was impossible.

Settling into the cab, William turned to her and said, "Have you been in touch with your dad yet?"

"We spoke last night. He's meeting me in Washington later today. We head out to Nova Scotia early tomorrow morning."

She was aloof and distant and unwilling to meet his eyes. Even after her rescue, she wasn't sure she could trust him.

"Listen, we should talk," said William. "Are you free for lunch or dinner?"

"Sure. Dinner would be okay. Call my room."

William waited several hours before dialing the front desk. "Can you connect me to Ms. Jordan's extension, please?"

After a moment's delay, the front desk said, "I am sorry, sir. Ms. Jordan has already checked out."

She ghosted me. I guess I deserved that, he thought dejectedly as he replaced the receiver into its cradle.

***

William was glad to be back in Canada, feeling an element of relief and satisfaction to be far from the machinations of Hong Kong. Getting back to his old life would be a respite from the turmoil in the former British colony. Even the students there were causing bedlam in the streets about the future of politics in Hong Kong keeping the police busy.

The driver of the black SUV from the carpool collected William from the airport. William picked up the newspaper left on the seat and read the front-page story on the *National Post.* The Canadian Government was detaining a Chinese telecommunications executive on the whim of the American Justice Department. The politics of both nations was not lost on William, and his only concern was that his actions in Hong Kong did not cause further conflict with Canadian foreign policy. He had plenty of time to contemplate his circumstances on the drive into downtown Ottawa.

***

The driver dropped William off at National Defence Headquarters. The building was situated on Colonel By Drive, adjacent to the muddy waters of the Rideau Canal, a National Historic and a UNESCO World Heritage site. Opened in 1832, the famous canal, faced northwest of the DND facility and was a sixteen-minute walk away to the Parliament Block. The Gothic Revival buildings are the powerhouse of the Canadian people, where political and military decisions are made.

William walked into John Abbott's office and sat down in the brown leather chair. He extended his feet across the beige carpet and pulled the chair forward on its rollers until it stopped behind the heels of his boots. This put him in front of John's desk with a direct line of sight to his certificates and degrees mounted on the wall. John was amused and smiled at William's theatrics. He shuffled loose documents into a file and placed them to the side.

"Glad to see you're back," said John.

"It's really nice to be back home," replied William.

John noticed William's sling. "What happened to your arm?"

"Ricochet. At the warehouse."

"You didn't mention this when we spoke."

"I didn't think it was a big deal." William shifted uncomfortably.

"I'll need to inform René," said John. "He'll probably put you on sick leave. Did you get a chance to remedy your situation with Tracy?"

"She left before we could talk."

"Maybe next time," said John. "Let's get to the report you owe me."

"Well, I met FBI Agent Patrick Reilly in Hong Kong, had a few drinks, and got to know him rather quickly. The next morning, we had a meeting with Superintendent Whang Yang at the Interpol office. We did our best to get involved with the investigation. After the superintendent identified Tang Dao and Ru Fa Zhong as the kidnappers, he stonewalled us and put us on the sidelines of the investigation. We decided to use the FBI cyber-operations at the US Consulate in Hong Kong. While there, we found a connection to Tang Dao through his girlfriend's cell. Our investigative team located him in a warehouse at the old airport in Kowloon Bay where Tracy was being held. Patrick drove me and two elite FBI agents to assault the warehouse and rescue Tracy. Patrick and I entered at the front and the two FBI agents from the rear. The pincer movement caught the triad gang in a crossfire. We eliminated two gangsters, saved Tracy, and because of the flash-bang grenades, a fire began in the warehouse. Ru Fa Zhong and Tang Dao escaped in the submarine. We did inform Yang that we were engaged in a rescue attempt and that he was to bring his SWAT team to assist. Which he did. Our decision was to include him and give him credit for the arrest. Patrick and I gave our reports to Interpol. Tracy was at the hospital getting treated. Afterward, we were escorted to the airport, and we left voluntarily. We arrived in Washington for a debriefing at FBI headquarters, and you know the rest."

"No, I don't," said John leaning forward, irritated. "Where are Tracy and her father?"

"They flew to Nova Scotia from Washington," said William.

John checked his watch. "You have just enough time to get to the airport and get home before dinner. Your country thanks you. Have a pleasant trip," he said, reaching across his desk and shaking William's hand.

"Nice to have met you. Maybe we'll see each other again," said William.

"Maybe."

William shoved the brown leather chair back, got up and walked out the door.

John pushed the button on his desk phone and said, "Get me the minister of national defense."

***

The minister coasted up the marble-laden hall away from the ruckus of parliamentary rhetoric. "I despise the grand standing and dirty political games. It just wastes taxpayers' money," he muttered. He could have said it's just another day in the Canadian political arena, but his sensibilities and loyalties remained with his constituents.

Poking his head into his office as if it was a bunker, he scanned the room, prepared to breach it. His military training still identified him as an experienced battle officer who had given up his command for a desk job. He readied himself for the constant onslaught of telephone calls, meetings, rules, and regulations.

His secretary stood up and straightened her dress, surprised to see him arrive so abruptly, as the wall clock indicated Parliament was still in session. She knew better than to ask why he was back so soon, as his acrimonious visual cues were quite evident. His secretary meekly broke the silence.

"Deputy Minister Abbott called, sir."

"Did he say what about?"

"No sir."

"Fine. Get him on the phone for me."

The secretary buzzed the minister, and said, "I have John Abbott on line one for you."

"Hi John, to what do I owe this pleasure?" said the minister.

"I wanted to bring you up to speed on a matter that may be used in Question Period to derail our office."

"Well, nobody wants to be blindsided."

"Let me begin with William Fox, one of our own RCMP officers that I put into an off-book operation as a favor for his father, James Fox. You may remember James as an ambassador to South Korea. To make a long story short, William Fox and Patrick Reilly, an FBI agent, saved Jeffrey Jordan's daughter Tracy who had been kidnapped by the Foo Dog Triad in Hong Kong. Rules were broken which resulted in their voluntary deportation. It is my belief that an international incident has been successfully contained. I'll send you a full report, so you are prepared."

"This sounds fascinating. Thanks for keeping me in the loop."

John Abbott's report intrigued the minister. He smiled with wry amusement. The sarcastic remarks made by the opposition parties' scabrous political hacks faded away. His day was getting much more interesting.

Twenty-Five

Cherry Blossoms

THE ARRIVAL OF Spring in Washington, DC transformed the state gardens from russet to green. The tulips, daffodils, and cherry tree blossoms surrounding the monuments had begun a triumphant transition, attracting Capitol Hill visitors from near and far to come and enjoy the history and season, host to the annual National Cherry Blossom Festival.

William caught glimpses of the crowds and flowers through the cab's window.

The taxi stopped outside the Willard InterContinental Hotel. The FBI had selected it because of its proximity to the White House. He was puzzled by Tracy's abrupt departure back in December after the debriefing, and other than the odd email or text, she remained distant.

William was surprised to receive Tracy's message saying that she would be in Washington to visit the Smithsonian the same week he was to receive the medal. Hoping to see her again, he started going over what he would tell her and repeatedly reframed his thoughts until he became exhausted. He grabbed a blended Scotch from the mini bar, snapped off the cap, and finished it in one swallow. A burning sensation followed, which warmed him and helped lift his mental fog. He called Tracy on her cell.

"Hello," she said.

"Tracy, it's William. How are you doing?

"Okay. Coming to terms with things... work helps."

"This... thing... between us... we should talk about it."

"It's been bothering me, too."

"After the medal presentation tomorrow morning, let's go for a walk."

"Yes. Sure, I suppose," she said with hesitation.

"Can you meet me at the Washington Monument at noon hour?"

"All right. See you then."

***

The following morning went quickly for William, and the FBI team. The ceremony for the Shield of Honor medals contained the usual dialogue about the bravery of the FBI agents. Special attention was spent on the collaboration with the RCMP and the participation of Inspector William Fox.

The president was immensely grateful for the rescue of Tracy Jordan and appreciated the international scale of the operation. It was a rare day a Canadian citizen was praised by a US president, especially one who was known for his outright dangerous and divisive policies.

The FBI director also commended Patrick Reilly, Aaron Fielding, and Randall Emmett with the Medal for Meritorious Achievement for their exemplary efforts in Hong Kong.

William was grateful to have the whole affair over as he was anxious to finally spend time with Tracy and talk about his feelings for her.

He said his goodbyes to Patrick Reilly and the FBI team. He would treasure the bond forged with Patrick for years to come and they promised they would stay in touch with each other.

"They'll be assigning me to a new embassy. I'll let you know where I land." Patrick shook his hand vigorously and patted him on the back of the shoulder like a brother.

William reciprocated. "See ya, pal."

"Mounties rock," said Patrick.

***

William approached the Washington Memorial wondering if Tracy would stand him up again. He was happy to see she was patiently waiting for him, dressed in silk cream blouse and a red floral skirt with matching red patent shoes. Her hair was fresh and shiny. He knew she expected a long and thoughtful explanation of their split-up years ago.

William reached her with a smile and a wave.

"How did it go?" she asked.

"The president was praiseworthy but couldn't stay long. He had other commitments. The FBI director was the one who presented the medals and gave the speech. He said we did a great job, despite the fact we should have been a little more cooperative with the local authorities."

Tracy stepped forward and put her finger to his lips.

"That's not important. What's important is that I'm here because you saved me."

Tracy placed her hands on his and looked into his deep, brown eyes. She moved her left hand forward, controlled his right hand, and pulled him along the sidewalk. "Come on, let's go."

Tracy stopped at the first park bench and said, "Let's sit down here."

"Oh, I had something else in mind," said William. "I wanted to take you along the Tidal Basin Trail. The Japanese cherry trees are blooming, and it smells and looks breathtaking."

"The walk can wait. I really need to hear what you have to say, and I need to hear it now." Tracy shifted her arm on the back portion of the bench and faced him. "Okay, Mister. Start talking."

William stiffened, looked intently at his Rolex, and fiddled with the crown. "Where do I start? How do I start?"

"You can start with why you ignored me in school and didn't return my calls."

William placed his hand on her exposed knee. "I was ashamed."

"What about?"

Annoyed, she slipped her right leg over her left knee. William removed his hand just in time.

"It's about when we got robbed in the alley."

"Go on."

"I was totally out of my element. I feel guilty because my brother is in a wheelchair. I wanted to save him. It was the worst day of my life."

An approaching whirling and clattering stopped their conversation. Tracy and William turned in the direction of the disturbance. A teenager flew by on a skateboard, his arms outstretched, and his knees bent as if riding a wave.

"My mother blamed my father, and they divorced. But it's really my fault for not protecting Jamey."

"William, you know that can't be true."

"She got a new job and moved to Toronto with my brother to take care of him. I couldn't face you. It could have been you in that wheelchair."

"Oh, William, I didn't know."

"I didn't call or talk to anybody. I threw myself into taekwondo."

Tracy looked away, then back again. Her eyebrows came together, and her eyes widened. She opened her mouth to say something but couldn't find the words at first.

"Do you know I would have done anything for you? I wish you had come to me. I could've helped you, comforted you. But you ignored me instead," she said. "Now all these years later..." Her voice cracked.

The clacking of red shoes echoed on the paving stones as she got up and walked away.

Tracy's reaction stunned William. Seconds passed before he composed himself and deftly paced after her.

"Tracy. Please."

He moved in front of her and stopped. She ran into him meeting him face to face.

"Are you going to be all right?" he asked.

"I don't know what I'm feeling right now."

"How about we go to the tidal basin? Let's just stroll and try to process this together. What do you say?" he said. "I do care for you. It's why I went looking for you when you were kidnapped."

"My feelings haven't changed for you in all these years. I would like to know everything about what happened to you since," said Tracy.

'You can tell me what you've been doing as well."

"All right," she said. Tracy slipped her hand into William's, looked up, and smiled. He looked over at her, smiled back, and they started wandering toward the tidal basin.

Twenty-Six

We Were Both Too Young

AS TRACY AND William entered the park, the midday sun warmed the afternoon air. Pink and white petals adorned the cherry trees, their cracked trunks and knurled branches nestled along the banks of the Potomac. The delicate scent of cherry blossom flourished amid the wooded promenade. In 1912, the Japanese government had gifted three thousand of these cherry trees to the city in a gesture of friendship.

Tracy and William walked together, searching their past for the link that would unite them in the present. The pathway was overcrowded with sightseers, day-trippers, and trekkers taking in the beauty of the trees in blossom.

They chatted, sauntering past the Jefferson Memorial. "Tell me what happened after I left Seoul," said William.

"You mean after I cried for a week?"

William blushed.

They continued to walk.

They consulted at the Franklin D. Roosevelt Memorial. "After the initial shock, I swore off guys and got into my studies. I admired my dad's work in archaeology, and now I am an associate professor at Stanford," she said. "What about you?"

"After graduating from McGill, I studied forensic accounting and joined the RCMP."

They consoled at the Martin Luther King Memorial. "I wish I'd understood what you were going through," she said. "All I could see was my own hurt at your rejection."

"We were both too young and immature, facing things that even adults would have trouble dealing with."

"You know, I never forgot you. I went on some dates in university, but no one really interested me. My work is what mattered to me most."

By the time they reached the White House, they had reconciled.

"Tracy, I never forgot you, either. Would you like to try again, now that we are so much wiser?" William acted nonchalant, but his brown eyes betrayed his longing.

"Yes, let's try." Tracy looked at her watch, hiding her own yearning. "I am really hungry."

"Let's go back to the hotel," replied William.

"What do you have in mind?" She flirted, batting her eyes.

"A room service date."

"Is that what I think it means?"

William stepped out and waved down an oncoming taxi. He pulled the rear door open and beckoned her in.

"How gallant!" exclaimed Tracy.

"My pleasure."

William barely had time to tell the driver their destination before Tracy slipped her right arm around his neck and drew his lips to hers. He closed his eyes and welcomed the sensation rushing in. His hands gently cradled her neck as she ran her fingers through his hair and kissed back harder.

The taxi ride seemed a blur, while the lobby and elevator became vague memories. The hotel door slammed shut after a well-placed push. The fresh sheets welcomed their arousal and desire as they joined together in a fury among throw cushions and chocolate truffles.

Their hurried embrace began as if an earthquake enveloped them. Its vibration erupted sensually, across and along exposed skin, without the calm of relief. It spread to the depths of animal lust and basic instinct without barriers or restrictions. Passion surmounted every obstacle of resistance. There was no return, only consummation, with all the swiftness and ferocity only the heart can conceive and deliver. That fervor went unrestrained until every ounce of lust was spent.

Two bodies lay tangled, an overlap of arms and limbs, glistening and exhausted, desire quenched and only their steady breathing was heard. They uncoupled and lay facing each other on the besieged bed. She placed a pillow beneath her head. He laid his head on her lap and peered up, took the crumpled bed sheet, and patted the moisture between her breasts. In a gentle motion he brought the bed sheet to his nostrils and inhaled. The trace of fabric softener, flinty iron, and musky scent made his head spin. He leaned up, keeping eye contact with hers. He was spellbound.

"You saved all this passion for me?" she whispered.

"I did, but I didn't know how much until now."

"You are full of surprises, Mr. Fox."

"I thought it was my allure and also my charm."

"It's a little of both, but I'm exhausted and hungry."

William shifted and reached for the phone on the nightstand and dialed room service.

"Champagne and a seafood platter, okay?" he asked Tracy.

Tracy pulled her knees up to her chest. At the same time, she tugged the bedsheets to the nape of her neck and nodded and said, "Great choice. I love seafood."

William replaced the phone back in its cradle. "Room service said they'll be about thirty minutes." He lay back down on the bed beside her.

Tracy ran her gentle fingers across the raised up fresh scar on his shoulder. "You were shot here."

"Yes."

"Does it hurt much?"

"Not that much anymore. Just a little stiff in the mornings, but the physiotherapy has helped me a lot."

"Will you be returning to work soon?"

"In a few days." He paused. "I suppose you'll be heading back to see your father?"

"Yes. These last few months we've been working on getting funding for our expedition," Tracy replied. "We have a few more details to work on before heading back to Nova Scotia."

"Could you postpone it for the rest of the week?" he asked.

She looked at him with astonishment.

***

Early the next morning, Tracy rolled over and saw William fast asleep. He looked so peaceful. She got up and put a pot of coffee on.

"That smells good," said William, disentangling himself from the sheets. He got up and placed his arms around Tracy.

Tracy pulled away from him. "Don't put too much hope into what happened last night."

"I thought we reconnected and could build on it."

"I thought so, too. I have second thoughts. After what I have been through, I am not ready." She paused. "Besides, my father and I have put a lot of work into the Zheng He project, and it's important we finish it."

"I thought I had made amends about my behavior."

"That's not it. Everything has happened so fast, and I need time to think."

"I am sorry you feel that way," he said. "Can we at least stay in touch?"

Tracy pulled her kimono tighter, crossing her arms against her chest. "Okay," she said. "Time to get going. My father and I have an appointment at the Smithsonian."

Twenty-Seven

April in Beijing

APRIL IN BEIJING was usually mild and dry during the day, but in the evenings, it was chilly and breezy. Ren Bo wore a two-tone baseball jacket, sweatpants, and upscale sneakers purchased on the black market. Wisps of black hair flipped down over his forehead as he moved through the rush-hour crowds.

The pollution in the city was heavy, and the smell of diesel was everywhere. Ren Bo took the Beijing Subway to Beikou Station about twelve kilometers north of the Forbidden City. He strolled alongside the Fourth Ring Road wearing a surgical mask. Many of the population used them for protection from the flu, colds, and pollution.

Unobserved, he slipped into the laneway between two low-rise apartment blocks. The back door adjacent to the parking lot and garbage bins had cameras scanning the entire area. Ren Bo's military training and diet left him with flat abs and muscular upper arms. Running long distances with heavy backpacks strengthened his legs. He was sufficiently agile to slide under the camera and through the door. Once in, he bounded up the back stairs to the fifth floor. He crouched in an unlit corner of the stairwell and withdrew his Norinco 9mm, the latest upgrade from the Chinese army. Pulling back the slide, a round rested passively in the chamber. Satisfied, he slid the gun between the belt of his pants and baseball jacket. He opened the hallway door, confirming the hall was vacant, and headed toward door number 512. He picked the lock in less than thirty seconds, his average time during training. Ren Bo walked in, expecting an empty apartment. He knew the occupant would arrive late. Right now, all he required were answers, essential answers only his quarry would have.

Ren Bo took deliberate steps to a modern-looking blue velvet accent chair. He placed it facing the door, turned out the lights, and sat prepared with his handgun. Then waited, like a spider ready to ensnare the unwary.

The apartment door opened effortlessly just before midnight. The hallway glare illuminated a man about medium height and build wearing a green military uniform. He looked into the room cautiously before stepping across the threshold.

"Suyin, I'm home."

"Come in, Captain Yuan Shao. I've been expecting you," announced Ren Bo in a low pitch. Ren Bo switched on the table lamp.

"Who are you? Where is Suyin?"

"She is all right. Nothing to worry about. But you can unholster your sidearm, drop out the magazine, and eject the round in the chamber."

Ren Bo pointed the Norinco directly at the captain's head. "Do it, or your brains will be splattered all over the hallway."

Captain Yuan followed the command. The magazine fell to the floor with a thud. The round flew out, thumped on the woodwork, and rolled before it stopped.

"Now close the door and sit on the sofa," said Ren Bo.

Shao sat down in the couch corner, visibly uncomfortable and angry.

"Who the fuck are you?" he said.

Ren Bo raised his voice to compensate for the surgical mask. "I work for someone very high in the office of our governing party. They want me to find out about General Po's death."

"It's plain and simple. The general committed suicide because he was caught in a bribe. Corruption will not be tolerated."

"Understood; we will get to that in a minute. Now let's discuss your situation. Your wife doesn't know you're keeping a mistress."

"This has nothing to do with the investigation."

"Your commander at Strategic Defense Force wouldn't approve of your little love nest."

"I know it doesn't look good. Why is it any of your business?"

"Let me help you with your situation, and you can help me with my part of the investigation," said Ren Bo. "I'll be involved in what you will report to your commander."

"Despite my situation, I can't with a good conscience let you interfere with my investigation."

"Your wife or your commander will destroy your career. If Suyin is that important, you should be motivated to help me, and your career can stay on track."

Shao paused for a few seconds. Ren Bo let his suggestion sink in.

"Let's get this over with," he finally said.

"You and your team interviewed General Po's wife."

"Yes, we confiscated the ancient scrolls. His wife didn't know anything."

"Take me through your procedures."

"As you know, our laws and constitution precede all individual rights. So, my team aggressively interviewed General Po's friends and military associates."

"During your investigation did you discover who may be involved?"

"We reviewed bank records, military, financial connections, and uncovered possible tax evasion."

Shao felt impatient because he was usually on the other end of the questioning. Indeed, he wanted this over quickly. His career and his girlfriend Suyin were in jeopardy. Looking over at his inquisitor, he noticed a pair of gold loops hanging on his right ear. His interrogator spoke like an army man but looked like a young radical from Hong Kong. *A dichotomy of status*, he thought.

"Why do you think someone would want to bribe General Po?" asked Ren Bo, scratching his ear in puzzlement.

"His position carried enormous responsibilities. He was in the General Staff Department, which had oversight of the Network System Department and Cyber Operations, with direct links to the Beidou Satellites Systems."

"I can see his role was vital to national security. The question is who offered the scrolls and for what information? Could they be national or foreign?"

Shao leaned forward. "The evidence points toward someone internal to the Party."

Ren Bo raised his finger, "Let me think." His eyebrows furrowed in concentration. "Satellite. Hmm. General Po was accountable for cyber and electronic warfare. But he was primarily in charge of our satellite systems.

"You continue with the investigation on your end. I will be following your progress. Assign one of your team members to proactively manage any negative publicity that might arise. The last thing we need is to have our president's corruption investigations look like a political purge."

Shao's torso sagged back into the couch with relief. He stopped clenching his teeth, sensing this matter was ending. Colonel Ren Bo decided the captain's cooperation deserved compensation and discretion.

"This Fourth Ring Road mandate is going to mess up your love life. The state is moving all middle-class citizens out to make room for influential millionaires," said Ren Bo.

"I don't like that I will have to drive so far to see my Suyin."

"I'll use my influence so you can keep your apartment. That way you don't have to leave Beijing."

"After all this, I'm supposed to forget that you were here?"

"You will go a long way in the People's Army."

Ren Bo stood up, backed up, and left the apartment. He guided the Norinco under his belt, pulled down his baseball jacket, and trod to the back stairs in the hallway. Taking off the surgical mask, Ren Bo took out a pair of black-rimmed glasses and snuggled them over his nose. He removed the earrings and tucked them into his front pocket. Brushed back his hair and dashed down the stairway. Soon he was on the street, hands in his jacket, walking toward the subway.

Twenty-Eight

Our Flight for Sydney Leaves at Daybreak

TRACY JORDAN had an insatiable curiosity about early history. Her father had introduced her to the pharaohs of Egypt while she was in grade school, inspiring her to become an archaeologist.

The Smithsonian National Museum of the American Indian was a brief taxi ride from the Willard InterContinental Hotel in Washington. They arrived in front of a sandstone-colored building formed in a geometric and circular design. A third-story portico overhang was fashioned as if milled by a 3D technology machine.

Tracy and her father Jeffrey had received initial funding from Stanford University to procure LiDAR equipment. Modern archaeologists now used this technology to produce three dimensional models of ruins buried beneath the ground.

They decided to meet Brenda Tadler, the curator responsible for Mi'kmaq Indigenous Canadian artifacts. They had emailed her that a prominent professor in Chinese antiquities and his assistant were interested in viewing the archives. The Jordans' plan was to find out as much as possible about the culture. While doing so, they would not reveal the project's true nature to anyone.

"It really is too lovely a day to be rummaging in a museum," said Jeffrey.

"This is important. Just go with it," replied Tracy.

After passing through security, they met Brenda Tadler in the lobby.

"Well, hello there. Glad you could make it," she said.

"We're delighted to be here," replied Tracy.

Jeffrey stuck out his hand and shook Brenda's, smiling and nodding his head. "It's my pleasure to meet you as well."

Brenda wore a gray business suit with matching charcoal pumps. Tracy thought she had been in charge for years and probably knew every nook and cranny of the museum.

"Let me give you a quick tour on our way to the archival rooms," she said.

Jeffrey was taken by her refined mannerism.

"I'm right behind you, Brenda," said Jeffrey.

As they moved through groups of students and visitors, they passed buckskins embroidered with beads and eagle feathered headdresses encased in glass enclosures.

"Very beautiful," said Tracy.

"Yes, our artifacts represent many North American First Nations and Indigenous cultures from around the world. The archives are downstairs." Brenda pointed to the elevator door.

The great room consisted of various cabinets and drawers, with a large viewing table in the center.

"Wait here, and I'll bring out some of the Mi'kmaq artifacts for your perusal."

Tracy and Jeffrey put on the white gloves that Brenda had given them. She returned with the trolly laden with ancient Indigenous relics.

"These are from the Mi'kmaq of the Chapel Island, part of Cape Breton. One of the original districts of seven, known as the Onamag or Unama'kik," she explained.

"My father and I are sympathetic toward the First Nations. The archeological evidence linking the Mi'kmaq to Nova Scotia for more than 10,000 years is of important historical value."

Brenda handed them the shallow wooden bowl with six stones. "This article was used as a dice and bowl game called waltes," she said. "It is still played today."

They passed it back and forth, while Tracy made notes.

Brenda passed Jeffrey a large bone fragment with an inverted tip that resembled a spear. "This was obviously used for big-game hunting," said Jeffrey.

The Jordans passed the weapon back and forth and placed it on the table. Tracy took a photo without flash.

Brenda replaced the spearhead with a fan made of bird feathers, an embroidered cap, and a porcupine quill–decorated drum. Then, she brought the final vestige, an embroidered chief's jacket. Jeffrey touched the sleeve with a delicate hand. "Loincloths and leggings from the 15th century are nearly impossible to find," he said in admiration.

Brenda smiled at the perceptive academic.

"Although we don't have very early examples of their culture, I can assure you that we can provide you with an extensive background to help in your research.

After reviewing the last historical pieces, Jeffrey took off his gloves.

"This was great. Thanks for all your help," he said.

"But there is more," responded Brenda. "Frederick Johnson is one of America's celebrated anthropologists. We have his field notes and photographs from his trips to the area in 1943."

"Let's have a look," said Tracy. She closed her notebook and followed Brenda and her father further into the archive room.

"Why are you being so nice?" Jeffrey whispered.

"Dad, it's obvious you're interested in her. Besides, shouldn't we look at all the data available before we get started?"

"She is rather regal and sophisticated. Should I ask her to dinner?"

"Really, Dad? You are asking me for love advice?"

***

Tracy and Jeffrey were in the cab on their way back to the hotel. Tracy studied the handwritten account about Zheng He and his relationship with the Mi'kmaq woman.

Jeffrey interrupted Tracy. "Brenda gave me her cell number."

"She's into you as well," replied Tracy. "It's been years since Mom passed away."

"Brenda said she'll help us if we need her expertise."

"Do you think she wondered why a professor of Chinese studies would be interested in Canadian Indigenous culture?"

"I think she's smart enough to put a couple of controversial theories together. Enough to satisfy her curious mind. She must think we are on some sort of adventure."

Tracy found it difficult to get back to Wang Jinghong's diary. *It would be nice if Dad found someone. Everyone needs someone in their lives, even me.* She was remorseful at how she had treated William.

Jeffrey resumed reading a brochure Brenda had given him with her business card and contact information. "It says here in this brochure that George Gustav Hayes, who was a great collector and contributor, is attributed for amassing a vast collection and is the forefather of the Smithsonian Museum of the American Indian."

Tracy was glancing through the cab's window, deep in thought. "Dad, when do you think the LiDAR equipment will arrive?"

"It's already in transit to Sydney, Nova Scotia, and should be there soon after our arrival."

***

In the hotel suite, Tracy downloaded the Reconnaissance Permit Application and submitted professional documents to the Nova Scotia Heritage Conservation Authority. By the time they procured the LiDAR equipment and helicopter, their initial permit would be ready.

Tracy felt the visit to the Smithsonian was helpful in getting a sense of Mi'kmaq culture but sifting through these relics was not enough. Frederick Johnson's photographs and field notes gave Tracy additional insight into Mi'kmaq shamanism and could provide the background needed to confirm if the eunuch Zheng He's manhood could have been restored using traditional herbs and barks.

"Dad, let's have dinner early," she said. "Our flight for Sydney leaves at daybreak."

Twenty-Nine

The Seneca

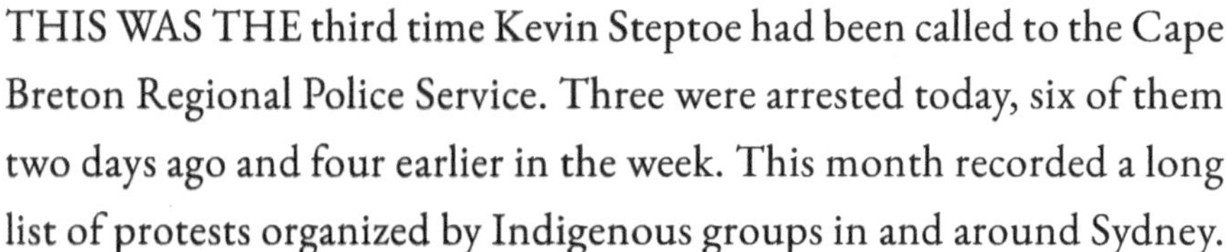

THIS WAS THE third time Kevin Steptoe had been called to the Cape Breton Regional Police Service. Three were arrested today, six of them two days ago and four earlier in the week. This month recorded a long list of protests organized by Indigenous groups in and around Sydney.

An international oil company had initiated fracking in the region, and a massive protest had ensued. A multinational gas company started washing salt into the Shubenacadie River, creating caverns to store natural gas. Today, at a downtown mall, three elders were detained for protesting Bill C-45, which they claimed disregarded Indigenous treaty rights.

Kevin was a civil rights activist and lawyer, presently bailing the latest First Nations members out of jail and getting them safely home.

He was motivated by his long ancestral lineage of the Mi'kmaq, who were advocates of change. His grandmother insisted he pursue higher education and he became a lawyer who could influence change and help First Nations people be recognized.

Kevin's professors at the University of Dalhousie said he was driven and focused, but they thought he was naïve and too candid. His experience of well-fought battles in courts and streets removed all doubt about his instincts and proficiency. The elders appreciated Kevin because he could match wits with the best of corporate and prosecuting attorneys.

As a youth, he spent his summers working at local archeological excavations. He enjoyed working alongside the scientists, getting paid in cash and in experience.

He escorted the three Indigenous grandmothers outside of the police station and past a group of local reporters. A national TV station journalist clamored for a statement.

"Mr. Steptoe, what about Bill C-45 and its ramifications to treaty rights?" asked a *CBC* journalist.

"The bottom line is Bill C-45 opens access for substantial environmental exploitation of Indigenous lands and our sovereignty. As custodians of our environment, we can form alliances to avert the misuse of our lands and the effects of climate change that come with it. That's all I have to say for today," he replied, as he guided the seniors away.

The door of the gray van slid open, and the elders stepped inside, followed by Kevin. The driver of the van sped away as the group of reporters wondered what information they could dig up to complete the attorney's terse statement.

***

Tracy had chosen the Mira Suites Hotel in the heart of Sydney. It was close to Grand Lake Road, which was Highway 4, the provincial road with direct access to the regional airport. The downtown area was teeming with eateries, a pizza parlor was within walking distance, and an Irish Ale House was a few doors away.

Tracy had contacted St. Mary's University to get permission to use its facilities for evaluating any artifacts they might find. St. Mary's had an archeological program where students participated in field research. Tracy and Jeffrey could use their help with the excavation.

Brenda Tadler had recommended someone who had extensive experience as a novice archaeologist and knew the area well. Jeffrey was pleased Brenda was contributing and staying in contact. The thought of starting a relationship with her was appealing. He texted Tracy the contact information Brenda had sent and asked her to call Kevin Steptoe, a lawyer representing Indigenous rights.

Tracy was mindful that part of the responsibility of procuring a Heritage Research Permit was consulting with the local Mi'kmaq community and accommodating their interests, including their treaty rights. Brenda Tadler explained that Kevin Steptoe was an excellent source to fast-track past the bureaucracy. The Mi'kmaq council gave him power of attorney to address tribal concerns and oversee indigenous sites. Getting him to join them would move the project along faster.

***

The gray van inched along in the local rush-hour traffic. Kevin's cell rang.

"Steptoe," he said.

"Hi Mr. Steptoe. My name is Tracy Jordan. You were referred to me by Brenda Tadler of the Smithsonian. We have an archaeological excavation I would like to discuss with you."

Kevin was interested in getting back into some archeological digs to extricate himself from the protesters, even just for a while. "Sounds intriguing," he said. "I'd like to learn more."

"That's great."

"Let's meet at the Irish Ale House tomorrow evening," he said. "Six o'clock, okay? We can sit down for a quick bite and discuss your proposal."

Thirty

Let's Keep This Professional

JEFFREY JORDAN LEFT the Mira Suites Hotel in a blue Mustang rental and drove the Grand Lake Road to the regional airport. The helicopter company had called him regarding the flight plans for the next day. Their pilot wanted to place the LiDAR unit onto the chopper, and he was concerned about weight distribution. Jeffrey had years of experience when it came to using the LiDAR's sophisticated electronics and knew how to place the unit to help enhance safety during hovering flight.

Suspending heavy LiDAR during airborne surveys can be dangerous for pilots who have not been trained in balancing the unit during flight. Once Jeffrey arrived, he immediately began preparing a detailed airborne LiDAR mission plan. He took over the manager's office desk and organized documentation and schematics, including accurate systems configuration, flight planning for every survey day, data-processing software, and calibration flight equipment.

The grant money from Stanford university would also cover the mission expenses such as aircraft leasing, the pilot, the LiDAR, the system operator, the data-processing, including software and hardware purchase, and miscellaneous items.

Jeffrey verified that all circumstances would be covered to ensure they would have an unencumbered flight in and out with minimal intrusion to the environment.

"

***

Tracy began her day with yoga as it was integral to her physical program. The breathing exercises helped control her asthma. While her father was at the airfield, she spent the day procuring field equipment, sending emails to colleagues at Stanford University, and preparing for her meeting with Kevin Steptoe. She ate lunch in her room, which consisted of Greek yogurt and honey, topped with banana slices. Glancing at her watch, Tracy realized she had less than an hour before her meeting with Kevin.

She bathed using the hotel soap and shampoos. On the way out, she waved at the service desk staff. She found herself walking downtown along the city's sidewalks, reviewing in her mind the informal questions she had prepared for Kevin Steptoe at the dinner meeting. It was crucial Kevin Steptoe would be discreet and willing to work with her and her father.

Tracy was preoccupied as she stepped off the curb to cross the street and was startled when the unrestrained blare of a car horn aroused her from her contemplations. She swiveled and mounted the curb as the traffic light changed and the Tesla bolted away.

Tracy reached Jubilee Elementary School on the main street and stopped to admire the weather-beaten bronze statue of World War I veteran Johnny Miles, who had won the Boston marathon in 1926. He became a member of the Order of Canada in 1982 for being one of the nation's top athletes.

She picked up her pace and changed direction toward the Irish Ale House. Groups of people were bunched together, strolling to eateries or bar crawls, cabaret comedy shows, or even karaoke. When she arrived at the pub, she was seated at a table near the brass bar. The floor was scuffed from years of traffic. Golden oak and dark brown ligneous tables were scattered about. The captain chairs were hard and stiff and belonged in a recreational room or church basement. The patrons were there for the food and drink, the Irish entertainment and, of course, the camaraderie.

She hadn't been seated a few minutes before a handsome Irishman offered to buy her a drink. His accent was pure Kilkenny, his scent fern and pine, and his temperament had a touch of vivacious spirit. Flattered, she smiled and refused, then turned her attention to the door as an Indigenous man was approaching her table. The Irishman stepped away as Tracy's guest arrived. He was angular, soundly built and he dwarfed the Irish admirer.

As an activist lawyer, she was expecting a disheveled-looking man with a bad taste in clothing. Kevin Steptoe, however, wore a black slim fit suit and black satin tie with a geometric design. He was about twenty-seven with his hair cropped short, his chin was square, and his eyebrows thin.

"Tracy?"

"You must be Kevin. Please have a seat."

"My pleasure."

"That's a beautiful tie," expressed Tracy as she placed her first compliment to make him feel comfortable.

"It's a Feral Fawn Canadian original, a tee pee appliqué."

"Unique and artistic," said Tracy as she lauded more flattery. Kevin cracked a smile, acknowledging that he was receiving a self-esteem boost. Tracy realized that Kevin was not fooled but even knowing this, didn't stop the flattery from working.

The waitress arrived on cue with the menus, two glasses of water, and a pitcher that started to sweat and drip on the coaster. "What can I get you guys?" she asked.

"I'll have the lobster flambé and a glass of California Chardonnay, please," said Tracy.

"For me, a kick-ass whiskey chicken with Jack Daniel's sauce and a Harrington Light," said Kevin.

Tracy felt that dinner was becoming awkward at times. She had decided to curtail her praise of Kevin. It occurred to her that her admiring comments had been misunderstood, leading Kevin to the wrong idea. Already he had reached over and placed his hand on hers. The touch of intimacy made her uncomfortable. She politely lifted his hand off hers. Her message was clear: let's keep this professional. Kevin discounted the gesture as a non-verbal cue and continued to regale her with stories of the Mi'kmaq.

Kevin spoke about the First Nations' oral history. "The Mi'kmaq traveled in seasonal migration patterns, spring and summer on the coast for fishing, then fall and winter inland for trapping and hunting, subsisting along rivers and bays and using teepees as shelters. Their first contact with outsiders was with John Cabot."

Tracy deliberated whether Kevin knew the Chinese explorer Zheng He had visited Nova Scotia in 1423, more than 100 years before Cabot. Her expression, deadpan, did not reveal her innermost thoughts.

She was still unsure about Kevin's motivation. Would he be comfortable with her and her father as they excavated the history of his people? She had ideas on gaining his loyalty. Only when she was satisfied could trust be a certainty.

Kevin continued to enlighten her on Sydney's past. "This city was a significant coal producer which shut down in 1975. During World War II, it was a staging harbor for convoys bound for England."

Tracy scrutinized his behavior. It was crucial to observe how he interacted with her and the waitress and whether he would be supportive. She recalled that Kevin had bailed the First Nations grandmothers out of jail earlier. It demonstrated he was honest, trustworthy, and supportive, worthy characteristics that signified a reliable and dependable person.

Kevin continued with exciting tales of Mi'kmaq battles. "The battle of Bae de Bic was re-counted by Jacques Cartier. One hundred Iroquois warriors disseminated two hundred Mi'kmaq camped at Massacre Island."

Tracy steered the conversation back to the present. "Do you have connections with the Nova Scotia Museum in Halifax?" she asked.

"Yes, I do. The Nova Scotia Museum has an ethnology collection, including a Mi'kmaq portrait gallery, Mi'kmaq petroglyphs, and a reciprocal research network of First Nations items from the Northwest Coast. I am acquainted with the curator, who I am sure would be pleased to be part of the excavation."

"Right now, we'll be working with St. Mary's University, but depending on the size of the excavation, we may need assistance from the museum as well."

Tracy's steel-blue eyes sparkled. She doodled absentmindedly in the melted chocolate ice cream with her spoon, convinced Kevin would be a suitable member of their team.

Kevin was unaware of her scrutiny of his character. He thought her doodling was an expression of her analytical mind.

The regular crowd was drifting in as the evening entertainment began. Tracy waved the waitress over to settle the bill.

While she was approaching, Tracy said to Kevin.

"Can you meet us at the Mira Suites Hotel tomorrow morning at six?"

"I'll be there," he said.

Thirty-One
Maybe Hong Kong Has Made You Soft

IT WAS NOT the first time Ru Fa Zhong had been to New York. He was in Chinatown ten years ago when he was making his way to the top of the gang structure.

His cousin was the head of the White Sharks Gang, running gambling and protection rackets in New York's Chinatown for many years. Today he found himself on old, familiar ground, walking down the main street looking at the diversity of people. Individuals who strolled the thoroughfare and dined in restaurants, used the body rub parlors, shopped at vegetable markets, the trade corporations, barbershops, and beauty parlors. Mott Street's rich history also included the famous People's Pharmacy with herbal remedies and concoctions. Ru ambled through downtown, studying architecture, and looking at the overhanging signage of the shops. The fire escapes dangling off each building looked like birdcages precariously affixed to old brick and mortar.

He made his way through Baxter Street and Canal Street and entered his cousin's Grand Temple restaurant. An edifice of modern design encompassing three stories of glass and tile, it was a conflicting paradox in a timeworn district. Ru's cousin was affectionately called "Big Wong" by the White Shark Gang members, and his influence in every breadth of the neighborhood confounded his enemies.

"It's good to see you, Big Wong," said Ru.

"You too!" the older man said, as he guided Ru to a table by the window. "Come. Have a seat. Have lunch."

"Your restaurant looks amazing. Who's the architect?"

"My daughter."

"Wow. You must be so proud."

"Yes, I am. I assume this is not just a social visit."

"I need a research ship and crew. Any recommendations?"

"Let me place a few calls." Big Wong left the table, while Ru nursed a drink.

A few minutes later he returned and sat across from Ru. "By the time we've finished lunch, I should have an answer for you."

The waiter was clearing the plates when Big Wong's cell rang. "Thank you." He turned to Ru and said, "The *Sofia's Odyssey* is for sale. You can see her at the South Brooklyn Marine Terminal."

***

Ru called an Uber to get him to where Sofia's Odyssey was moored. He was ecstatic with the ship. It was exactly what he needed. The research ship had been built in France forty years ago and was recently refurbished to state-of-the-art capabilities. It had taken some shrewd bargaining to procure the vessel since the Shoals Marine Laboratory was also interested in its procurement. He bought the ship with the ill-gotten loot he had extorted from the billionaire. Big Wong would help choose a tough crew to help him get the ship underway.

Chinese archaeologists had a dig site in Chinatown exploring cultural resources from the earliest settlers in the 1800s. Big Wong explained to them that there was a potential cultural discovery in Canada and that his cousin Ru required their assistance in uncovering a significant find dating from the 15th century. They were more than excited to postpone their digging for a worthier cause.

It was a notable time for Ru to come to New York and see Big Wong. He had missed his cousin and mentor from the early days of their gang activities. They were halcyon days until the power struggle for control of the neighborhood with another gang forced Ru to leave.

Ru had been young, ambitious, and hotheaded. Not that he had changed much over the years, except for becoming sophisticated, clever, and wiser. Finding himself in New York, his troubled past had come back to haunt him. Members of opposing gangs had been muscling in on the White Shark Gang's turf. As a street thug working for his cousin Big Wong, he was told to beat up Lou Kirin, the lieutenant of the Sichuan Boys. Ru was a psychopath and combined with lethal Kung Fu, was unstoppable. Kirin was hospitalized for many months and still walked with a noticeable limp.

***

Ru was having dinner with Big Wong when a courier came into the Grand Temple restaurant and interrupted them. The messenger said, "Lou Kirin is looking for Ru Fa Zhong and demands they finish what they started ten years ago."

Kirin now headed the rival gang and wanted to avenge Ru's battering. Kirin's rematch was to save face and prove his authority.

"Ru, you must fight, so the White Shark Gang retains respect in Chinatown," said Big Wong.

***

The fight was organized very quickly and took place at Wings Kung Fu Club in the back alley off the main street. Ru and Big Wong arrived in the alleyway and made their way to the fight club entrance. The steel rollup door with two gangsters outside was opened on their arrival. Big Wong brought a few of his men with him in case the situation got out of hand. Soon after they entered the kwoon, Kirin took a position on one side of the mat and some of his gang leaned against the kwoon walls. Big Wong was with his crew, and Ru positioned himself opposite Kirin.

"I haven't seen you in ten years. You've become mature but are you tougher? Or maybe Hong Kong has made you soft," sneered Kirin.

"I'm glad to see you've become a success. I would've thought this confrontation would be behind you," replied Ru.

"My honor is at stake, especially now since I run the second largest gang in Chinatown."

"Well, I'm not staying because I have other interests. But I will not embarrass my cousin by leaving this business undone. I also have our honor to defend."

Ru bowed, and Kirin followed him with an appropriate bow. Kirin stepped into cat stance, then jumped toward Ru with a flying front kick. Ru backstepped and palm blocked. Kirin executed three brutal flying front kicks. Ru back stepped each time, finding his opponent's range. Kirin connected a sidekick to Ru's midsection. Ru flinched, his left foot swiveled, his back fist cracked Kirin's cheek, throwing him off balance. Kirin threw a punch which Ru blocked. Ru retaliated with sledgehammer punches to the stomach. Kirin gasped in agony. His men murmured in bewilderment.

"How is that for a Hong Kong shuffle?" said Ru.

"What else do you have, you coward?" said Kirin.

Ru punched, crunching Kirin's nose, spurting blood everywhere. He staggered, wiped the blood with the back of his hand, then front-kicked left, right, left. Ru sliced away each kick with knife-hand techniques and delivered a flying spinning kick striking Kirin's temple.

Kirin fell to the floor, stunned. Confused, he rested on his elbow, supporting himself. Big Wong and a few gang members started to snicker at the outcome.

Kirin's lieutenant threw two sets of Wing Chun broad swords on the floor. "This should separate the king from the puppet," he said in disgust.

The fight escalated from a grudge match to a death match. Kirin got up, wobbled on his poor leg, and picked up the blades. Everyone could see he was exhausted. He swung sloppily, the swords crossed Ru's chest, missing the strike. Ru withdrew, slid his swords past Kirin's defense, slicing his forearms. Hemorrhaging, Kirin panicked and thrust back.

Ru blocked low, deflecting both Kirin's swords up and away. Ru accelerated the blades like the wings of a hummingbird. Kirin was mesmerized. Before he could react, Ru severed Kirin's hands at the wrists. He screamed in shock as Ru sliced one blade across the throat then thrust the other blade into his abdomen. Kirin fell off the sword to the mat, lifeless.

Kirin's crew wrapped up his warm body and removed him. Big Wong, as a courtesy, let his enemies go. He explained he would clean up the mess.

"Ru, you must leave Chinatown now. The White Shark Gang will arrive at the ship with equipment in the morning, and you will have your crew," said Big Wong.

"After this, I will never come back again."

"The vendetta has ended."

"I hope there will be peace in Chinatown now that Kirin is gone."

"His lieutenants will need to sit down with us and hammer out some sort of peace arrangement to keep both our interests in Chinatown running smoothly. Most importantly, keeping the New York Metro Police out of our business."

Thirty-Two
Washington Was Miles Away

AS WILLIAM SHUFFLED off the plane, he smiled half-heartedly at the flight attendant. Once outside of the terminal, the balmy spring weather reminded him of his romantic walk with Tracy along the Potomac. William and Tracy left each other on uncertain terms. He felt severely rebuffed by Tracy's reluctance to renew their relationship. His passion and energy levels were drained. For a usually open and frank man, this funk had made it difficult to socialize with people. He was anxious to get back to life in Montreal and try to move on.

***

A heavy beat of pop music blared from the Crowbar Club. Part of the local nightlife in downtown Montreal, which was a favorite karaoke hangout for William and friends.

Philip White had organized William's party, first to welcome him back home from Washington and to celebrate his Shield of Honour medal. Philip had invited supervisor René Bouchard who made sure he had a sitter for his French mastiff named Hooch.

Walter Smith was happy to join them for a few drinks as well. Being recently freed from prison, he had a lot of carousing to catch up on. Mr.

Kim insisted his two junior black belts get experience, instructing the evening classes, and was also present.

Philip wanted to know how things had gone with Tracy. He thought the best way to loosen most people up was by plying them with plenty of good drinks, then waiting for a moment of extreme vulnerability before asking the probing question.

Philip's eyes fixed on the crowd parting like the Red Sea as Williams's tall and lanky frame cleared the group. As William closed the gap, Philip noticed a sagacious expression on his face, and he smiled back as William approached. The two men gave each other a firm hug. René and Walter turned around after lifting their cues from the pool table. Mr. Kim walked over to the bar, ordered an ice-cold beer and handed it to William. Everyone was pleased to see each other here for the celebration. The festivities continued with the arrival of a tray of whiskey shooters.

The party took on an exuberance of its own, revving into a lively celebration. The guests were mainly RCMP officers who were typically responsible, evidently not tonight as the noise at the back of the bar became riotous. The karaoke vocals were discordant, and patrons were heckling the constables. Their performance of the Backstreet Boys' top hits would be remembered as enthusiastic but flawed. Some customers recalled that some redemption was warranted as downtown Montreal police were worse.

***

The next morning, William awoke with a massive headache with a matching scowl reflected in the water-spotted mirror. Having a wild night with the boys was precisely what was vital to alleviate his emotional letdown from Tracy.

Washington was miles away, and so was she. The entire evening was a better experience than picking up a woman in a bar and waking up in a strange bedroom. At least his friends distracted him when he needed it the most. There was no better way than to get blitzed and bond with his mates. He rummaged around the bathroom until he found a couple of Tylenol. He took them with a fruit smoothie, followed by a freshly brewed dark roast coffee.

William grabbed his gym bag, containing his gi and headed toward St. Catherine Street to Mr. Kim's dojang. The best recourse for a hangover of this magnitude would be training extra hard on the punching bag and throwing the taekwondo students around the mat until they learned something.

The hard exercise alleviated his weariness during class and his efforts cleansed out the toxins from his body. He was ready to start his workday at C Division.

Most of the office staff had heard about the sorrowful singing. The gossip flowed from the water cooler to the kitchenette to the division head. The captain of C Division smiled and mused that "boys would be boys." William walked past his desk, nodding acknowledgment at his coworkers until he entered René Bouchard's office. They exchanged that look men have regarding secrets they would rather not share with others.

"Take the load off. You look like a train rolled over you," said René.

René was dressed in a somber gray suit with an equally soulless blue tie. He looked tired and sallow as he waved William over to a leather chair.

"I don't know if you should be in the coffin or carrying it," said William.

"Mind your place. We are in the office now."

"Yes, sir."

"Now that you are back from sick leave, protocol normally requires me to debrief you." René waved a file. "No need, though; John Abbott copied me on your report." He paused. "How is the physiotherapy going on your arm?"

"Much better. I am back to full workouts again," he said. "What do you have for me on the duty roster?"

"I do have a new assignment for you. Far less exciting than Hong Kong but perfect for your forensic accounting skills. We have a scam case our fraud department needs assistance with. They asked for you specifically. They want you to look over the books and statements and see how much money was funneled offshore to Belize," said René reaching for aspirin and water.

***

William sat at his desk, opened his computer, clicked a few keys, and the screen launched to a file of surprising proportions. The RCMP forensics department was made aware of the fraud by the chief financial officer of a mortgage company. He had asked the auditors to review some minor discrepancies. This led to the investigation William was assisting with now. Going over the initial investigative report revealed a syndicated mortgage fraud built on a Ponzi scheme. Amicas Mortgage Company collected funds to build students' residences, which were started but not finished. The builder asked the mortgage company for capital on another project, a large plaza, which was started but not finished. Twelve projects were created and never completed. William's initial impression was that the monies were loaned between projects and bonuses were paid to the principles of the construction company. In this way, funds were diverted away from projects and hidden in offshore assets.

Hunching over the computer screen, the bright light caused William's peripheral vision to blur in a kaleidoscope of colors. This unnerved him to no end as he realized he was getting fatigued. He decided to take a break, shut down his computer, and made his way to the kitchenette for a coffee.

William's involvement in the case file was wearing him down as he hadn't done this kind of desk work for several years. Fieldwork was looking better and better.

Thirty-Three

Sofia's Odyssey

THE MORNING WAS brisk at the South Brooklyn Marine Terminal. Dock men were loading supplies onto *Sofia's Odyssey*, Ru's research ship. Rundown warehouse lights were ablaze, illuminating the wharf. The dawn air was damp from the influences of the Hudson River while a yellow haze hung above the city skyline. True to her name, the ship seemed awash in the golden fleece of Greek mythology.

Three black Range Rovers approached the glowing miasma and came to an abrupt stop. One driver emerged, yelling to the gantry operator, "Drop the cable." He summoned two dockworkers to place slings front and back of the last Range Rover. The vehicle was raised in the air and effortlessly positioned aft of the vessel's submersible platform. Ru's luxury four-wheel-drive SUV was a gift from Big Wong.

RPGs, AK-47s, and tactical handguns were concealed under the floor of the Range Rover. Ru and his renegade crew would be pleased with the arsenal, trigger-happy assholes that they were.

Ru summoned Captain Bush. The burly fellow had been recruited from another freighter laid up for repairs. Big Wong vouched for his character and experience.

Captain Bush advanced onto the bridge wearing casual apparel. He was Eurasian, his sea-weathered features were striking. His crew were among the toughest sailors in New York Harbor. Just the kind of men Ru and associates would consider equals.

"Captain, it's time to be underway," said Ru.

"Yes, sir! Men, release ropes and lift anchor," said Captain Bush.

Two crewmen vaulted onto the deck, pulling ropes from the piling as the winch lifted the anchor. The chain clanked with the whine of the electric motor. Lubricated gears lifted the ballast, dripping seawater as it broke from the deep.

Captain Bush said, "Slow ahead."

The vessel proceeded into the Hudson River, churning the frothy water gray and white.

"Helmsman, keep her steady in the channel," he commanded.

The ship turned to port, steaming away from the terminal. Ru stood beside Captain Bush on the bridge and observed the vast harbor. Then faced starboard at the Statue of Liberty waving goodbye. Safe aboard and fortunate to have evaded the hangman's noose for now, he knew that inevitably, the authorities would come searching for him.

Lights on the Brooklyn Bridge were cascading in the distance, strung along from abutment to abutment. Car lights flashed between telephone posts as a determined parade of morning commuters drove the highway along the river.

Goodbye, New York. Goodbye to the Big Apple. Thanks for the memories. Ru felt it was ironic coming to New York to buy a ship. Then killing Kirin. It was satisfying, especially after waiting ten years. The victory was sweet, and he felt invincible.

The archaeologists couldn't contain their excitement about the journey. They were on deck discussing the project. Ru's musings about stealing the treasure brought his thoughts to Bojing. He expected Bojing would return some of the artifacts to the communists to secure his continued position as culture minister.

Ru's thoughts were interrupted when the captain barked, "Helmsman keep starboard of the West Bank light."

"How are we making out?" asked Ru.

"Long Beach is on your portside." He pointed to the landmark. "We are headed into the Atlantic."

"Good. I'll be in my cabin if you need me."

Thirty-Four

Perhaps a Vendetta?

THE FBI HEADQUARTERS in New York City was in constant threat of terrorism barking at the heels of democracy. The intelligence community was scampering to stay ahead. Today was no exception as video from John F. Kennedy airport was scanned by experienced agents, intent on exposing any risk.

The facial recognition programs spotlighted individuals who matched database photos on watch lists. An investigator with a sixth sense developed after many years of experience remembered a request made by an FBI agent weeks ago to watch for specific individuals. The image he recognized matched the passport photo of a gangster from Hong Kong.

The investigator isolated the information and photos and emailed them to FBI agent Patrick Reilly who paired it with the Interpol Red Notice to arrest and extradite Ru Fa Zhong.

Hoping Ru was still in New York, Patrick immediately called his contact, Chief of Detectives Palmer, at the NYPD 5th Precinct, which serviced Chinatown, Little Italy, and the Bowery. He asked if his detectives could inquire if the suspect had visited Chinatown.

A short while later, Palmer called Patrick on his cell and said, "I have heard back from my detectives."

"Go on," said Patrick.

"For many years, there's been a bitter rivalry between Lou Kirin of the Sichuan Boys and Big Wong of the White Shark Gang. Shortly after Big

Wong's cousin Ru Fa Zhong arrived from Hong Kong, Kirin died under unusual circumstances. Chinatown came to a standstill at his funeral."

"Will there be a turf war?"

"Maybe. I am concerned about the neighborhood dynamics."

"What do you think happened?"

"Who knows for sure? Perhaps a vendetta completed in a grisly fashion? A ceremony kept secret, guarded from reprisal? No one is talking. Members of the Chinese community fear revenge from the gangs more than American justice."

"This is helpful information. Do you have anything more?"

"Not yet. But I am waiting to hear back from one of my undercover officers."

When Patrick returned from lunch at his favorite restaurant, his phone rang, before he even had a chance to sit. "Agent Reilly, here," he said.

"Patrick. It's Palmer. Got additional info for you," he said. "Our informants confirm that Ru killed Lou Kirin in a vendetta fueled fight to the death," said Palmer, a veteran street cop who knew the Asian gang mentality and was aware of these fights of honor.

"It seems he has no qualms leaving the occasional cadaver."

Chief of Detectives Palmer smiled at the dark humor.

"Any word of where Ru is now?" asked Patrick.

"Ru has left the city, along with a team of Chinese archaeologists. He bought a research ship called the *Sofia's Odyssey* and sailed out of New York Harbor early yesterday morning," said Palmer, unfastening the top button of his shirt, the season too early for air conditioning.

"Thanks, Chief, leave him to me. I owe you a few beers," said Patrick.

"Make sure you follow through on the drinks. I'm still waiting from the last time." Palmer picked up a case file and wafted it in front of his glistening face, the coolness temporary.

Patrick relayed this development to his superiors in the Tracy Jordan kidnapping case. With this break, the FBI had a good chance of arresting the key suspects.

He strolled out of the FBI office wearing Levi's jeans and a navy-blue polo shirt and took the elevator to the underground garage where his classic car was parked. He slid into the Camaro's blue and white vinyl seat. The muscle car belched and burbled Detroit's most pleasing symphony. Its wheels chirped on the concrete floor as Patrick steered the powerful coupe to the street. He directed the Camaro through traffic across the Brooklyn Bridge and directly to South Brooklyn Marine Terminal. Patrick drove along the wharf and located the berth where Sofia's Odyssey had been moored. He discovered a security camera mounted on a nearby warehouse.

Patrick was disappointed the tape was grainy, but he could still identify Ru boarding the ship with his crew and the archaeologists.

With this new information, it was time to involve the RCMP to assist in the ongoing pursuit of the Foo Dog gang members who were responsible for Tracy Jordan's kidnapping.

The FBI director had already established a rapport with John Abbott, who immediately said yes to Patrick's request to work with William.

Patrick was looking forward to collaborating on the case with William because they had built a valuable foundation of trust. He palmed his cellphone and made the long-distance call to Canada.

Thirty-Five

A Den of Sober Reflection

THE COMPUTER WILLIAM was typing on was standard government issue. He was hunched over in the final stages of completing his report. There were Excel spreadsheets with years of expense claims and bank statements. There were phone transcripts, thousands of emails, and hundreds of witness interviews. There were raids on the offices of the cunning executives as the probe took many paths. Residences were searched, personal travel was investigated, and contracts with family members were examined. Data mining was thorough and SWIFT transaction logs were checked for financial transfers to offshore accounts.

William typed forty-two words per minute. Not exactly stellar, but average, not one of his best attributes. His forensic accounting expertise had been essential as his final comprehensive report unfolded on the computer screen. The administrators were in bankruptcy, and the court-appointed trustee was selling the uncompleted properties or finding builders who would complete the projects. All recaptured funds, minus professional fees, were to be returned to the investors. The unwitting financiers had been fleeced like sheep, unprepared for the sophisticated dealings of complex investments.

When William had finally finished his report, he picked up his coffee cup, and looked at the empty bottom, covered with brown sludge. He had consumed six cups of brew in four hours, was irritable, and in a bleak mood.

His office's negative mise-en-scène depressed him; it was a den of sober reflection. The results of the financial devastation had proven too much, even for him. He pressed the button and waited for his final report to roll onto the printer tray. Satisfied there wasn't any more he could do, William slipped the report into a file folder and placed it in his outbox.

The fraud squad would have a copy, the evidence compelling. Multiple charges would be pending as the Crown prosecutor expected to bring criminal charges against the swindlers, who thought white-collar crime would be a cinch to evade. *Not in this country. Canada's system of justice would make sure white-collar criminals got their punishment.*

"I have a message for you," he heard in Québécois.

William had not noticed René come into his office. He waved a printed copy of an email he had received in front of him. He placed it on William's desk and sat down in an armchair opposite him. William read it quickly, put the email down, and looked at René, with concern.

"I take it this has been cleared by the chief's office?" asked William.

René nodded in the affirmative. "John Abbott wants this case wrapped up. You can expect a phone call from FBI agent Patrick Reilly. He asked for your help." René stood up, adjusted his suit, and turned to leave.

William watched him go. This time he would be ready for Ru and the Foo Dog Triad. *This time the fox would devour the rabbit. He would not be outfoxed again.*

William threw his leather jacket over his lanky frame and exited the stale, airless offices of the RCMP building on Dorchester Boulevard. He mounted his Triumph Rocket 3 and drove his bike through Montreal's crowded roadways to his home in Mercier Ouest. His neighborhood consisted of working-class people. Italians and Vietnamese immigrants had a conspicuous presence. Both sides of Rue Baldwin overflowed with duplexes and triplexes, with walk-ups and balconies on each floor. Older dwellings had remodeled façades with new brick, giving the old block a fresh look. Mature maples dotted front lawns, providing shade in summer and a blaze of color in the autumn.

William parked in the driveway of his recently renovated duplex which stood at the southern end of his property, facing the Greenbelt and the St. Lawrence River.

He unlocked the front door and let himself in. He prepared his kit bag and packed his carry-on luggage with essential clothing. Then poured himself a Jameson Irish on ice, dropped his tired body onto the battered couch and ordered a meat lover's pizza. He managed to enjoy several sips of his drink before he received a text. Patrick had finally decided to contact him regarding Tracy Jordan's kidnapping case.

Tried to call you didn't pick up.

Was driving home.

Are you ready?

All packed.

Ru has a ship and is sailing to the Maritimes.

When did he leave?

Yesterday morning.

What's next?

John Abbott arranged your flight to St. John's. You will meet the Canadian Coast Guard there.

William felt a sense of trepidation and wrote:

O shite and onions.

What does that mean?

William sipped his Irish whiskey and wrote:

'When is this bloody state of affairs going to end?' It's from James Joyce.

Just get your ass on the ship.

Great.

It's a big ocean. You start from your end, we'll meet.

Will send details when ship bound.

Keep the faith.

William opened the contacts on his phone and called John.

When the phone rang, John put down his dossier, picked up, and spoke to William about his mission to St. John's, Newfoundland.

He was booked on the Air Canada flight out in the morning. John had arranged for William to travel undercover and act as an in-flight security officer. This would ensure that he could carry a loaded firearm on board as part of his legal duties.

After 9/11, public safety and security became paramount to deter international terrorism. William had read the RCMP's internal Report on the Terrorism Threat to Canada and was versed on right-wing extremism, a path many radicals take.

The following day, he sat down at the rear of the airplane, scanning the passengers, on the alert for suspicious behavior. The exercise sharpened William's mind as he prepared for the upcoming dangerous assignment.

Thirty-Six

A Common Interest in Revealing the Truth

JEFFREY WAS EXCITED about the airborne survey. He and the pilot set out with the helicopter and LiDAR equipment sooner than originally planned.

When they reached their destination, the LiDAR unit started firing invisible laser beams in all directions, catching the reflections and measuring how long the beams took to return. The data collected could extrapolate the topography and build a real-time map. The flight took at least twenty checkpoints for each land cover class and used the flat areas to minimize horizontal errors. The XYZ points were interpreted by the LiDAR data and downloaded into a 3D visualization program. A pale yellow and green terrestrial map of the earth's surface illustrated manmade structures, vegetation, roads, and paths.

Jeffrey assiduously reviewed the information on the 3D rendering and closed the program. He leaned back and stretched, relieving the tenseness in his back. Four hours in a cramped helicopter had taken a physical toll on his maturing torso. Relieved, he thanked the manager for using the office.

He had been the only occupant during the foray to the ancient forgotten area. Tom, the pilot, had been instrumental in pulling off a successful flight there and back. The stubby man was gracious and thankful to Jeffrey because he had provided professional experience on LiDAR application and hovering maneuvers. Overall, the experience for both had been positive.

Looking at his watch, he realized if Tracy was on schedule, she'd be finishing dinner with Kevin Steptoe and returning to the hotel. He bid goodbye to the manager of Sydney Helicopter Service and settled into the Mustang. Driving like a man possessed, he took advantage of empty lanes, speeding directly to downtown Sydney.

Jeffrey needed something other than the green tea that had sustained him all day. In retrospect, skipping lunch to complete the terrestrial mapping had been a dreadful idea. Room service would have to suffice as Tracy would be arriving presently. Time enough to eat and rest up for tomorrow's trip.

***

The morning delivered bright and clear skies, a blue reminiscent of a robin's egg. Very little wind and moderate conditions were in the forecast. Ideal conditions for an excursion in a Bell 421 HP helicopter.

Kevin managed to squeeze his towering frame into the back seat of the Mustang. Tracy sat beside Jeffrey in the front. He drove at a moderate speed to the airstrip.

Arriving at J.A. Douglas McCurdy Sydney Airport, Tracy, Jeffrey and Kevin entered the offices of Sydney Helicopter Service. An extensive overview of the 3D map was essential for planning their day of digging.

"Let's look at what we have so far," said Jeffrey.

He was in the executive office chair facing the computer screen. Tracy sat next to him, and Kevin stood behind them, focused on the monitor.

The 3D computer representation of a geometric map rendering filled the screen. Several large foundations were centralized in a grid of half a kilometer square. The rest of the area consisted of roads, paths, and gardens.

Kevin looked mildly amused, a smile forming on the edge of his mouth. "Astounding. Who built it?"

Tracy and Jeffrey turned to face him, half expecting shock, and betrayal. They should have explained every aspect of their involvement in this unusual initiative.

"We were going to tell you more when we discovered the settlement." Jeffrey was apologetic and eliciting sincerity.

"Please forgive us. We thought it strictly necessary to be guarded until we were sure," explained Tracy. She turned to stand between Kevin and the monitor.

"I must say, at dinner last night, your conciliatory manner sparked my interest. As an inquisitive lawyer, I made a call to Brenda Tadler. It was a revealing conversation, to say the least."

"She could hardly have told you very much," said Tracy.

"No, but she was confident you were searching for a mythical Asian fleet that landed in Canada. And maybe made first Indigenous contact."

"Are you going to expose us to the Ministry of Culture and Heritage?" asked Tracy, realizing she had misjudged him.

"Try not to be too harsh. Your paper on Admiral Zheng He convinced me otherwise. Your professor at Stanford emailed me a copy last night."

"Was it necessary to go behind her back?" asked Jeffrey, who now turned to face Kevin.

"Let's just accept that we have a common interest in revealing the truth."

Footsteps were coming closer as the rhythmic thud of heavy boots filled the hallway.

Everyone became quiet. Tom, the helicopter pilot, poked his head into the office.

"We are fueled up and ready to go," he said.

"We'll be right with you, Tom," replied Jeffrey. Tom retraced his steps back to the tarmac.

"Before we fly out don't you think you should explain the site demographics and settlement structures?" asked Kevin.

Tracy and Jeffrey reverted their attention to the eerily green and yellow map on the screen and explained to Kevin what they believed they had discovered.

Thirty-Seven

Why is Your Computer Damaged?

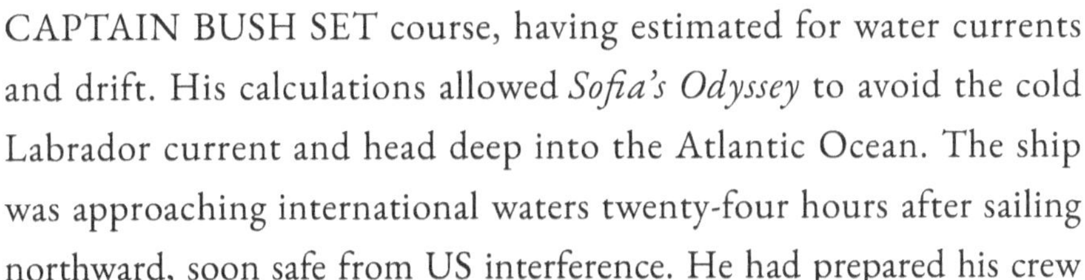

CAPTAIN BUSH SET course, having estimated for water currents and drift. His calculations allowed *Sofia's Odyssey* to avoid the cold Labrador current and head deep into the Atlantic Ocean. The ship was approaching international waters twenty-four hours after sailing northward, soon safe from US interference. He had prepared his crew and passengers for a four-and-a-half-day passage to the GPS coordinates that Ru had given him. Bush reckoned the weather and the sea would cooperate during the voyage.

The team of archaeologists' interest was piqued at starting a new assignment. The six of them had been educated in China and had been granted green cards to work in the United States for Big Wong. When he had decided to extend the subterranean basement beneath his restaurant, the construction crew had discovered relics from old Chinatown while removing the brick and debris. Big Wong postponed the development and contacted Deshan, the principal investigator, and his team to continue excavation, and to chronicle the ancient heritage beneath his buildings. As senior historian, Yulan had already compiled a brief history, the computer graphics specialist and photographer June Fields had been processing her work, and the field director Kian had categorized a few artifacts and sent them for cleaning. It was routine work, so when the opportunity to join a more elaborate and rare expedition presented itself, the scientists were very enthusiastic with Ru's proposal.

Ru summoned the field crew to the mess hall of the research ship. The information session began while the galley chef served coffee, tea, and cookies.

During the raid on the airport warehouse, everyone had been assaulted by smoke and flash, with each person compelled to save themselves in the confusion and subsequent fire. Ru, in a desperate course of action, had retrieved Tracy's computer. With all the vital information she had researched, this data was key to moving forward with the expedition.

Ru was standing in front of the scientists, seated around the mess hall table. All eyes were on him and the scorched exterior of the computer. Ru was ready to project the video images of the data on the screen behind him. The science team had to be familiarized with the details of Zheng He's many voyages.

Ru felt nervous. He knew his usual intimidation tactics should only be used as a last resort. He understood that motivating his gangsters took a certain streetwise finesse, but these archaeologists would require a different approach to remain motivated. He stepped away from the screen and cleared his throat.

"Thanks for being here today. As you are aware, my name is Ru Fa Zhong, and I am sponsoring this expedition."

The stuffy room became silent as the onlookers faced him. Ru felt restless, his heart rate increased, and his breathing became rapid. He reached behind his sport coat, touching the grip of his pistol, his trusty business partner. His symptoms faded and his confidence was regained.

"The purpose of this endeavor is to bring rightful artifacts of historical value back to our homeland," said Ru.

The academics murmured as Yulin whispered in agitated Mandarin. Field director Kian looked at the disfigured computer and stiffened. "Before you continue, we are disturbed. Why is your computer damaged?"

Ru closed the computer at the unexpected interruption. An explanation was warranted. "The computer was in an office fire, and I managed to save it."

"Is that your computer?" asked the field technician.

"No, it belongs to a former colleague who is no longer with us."

"I believe I speak for all of us here when I ask. Is there something you're not telling us?" asked the principal investigator.

Ru composed a compelling story with certain facts altered and others absent.

"A young American professor approached me with a historical account of Zheng He's voyages. Her name was Olivia, and we were attacked by a gang of criminals who was after her research," he explained.

Ru's forehead was glistening as his unbridled bullshit was convincing the unsuspecting and gullible pawns.

"Olivia perished in the inferno, and I just barely escaped with the computer before the building collapsed."

As he continued, his embellishment became easier, his charisma dominated the room, and the science team was hypnotized by the perversion of truth. The tone in the room was laden with relief as Ru had succeeded in regaining their trust.

"If you don't have any further questions, then we can proceed."

In the confined mess hall, the parties relaxed, expressions of interest were rekindled, and Ru continued with his presentation.

***

The engine's steady drone and rolling waves that Captain Bush watched through the bridge window were comforting and he almost drifted off. One of the crew members brought him some Colombian coffee. Even the strong brew was not enough to deliver him from the gentle calm in which he was embraced. It had been twenty-four hours since Bush took the helm at the Brooklyn Terminal, and he had never relaxed for a moment. He could make a critical mistake if he didn't get the necessary rest. A crackle over the ship-to-ship radio broke the silence on the bridge.

The constant vibration of the primary propulsion system had suddenly stopped, and the ship was at a standstill.

Ru scowled. "Everyone stays here. I need to go and speak with the captain."

He compared the sound of the propellers' cavitation to nuts and bolts rotating in a coffee can. After a full day cruising in the Atlantic Ocean, the thought of stopping so soon alarmed and agitated him. He left the scientists murmuring and marched up to the bridge.

"Northbound vessel, Northbound vessel, this is US Coast Guard vessel, Seneca, on channel 16. Over."

"Full stop. Don't do anything until I say," shouted Captain Bush, instantly awake. "For fuck's sake, what's our position?" He picked up the binoculars then scanned the horizon to identify the intruder's position.

"We're about one hundred nautical miles from the coast and just shy of the international waters, Cap," replied the helmsman, his hands resting on the ship's wheel.

Captain Bush panned the skyline again. The morning sun was illuminating the vastness of the Atlantic. Bush spotted the Coast Guard cutter astern.

"I see her," said Bush.

Ru opened the door and stepped onto the bridge, breathing heavily. "Why have we stopped?"

"Northbound vessel, northbound vessel, do you copy? Over."

Captain Bush put up his hand for Ru to stop talking and responded to the hail.

"*Seneca*, this is *Sofia's Odyssey*. Over."

"*Sofia's Odyssey*, switch to channel 71. Over."

"Roger that. *Sofia's Odyssey* switching to channel 71. Over."

"Prepare for boarding and inspection. Over."

"Preparing to receive. We are dead stop. Out."

A sense of dread overcame the occupants of the bridge. The outcome of a search of the ship could decide whether they would be escorted back to harbor or allowed to continue. It would be a significant setback, if not a total failure.

"Let's start the ship and run her into international waters," said Ru. He was fuming and irrational, the behavior that marked him as unstable and prone to recklessness.

"No can do," replied Captain Bush.

"I'm giving you an order!"

Bush ignored his outburst and focused the binoculars onto the fast-moving cutter.

"We can't outrun her. The best scenario is to organize yourselves and comply."

The USCGC *Seneca* stopped portside. A small boarding skiff, blue light flashing, skimmed across the surface of the water rhythmically before halting alongside *Sofia's Odyssey*. The crew tied up and climbed onto the ship. One Coast Guard member stayed on the skiff while the rest fanned out to examine the vessel. Dressed in blue fatigues, orange life vests, and baseball caps, they followed the lines of command and protocols. The ship was examined in various sections for safety violations. A Coast Guard member monitored the crew in the recreation room, another secured the scientists in the mess hall, and another ensured the captain, and his crew on the bridge were detained.

The chief officer asked Captain Bush. "Any weapons on board?"

Ru had had ample time to reassure himself that the firearms in the Range Rover remained hidden.

"Yes, we have a chrome barrel shotgun located on the bridge," said Bush. "It's securely locked away, and there is a permit."

The crewmembers' identification was checked, and the captain's documents and logbook were inspected. All vital survival equipment, including the freefall lifeboat were scrutinized and deemed compliant with federal laws and regulations.

One member of the boarding team searched the Range Rover but missed the hidden compartment. Ru quivered in relief, as the cache of arms had not been discovered.

The chief officer was satisfied with the ship's condition and filled out a boarding report. Two minor infractions were corrected on the spot. He handed Captain Bush the yellow copy of the CG-4100 report of boarding form and bid them a good day. The skiff returned to the Seneca.

Bush stood on the port side deck long enough to see the skiff loaded onto the Coast Guard vessel. He stomped up the metal stairs to the bridge and took control of the helm. He increased the pace of the engines to twelve knots and rechecked the course guiding the ship into the open seas.

Ru's uneasiness behind him, he returned to the mess hall to reassure the scientists they were proceeding on schedule. He could hear the familiar sound of nuts and bolts revolving around in the coffee can. The constant vibration of the propellers churned unbridled by the interdiction of the US Coast Guard.

Thirty-Eight

Louis St. Laurent - The Ice King

THE AIR CANADA flight to St. John's was on schedule as William stepped on board at 7:30 a.m. The flight was two hours and 27 minutes in duration, giving him ample time to study the members of the Foo Dog Triad. Occasionally he would look up from his tablet, glancing around the cabin for passengers exhibiting atypical behavior. His observations confirmed that an orderly group was aboard the aircraft.

He continued reading the background notes. Much of the information seemed thin compared to RCMP standard files but included arrest records and time served in maximum security. There were six penitentiaries located on Lantau Island, which was one of the biggest islands in Hong Kong. Shek Pik Prison housed the prisoners receiving middle to life sentences and was frequently occupied by Foo Dog Triad members.

William found it ironic that the Hong Kong Disneyland Theme Park and many other tourist attractions were nearby. He thought a more desolate, far-removed location would have been better suited, although the Shek Pik Prison was situated in a remote area of the island.

William resumed his examination of the case files of the principals in the investigation and became utterly immersed. Someone midway in the aisle yelled in an outburst of anger, and William's posture stiffened. From his obscured position, he observed a passenger shouting at the female flight attendant doing her utmost to calm him. Her voice, shaky, halting, and filled with restraint, was drowned out by the temerity of a Newfoundlander.

William folded up his table tray, preparing to intervene but sat back promptly as the flight attendant defused the situation by apologizing. Another cabin attendant rushed over and offered the jerk a towel and a can of beer. Weary, William decided the flight attendants could handle the offensive oaf.

***

The Grand Banks off the east coast of Newfoundland and Labrador is the foggiest place on earth. That distinction is another attribute to the elements and conditions that seafarers must endure as they pass over the submerged plateaus of the continental shelf. Dangerous meteorological conditions, which are often the norm off the coast of Newfoundland in May, can confound even the best sailors.

The *Louis St. Laurent* is the biggest ice breaker in Canada. Dubbed the *Ice King* by the Canadian Coast Guard, it patrols the Atlantic and goes where needed. The thick bow is made of hardened steel, allowing the ship to traverse the thick ice where other vessels cannot. She regularly voyages from the Gulf of St. Lawrence to the Arctic Circle. The vessel often carries out multi-disciplinary scientific expeditions. The ship's visibility confirms Canada's sovereignty in its surrounding waters.

Besides patrolling the Atlantic for environmental and fishing infractions, the Canadian Coast Guard provided platforms to support other government departments involved in maritime security by providing ships or aircraft to the Canada Border Services, the RCMP, and the Royal Canadian Navy.

Jimmy Kim, the third mate and watch stander, held his binoculars, and peered into the gaps of the shifting fog. Chief Officer Paul Goyette approached him with a mug of coffee.

"Got you something hot. Hopefully, it will take off the chill."

"Thanks, pal," said Jimmy.

"See any icebergs?"

"No, but it's the season. We may see some soon," said Jimmy.

Paul was the first to hear the thumping. He jabbed Jimmy in the ribs and pointed a finger into the fog.

"There's a helicopter approaching."

"Yeah," exclaimed Jimmy. "What on earth is the pilot doing out here in this pea soup?"

"He must be about 300 kilometers offshore!"

"Could be headed for one of the oil platforms or this here ship," said Jimmy with concern crossing his face.

Following what seemed a rather intense wait, the helicopter gradually put down on the stern of the *Louis St. Laurent*. As soon as the engine was shut down, pilot Victor Stupendski and RCMP officer William Fox simultaneously jumped to the deck. They sprinted up the staircase to the upper deck, where First Mate Carl Rogers and Captain George Carter waited.

"Permission to come aboard," queried William.

"Permission granted," barked Captain Carter. "We just got the message you were coming."

Victor stood, his posture stiff, his demeanor tense, a mixed feeling of euphoria and relief after having relied on instruments to fly through the dense fog.

"Captain, can we gather the officers and the search and rescue team? I'd like to explain our mission," said William.

"Consider it done," replied Captain Carter, a stout and sturdy man who loved his job. Carl motioned William and Victor to follow him down into the conference room three levels below. Fifteen minutes later, the crew was assembled.

Captain Carter stood before the officers and staff, and said, "I'd like to introduce you to RCMP Inspector William Fox."

"Hey everyone, I have been tasked by the Canadian government to cooperate with the FBI on the apprehension of dangerous kidnappers and murderers. As we speak, they are out there on the Atlantic. We will be collaborating with the US Coast Guard to locate them."

William continued, "Right now, there is a research ship called Sofia's Odyssey in the Atlantic that has a Hong Kong Triad boss aboard. He has been identified as a person of interest, and we intend to arrest him the instant he arrives in Canadian waters."

"Excuse me, Inspector Fox, it's a vast ocean. How do you expect to apprehend this gangster?" asked Carl.

William measured the man and surmised his concern was a legitimate one. The first mate was straightforward, and his handsome looks had the same intensity: black skin, high forehead and square chin. William sensed this was a man he could rely on if the going got tough.

"Thank you, Mr. Rogers. Let me explain. We are expected to rendezvous with the US Coast Guard and catch *Sofia's Odyssey* in a pincer movement. Patrick Reilly, an FBI agent from New York, will be onboard the US Coast Guard Cutter Seneca coordinating from his end. Together, both ships and personnel should be able to apprehend the gang. The US Coast Guard cutter is armed and ready should the situation become tenuous. Of course, only we can arrest a criminal in Canadian territory."

"What happens in the event we reach *Sofia's Odyssey* before the Americans? Most of us on this ship don't have assault training," said Paul.

"Precisely, the situation on the ocean can shift dramatically, catching us off guard as well," added Captain Carter.

"Captain, how far away are the CCGS *Cape Roger* and the CCGS *Cygnus*?" asked William, splaying his fanned-out left hand against the desk.

"As of their last positions, CCGS *Cape Roger* is anchored in Shelburne, Nova Scotia, and *Cygnus* is being refitted in St. John's Dockyard. No help there," replied the captain.

"Too bad; those two vessels have armed boarding teams and are equipped with .50 caliber machine guns. What other options do we have?" asked William, his muscles tensing as he breathed in deeply and expelled slowly.

"There is the *Leonard J. Cowley*. She's got armed boarding teams," said Carl. I was a junior crew member when she was the command vessel in the Turbot Wars of 1994. Her crew fired machine-gun bursts across the bow of a Spanish ship that was fishing illegally."

"I remember the ship was escorted back to Canada and her nets examined for proof." William paused and asked, "Captain, can we contact the *Cowley* for assistance?"

"I'll ask the helmsman to hail her," said Captain Carter.

"We will reconvene later. Let's just see if the Cowley is available," said William as he adjourned the meeting.

***

William went up on deck for some fresh air before dinner and to get his duffel bag. Now, it was a waiting game. Jimmy was patrolling the deck and ensuring the helicopter remained strapped down. He was resecuring one of the tie downs when a gust of wind bounded over the aircraft, dislodging it from Jimmy's hands.

"Tie her down tight. My gear is still on board," said William.

"Not to worry, the Coast Guard taught us not to catch our fingers," replied Jimmy and turned around and gave a wink of his eye.

"That's why you're a Coastie. They had to teach you," said William bemused.

"I was going to join the RCMP but was overqualified," said Jimmy as he escalated the banter. William rolled his eyes up and gave a quick snort.

They both moved over to the ship's railing and took in the foreboding weather. It had not changed, and Environment Canada was warning of an approaching gale.

"So, what do you do for fun when not on assignments?" asked Jimmy.

"Well, I like going out in my cigarette boat," said William. "I was lucky to select good stocks, which let me afford it." Retrieving his phone, he showed Jimmy pictures of his speedboat.

"Incredible, and what an interesting name!" he said. "The *Midnight Fox*," rolled off his tongue. He was in awe of the boat. "Why did you name her that, eh?"

"My grandfather had a speed boat with the same name. He was an undercover RCMP agent during Prohibition. His job was to run Canadian whisky from Pelee Island in Lake Erie to the US to gather evidence against Al Capone and the Purple Gang of Detroit."

"What happened to him?"

"On one of his midnight runs, a US Coast Guard cutter ambushed him, rammed and cut his boat in half."

"Did he make it?"

"Well, I am here, aren't I?" grinned William. "He swam to shore, eventually met my grandmother, and was reassigned to Montreal."

"You sure sound proud of him."

"Yes, he was a good man. During the Second World War, he became a captain of a destroyer in the Royal Canadian Navy. Later, he was awarded a medal for sinking a German submarine."

Paul found them on deck and informed them that dinner would be in about ten minutes. "Cookie is going to fire off a scoff and prep some figgy duff."

"You know I've lived most of my life in Canada and never heard of that," said William.

"I'm just about gut-founded," said Paul.

William placed his hand on his forehead and squinted in bewilderment.

"It means I'm hungry, eh," Jimmy belted out in his best Newfoundlander accent, despite being of Korean heritage.

Let's have some figgy duff
Some nice piece of stuff
Eat till we had enough
Keeper down when the sea is rough.

They all laughed at Jimmy's sea shanty. Jimmy and Paul headed to the mess hall. William unsure of this new culinary experience, said, "I'll catch up with you guys in a minute."

Thirty-Nine
Why Didn't I Bring Gravol?

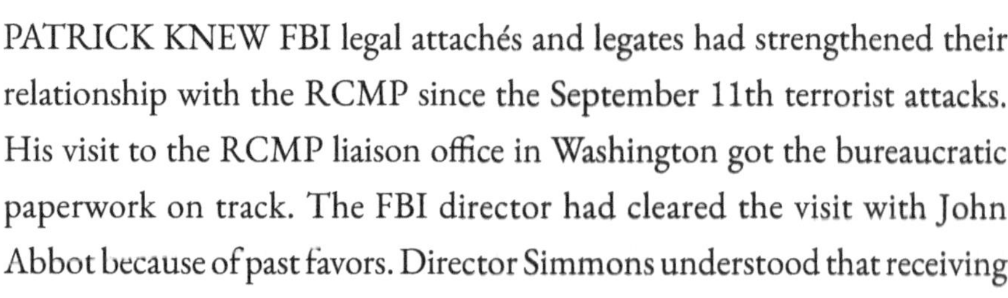

PATRICK KNEW FBI legal attachés and legates had strengthened their relationship with the RCMP since the September 11th terrorist attacks. His visit to the RCMP liaison office in Washington got the bureaucratic paperwork on track. The FBI director had cleared the visit with John Abbot because of past favors. Director Simmons understood that receiving diplomatic clearance from the US ambassador in Ottawa was essential. Patrick was now officially permitted to take on the assignment with William Fox.

After Hong Kong, Patrick had invited William to the Farm, but he was on sick leave and later temporarily reassigned to the forensic fraud department. Perhaps a day would come when this would happen.

The last item on Patrick's list was contacting the US Coast Guard and asking the senior officer at Base Boston for transport to the *USCGS Seneca*. Ship Commander Tommy Green had a good laugh that the FBI wanted a ride. It was the most refreshing request for cooperation between law-enforcement agencies he could remember.

It took the FBI Bell 407 helicopter a little over an hour from New York Bureau to Base Boston. On arrival at the base, Patrick was informed that the *Seneca* was midway between Rhode Island and Nova Scotia, and that his ride to the *Seneca* was waiting.

After clearing Boston air space, the helicopter headed over the open ocean. Patrick began to squirm in the comfortable cabin. His heartbeat increased, and his jaw muscles clenched. Patrick understood that the dread he felt would overwhelm him if he let it. Flying over deep bodies of water left him feeling defenseless. He suffered from thalassophobia, terror of the ocean that's deep, murky, and vast, coupled with the fear of drowning. It would be hours before he would reach the *Seneca*. *Why didn't I bring Gravol?* Patrick shifted his body and practiced cognitive behavior therapy to counteract his negative thoughts. Before long, he was wiping the sweat from his brow with a paper napkin. His upset stomach felt relieved, even with the jarring and uneven flight of the helicopter. Patrick was recovering. He looked forward to seeing William and getting on with the assignment.

Patrick was grateful when the chopper dropped to the deck of the *Seneca*. The ocean vessel was as long as a soccer field and was designed to take its crew for extended missions.

The ship's commander sent a crewmember to welcome him on board and escorted him under the helicopter backwash toward the bridge. Once Patrick arrived on the bridge, Commander Tommy Green and crew were introduced. Patrick explained to the commander and the lieutenant commander his plan. They in turn described the capabilities of the Shipboard Command and Control Centre. The advanced technology would enable them to locate the research ship.

When Patrick conveyed the ship's name in question, both men were shocked and dismayed. The FBI agent was irate when he learned that *Sofia's Odyssey* had been boarded in a routine check the prior day, then allowed to proceed with two minor corrections. Patrick's stance stiffened, and his facial muscles became rigid with anger. Even the seasoned Navy men were surprised by the level of language directed at them.

Taken aback, they changed course as quickly as possible to the last-known coordinates of *Sofia's Odyssey*. Bridge crew became busy with radar sensors while radio transceivers collected vital information. To appease the fiery Irishman, the lieutenant commander ordered, "Full steam ahead."

The chase was on, and Patrick wanted to get to *Sofia's Odyssey* before the Canadians. It was a matter of pride. The *Seneca* was already a formidable ship with a record of stopping many go-fast drug boats and taking millions of dollars of drugs off the street. Another feather in her cap would improve the ship's morale and pride. So, the entire squad got behind Patrick's goal to take down the murderous triad gang leader.

Patrick turned to the captain and said, "I'd like to contact Inspector William Fox on the *Louis St. Laurent* and let him know we are underway." *This was going to be an interesting conversation.*

Forty

Bring the Sub to an All-stop

THE SUBMARINE TRIP from Macau around Africa and north to the Azores had taken two weeks. Sailing outside normal shipping channels and running at snorkel depth allowed the vessel's engines to draw air and remain concealed.

With a short layover at the Azores, they crossed the Atlantic and arrived on the Grand Banks off Newfoundland and Labrador. Although they were in international waters, a foreign submarine close to the coast would be considered hostile, bringing a swift and deadly response from NATO forces who patrolled the area.

Captain Ho Chan believed that the Coast Guard vessel was too close for comfort and retracted the periscope. The Coast Guard vessel's radar or sonar could track conventional submarines and, if necessary, call a naval destroyer and intercept them. The new US Naval destroyers were equipped with depth charges and sonobuoys that could destroy them. *Would the submarine's cloaking technology help them remain hidden?*

"There's a Coast Guard cutter moving toward us at approximately ten knots. Are they transmitting any sonar?" asked Chan, addressing the sound technician.

"I can't make out anything over the sound of our propellers, Captain."

"Check again. Keep trying."

"The ship is slowing down and making a wide turn toward us," said the sonar technician.

The submarine's crew were silent as the interior became unearthly, like a child hiding in a closet, afraid of an apparition.

"Bring the sub to an all-stop," said the captain.

The technician stopped the submarine's engines and heating systems, reducing noise. A pall overcame them as the interior became bone-chilling and claustrophobic. The gangsters were concerned they would be sunk but the former Chinese Navy crew were accustomed to operating under these circumstances. The tense atmosphere in the unventilated chamber was stifling and made breathing difficult for everyone.

Most captains, when faced with a crisis, decide whether to rely on instinct or training. Chan's naval experience was invaluable when combined with instinct, it was a significant factor in favor of their survival.

"Fill the ballast tanks and let her sink. Keep me apprised of depth," said the captain.

The technician engaged the ballast tanks, and the submarine began to descend into the lower reaches beyond the thermocline into the sea's cold arms.

Dao observed the performance of the crew and captain. He knew that the submarine could take out a vessel the size of the Coast Guard ship that was pursuing them. The submarine's defenses consisted of surface-to-air missiles of Chinese design, which were versions of the French Exocet missile, notorious for sinking the *HMS Sheffield* in the Falklands War. If needed, anti-submarine torpedoes could be deployed. Dao regarded the advanced communications systems and satellite dish as a bonus. It could recognize the electronic fingerprint of radar and identify the pursuing ship and its electronic defense system.

Although the submarine was capable of modern warfare, Dao knew better than to engage the American Navy. The prize the triad gang was after far outweighed the success of a Sardine missile launch. Once the systems came online and the Coast Guard cutter radar found the signal, the ambush would alert them. On the other hand, if the Sardine missile sank the vessel, every ship nearby would arrive to rescue survivors, ruining any chance of escaping.

"Captain, let's take it easy. Maybe the ship moves away," said Dao.

"I'm not about to start a war." Chan spun around, his lip in a snarl.

"Good. Ru would likely kill you and your family if you messed up his plans."

"Ha, ha. Not likely if the US Navy gets us first." Chan looked around to establish whether he had lost any respect from his crew.

"Two hundred meters and falling," said the helmsman.

"Any sound in the water?"

The sonar technician, ready to report underwater sound pulses to the captain, wedged the left headphone so tightly to his ear it became numb. The control center crew members watched him as he spoke.

"Picking up propellers," he said with an urgency in his voice.

"Keep a steady plane."

"Steady plane, Captain," replied the helmsman.

"Sonar, report."

Time stood still like an eternity. Everyone was uneasy, waiting for the subsequent callout.

"Sir, propulsion is moving away."

Tension in the control center subsided and murmurs of relief drifted through the space.

"The cloaking technology worked," said the captain. "Prepare for a new heading."

"Aye, aye, Captain."

Dao put his hand on Chan's shoulder. "Good work," he said. "Captain, in a couple of hours, surface. I need to contact Ru via secure satellite feed."

Chan shrugged his shoulder to remove Dao's hand. He despised being patronized. He headed toward his cabin, head up and shoulders back.

Forty-One

This is Not About Us

WILLIAM LEANED AGAINST the railing, glancing eastward at the horizon. It was vast and empty. He knew many flagged ships sailed from New York to Halifax, past Greenland, and further to the UK. The Gulf Stream lanes were filled with them. Icebergs floated down the shipping lanes from the north, amusing tourists and panicking ships' crews.

Jimmy and Paul had left the deck for dinner. William was occupied with his thoughts when the external speaker system beckoned him to the bridge. He rubbed his hands together for circulation. While preoccupied, the Atlantic wind had swept across the handrails, chilling his fingers. William walked to the edge of the bulkhead, grabbed the handrail, and ran up the flight of steps to the bridge.

He nodded to Carl as the radio handset was handed to him.

"This is Inspector Fox. Over."

"It's Patrick Reilly on the *Seneca*, What's your status? Over."

"Good; what's your plan? Over."

"Captain Green says *Sofia's Odyssey's* AIS is shut off. Over."

"What is that? Over."

"It's the automatic identification system, tracks ships in real-time. They also shut off the GPS system. Over."

"Suggestions? Over."

"Speak with your captain about an irregular east–west pattern heading southward. Commander Green will sail the *Seneca* northward in a zig-zag pattern. Our radar should be able to locate the ship. Over"

"Roger that. The *Louis St. Laurent* can locate icebergs with the assistance of satellites from the Canadian Space Agency. We'll try that method too. Over."

"Let's have the captains run the show. They know their sophisticated equipment and systems. Over."

"Roger that. Leave it to them. Speak to you in eight hours closer to the Nova Scotia coast. Over."

"Will do. Out."

William turned to Carl and said, "Thank you." He and Carl left the bridge and headed for dinner and the famous figgy duff. William sat with Captain Carter and Carl, and during supper, discussed the operation. They were curious about William's partnership with FBI agent Patrick Reilly. William explained the Tracy Jordan kidnapping in detail. His thoughts drifted toward his relationship with her. A prickly issue for him as he was still smitten with her and hurt by her rejection.

His thoughts were interrupted by Captain Carter who asked, "Do we know the location for this presumed archaeological site? It might help pinpoint where they're headed."

William and Tracy hadn't spoken since Washington. Extrapolating *Sofia's Odyssey's* position might be faster if Tracy gave him the coordinates.

"Good point. I'll call Tracy and ask her," said William.

***

William stood below the foremast and yanked out an Iridium satellite phone. Compact like the iPhone, it was encrypted and had global coverage.

John had given it to him for updates. William dialed up Tracy's number and waited for it to connect. The wind howled across the ship. He cupped the Iridium in his left hand as he paced back and forth. His gut was in knots. His pride strained. His emotions pulled him apart. His face was hot and sticky. Even the freezing crosswind provided no relief.

"Hi, Tracy. It's William. Is this a good time?" He heard static. Maybe he was too close to the radar unit. He moved away.

"Look, I didn't mean for us to leave it the way we did..." her voice trailed off.

"This is not about us."

"Oh?" Tracy tried to hide the disappointment in her voice.

"I'm on an icebreaker in the Atlantic searching for Ru. They are sailing to the coordinates you gave them. Tell me they are not headed your way," said William.

"No. I sent him to a different location."

"Can you send the false GPS coordinates to us? It would improve our chance of capturing Ru."

"Of course."

William gave her the number of the satellite phone. He heard the text arrive and looked at the display. The screen was like a gray void he felt he could fall into and disappear.

"Thank you, Tracy. I hope we have a chance to catch up again. Bye."

"William, wait..." He had hung up before Tracy could finish.

William called John next. He left a brief message, saying that they were making progress and pocketed the phone. He arrived at the bridge and gave Captain Carter the coordinates Tracy had texted him.

Captain Carter and William contacted Captain Green and Patrick on the Seneca and relayed the coordinates to them.

"Knowing the *Sofia's Odyssey's* destination will help in our search," said William.

"I suggest we confer again in the morning and decide whether we need both ships, or if we should adopt another plan.

"It looks like things are coming together," said Patrick.

"Images from RADARSAT-2 are starting to come in," said Carter.

"How can you tell the difference between an iceberg and the ship?"

"Our technicians can tell a ship target because it appears brighter than the surrounding area and dissimilar from an iceberg."

"If we discover an image of interest, we can send a helicopter for visual confirmation," suggested William.

"That's right." Carter added, "It will take about seven hours to reach Ms. Jordan's coordinates. Best get some rest."

"Thanks. Will do."

William left the bridge, the engines' vibrations reverberating through his boots. He tried desperately to organize his thoughts. Sleep would be a comfort.

Forty-Two

These Boots Will Do in a Pinch

TRACY, KEVIN, AND Jeffrey sat in the helicopter, adjusted their headphones, and continued their discussion about the LiDAR mapping. Tracy was confident Jeffrey had located the settlement site, noted in the ancient diary.

Tom, the pilot, clicked on the microphone. "It will take one hour from Sydney airport to fly south to Gabarus Wilderness Area."

"Thanks Tom," said Jeffrey.

"What we have discovered is a cluster of old stone foundations. A design pattern similar to a type of Chinese architecture from the 15th century. Simply put, a blockhouse with a doorway and possibly a peaked roof," Jeffrey explained.

"The typography indicates plots of gardens, rice paddies, roadways, and structural networks a kilometer in scope," said Tracy.

"When we land, I will explain the rest of the LiDAR mapping and what we plan to do," said Jeffrey.

Tracy noticed Kevin looking at her, and she broke eye contact. She peered out the window. Flying over the shore, she recollected as a child running free on the sands chasing sandpipers, squealing in delight, as they flew away squawking. She missed that feeling of innocence.

"Do you see any issue with the Indigenous community?" Jeffrey asked Kevin.

"The area is protected by the Nova Scotia government. Some Indigenous peoples will have objections, but that's why you have me here. I do represent my people," Kevin reassured them.

Tom guided the aircraft to a gentle landing. The group disembarked and located a place for their mobile headquarters. The equipment they needed for the day's survey was unloaded and a tent erected to serve as a temporary office. Fold-up chairs and a portable table with laptop computer completed the arrangement. Tracy clicked on the LiDAR map and directed Kevin to an area that exhibited various anomalies.

"Kevin, if you'll notice, the buildings are constructed around a central room or hall. The front gate, the courtyard, and rooms to the cardinal points. This design is influenced by Confucius and the principles of feng shui. Imagine large structural timbers to support the roof and walls made of bricks over foundation stones. These designs are very similar to the Ming dynasty, circa 1368 to 1644. I'm convinced this settlement is of Chinese origin."

Around them, everything was overgrown. Loose vines dangled from pine trees and wild shrubs. They walked through swampy areas with bulrushes and yellow wildflowers, bending with the breeze. The area looked bleak and deserted, not a hospitable place to live.

Kevin was anxious to get started. He had dressed in hiking boots, blue jeans, a plaid shirt, and a Levi's trucker's jacket. He carried work gloves and was ready to get into the heart of the dig.

"Just a recap of what we're looking for," said Tracy. "Begin in a rectangular grid and collect your data that way. We're looking for shallow, medium, and deep targets. The unit should give you 3D depth slices on any buried anomalies. We'll save the data on a memory stick."

"I could email the data to the museum so they can start some analysis," said Jeffrey.

"We shouldn't give them that information so soon. I'd like to keep this under our control. All right, Dad?"

"Sure thing."

Tracy turned to Kevin and said, "You can start digging test pits based on what evidence the radar images provide."

Tracy slipped into coveralls and pulled on tall black riding boots.

Kevin noticed. "Do you have a horse hidden around here someplace?"

"I didn't take you for a smart-ass, Kevin. These boots will do in a pinch. Aren't there some holes over there that need digging?"

"On it," he grinned. Kevin went off with the shovel and trowel toward the yellow wildflowers, unable to hide his amusement.

***

Tracy walked over to the first test pit Kevin had dug. She passed soil through the screen and found shards and remnants of bowls, iron nails, some wild rice, and hops. At the second test pit she uncovered bones of birds and fish. She packaged, numbered, and indexed where the items were found. These items would be a narrative to the way of life of the inhabitants and would help interpret local history and eventually would be donated and displayed in museums.

As mid-afternoon approached, the equipment was collected, and the team prepared for a short meeting before leaving.

"What do you think we have here?" asked Tracy, seated and pulling off her riding boots. Kevin responded first. "Definitely looks like this was a serious settlement, although some artifacts can be attributed to my ancestors being here."

"Dad, what's your take?"

"My preliminary radar scan is affirming substructures. I think there must be a tomb near the house foundation," said Jeffrey.

Tracy groaned as she removed the other boot. "I think Zheng He's treasure is buried in a tomb, similar to that of the Terracotta Warriors. I believe the admiral dismantled his ships and used the timber and the ballast to build his settlement. He would have used the treasure to barter goods with the locals," said Tracy.

"Interesting. But my people have no oral history of this," said Kevin.

"The Chinese settlers would have integrated and dissipated amongst the Indigenous peoples in just one generation," Tracy answered.

"Severe famine could also have disseminated the Chinese population. That is why there is no evidence in traditional historical literature," added Jeffrey.

"I agree to some of your hypotheses, but it's getting late. We should fly back." Kevin's comment had broken the spell.

They boarded the Bell helicopter. Tom settled everyone in, took control, and brought the big bird back to Sydney.

Forty-Three

My Original Order Still Stands

REN BO'S ASSIGNMENT to find the person responsible for poaching Dr. Chen Hao began by accessing the data files President Wei Lei had compiled. Ren Bo opened his laptop, adjusted his office chair, and prepared for a long session. He accessed the list of delegates that had attended the Second International Conference of Environmental Chemistry and Engineering.

Adopting a method of elimination, he removed all the candidates who had not been teaching at an accredited university, then anyone not lecturing or having policy-making influence. Ren Bo focused on individuals who had given a keynote address, an oral workshop, or an academic discussion.

After eliminating many academics from various countries, he was sure the recruiter must have been an American professor who had spoken at the conference. A few names emerged, like Jeffrey Jordan and other academics. How would he prove whether one of them had been a CIA or FBI operative in 1985? President Wei Lei said the conference was a CIA front.

Dr. Chen Hao had specialized in material physics that could be applied to the study of atoms and their interaction with nanotechnology biomaterials for space research. Ren Bo suspected that the space shuttle program overseen by NASA needed the CIA to recruit scientists of this caliber.

Ren Bo's training enabled him to break down specific characteristics of intelligence officers. The Chinese intelligence network provided a background check on Jeffrey Jordan. Ren Bo's analysis of his quarry showed that Jeffrey Jordan's skills included steering conversations and mastering languages like Russian, Mandarin, Farsi, and Korean. Also, in his record, he had worked undercover in many underdeveloped countries as an archaeologist. With Jordan's high level of intelligence, it would not be a stretch for him to have taken a primer on material physics so that he could instigate a conversation with Dr. Chen, then gain his trust.

In 1985, eight space-shuttle missions were scheduled and could have been an incentive to motivate a defection for a scientist living under an autocratic regime. The promise of living in a democratic society and participating in NASA programs must have given many academics sweats and palpitations. Bringing an accomplished scientist such as Dr. Chen to the US space program would have been career advancing.

Ren Bo was positive that Jeffrey Jordan was the man he was looking for. He felt there might be more depth to what had happened and wanted to confirm some facts before submitting his report to President Wei Lei, especially when he wasn't sure where this assignment would lead.

Ren Bo decided to refocus his assignment on locating General Po's manipulator. He was tired, exhausted, and a fierce headache forced him to finish early. He needed to recover his strength and go at it another day.

***

The alarm-clock radio blared out C-pop music. The melodic rap penetrated Ren Bo's dozy state of bliss. He sat up on his elbows, away from the pillow, and realized one of his favorite groups was waking him up. A Crush was the latest hot band on the Chinese mainland. The girls dressed in boys' clothing and mimicked boy bands of North America and South Korea. After the song finished, local Beijing news reported traffic congestion downtown, followed by the weather report.

Ren Bo reached over and hit the alarm button to stop the onslaught. Today he would provide an interim report to President Wei Lei.

He dressed in casual clothes and prepared his breakfast. He left a few voice messages. One of them was to Minister of State Security Guan Yin, informing her about his pending meeting with President Wei Lei. Then he made his way from his apartment to the underground to his Knight S12, a cloned Jeep. He made the hectic drive through the city and avoided the traffic jam he had heard about earlier on the radio.

The morning was crisp and clear, and the sky an intense sapphire blue. The trees lining the streets were cloaked in soft emerald green, the city's mood seemed cheerful and reflected his state of mind.

He turned off the road and proceeded toward Communist Party Headquarters. He parked his Jeep and walked to the rear of the building, where two guards from the Central Guard Bureau escorted him to President Wei Lei's office.

On entering the office for the first time, Ren Bo nodded his head respectfully to the Communist Party chief. Wei Lei gestured with his hand for Ren Bo to sit in the pale-yellow cushioned chair. A low-level coffee table was between them. The room was filled with classically crafted mahogany furniture. The main desk was Ming design, and the black lacquered bookshelves were laden with literature of the ages. Period statues and vases were distributed throughout the room, with elaborate silk screens partitioning off a quiet corner. Conceivably, clandestine conversations took place there. Behind the ornate desk and on the wall were portraits of two heroes. One of Mao Zedong, the father of Chinese Communism, the other, Lei Fang, a propaganda icon who represented the ideal citizen.

Ren Bo sat down, and the president feigned mild interest in his presence.

"I understand you have something important to relate to me. Be as quick as you can. I have foreign delegates waiting," said Wei Lei.

"I interviewed Captain Yuan Shao who was central to investigating General Po's death. He and his team interviewed General Po's friends, military associates, then questioned his wife and examined his financial records."

"I expect no less from my investigators. I presume the scrolls have been donated to the Ministry of Culture?"

"Yes, sir, they were delivered into the minister's hands. You are probably aware that as chief of staff, General Po had access to the satellite systems and the cyber operations."

The president nodded his head in understanding.

"That's where he was most vulnerable and became compromised. In exchange for the scrolls, he committed fraud and treason against our country. All evidence is pointing to someone wanting unlimited access to the satellite system. It seems they were tracking someone."

"So, you want access to classified information? That's why you're here today?"

"Yes, sir. This would help me expedite this assignment for you."

"I'm calling my secretary. She'll get the information you've requested. Just hold on."

"Joy, explain to the North Korean delegation that I will be a few minutes late. Next, find out who oversees the satellite tracking information and give me his name and number. Make it fast."

Ren Bo's eyes drifted around the office and then back to the president who was still holding the phone to his ear, waiting for the information. His annoyance was beginning to become perceptible.

"Colonel Hu. Okay, thank you."

President Wei Lei picked up his pen and jotted the number down on a pad. After replacing the receiver in its cradle, he tore off the sheet and handed it to Ren Bo.

Wei Lei looked at Ren Bo expectantly. "Do you have anything to report on the other matter?"

"No sir, not yet, but I expect to identify the person involved soon."

"You know what to do. My original order still stands."

Ren Bo stood up, nodded to the president, turned around and left. The same two government agents escorted him out of the building.

***

Wasting no time, he sat in his Jeep and phoned Colonel Hu.

"This is Colonel Hu."

"Hello. My name is Colonel Ren Bo from the Ministry of State Security."

"How may I help you?"

"I am investigating inconsistencies in the record-keeping of satellite positioning. It is important I meet with you immediately. This is on the president's orders."

"Your timing couldn't be worse. Our space administration is preparing a launch in a few days," said the colonel.

"I must insist that we meet. Our national security is at stake."

"I can make time during my lunch."

"I'll bring something to eat. You're not allergic to anything, are you?"

"No, but can you bring some pearl milk tea?"

***

Ren Bo drove out of the park along West Chang'an Avenue. The space agency was in Haidian District. Along the way, he stopped at Sanguine Restaurant and ordered sweet shrimp, garlic scallops, fried vegetables, and pearl milk tea for two. Picking up the takeout lunch, he resumed his journey to the space agency and arrived just before noon.

Colonel Hu escorted him into his office. They tore open the lunch bag and began to eat. During the indulgence of good food, Ren Bo got to the details.

"Did you review the satellite logs leading up to the months prior to General Po's arrest and subsequent suicide?" asked Ren Bo.

"Yes, I did. It looks like General Po was repositioning one of our military satellites for some interested party. The logs, when retrieved, indicated he used the system to track a cellphone."

"Can you tell me what the cell number was?"

"Not if they removed the SIM card. But China Mobile might still be able to trace it."

"What about the location of that cellphone?"

The colonel began to click his curser until the evidence scrolled across the monitor.

"Hong Kong International Airport." He picked up a sweet shrimp with his fingers and popped it into his mouth.

"Would the system still have a picture of the area in question?"

Colonel Hu wiped his hands and his mouth with a tissue. Then started tapping on the keyboard to bring up the coordinates and high-resolution photographs captured by the satellite that day.

"What does that look like to you?" said Ren Bo.

"A young woman carrying a tote bag."

"I have plenty more frames that we can look at. There, two men in black suits are picking her up and putting her in a late-model Range Rover."

"Our satellite optics are as good as the US, aren't they?" said Ren Bo, pointing at the vehicle.

"Better. Focusing on the license plate. Clear, clearer, there it is."

Ren Bo took a picture of the license plate shown on the computer screen. He texted the image to his contact at the Ministry of State Security as a high priority. The plate would be run, and Ren Bo would locate the owner's address. It would bring him another step closer to the person responsible for the ruin of General Po.

"Thanks, Colonel Hu. I will put in a good word with your superiors for your cooperation."

"I really appreciate you buying lunch, but I must go. My team is waiting on the prelaunch preparation."

***

Ren Bo was driving from the Haidian District back to headquarters when his cell rang. He engaged the hands-free option. It was his contact regarding the Range Rover's license and ownership. The Range Rover was registered to Lucky Star Enterprises.

Arriving at headquarters, he walked to the cubby hole designated as his office. He contacted the head of security at the Hong Kong International Airport and demanded the security tapes for the date and time in question. Then, he called up China Mobile, gave them the coordinates obtained from the military satellite and asked for the phone numbers used at that location and time. He was determined to use all possible tools at his disposal to expand his investigation. The security tapes would make it possible to identify the individuals with facial recognition. The phone numbers would help find the suspects.

Information started rolling in faster than Ren Bo would have thought.

His cell rang, he picked up and said, "Colonel Ren Bo."

"This is Mr. Jinn from Hong Kong International Airport security. I have sent you the videos. Is there anything else that I can do for you?"

"No. This is good. Thank you."

Ren Bo loaded the videos, set them up in the facial recognition program, and waited again.

His computer beeped. He had an email from China Mobile. There was a list of at least four phones active at that precise time.

He decided to go to the cafeteria for a cup of tea. By the time he returned, the results of the facial recognition program would be available.

Forty-Four

Sofia's Odyssey Would be Taking a Huge Risk

WILLIAM WAS TENSE and nervous as the constant vibration and swaying of the icebreaker prevented him from getting the rest he needed. He was listless and irritable. He straightened his crumpled clothes and headed to the cafeteria for a quick breakfast and fresh coffee.

He entered the bridge and smiled at Captain Carter seated in the command chair, who was sipping his morning cup of coffee.

"Sleep well?" asked the captain.

"It was a good snooze," William stretched the truth because he didn't want to sound like an ungrateful guest.

"We've been in radar contact with the Seneca, and she is closing the gap between us."

William responded, "Any success locating Ru's ship?"

"Regretfully, no, even with our combined efforts."

"What a bloody shame."

"Captain Green would like to return to his assigned patrols," said Carter.

"I'd like FBI agent Patrick Reilly to join us as we sail north. Tracy's coordinates are not far from Newfoundland," said William.

"All right, I'll make a request to the *Seneca* to fly him over," said the captain.

William pulled back his left shirt sleeve. The Rolex's hands swept minutes away, reminding him of their squandered timetable.

The captain turned to his first mate, "Mr. Rogers, when agent Reilly arrives, bring him to the bridge."

Captain Carter swiveled around in his chair and pointed toward the radar screen. A man scrutinizing the monitor turned around when the captain cleared his throat.

"Dr. Chatterjee, have you met our guest? This is RCMP Inspector William Fox from Montreal."

William shifted his weight from one foot to the next and turned around to face the gentleman in question. The doctor's skin was bronze, he was of medium height, with cropped hair. Narrow, black-framed glasses sat over a squat nose, and a goatee surrounded a generous mouth.

"Pleased to meet you," said Dr. Chatterjee.

"Likewise."

"I understand my assistance is required in a criminal investigation. Normally, I am in the lab."

William stifled a sneeze as the man's strong cologne drifted toward him. Dr. Chatterjee's excessive grooming suggested the importance he placed on his appearance. The better you look, the further you get. *He'll probably try to impress us with his knowledge,* thought William.

"Doctor, can you update us as to what you've been able to discover on the satellite images?" asked William.

"The RADARSAT-2 images indicate massive ice floe around the southern tip of Newfoundland. Let me explain this phenomenon further. Glaciology is my specialty. Our research suggests climate change is forcing our global temperatures higher. So far, twenty trillion tons of ice have melted worldwide since 1990. The annual melt rate is about fifty-seven percent faster than thirty years ago. For example, a massive ice cap broke away recently from Greenland and is fragmenting, causing shipping concerns."

Carter nodded. "It's true. A couple of weeks ago we rescued a freighter with rudder damage, directly linked to massive ice chunks."

"How dangerous is it for us if *Sofia's Odyssey* heads into the ice floe to elude us?" asked William.

"It's no concern for us. We are quite capable of punching our way through," said the captain. "But *Sofia's Odyssey* would be taking a huge risk."

Everyone on the bridge was still as the helicopter's distinctive sound became apparent. Moments later, the bridge door opened, and Patrick came in with Carl.

"Permission to come aboard."

"Permission granted," replied the burly man. "I'm Captain Carter. You've already met first mate, Carl Rogers." He pointed at the helm. "This is our resident scientist Dr. Chatterjee. And of course, you know William."

"It's a pleasure to meet you all. Captain, thanks for the hospitality. Also, the FBI appreciates your cooperation in this matter," said Patrick.

"I'd like a few minutes to bring Patrick up to speed," said William.

William and Patrick moved toward the back wall of the bridge to speak privately. After a brief discussion, they returned to stand near the instrument panel close to Captain Carter's command chair.

"How long before we arrive at Saint Pierre Island?" asked William.

"With our current speed, we should be there in about seventeen hours. That's assuming headwinds remain stable and the weather cooperates," said Carl.

Carter addressed William and Patrick. "My recommendation is both of you go to the crew lounge and review your plans. There is a good chance we can overtake them."

"Thanks, Captain," said Patrick. "The lounge is a great idea. Don't worry about us; we'll be ready. You just get us there."

Forty-Five

Who Can Eat After This?

THE WEARY EXPLORERS landed at the Sydney airport late afternoon. Everyone was exhausted and hungry from the day's exploration. Tracy unloaded the plastic bins containing the artifacts they had collected and placed them in the trunk of the Mustang, while Kevin and Jeffrey unloaded the radar unit from the helicopter and brought it to the manager's office. Tom secured the aircraft.

It felt good to have had a successful dig that unearthed samples of value and radar images to support their thesis. Tracy's entries in the site journal would be the foundation to initiate a widespread probe during subsequent trips to the secluded location.

Twenty minutes later, Jeffrey steered the rental car safely back to the hotel's car park and slid it in the space beside Kevin's van.

"Kevin, would you mind transferring the artifacts to your van? I think they'll be safer there than in the Mustang," said Jeffrey.

"Sure. No problem."

After a quick bite at a burger joint, the team decided to get some much-needed rest and agreed to meet again in the morning.

Tracy and Jeffrey went through the lobby of the Mira Suites Hotel and took the elevator up to their room while Kevin headed to the parking lot to retrieve his van.

Kevin felt conflicted. He wasn't sure if he was thinking straight or what was motivating him to drive to Membertou Heritage Park, but he needed to speak with the grand chief and the elders at the Indigenous Cultural and Interpretive Center.

The center had closed a short time ago, but he knew that the secretary was probably working late. Noting the lights were still on at the center, he banged on the glass door to gain attention. Eventually, Kayla noticed him, opened the door, and let him in.

"Don't you know how late it is?" said Kayla.

"I'm dropping off a couple of bins." Kevin piled the plastic bins outside the grand chief's office door. "It will be okay, don't worry," he assured her.

Kayla felt this was unusual and called Grand Chief David McDonald. After speaking with him briefly, she said, "Kevin, the grand chief would like to talk with you. He's on line one."

"Kevin, what's going on?" asked the grand chief.

"Remember that dig I was telling you about?

"Yes?"

"We found some Mi'kmaq First Nation artifacts. I recommend a cease-and-desist order before excavation continues."

"I concur. Get this arranged as soon as possible."

A few minutes after 7:00 p.m., Kevin shut the door behind him. He left the cultural center, feeling the artifacts in the bins would be safe for the night. As he was driving home, he wondered how the Jordans would react to the cease-and-desist order.

***

Tracy was up at dawn. The previous day's excitement had not worn off yet and she was busy making notations in the site journal. Jeffrey joined her in her adjoining suite while they waited for room service to bring their breakfast. A heavy knock of impatience on the door roused them.

"I think it's room service. Dad, can you get the door?"

Jeffrey opened it to find a young man dressed in a leather motorcycle jacket holding his helmet.

"Are you Jeffrey Jordan?" he asked.

"Yes, and you are?" replied Jeffrey.

"This is for you." The young man handed Jeffrey an envelope. "You have been served."

Jeffrey grimaced. Served what? he thought. Before he could respond, the fellow had disappeared.

"What just happened, Dad?" asked Tracy.

"We've been served with a cease-and-desist order from the provincial courts."

Jeffrey closed the door, walked back into the room, used his fingernail to tear open the envelope.

"It's from Grand Chief David McDonald. And get this—his legal representative is Kevin Steptoe."

"That little shit head!"

Jeffrey read out loud:

This letter is served due to trespassing and excavating on Indigenous lands. The property in question is the Gabarus Wilderness Area. The region is sacred and has significance to the Mi'kmaq community since ancient peoples have passed away on the land. Also of concern is the looting, theft, and destruction of our cultural heritage for private gain. If you do not cease the activity mentioned above, a lawsuit will be commenced against you. If the activity continues, we will immediately seek a temporary restraining order in the provincial courts against you and any accomplices in this matter. We will also seek monetary compensation. Hopefully, this recourse will not be necessary. We have our own interests to protect and will vigorously do so.

"It goes on and on, and it's signed by Judge Henley of the Nova Scotia provincial courts."

Another quieter knock at the door drew their attention away from the cease-and-desist order.

"That must be room service," said Jeffrey.

"Who can eat after this?" said Tracy. She felt agitated. She rummaged through her purse for her asthma inhaler and took a puff to stabilize her breathing.

"I'm totally perplexed. Kevin had me convinced that we were working together," said Jeffrey as he sipped lukewarm coffee.

"He won't get away with this. If there's anything I can't stand, it's dishonesty."

"Besides, we are clients. This smacks of conflict of interest," added Jeffrey. "Should we call Kevin?"

"No. We should call the police."

Tracy explained to the Cape Breton Regional Police that Kevin Steptoe was part of her team working on a dig at Gabarus Wilderness Area and that they had collected some artifacts, and that Kevin had disappeared with them. The police sergeant knew Kevin and promised to locate him.

Tracy's phone rang. "Hello, this is Tracy Jordan." Her expression darkened. "Yes, well, we didn't expect to report so soon. The funding depends on it. I realize that." Tracy squirmed as her mouth opened in surprise.

"How, how much time will the committee extend to us? Twenty-four hours hardly seems fair. Yes... Yes, we can accommodate the deadline, I think. We have some physical proof there was a settlement. But we really need more time to review the initial materials. Okay. Okay. Let me talk with Professor Jordan and get back to you."

"What on earth is going on?" Jeffrey asked.

"Dad, we've had another major setback; the university has delayed our funding until they have a progress report. We only have twenty-four hours to accommodate them. It's so frustrating."

"We can try and locate Grand Chief David McDonald and get to the bottom of this mess ourselves."

Tracy called the Nova Scotia Heritage and Cultural Society. Jeffrey and Tracy felt it would be better to talk to the person who had issued their permits. She explained that artifacts discovered at the site had gone missing and that the Cape Breton Regional Police were investigating.

***

Kevin arrived at the provincial courthouse precisely at eight. He had cajoled Judge Henley into an early morning meeting to prepare the cease-and-desist order. Kevin purchased an expensive bottle of Bordeaux for Judge Henley's cellar and insisted it was not a bribe. The judge was amused and promised not to hold him in contempt. A win-win situation not discussed within legal or social circles.

Kevin used his office delivery service to serve the cease-and-desist order. Then drove across the city to Membertou Heritage Park to meet with the elders at the cultural center.

He parked his van next to Grand Chief David McDonald's Hyundai Santa Fe.

Kayla opened the front door, and Kevin stepped in briskly. "The grand chief is waiting for you in his office," she said.

Grand Chief McDonald was dressed in a black shirt and his favorite embroidered vest. He believed in bringing the traditional ways to council meetings.

Kevin noticed that some of the objects from the bins were on the grand chief's desk. Placed there meticulously after being carefully examined.

"Good morning, Grand Chief. You have part of the story, but not all of it," said Kevin.

Kevin reached into his pocket, retrieved a small bluish fragment, and placed it carefully on the writing desk. The grand chief held the fragile piece gently between his forefinger and thumb, rotating it to take in all its surfaces.

"Is this what I think it is?" asked Grand Chief McDonald.

"What do you think it is?"

"It's a porcelain shard of Asian manufacture. It looks rather ancient. There is a Chinese character on the bottom."

"I haven't had time to get it deciphered. But it certainly says enough."

"Yes, indeed, it does."

"So, what should we do?" asked Kevin.

"You found this at Gabarus Wilderness Area?"

"Yes. I should have handed it over to the Jordans. But I didn't because I realized how significant this piece of porcelain is. And how it could impact our history."

"It's probable our ancestors had encounters with Vikings. However, it is unrealistic to believe that early Asians intersected with our culture. Especially in the early development of language, literature, and medicine. And it's not going to sit well with our community," said Grand Chief McDonald.

"I agree. So, we must get ahead of this before it becomes public knowledge."

"This is why you brought the artifacts here?"

"Yes, it is. I don't think this is going to stop them. But it should slow the Jordans down enough to discuss the situation with the elders and provide a solution to accommodate everyone."

"When will council members arrive?" asked Grand Chief McDonald.

"The meeting should begin at 10:30 this morning. Not everyone can attend because of the short notice, but we will have a quorum for a legitimate proceeding."

***

It was late spring, and a balmy breeze warmed the air. Tracy was dressed in a peach blouse, beige jacket, a blue scarf, and denim skirt. Her features were framed with aviator glasses and loop earrings. It was the first time she wore earrings since the damaged earlobe had healed.

Jeffrey and Tracy left in the Mustang and headed to Membertou Heritage Park. They had prepared questions for the grand chief and council concerning the cease-and-desist order, in particular the disappearance of artifacts and the questionable behavior of their legal counsel.

When the Jordans arrived at Membertou Heritage Park at 1:00 p.m., they were surprised to see a gathering of members of the Mi'kmaq community and police in the parking lot outside the center. A barricade of park benches and picnic tables surrounded the front doors. A dozen First Nations members were standing behind it with kerchiefs covering their faces. Some even had hockey sticks and baseball bats borrowed from the sports center. Grand Chief David McDonald insisted that firearms be locked up and that this would be a peaceful demonstration. For now, emotions and tempers were in check, but the situation could deteriorate rapidly and become violent.

At least two Cape Breton Regional Police cars and an RCMP cruiser were strategically angled in front of the cultural center. Six officers were back of the vehicles and focused on the group, hoping to avert a disaster. Miraculously, the local media had not yet arrived.

After parking the Mustang, Tracy and Jeffrey asked for Sergeant Rideout, the officer who had taken their initial theft report.

"Good afternoon. My name is Tracy Jordan, and this is my father, Jeffrey. We want to thank you for responding so quickly."

"I take it he's inside the cultural center," said Jeffrey.

"Yes, he's inside. We can't go in without causing a disturbance," replied Sergeant Rideout.

"If you let us make our way in, I'm reasonably sure Kevin and Grand Chief David McDonald will speak with us. Perhaps we can negotiate a solution before it gets out of hand out here," said Tracy.

"Okay, Tracy. I'll ask my men to stand back. But make it quick. This situation could unravel and become very serious," said Sergeant Rideout.

Tracy pulled out her cellphone and called Kevin Steptoe.

"My father and I are here to see if we can come to some sort of resolution. Please let us come in," said Tracy.

Approximately two minutes later, the front door opened, and Kevin was standing there, waving them into the center. Jeffrey and Tracy scrambled over the picnic tables past the armed police. Kevin directed them into a meeting room where six elders were seated comfortably. They were ready for meaningful dialogue.

"Let me introduce you to the members of our council. This is Grand Chief David McDonald. At the end of the table, Dr. William Underwood, and beside him, Olivia Francis. Next to him René Doucette, then Eva Prosper, across is Amelia Meuse, and Jacob Basque," said Kevin.

"We are pleased to meet you all," said Tracy.

Jeffrey nodded in their direction. "We are genuinely sorry for any misunderstanding."

"Please have a seat so we can start the proceedings," said the grand chief.

Tracy and Jeffrey sat down opposite the elders.

What's Kevin's end game? Tracy wondered.

Kevin stood up to address the group. "First, I would like to explain that the elders are here because of their knowledge of traditional First Nations ways. They wish only to guide us in respect to the natural world around us. Essentially to connect, events, customs, and safeguard the history and ceremonies of our peoples to steer us to a better place."

"Before we begin, how can you represent both the Mi'kmaq peoples and us? It certainly must be a conflict of interest," said Tracy.

"I was anticipating that. Here is a letter stating that I no longer represent you. You can file a complaint with the Nova Scotia Barrister Society if you like. But please, let's conduct our meeting today. Then you can decide what's in everybody's best interest."

"This case raises a lot of legal, environmental, and historical issues," said Eva Prosper. The elderly stateswoman had been a member of council for years and took the minutes.

"For the record, my name is Kevin Steptoe, and as the legal representative for the Mi'kmaq First Nations, I would like to begin my statement. First Nations must be involved in any development or encroachment affecting them."

Tracy stood up, brushed down her skirt, looked around the table, and spoke.

"On behalf of Stanford University, we obtained all provincial permits from the Nova Scotia Heritage and Culture Society, and we did consult with a First Nations lawyer—you, Mr. Steptoe—for guidance."

"May I point out. Canada's constitution and recent court rulings have affirmed that treaty rights override any provincial permit process by which those permits were issued and are a breach of the Crown's obligations," said Kevin.

Grand Chief David McDonald stood up, took the floor, and said, "The permit from the Nova Scotia Heritage and Culture Society, and the consent from our community are significantly different. That process worked in the past, but it no longer works and should be based on a more empathetic approach to treaty rights and First Nations considerations."

"We don't want people just moving in without proper notice. Furthermore, non-First Nations people should not rewrite history regarding contact with the Chinese. These are not colonial times," said René Doucette in a frosty tone.

"In any project affecting the Mi'kmaq First Nations, you absolutely need to have the local communities as partners. There will be no project without the buy-in from the community," said Dr. Underwood.

"It's important to develop a personal relationship with the chief, the band members, and all the community members," said Olivia Francis reinforcing the doctor's statement.

Eva Prosper looked up from her notes, occasionally taking in the tension building in the room.

Tracy did not bother standing. Her body language got everyone's attention around the table. "All my research plus the journals have led me to the location in the Gabarus Wilderness Area. There is no turning back from the reality of what we have found on this site. The First Nations may have encountered the Chinese and their culture could have been influenced. There is no proof for or against, only that there was contact for some time," explained Tracy.

"Well, that brings up that piece of Chinese porcelain I found at the site and its ramifications to our ancestral history," said Kevin.

Tracy's eyes widened in surprise.

Kevin retrieved the artifact from his pocket and passed it amongst the elders. Each examined the shard and passed it to the next person until it reached Tracy.

She rotated it completely, taking in all surfaces and fracture marks, and examined the bottom. The cobalt blue floral pattern was recognizable.

"This is a Chinese character from the Ming dynasty. The characters are called hanzi and are logograms developed for writing Chinese languages. Similar but not exact duplications of Mi'kmaq ideograms," said Tracy.

"There may be some similarity. But enough to create a culture clash? After all, we are a proud people who would find it difficult to acknowledge even more interference beyond the 17th century Jesuits who had influenced our hieroglyphic language," expounded Amelia Meuse, an elder with a fiery temperament.

Jeffrey realized that all the women elders had made compelling arguments. He tapped Tracy's shin under the table and slipped a note stating the observation. Tracy, coolheaded, never missed a beat in her presentation. She smiled at everyone around the table as she discussed her knowledge of the language issue and focused on the women.

Tracy hoped her mediation skills would convince the elders to agree with their proposal. Taking the cue from her father, Tracy looked at the women one by one. She had to convince them excavation of the archeological site would be a good thing for the community. The funds from the university were also in jeopardy. Now she needed to bring it together... today of all days.

"After examining the facts, including the fragment of Ming dynasty porcelain, we should agree that there was some Asian influence at this site," said Tracy. "My findings indicate there is a sizable treasure. My proposal is to permit us to continue with this important find. It will enrich Canadian history and, in particular, raise funds for the Mi'kmaq First Nation, improving quality of life for your community. One of the suggestions is to involve Sotheby's. Their experts would evaluate any Ming dynasty porcelain and other treasures found. The invested money could provide pensions or grants for your community."

Grand Chief McDonald stood up and said, "Thank you, Tracy. We will take your request under advisement. I must admit that your impassioned speech has moved me. And I know I speak for all of us. Please wait in the lobby while we make our deliberations. Kayla will escort you out."

Forty-Six

Like He Was in High School

WILLIAM WAS DISAPPOINTED that the *Leonard Cowley* could not be diverted to assist them, and that their armed boarding team would not be available. William and Patrick needed to devise a new plan to apprehend Ru and his vessel. They would approach Captain Carter for volunteers since it was within the captain's purview to assist a government operation.

In the day room of the *Louis St. Laurent*, William and Patrick refined their tactical plan, called their superiors, and mingled with some of the crew. Most crew members were in their cabins, spending time on personal computers, leaving the day room mostly unoccupied. William and Patrick were surprised at the sound of an acoustic guitar. It had the earmarks of the camaraderie of the old days. The walls were adorned with hockey jerseys from the NHL and taped-up hockey sticks were in the corner. They both sat down with sodas, enjoying the Spanish riffs from the vintage Gibson.

Amenities onboard the *Louis St. Laurent* were contemporary, comfortable, and relaxing. The ship's complement included a library with films and books, a workout gym, and a day room accessible to everyone. Crew cabins were well-appointed, including televisions and wall phones. The ship provided Wi-Fi signal via the egg-shaped dome perched on the foremast. This made family members and friends easily accessible every day.

During shift rotations, the able crew performed heavy duties in compromising conditions. Often, they'd have to clean snow off the decks at sub-zero temperatures, usual conditions when the ship toured in the extreme regions of the north.

After a demanding day, crewmembers looked forward to mealtime as the benefits of a good meal could lift the spirits. Sometimes the chef would spoil someone with a birthday cake or a gourmet pizza. The team's overall cohesion was due to Captain Carter's training and leadership. He encouraged self-reliance in each team member, and believed it was a testament to the crew when they performed their duties well.

***

It was 1:00 a.m. when the ship arrived at the expansive ice floe Dr. Chatterjee had mentioned. The ship beat expectations arriving in the vicinity in record time.

The night helmsman reduced power to the diesel engines, gaining more control over the approach through the ice floe. The large vessel pushed the glacier mass aside like the brute strength of a bull elephant crashing through the jungle.

Radar signals were rebounding from an anomaly fifty nautical miles away. The satellite imagery from the passing RADARSAT-2 would be arriving early morning and would confirm if it was *Sofia's Odyssey*. In anticipation of the operation, the captain ordered the night helmsman to prepare the ship for the offensive maneuver. The pre-dawn assault on the research ship would begin when the helicopter landed them on the vessel. The responsibility of seizing Ru and *Sofia's Odyssey* would fall to William, Patrick, Carl, and Jimmy.

***

Very early the next morning, the engine turned over on the helicopter. Victor Stupendski prepared for takeoff. Everyone was belted in and hooked up to the communications array.

"We are sure it's *Sofia's Odyssey?*" said Patrick.

"The satellite images confirmed it's the ship," said William.

"Then let's get these bastards!"

"Paul, Jimmy, you good to go?" asked William.

They were sitting butted together and regarded each other apprehensively. Both looked at William and nodded affirmatively.

"It's okay to be nervous. I know you haven't done this sort of thing before. Patrick and I will keep an eye on you," William reassured them.

"Just follow the plan, and we should all come out all right," said Patrick.

"Copy that," said Carl.

"You both had some practice with the handguns. Protect yourselves, when necessary," said William.

"It was great the armory was stocked with sidearms in case of an emergency," said Carl.

"I'm concerned about sliding down a rope," said Jimmy.

"Just like being at high school. Remember when you had to shinny up to the ceiling in the gym class," said William.

"Only this time you slide down dodging some pot-shots," said Patrick.

"That's not quite the same! Is it?" retorted Jimmy.

"Patrick and I will be down first and cover you," said William.

William turned around from his position in the co-pilot's seat and scrutinized both volunteers. He nodded at Jimmy. "When you hit the deck, run to the bulkhead, and cover fire for Carl. He will be last."

"Yeah, cool," said Jimmy.

"You will be with me," said Patrick. "Carl will follow William to the bridge," said Patrick.

"Good. I'll be right on his ass," said Carl.

Flying through the early morning, their eyes could barely distinguish between the sky and the sea. It was if they were sitting in a vacuum. It was a strange perception as the craft skimmed across the black surface. A flickering gray cap occasionally violated the monochromatic seascape while the crew sat in ghostly stillness.

"Victor, are we making good time? I want to make sure that we can surprise them," said William, breaking the solemn mood.

"We should arrive in five minutes," said Victor.

Moments later, there was relief in the cockpit as a thin bright line of reddish-yellow split the two realms.

"We are on the mark. There's the silhouette of the ship."

"Okay, guys, you know what to do. Victor, get us over the top of the ship. Patrick and Carl drop the lines on either side of the doors and get ready to rappel," said William.

"We're in position," said Victor.

"You see any activity yet?" asked Patrick.

"Nothing. Drop the lines. Good luck, guys," shouted William.

Then he dropped off the side and disappeared into the darkness. The thump of his boots hitting the bulkhead was drowned out by the sound of the helicopter.

"Meet you down there, guys," barked Patrick.

He disappeared into the darkness. Jimmy gave a final nod to Carl. He checked his leather gloves and slipped his legs around the rope. Grabbing the halyard, he descended like he was in high school, traveling the first twenty feet in seconds.

Whirrrrrr. Crack. Whirrrrrrr. Crack. Jimmy immediately stopped. His body cowered at the sound of slugs ripping by. "Crap, crap, crap," he muttered under his breath. Startled, he released his grip and fell the last segment. His left ankle took the brunt of the impact.

"I hit one!" someone from the triad gang shouted. Now, several of the triad enforcers were awake and fighting back.

"Stay down," William shouted. He stepped out and fired rounds at the gangster, barely visible in the breaking light.

"Carl, get moving," urged Stupendski.

Carl cascaded one hand around the rope and a Smith & Wesson 9mm, barking rounds in the other.

William had already reached Jimmy, who threw an arm around his shoulder, and they blasted their way to the stairway leading to the bridge.

As Carl landed, he realized the plan's dynamics were altered and joined Patrick.

"Follow me," commanded Patrick. They entered the bulkhead door under the gantry crane at the stern and scampered down into the heart of the ship.

"Let's secure the science team first," said Patrick.

Carl and Patrick cleared the rooms in the hallway. They returned fire at the only gangster left to guard the scientists. He surrendered after suffering a gunshot wound to the leg.

"Room is secured," said Carl.

The scientists were all huddled in the meeting room. When the shooting started, it seemed the safest place. Carl pushed the injured thug onto a chair and secured him.

"Hold them here. I'm headed to the bridge to back up William," said Patrick.

The excited scientists asked a barrage of questions Carl could not answer.

"Hold on. One at a time! Please! Just stay calm. Okay?" Carl holstered the sidearm, raising his hands and lowering them like a kindergarten teacher calming children.

Forty-Seven

Victor... Rest Now

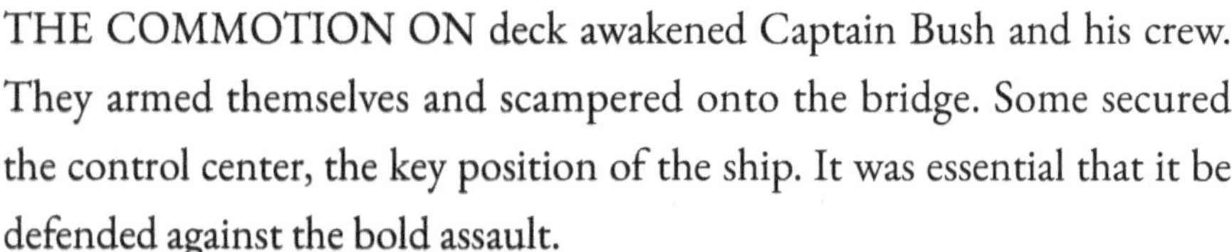

THE COMMOTION ON deck awakened Captain Bush and his crew. They armed themselves and scampered onto the bridge. Some secured the control center, the key position of the ship. It was essential that it be defended against the bold assault.

"How did they find us? You turned off the GPS and the automatic identification system?" said Ru.

"I did. The Coast Guard must have used satellites," answered the captain.

"Too late to worry about that now. We have to get off this ship."

"Full ahead," commanded Bush. He swung the helm's wheel toward the coast of Newfoundland and into the ice floe.

"They must have a ship in the vicinity. That chopper has to have a base," said Ru.

***

Victor pulled the chopper away, avoiding the bullets being fired. The brilliant jewel of daybreak gave a clear view as the sunrise broke the horizon.

William and Jimmy descended the staircase and arrived in the galley way leading to the bridge.

"Stay here and keep them pinned down. I'm heading to the bridge," said William.

"My ankle's killing me. Make it quick," said Jimmy, his face tortured in agony.

William advanced on top of the ship's superstructure, avoiding gunshots and a deck littered with equipment. Seizing the safety rail above the bridge, he leaned forward and fired two rounds into a window. William heaved himself through the window, shattering it on contact. He rolled over the floor and sprung up with gun in hand, facing Captain Bush and Ru, who held a gun to Jimmy's head.

"Drop the firearm if you want to keep him alive," said Ru.

"Don't do it, man," said Jimmy, looking pale. In an untenable position, William clicked the safety and dropped the gun. Its clatter broke the tension in the room. Captain Bush now had his weapon pointed unwaveringly at William.

"Good move," said Ru. He wiggled on brass knuckles and threw two successive punches to William's rib cage.

"Argh," bellowed William, grabbing his abdomen as he doubled over. He sucked in air and tried to stand up. Ru executed a downward hammer blow, and William collapsed.

Ru adjusted the brass knuckles to deliver the killing blow to William's temple, when Bush shouted, "There's no time for that! Let's get out of here!"

Bush smacked Jimmy at the back of his head with his pistol, and he crumpled to the floor, then pushed the Chadburn to full throttle and steered the ship into the ice floe. "That should keep them busy when they come to."

Bush and Ru bounded to the stern. They grabbed the two grenade launchers and Kalashnikovs from the Range Rover and transferred the munitions into the rigid-hull inflatable boat.

"Over the side, quickly!" shouted Ru.

***

Victor watched their escape and called Captain Carter for instructions.

"We will try to intercept," said Carter. The boat with Ru and Bush was plowing toward the horizon and the Newfoundland shoreline. Patrick reached the bridge too late to apprehend the escaping criminals. He tried to rouse William first.

"Are you all right?" he asked.

Unsteady, William responded, "Help Jimmy; he's hurt."

Patrick tended Jimmy and got him upright. William hung onto the captain's chair as he raised himself.

Jimmy was rubbing the lump on his head. "This is so uncool. Screwed up ankle and a concussion too. What a fuck up," he complained.

William realized Ru had escaped. He picked up the binoculars, headed to the open window, and peered at the wake left behind by the rubber boat. He was joined by Patrick and Jimmy. Victor lowered the helicopter to a level just above the ocean and was in pursuit.

William dropped the oculars and cursed, "Those bastards just launched an RPG at our helicopter!"

Jimmy, Patrick, and William watched the rocket-propelled grenade as it zoomed toward its target. Their eyes followed, knowing nothing could be done. The projectile blew the chopper into pieces, an intense burst of explosives ending Victor Stupendski's life. The surprise offensive on *Sofia's Odyssey* was only a partial success.

A sudden dread overcame William, then coldness and anger. He was resolved Ru would pay, one way or another. He whispered, "Victor... rest now."

Forty-Eight

What is it About Her Last Name That Disturbs Me?

REN BO'S EXCURSION to the cafeteria was noneventful as he preferred to keep conversations with his contemporaries as brief as possible. His green tea was too hot to drink, so he placed it on his desk, sat down, and manipulated the cursor on his computer screen. The facial recognition program had completed its search and identified a triad gang leader named Tang Dao and two other gang members. Their criminal records were significant but did not rival that of Tang Dao's, whose rap sheet was extensive. Ren Bo printed the photos. Transfixed by the screen's contents, he took his first sip of green tea and scalded his tongue.

The security pictures rendered from the Hong Kong International Airport video had provided a significant clue. General Po had been approached by the triad leadership and blackmailed into finding the young woman in the surveillance tape.

Ren Bo was contemplating his next step when he received an email from his investigative team. The message said that Lucky Star Enterprises was owned by Ru Fa Zhong, leader of the Foo Dog Triad. His company owned restaurants, nightclubs, kwoons, and a gambling ship called the Lucky Star.

He took another sip of tea, but it was tasteless after having burned his tongue earlier. His back ached, and his eyes burned. Sitting and staring for hours at a computer screen brought him results, but it was exhausting.

Then another email arrived in Ren Bo's account. This one was from China Mobile, identifying the owners of the four cell numbers triangulated at the airport. Three belonged to triad members, but the fourth one belonged to Tracy Jordan. *What is it about her last name that disturbs me?*

Ren Bo pushed away from his desk and rubbed his temples as he thought about the information he had obtained so far. His next step was to access Tracy Jordan's Facebook profile for leads.

Within minutes of browsing Facebook, Ren Bo had downloaded Tracy Jordan's profile. In her social media, he discovered her father was Jeffrey Jordan, the man he was tasked to find for President Wei Lei. He noted that she had made numerous trips within China. After reading her published papers on Admiral Zheng He, his interest was piqued. Following her kidnapping at the airport, he surmised, she had been flown by helicopter to the Lucky Star casino ship.

Ren Bo decided his next step was to go to Hong Kong to interview additional suspects. His key witness was the gambling ship's captain.

***

Ren Bo's Air China flight took three and a half hours, allowing him to arrive in time to board the ship. The day-long battle against his exhaustion was dissipated by meditating on board his flight. His meditative state allowed him to establish a powerful *qi,* which gave him renewed energy. A necessity in the event Captain Li was protected by triad members making access to him difficult.

Dressed in his two-tone baseball jacket and his upscale black sneakers, Ren Bo puffed on a cigarette like a nervous player, even though he disliked the taste and pretense.

He boarded the ship, immersed in a crowd of carnal seekers and excited gamblers. Ren Bo slipped away from the group and proceeded to the bridge. He planned to reach Captain Li before the Lucky Star slipped away into the night. It was a get in and get out with the information before the ship's departure. He had no intention of being trapped on board for hours without an exit strategy. The possibility of being captured and interrogated was more likely the longer he remained on board. He was sure the triad gang members would enjoy taking him apart and disposing of him over the side. His body would never be found, and the mysterious circumstances leading to General Po's suicide would never be discovered. That scenario was sufficient motivation to make sure he followed the details of his scheme meticulously.

Ren Bo burst into the bridge and aimed his Norinco pistol at the man sitting in the commander's chair. "Nobody moves," he said.

Two sailors standing in front of the control panel turned around at the sound of the man's deep voice. "Don't move a muscle. Place your hands on the panel," Ren Bo said.

They stood frozen, aware the pistol with the suppressor was aimed at them. Ren Bo looked over at the man settled comfortably in the captain's chair.

"Captain Li, your photo doesn't do you justice," he said.

"Compliments, really; with a gun to my face? Just who the hell are you?" asked Captain Li.

"I deal in justice, and this is my gavel," said Ren Bo, gesturing with his pistol.

"A mystery avenger. How appropriate for a dead man. I have twenty men on board who will kill you slowly... painfully until you scream for the end," said Captain Li.

Ren Bo sneered at the detailed threat. *Is this where an attempt would be made to change the dynamics of the standoff?*

The small gesture from Captain Li toward his men was not lost on Ren Bo. He raised the Norinco, and two double taps splattered the control panel with blood and human fragments. The two men fell heavily to the linoleum floor. Captain Li leaped from the armchair and was stopped abruptly by Ren Bo's front kick, which snapped off like a cannonball, catching him in the abdomen. The middle-aged man doubled over and fell to his knees, starving for air.

"Now that I have your absolute attention. You will answer my questions. As you see, I have no time for frivolous formality," said Ren Bo.

Captain Li hacked and settled back into the armchair. Ren Bo zip-tied the captain's arms and ankles to the chair. Li was quite spry; being on the other side of fifty didn't necessarily equate to a man whose vitality was diminished by time.

"So, Captain Li, let's begin with why Ru Fa Zhong kidnapped Tracy Jordan."

Fifteen minutes later, Ren Bo had the complete story about Ru Fa Zhong's involvement in the kidnapping of Tracy Jordan and the search for Admiral Zheng He's supposed treasure in Eastern Canada.

He had it all. Finding Tracy Jordan would lead him to her father Jeffrey Jordan—the man he wanted.

Banging on the bridge door brought Ren Bo's focus back to his assignment. He bashed the pistol grip against Captains Li's temple. He dashed out the portside door and sprinted off the vessel and ran across the wharf to the car rental. The yelling faded away.

Forty-Nine

One Hell of an Iceberg

THE RESEARCH VESSEL slammed into the iceberg like a freight train hitting an embankment. The collision reverberated along the axis of the ship. It had not been designed to handle this kind of impact. The metal buckled and screeched as the hull careened across the floe, throwing William and the boarding party to the bridge floor.

A large piece of ice was dislodged and fell alongside the ship, plunging into the ocean like an erupting geothermic geyser. The resulting crash wobbled Sofia's Odyssey. The vessel found itself wedged on an iceberg of considerable size and depth. Ocean water sprayed and pieces of ice and snow fell on the foredeck of the ship.

Momentarily stunned, all three men found their bearings and got to their feet.

"What the hell was that?" asked Patrick.

"One hell of an iceberg," said Jimmy pulling the engine order telegraph to full astern. "They changed course while we were unconscious."

"Patrick, go below and see if we are taking on water," said William.

"I'll go and check on Carl and the scientists on the way. I'll be back with a report shortly," replied Patrick.

"Where is the *Louis St. Laurent?*" asked William.

"I'm checking her last radar position," said Jimmy.

"Open up a channel."

"Got her. VHF Channel 16."

Jimmy winced as he shuffled on his ankle and added "But we are not moving astern, eh. We're stuck."

"Shut the engine down until we can figure this out," said William.

"Aye." Jimmy pulled the Chadburn into the neutral position, stopping the propellors. "Captain Carter just responded. They are at full steam, heading here."

Carl threw open the bridge door. "Where is the flare gun? We should send a distress flare off." He was focused on saving the stranded ship. Carl aimed the flare gun at ninety degrees and fired two rounds skyward. "We should check the bilge water levels. I don't hear an alarm, so we are probably okay," he added.

"Patrick is already on it," said William.

Patrick arrived back at the bridge. He bent over, placed his hands on his knees, and took in two breaths. Huffing, he regained his composure.

"We don't seem to be taking on water, but it looks like some of the hull is bent. The engineer and the rest of the crew are okay. The science team members were shaken up, but they're all right, too," said Patrick.

"Someone should check the storage room and see if there are cold-water immersion suits," said Jimmy. "I'd do it, but..." he gestured toward his swollen ankle.

"We won't need the suits if we get evacuated," said Carl. "Captain Carter and the crew will pull us off. We should consider towing the ship into St. John's," he added.

"I'll leave that to you and Captain Carter. We need a patrol boat as soon as the ship arrives. Patrick and I are going after them," said William.

"It's unfortunate we can't help with the evac. William and I will catch these bastards," added Patrick.

As they waited for their patrol boat, William contacted the RCMP office in Newfoundland to coordinate a land operation with them.

William and Patrick packed their knapsacks with power bars, water bottles, ammunition, and a satellite phone.

The ice king, *Louis St. Laurent,* arrived and held steady as its vigilant crew swung into action. Captain Carter directed his team in the rescue efforts. Their efforts bore fruit as ropes thrown aft of the ice breaker were secured. Two patrol boats arrived alongside the stranded vessel, one for the evacuees and the other for William and Patrick. Carl and Jimmy, despite his injuries, remained on board to man the ship once it would be pulled free by the icebreaker.

While the rescue efforts by the crew of the Louis St. Laurent continued, Patrick and William embarked on the patrol boat. William guided the boat northwest toward the outline of the coast, to Ru's last know position. There was a small window of precious time to find their adversaries' trail before they disappeared on "The Rock," as the locals called it.

William was comfortable on the water. Patrick, not so much. The rocking of the patrol boat increased his fear again. The anxiety was nothing to be ashamed about as thalassophobia was common and treatable. William could see Patrick's expression change from self-confidence to trepidation. He was trembling and sweating, obvious signs of a panic attack.

"Whatever is plaguing you, get over it." William was determined to refocus his friend. Tough love of sorts; he expected Patrick to concentrate on the mission.

"Thanks," Patrick replied.

He knew William was right, so he focused on cognitive behavior as his go-to remedy. It worked before and should be enough to pull him out of it.

"What are we waiting for?" shouted Patrick.

The patrol boat lurched forward as William steered along the shore. Patrick felt better. William smiled. Whatever was on Patrick's mind had disappeared; he was back.

William used dead reckoning to follow Ru to a likely landing point. It was a long shot. He knew Ru's escape was spontaneous. Finding the rubber boat onshore would point William and Patrick in the right direction. Once on land, William would send Captain Carter the coordinates to retrieve the patrol boat.

***

Canadian Coast Guard seamen are adept and experienced at ice navigation and coordinating ship rescue. Removing *Sofia's Odyssey* from the iceberg was routine for the crew of the *Louis St. Laurent*. First, they attached tow lines to her stern and then backed her off with a close-coupled tow. The Louis St. Laurent engaged full reverse, enabling the disabled ship to break free from the icy hold. Everyone on both vessels breathed a sigh of relief.

Once the vessel was detached, Captain Carter's crew attached tow lines to its bow. Then, the rescue ship hauled *Sofia's Odyssey* from the icefield and tugged her toward St. John's, Newfoundland.

Captain Carter's efforts to move the ship through the rugged stretch of ice floe would be a painful and dangerous process. He counted on his team's many years of experience to complete the task professionally. Jimmy and Carl operated the bridge on the damaged ship applying minimal power to assist towage. The weather forecast was optimistic and predicted good conditions.

***

After the recent altercations with Ru, William began to understand how Ru's reasoning worked. Under pressure, Ru was prone to being impulsive and irrational. All it required was a mistake on Ru's part for William to seize the advantage. This insight was immeasurable in outfoxing his adversary. William always enjoyed that phrase: *To outfox is to be cunning!*

William slowed to a low cruise and skirted the rocks while Patrick scanned the shore with field glasses.

"What are these two goons planning to do here?" asked Patrick.

"Right now, they're running for their lives. My guess is they're going to make us chase them all over the island."

"I don't get it. Is there a part of the puzzle that we're missing here?"

"Tracy gave Ru the wrong directions. That's why we're here. If they elude us on Newfoundland, we can catch up to them in Saint-Pierre."

"You should put on some of that French Canadian charm and fix things with Tracy."

William patted Patrick on his back. "Thanks for the brotherly advice." William was unwilling to talk about how Tracy had rebuffed him.

Even though the future looked a little sketchy, both men were bound by a code of honor to finish their assignment. Neither one was willing to quit. Ru and Bush would continue to inflict death and destruction in their path if they were not apprehended.

Fifty

Could You Drop the Theft Charges?

EXCITED VOICES were emanating from the participants in the conference room. A weighty discussion was underway, the fate of the excavation was hanging in the balance while Tracy and Jeffrey waited for the elders' decision. It appeared to be taking hours for a resolution to be made. Jeffrey paced the corridor relentlessly. Tracy's resolve was waning as she bounced her right knee, puffer in her hand, just in case.

The conference room door opened. Tracy stopped bouncing. Jeffrey stopped pacing.

"Would you join us, please?" asked the grand chief. They followed him in and found empty chairs and sat down.

The grand chief stood up and took the floor. "First, we are going to accept your proposal, however, we need to clear the air first."

"As do we," said Tracy. She tried hard not to hide her disappointment in Kevin's behavior. She set her muscular shoulders back in a confident manner, her eyes telegraphing her vexation and annoyance with the legal hellion. "Wouldn't it be good form for Kevin to apologize for taking the artifacts? Besides, the police are outside and ready to arrest him," said Tracy, glaring at Kevin.

Kevin blushed. "For the sake of all of us involved. Could you drop the theft charges, please? I am deeply sorry about what I did. My primary intention was to help my community get a fair shake."

"Let's give Kevin some slack. He knows he stepped way out of line on our behalf," said Grand Chief McDonald.

"Okay," Jeffrey replied, calmly. I agree it's been a bit prickly. Let's start with a fresh perspective and consider this a learning experience."

The mood changed from adversarial to conciliatory as murmurs swept through the council room.

"Where would you like to start?" asked Grand Chief McDonald.

"Let's inform the police that Professor Jordan and I will drop the theft charges. That should deescalate the standoff outside," said Tracy.

The grand chief and Jeffrey went outside to explain the situation to the authorities. Sergeant Rideout called off the defensive measures, as the Cape Breton Regional Police had other duties. The standoff ended peacefully as the police and the RCMP left.

First Nations members put the picnic tables and the park benches back in place. The makeshift weapons were returned to the sports locker, and the group broke up. Grand Chief McDonald thanked them for their commitment as many of them could have been hurt or worse.

The First Nations community and the authorities were grateful to dodge a potential conflict, and the Jordans had saved Stanford University from embarrassment since the educational institute was a well-known supporter of Indigenous peoples.

The media was arriving in a convoy of camera trucks. They had just missed the story of the week. "Hockey Sticks and Baseball Bats Against Bullets," a David and Goliath cliché, could have been the headline of the day if the situation had not been diffused.

The first journalist from CBC arrived with a cameraman and a microphone. The grand chief turned and walked away, closed the community center door, and locked it, leaving the reporter standing outside, bewildered.

"Doesn't look like we're going to get an interview," said the journalist.

"We just got ghosted," said the cameraman.

***

Grand Chief McDonald and Jeffrey rejoined the group, each satisfied privacy was restored.

"Let's get started before the media speculates what this meeting is about," said Jeffrey.

The grand chief nodded and said, "Eva, would you please distribute the list to everyone at the table?"

"These are the items we wanted covered," said the grand chief. "Of course, Kevin and Tracy are to work out the finer details."

Tracy and Jeffrey reviewed the list. Tracy spoke first. "This looks very reasonable. We are comfortable with Kevin handling the trust fund and drafting up our partnership agreement."

"Kevin will have the documents ready within the next few days," said the grand chief.

There was a rustle of fabric as people nodded in a show of mutual agreement.

"This is a milestone for our community," said Kevin.

Tracy, Jeffrey, and the council members smiled at each other. Admiral Zheng He's treasure would bring prosperity again, centuries after the last blue porcelain piece had been fired.

Fifty-One

These Pricks are Bloody Dangerous

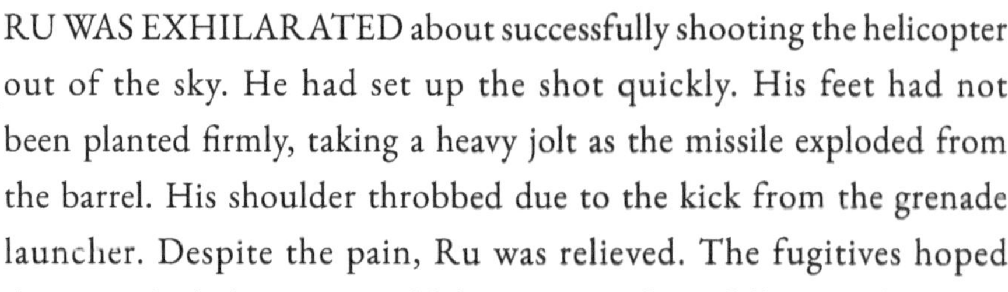

RU WAS EXHILARATED about successfully shooting the helicopter out of the sky. He had set up the shot quickly. His feet had not been planted firmly, taking a heavy jolt as the missile exploded from the barrel. His shoulder throbbed due to the kick from the grenade launcher. Despite the pain, Ru was relieved. The fugitives hoped downing the helicopter would deter anyone from following them.

While Bush piloted the boat, Ru used the compass and map to plan an escape route across Newfoundland. Bush and Ru had not been appropriately dressed for the elements. Wet suits should have been worn to protect themselves. The boat's high speeds intensified the effects of sea spray and the cool air as they traveled past Point Lance and across Placentia Bay. Ru and Bush landed on an inlet in Burin Peninsula near Rock Harbour, a hamlet with houses, barns, and outbuildings.

Ditching the boat on the rocky shoreline, they scrambled to the roadway. After a few hours riding the rough waves, both men were relieved to be on land. Wet clothes chafed as they walked through the quiet village. Transportation and dry clothing were on the top of their list.

While scouting the hamlet, they discovered a Bronze Ford F-150 in a driveway and clothing flapping on a clothesline. They startled a retired couple and hit the old man when he refused to give them the keys to his truck. The clothing fit Bush, but Ru was swimming in his. He rolled up the shirt sleeves and pants legs. He felt comfortable, apart from looking absurd.

Ru stopped the F-150 on the side of the road and switched the flashers on. He looked over at Bush and asked him to hand him his phone.

"It's time to call Dao in the submarine," said Ru.

"They should be between the Azores and Saint Pierre," replied Bush.

"I can't get through. The submarine must be submerged."

"Let's get going. We'll try later."

"I'm sending him a text. He'll get it the moment he surfaces." Ru started the F-150 and drove to Highway 210 for Marystown.

"I am hungry. Let's grab something to eat," said Bush. The truck's navigation system displayed a nearby Mary Brown's Chicken location.

"Okay, but no lingering in case the truck has been reported stolen."

Ru drove carefully, not exceeding the limit. They arrived at the restaurant, ordered fried chicken, and left. Munching, in the vehicle, they observed the townspeople and looked for suspicious activity. Sensing, they had overstayed, they finished up their meal and pulled into traffic. Ru searched the vehicle's navigation for a route to the ferry which was located in the town of Fortune. From there they could take the ferry to Saint-Pierre Island. According to Tracy's coordinates, the French protectorate located off the coast of Newfoundland was their destination.

***

William's cellphone vibrated. He slowed the patrol boat and answered it. The RCMP officers relayed the grim details. Two seniors had been pistol-whipped and their Ford F-150 stolen. They requested William and Patrick land at Rock Harbour to rendezvous with the RCMP, where a cruiser would be waiting for them. Through choppy gray seawater, they headed for their destination, northwest of their current position. William called Captain Carter on the *Louis St. Laurent* and sent them the coordinates for his crew to retrieve the patrol boat in Rocky Harbour.

After docking the boat, William and Patrick trudged to the RCMP cruiser and were greeted cordially. The two cops stood by, waiting for their arrival. Both wore tan shirts, yellow stripe black pants, and utility belts. No hats. Their protective vests had name tags. They were officers Garber and Fellows. Garber palmed his hip holster like a veteran. Fellows was younger, probably a newbie. Nosy neighbors mingled beyond the yellow tape. One of them had called the assault in.

Based on the older couple's description, William realized Ru and Bush were the ones who had stolen the truck. Knowing that Ru and Bush's destination was Saint-Pierre Island, William asked Garber for the fastest way to the ferry in Fortune.

"We'll take you there," said Garber. He opened the rear doors to the cruiser. William and Patrick sat behind the plexiglass barrier like prisoners.

Arriving at Route 210, Fellows answered the radio. "The rolling patrol just got a hit off our new automatic license plate recognition scanning system," said Fellows. "They've identified the stolen Ford F-150 traveling toward Frenchman's Cove. Two men matching the description of Ru and Bush were in the front seats."

"Nice. That ALPR just saved us a lot of time," William said.

"Heading there now," said Fellows. Garber switched on the red and blue overhead lights and raced through the busy core of Marystown, avoiding traffic and pedestrians. Fellows radioed to the RCMP in Fortune to establish a roadblock and gave a vehicle description.

William tapped on the plexiglass barrier. "How long from Marystown to Fortune?"

"It's about forty-five minutes. Unless we really shake it up," said Garber.

William tapped the plexiglass again. Garber didn't turn around and kept his eyes forward.

"Can you shake it up? These pricks are bloody dangerous."

Garber gave a thumbs up and turned right onto Columbia Drive. It linked up with the road to Frenchman's Bay. Now, the cruiser was flying, the landscape a blur. Garber expertly controlled the unruly rear.

Fellows received another radio call from the RCMP patrol. The F-150 had disappeared onto Route 213 to Garnish. They lost them.

At Columbia and Creston Causeway, two Targa rally cars on a dry run squealed into the intersection. The first rally car smashed the cruiser into the ditch, then spun around in a semi-circle and stopped on the highway's yellow lines. The second rally car halted one car length behind the wreckage.

Airbags on the cruiser deployed, pinning Garber and Fellows. Both were safe. The damaged rally car was equipped with a harness and roll cage protecting the driver and navigator. Everyone seemed fine but shaken up.

Patrick and William extricated themselves through a damaged rear door. William reached in through the window and knifed the airbag, releasing the gas.

"Are you okay?" William asked Garber.

He managed to nod, but the pain was evident in his grimaced expression.

"I'm going to send for help," William said. He looked over and was relieved to see Fellows was lucid and unhurt.

William retracted the Motorola police radio from Garber's vest and utility belt. He called in to dispatch for an ambulance. Patrick checked the drivers in the busted rally car and pronounced them unharmed.

The other Targa rally car drivers were already out and tending to their friends. William approached them, displaying his badge. "Guys, we're going to need your car. Sorry for the inconvenience, but we've got murderers to catch. We'll return the car when we're finished."

The racers wore Nomex overalls arrayed with sponsor badges like an active billboard. The driver removed his helmet and reluctantly handed it to William. His navigator did the same for Patrick.

The Targa Newfoundland was an annual event allowing classic cars to compete in a time, speed, and distance rally. The white wedge-shaped rally car had six huge headlamps and a green racing stripe. Sponsors' labels from tire, oil, and air filter manufacturers bedecked the car.

"It's a Lancia Stratos, tuned to 560 bhp," said the driver.

"That's ferocious rallying performance. So please be careful," added the navigator.

"I'm no stranger to speed," replied William as he pulled on the sweaty helmet and slid in the seat. Patrick connected his five-point harness. William pushed the starter button, and the engine bellowed.

Patrick was confounded by the complex instrument panel. He adjusted the headset intercom and said, "What do I do with all this shit?"

William threw the lever into first gear, gassed it, and painted double rubber bands across the asphalt. The car fishtailed across the yellow lines, throwing both men hard into their seats.

"Just get me to the cut-off for Garnish and Frenchman's Bay," said William.

"There's a rally computer. Looks complicated to use," said Patrick.

"There's a clipboard with a map on it. Use it instead."

Patrick eyed the clipboard guide sheets and started to map out the route.

"Keep straight on this road. It should be around twenty-two minutes before the next turn."

"With these good roads, I can get us there in ten minutes."

***

Ru and Bush were no strangers to being chased. They saw the RCMP sports utility vehicle in their rearview mirror. It was not hard to miss the light bar and the brush guard over the grill.

Ru spun the wheel and turned left onto a gravel road.

"That was a good move," said Bush.

"Pursuers look right almost every time because it's an easy turn. And the odds are lower for a left turn since it takes longer for oncoming traffic to pass."

Ru frowned and drove hard over the sandy soil. He parked in front of a military green Quonset hut. They had broken through a rust-laden rail gate and were regrouping at an equipment yard.

"What's the next move?" asked Bush.

"I think we have to assess how many cops between us and the ferry to Saint-Pierre."

"I don't want to spend any time in a Canadian jail."

"Okay, let's consider this. The cops have a good communication system. Collaborating with local forces, they can converge from any direction."

"Like roadblocks, multiple units, and maybe a helicopter," said Bush.

"Exactly, which is why we must outthink them. Do something the cops won't be expecting."

"Let's check the Quonset hut and see if there's anything we can use."

Ru found a crowbar in the back of the pickup. He broke open the lock between the two doors. Once inside, they were astonished.

"Buddha favors us," said Ru.

"Got a plan?" asked Bush.

"Yeah, got a plan."

They drove across the limestone driveway back to Route 213, where they joined Grandview Blvd. and headed to Fortune.

"Let's keep a low profile until the last minute," said Ru.

"Yeah, by the time they realize it's us, it will be too late."

***

"Got a message from the RCMP following the suspects. They lost the pickup on an obscure driveway. Officers now heading to the town of Fortune," said Patrick.

"Okay, time to put the hammer down," said William as he shifted to second gear.

"The challenge is keeping this monster on the road," said Patrick.

"Keep the directions coming. Leave the driving to me."

"Blind curve, small dip, keep straight, and then an S-turn!"

Shifting gears was precise and measured acoustically in the howling engine. William completed the dip and hit two bumps, causing the rear tires to slide into the turn. He shifted again, spun the wheel, tapped the brakes, and straightened. And avoided a car in the opposite lane.

"This car has a tendency to oversteer," said William.

"Try to stay out of the ocean."

The Lancia Stratos accelerated and double-crested, made a fierce right, missed the turn, then headed straight for the brush on the roadside.

"Holy shit!" said Patrick.

William managed to spin the car off the shoulder and shrubs. His flamboyant and adept skill derived from his years of motocross.

"You have to admit at least I didn't roll it," said William.

"We had at least three wheels off the ground!"

As the car crested the hill, Patrick heard a clunk as William fixed first gear; the tires chirped, and the rear sashayed. William and the Lancia were moving as one.

"You drive like Colin McRae."

"Compliments are always welcome."

William dodged a rock cliff, then a house with a white picket fence on a stretch of unrepaired road. Near Grand Bank, the Lancia vaulted a ridge, almost shattering an Anglican church close to the highway. The speeds were ferocious. William kept the car maximized using the entire powerband.

"Are you getting jacked up? Can you tone it down?" asked Patrick.

"You're right. I'm taking chances."

"Good. Let's get to the roadblock in one piece."

"Reach the rear patrol, see if they've found our guys yet."

They arrived outside of Fortune where the RCMP had blocked the straight section of Grandview Boulevard. Two cruisers were diagonal, front grills opposing each other. Another one faced uphill as a pursuit car in case the F-150 escaped. That remote part of the road had an ample site line obscured by a hill until crested. Further on, it was ocean on one side, marsh on the other, and a tight turnaround. Ideal conditions to stop a runaway car, especially when spikes were laid across the roadway.

The Lancia Stratos stopped beside the police cruisers. William and Patrick introduced themselves and explained why they had the rally car. The officers got positioned behind the cruiser and waited for Ru and Bush. After being briefed by William, the policemen were doubly cautious.

Voices became garbled on the radio as an urgent message drifted through the cruiser window.

"They changed vehicles! The F-150 was spotted on the flatbed of an eighteen-wheeler!"

"They are coming in fast!"

Patrick tilted his head slightly as he captured a faint sound. It wasn't a bird or animal he was listening for but something mechanical. Everyone became sharp. The rumble of a diesel transport truck became loud. Then it blasted over the crest of the hill, exhaust stacks belching black smoke. The truck was being driven flat out.

"Now," the sergeant yelled into his mobile radio.

Below the hill, a constable heaved a spike strip over the road seconds before the eighteen-wheeler rolled over them. The ribbon was designed to allow a slow release of air from the tires to prevent loss of control. Once fully deflated, the rims tore the tires to shreds, the friction creating sparks on the asphalt. Ru disregarded the chance of fire and kept driving.

"They're not gonna stop!" said Patrick.

"These are desperate men," said William.

Everyone jumped aside as the truck smashed through the cruisers. The cars were thrown asunder, sparks flew from steel rims, creating fireworks. The transport truck stopped and both men jumped out.

They unhooked the F-150 pickup truck and drove off the trailer, heading toward the ferry at Fortune. The plan was well executed. The police cruisers were rendered useless. The Lancia Stratos was flipped on its side, a result of the domino effect. The barrier had failed to stop them. The officers were stunned at the outcome.

The RCMP vehicle chasing the criminals was also speeding. The officer spotted the spike strip and braked the car a few feet before. His partner rolled up the spike strip and threw it to the side. They proceeded toward the upturned police cars to evaluate the damage.

The constables were shaken and humiliated. Everyone had underestimated the resourcefulness of the Hong Kong triad boss.

William and Patrick were not wallowing in self-pity as they commandeered the RCMP SUV and drove to Fortune. In their dogged pursuit, they anticipated arresting the gangsters before they boarded the ferry.

When they arrived at the harbor, the ferry was still being loaded. Searching front to back, the F-150 was not on board.

On Harbour Street, William retrieved the binoculars and swept the harbor for clues. The ferry departed. He was perplexed that Ru and Bush were not onboard.

Watercraft make a distinctive sound as they bounce across the water. It piqued William's attention, he looked over and saw Bush piloting a power boat. "Those bastards. They are heading out to sea!"

Patrick scrunched his face in disgust and turned away.

"This is not over yet. We'll get them," said William.

Fifty-Two

This is Mind-Blowing

THE JORDANS' RENTAL Mustang left the downtown core and headed toward the cultural center at Membertou Heritage Park. Grand Chief McDonald had provided an operations room for them to conduct their work. Tracy and Jeffrey were pleased the artifacts were being guarded by community members.

They reviewed reports prepared since their first trip to the site. This included the initial LiDAR mapping and the notes from Tracy's journal.

Stanford University approved Tracy's report and granted financial backing with the understanding the Mi'kmaq peoples were partners in this project and represented by Kevin Steptoe. Earlier in the month, he had drafted a partnership trust fund for them, and would be supervising the project along side Tracy.

Jeffrey convinced the Canadian government to permit the Chinese science team that had been on the *Sofia's Odyssey* to participate in the dig since their knowledge of Asian archaeology would be indispensable. With sponsorship from John Abbott at the Department of National Defence and assistance from the Canadian Immigration Department, the archaeologists' work visas were fast-tracked. The bureaucrats in Ottawa recognized the importance of the discovery and were willing to bend the rules.

Tracy reviewed the site map that included the building, roads, bodies of water, and survey points. She organized a list of duties for the scientists and Indigenous university students of archaeology.

"Everything is prepared and ready to go," said Jeffrey.

"Okay, let's get to the airport," replied Tracy.

Arriving on the tarmac, Tom waved them over to the upgraded helicopter.

"Is that what you call the sky crane?" asked Tracy looking over, her blue eyes expressing excitement.

"Yes, that's the Sikorsky S-64 that I ordered from Halifax. The Bobcat is local equipment," Jeffrey said, sensing her energy.

"Let's get going!" said Tracy. They both climbed into the helicopter.

Tom flew the Sikorsky south, arriving at Gabarus Wilderness Area an hour later. The Bobcat hung below like a plumb bob defying gravity. Kevin Steptoe, the archaeologists and excited university students were already on site and had begun to set up.

Tom lowered the front-end loader to the ground and the students released the cables from the excavator. He landed the chopper a short distance away so that Jeffrey and Tracy could disembark.

They walked toward the staging area where the group was assembled. "Can I get everybody's attention?" said Tracy waving a floppy orange hat.

The team wore pale blue coveralls and canvas shoes. Tracy handed out itineraries to the team leaders. They had specific duties and areas on the grid to take charge of.

"There are bins to be unloaded which contain excavation tools. Make sure you equip yourself properly. Take tape measures, grapefruit knives, dental picks, whisk brooms, and dustpans. Whatever you require.

"Professor Jordan and I will tackle the sub-surface anomaly that we discovered with the radar unit. Our static data indicate intervals of medium and deep targets that will require initial soil removal using the bobcat. From there, some of you will help with trowels and shovels. Check your itineraries for your assigned grids. When we're ready, we'll call on some of you to hand excavate," said Tracy. "Any questions?"

When no one replied, she wrapped up the meeting and said, "Get started on your section."

The team dispersed and was busy in the field while Jeffrey instructed field technician Liao to drive the bobcat to the location marked for excavation.

"Remove a meter of soil. But proceed carefully following the radar readings," said Tracy.

"Will do," said Liao.

"I'll monitor the soil and gravel in case any artifacts are unearthed."

After an hour, Liao reached the targeted depth and felt resistance. The skid steer shovel hit something. Tracy and Jeffrey heard it as well.

"It's time to back off and dig by hand. Let's bring in the students to assist." Tracy grinned with enthusiasm.

Jeffrey cupped his hands and shouted, "Helpers over here!"

Students and archaeologists ran, in anticipation of the discovery.

"Okay, this is it. Everyone knows what to do," said Tracy.

Half a day passed as the final layer of soil was cleared. Students removed ancient bullrush reeds to expose the remnants of pine logs. The logs formed the ceiling, and the bull rush reeds served as roofing.

"This type of structure is similar to the terra-cotta warrior tomb," explained principal investigator Dashan.

"Yes, I agree. My professor was on the original dig and taught this technique in university," said senior historian Yulin.

"The easiest way into the chamber is to find the most decayed pine log. Then gently chisel an opening," suggested field technician Liao. He scoured the toolbox for the right tools.

Liao chose a chisel and a mallet, hammered into the logs, and found one with the most deterioration.

"This one is rather soft. It's water damaged and vulnerable," said Liao. He wiped the sweat dripping from his forehead.

With everyone's efforts, the pine logs were pried loose until the opening to the sepulture was large enough for a person to enter.

"What is that ghastly smell?" asked one of the university students.

"That musty sweet mothball smell is indole," said Tracy as she placed her hand over her nose and felt her lungs constricting. "Indole is a decomposition by-product of decaying organic matter."

"Just breathe through your mouth until you get used to it," said Jeffrey as he put on a facemask.

"I'm picking up camphor, pine resin, and wild rose," said Tracy. She took a deep breath from her inhaler and peered in. Her LED headlamp illuminated antiquities.

"We've got to get down there! Get me a rope ladder," said Tracy.

A couple of students attached the rope ladder lowering it gently into the tomb.

"We have to be methodical. And constant care must be taken to preserve whatever we find," said Kian.

Tracy lowered herself, one foot at a time, one rung below another, pushing deeper, piercing the darkness with light. The flashlight revealed elaborately painted murals.

"This is amazing," she yelled out, euphoria overcoming her usual self-restraint.

Tracy was attentive as she stood on the packed ground. Her first exciting find. Where to start cataloging these amazing treasures? She swallowed the lump in her throat.

Jeffrey landed beside Tracy with his Fenix lumens flashlight. The ornate room shone as if lit by floodlights at a stadium night game. Everything in the wide beam had not been seen in six centuries. Jeffrey crossed the floor. His eyes met Tracy's. In their excitement, they executed a high five.

"This is totally mind-blowing. I don't even know where to start," said Jeffrey, his face flushed.

Yulin made his descent into the enclave. An experienced archaeologist, Yulin was well acquainted with most of the antiquities in the chamber. June Fields followed, ready to photograph.

"June, please start on the left wall and then go clockwise," said Tracy.

As a precaution, June took her photographs without flash.

All four walls were overlaid with murals depicting various forms of activity. Yulin described the story portrayed on the far wall. To him, it was more important than the objects displayed throughout the room.

"The occupant of the chamber, most likely Admiral Zheng He, would have needed these things in the afterlife," he said.

Tracy added her expertise. "The craftsmen who created these exemplary works of art were exceptional." She pointed at the left wall. Everyone gasped.

"Yes, Tracy, these frescos are recreating scenes that depict everyday life in the courts of the Yongle emperor," said Yulin.

"See the guards and dancers? And illustrated here are ambassadors, merchants, traders, and emissaries," said June as she took another vivid shot with the Nikon D850.

Tracy turned around slowly, feasting her eyes on the far side fresco. "This is extremely interesting over here. See, a person is holding a Persian cup.

Those are high-ranking foreign dignitaries. Over there is a musician with instruments from far-off lands!" she exclaimed.

Tracy stepped closer and put on her white cotton gloves. She caressed a wall where cheetah, camels, and giraffes were depicted in naturally brilliant colors.

"These walls are plaster with woven silk fibers pasted to it, and the paintings are directly on the fabric," she said.

Kevin Steptoe kneeled and poked his head in the opening. "Can I come in? I'd like to make a report for Grand Chief MacDonald," he said.

"Can you wait till we are finished? We need to limit the number of us in the room at one time," said Tracy. "The carbon monoxide from our exhalations could damage the murals." She had almost forgotten about the annoying lawyer. "I'll give you a tour afterward," she added.

"Sounds good, Tracy," replied Kevin.

Yulin tapped Tracy's shoulder. He pointed over to the south wall. A wooden engraved coffin was lying on a pedestal. Tracy was sure of the occupant's identity. She walked toward it, careful not to disturb any relics.

"The mural beyond the coffin is illustrating hundreds of ships." Tracy brought her hands up to her face in astonishment.

"The artists' panorama links this room to travel by sea. Look at the map featured beside it," said Jeffrey.

"There is no doubt as to the imagination of the artist," said June Fields.

"Oh, this is real. These murals are historical chronicles and I consider them accurate," said Tracy.

"Ahem. Let's examine this coffin," said Yulin.

"The coffin is orientated east, facing Mecca. It makes sense; Zheng He was Muslim," said Tracy. "However he was placed in the tomb according to Chinese funerary custom as opposed to being buried directly in the ground."

On the coffin was a jade encrusted book. Tracy bent and blew off surface dust. The fine particles muddled in the light, then dissipated upwards to the opening in the ceiling of the tomb.

Dashan set the half-meter bronze goose on the floor. Then entered the dimensions in a notebook, beside his sketch of the bird. "Tracy, this jade-covered book is in all probability a record of the admiral's life in this new world."

Tracy picked up the journal delicately. Dashan opened a specimen bag. With gloved hands, Tracy placed the book inside and sealed the bag.

"We can examine this curio better in the lab. Right now, let's resume," she said.

The room was filled with period furniture, assorted ceramic figurines, carved lacquerware, bronze swords, helmets, and body armor.

Examination of the south wall exposed an opening into an anti-chamber where the great Admiral He's attendants had placed the bulk of the treasure.

"I'm amazed again. This experience beats everything," said Tracy.

"I think we all feel that way," said June.

Everyone was in shock. Only the Nikon camera clicking like Morse code interrupted the room's silence.

The entire area was dry as a bone. The Chinese engineers had sealed it so that water could not enter. Crafted wooden shelves were stacked with Ming dynasty imperial blue and white porcelain plates and vases. Crates held gold statues, jewel-encrusted hairpins, gold bowls and cups, boxes of gold coins, and jewelry boxes. The list was endless.

Tracy realized the team was overwhelmed. To ground everyone, she chose to pause further examination until the next day. "May I have everyone's attention? We've covered enough for now. We need time to secure the roof opening," she said. "Let's set up camp and get some dinner going. Then we can evaluate today's work over our meal. I expect no discussion about our discovery outside of our team. That means family, too. So, everyone let's get out of here," she said. "Thank you for your work. It's been a wonderful day."

She took a deep breath, left the anti-chamber, and grabbed the rope ladder. The rest reluctantly followed her out.

Kevin was waiting at the top. "My turn?" he asked.

"No, I'm sorry, your turn tomorrow. We're wrapping it up for today. It's late and we need time to secure the site."

"That's too bad, but I understand," said Kevin. "I will send over my security men to guard the site overnight," he added.

"Thanks Kev," said Tracy. "You can join me in the morning for a personal tour."

The students assembled metal rods for the canopy over the entrance to the tomb while Kevin waited for the security team to arrive.

Fifty-Three
His Name is Jeffrey Jordan

REN BO ENTERED the Ministry of State Security building to visit Guan Yin. He was enamored with his boss, an intelligent, middle-aged beauty. Her office was dusty and cluttered. Yin was determined to operate through the construction and renovation of her workplace. Plasterboard and materials were piled in the corner under a tarp awaiting workers who, after business hours, would transform her enclave into an upgraded control room.

"Good morning, Ren Bo. Please be seated," she said. He brushed the dust from the chair and sat.

"I heard President Wei Lei increased national defense spending across the board."

"Yes, I am very pleased." She shifted some files around her desk, her eyes blinking as the dust floated. "What are you sharing with me today?"

"Minister, I have determined the identity of the man for whom President Wei Lei has been searching. His name is Jeffrey Jordan, and I have located him and his daughter Tracy in Sydney, Nova Scotia, Canada."

"I'm pleased you have kept me informed. How did you come by your information?"

"His daughter Tracy Jordan was enrolled at the University of Nanjing. I tracked her using her credit card activity. Airline tickets purchased prove she and her father flew there from Washington, DC. They are at a hotel in Sydney.

"I found out from other sources that they are after treasure they believe was left behind by Zheng He," he explained, catching surprise on her face. "You know the famous admiral from the Ming dynasty?"

"I know the history. Despite this revelation, how do you propose to apprehend Jeffrey Jordan and bring him to Beijing?"

"I have contacted the *Xin Feng*, a cable-laying ship, and plan to join the crew as my cover." He sat wearily and rubbed his bloodshot eyes.

"Where is the ship currently?"

"It left Zhoushan Garrison Naval Yard a month ago and is repairing internet cable in the North Atlantic for Chinwah Optics Electric."

"I like this idea. I will contact the ship's commander to ensure the marines on board will be at your disposal."

"Thank you. By the way, I wanted to add that General Po's case is ongoing."

"That's interesting. But let's place the General Po investigation on the back burner as the president is anxious to have Jeffrey Jordan apprehended."

"Yes. I will focus my full attention on bringing him to Beijing."

"You should know, the executives at Chinwah Optics are grateful for your help in North Africa. Your efforts resulted in a lucrative contract for them."

"I look forward to working with them again."

"You are going to find out anyway, so I will tell you now. The Xin Feng is a state-owned spy ship. It has a legitimate reason to be in the mid-Atlantic to inspect the cables. What international authorities don't know is that the ship, under my orders, is to tap into the cable to gather classified information."

"Once Jeffrey Jordan is apprehended, I will need to move fast. I am concerned the two operations may be in conflict," said Ren Bo.

"Your mission is top priority. The captain has orders to immediately sail within helicopter distance of Senegal. Arrangements will be made for you and Jeffrey Jordan to fly from there to our military base in Djibouti. From there, a military flight will take you to Beijing. Then you will escort him to the president."

"Should I question him regarding his CIA past?"

"No. President Wei Lei will question him personally," asserted Yin, placing her chin on her folded hands. "You have your assignment." She nodded toward the door, indicating the meeting was concluded.

Ren Bo gave her a smile, zipped up his jacket, and left the room. He thought about his mission. Then felt a tinge of excitement that only a woman like Yin could inspire.

Fifty-Four

Don't Forget I Expect My Share

THE OFFICE STAFF had gone home. But not Chu Bojing. He shifted his slender physique, relaxed in his chair. Then, he scratched the itch above his eye and flipped his hair over the bare spot with his fingers. He had just completed his list of literature and music that he felt should be banned.

He was tired of evaluating distasteful comics and animations and reached for his lyric book and read his favorite poem, *A Faithless Husband*, by Zhou Wenjun from the Han dynasty. He recited it out loud, pronouncing the old Chinese distinctly.

Plain as snow on the hill, clear as moon among the clouds.

It's your change of heart, they tell me, and so I've gone to bid you goodbye.

Today we've drunk a measure of wine, tomorrow we must part by the canal.

His oratory was disturbed. He reached for the phone, lying on the credenza behind him.

"Hello, this is Minister Chu Bojing."

"Minister, this is Professor Peng Lixin."

"To what do I owe this pleasure?"

"What progress are you making on our project?"

"Professor, there's nothing at the moment unless you have important information."

"I have learned the Yongle Emperor who overthrew the Jainwen Emperor sponsored Zheng He to secretly search for Jainwen on these voyages as it was believed he had escaped," said Professor Tain, overplaying the facts.

"I don't think this is relevant," replied Bojing, who expected better but got nonsense instead.

"If that's not important, then let me remind you that I delivered Tracy Jordan to you."

Bojing realized the real reason for the call. "So, you did, and we will reward you for your efforts, but please refrain from contacting me in the future as it's dangerous. Do you understand?"

"Yes, but don't forget I expect my share."

Bojing said goodbye, disconnected, and returned his phone to the credenza. *This man is a liability. His usefulness is no longer required. Time to eliminate this little ant.*

The phone rang again. Ru Fa Zhong's name flashed across the screen.

"Hello, good to hear from you. I was beginning to become concerned."

"We have been busy trying to keep ahead of the police."

"You are? What the hell's going on?"

"Captain Bush and I are on Saint-Pierre Island, just off Newfoundland. The coordinates for the treasure are nearby." He changed the subject. "Have you heard anything about the investigation concerning General Po's death?" Ru was worried if he and Bojing were under suspicion.

"No, there's nothing new. Any findings from the investigation are usually relayed to me. Should we be implicated, my sources will advise me."

"That's a relief."

"Now, onto the issue at hand. You are on foreign soil. The police pursuing you will ask the local authorities for help."

"We are aware of that. We'll fit in as tourists until the submarine with Chan and Dao arrives. Then our plan is to explore the area."

"It's imperative we succeed. You must recover the antiquities at all costs."

"When Dao arrives, we will have the manpower to carry it out. You must trust us." Ru said goodbye and pocketed his cellphone.

***

After escaping William and Patrick in Newfoundland, Ru and Bush landed at a small rocky inlet away from the city, bypassing French Customs. They knew little about the French Territorial Collective.

Trekking across the flattish, rocky, and barren landscape they had time to think. Their only hope was to blend in, expecting the tourist industry to be strong with worldwide visitors.

Using false identification, they rented a Jeep and registered at Chez Calvin, a trendy hotel downtown. Both men took separate rooms and went shopping. They bought a Canon camera, some floppy hats, and comfortable clothes to replace the ones they had stolen.

Ru admitted his phone was too small for surveillance purposes and asked the concierge to direct him to a computer store.

Ru observed bright colors on buildings as he walked to the computer center near the waterfront. He passed purple and blue bay windows along the streets parked with various European cars.

"What kind of computer do you need?" asked the French woman behind the counter.

He pointed and said, "I'll take the HP computer and this drone."

Both men returned to their hotel room as it was vital Ru access his cloud account. The abrupt departure from *Sofia's Odyssey* meant he had left Tracy's scorched computer on the ship. It was also paramount he make contact with Dao and Captain Ho Chan.

***

"Just got a message from Dao. They received the coordinates," said Ru. "We should finish our breakfast and get to the rendezvous point."

Captain Bush understood the complexity of the situation. "The sooner we meet with our teammates, the more comfortable I'll feel."

"I've checked our cloud data and conducted background searches. I hardly got any sleep. But there is a suitable way across this island on back roads." Ru looked tired and edgy.

"You navigate, and I'll drive," said Bush, concerned about the welfare of his boss.

They checked out of the hotel, loaded the Jeep with their equipment and left. Rue Boursaint was one of the main thoroughfares out of the city. After leaving the paved road, Bush engaged the Jeep's four-wheel drive. They drove across the barren landscape, craggy hills, and outcroppings to the furthest point of the island. Bush stopped the Jeep where the trail ended on a spearhead of rock jutting into the ocean.

Ru gazed through binoculars across the strait to Grand Colombier Island. Then he opened the computer and checked the coordinates that Tracy had given him. Yes, they were right where they were supposed to be. "How can this be?"

Bush could sense that Ru was becoming agitated. "What's going on?"

"I'm looking at a treeless steep-sided hill with a rolling ridge covered with grasses and ferns. There are black, indigo-colored birds and Atlantic puffins and seals. It doesn't look like any settlement could ever have been here. It's deserted!" Ru was angry and disappointed.

Bush looked through the binoculars "Yes, I see what you mean." There's no point sending up the drone. It would be a fruitless pursuit."

"Tracy outplayed us. She diverted us from the real location!"

"The submarine should be arriving any time now. What are you going to tell the team?"

"They will be pissed off. If Tracy was here, I'd kill the little bitch!"

Bush tried to hide his shock and disgust.

"Let's leave the Jeep, board the submarine, and find Tracy's location. This is to be kept quiet. I don't want to be embarrassed in front of Bojing."

They heard water gurgling and splashing in the channel. Both men stopped and turned toward the sound.

"They're here," said Bush.

The submarine was surfacing almost on point. Ru was impressed with Captain Ho Chan and his navigation skills. They'd come halfway around the world—a feat Admiral Zheng He was thought to have accomplished.

"Locating Tracy is going to be challenging. I wonder where she is?" said Ru.

Fifty-Five

We're Too Late

WILLIAM AND PATRICK boarded the ferry to Saint-Pierre. They had failed to apprehend Ru and Bush, but it didn't matter because there were only two ways off the island. The ferry or the airport. Both were monitored with security cameras.

"You have to put disappointment into perspective and identify the next opportunity," said Patrick, cupping his hands around a steaming cup of coffee.

"Success is being persistent and focused," replied William. He leaned on the handrail glancing over the choppy blue sea.

"Looks like we've gone to the same motivational seminars." Patrick laughed. "Was that close or was that close?" he asked, changing the discussion away from the philosophical banter.

William adjusted his submariner dive watch since Saint-Pierre was thirty minutes ahead of Newfoundland. A brisk wind created long white caps. Patrick paced the deck, then froze at the roar of a powerboat. William noticed its actuation across the ferry's bow.

"Smugglers," said William.

"Must be pretty lucrative if that's still happening." Patrick returned to the handrail beside William.

"Rum runners have been here since Al Capone used the island during prohibition. And now there are drugs as well."

"What else do you know about Saint-Pierre and Miquelon?"

"It was settled by the Basques in the 17th century. The British had it. Then the French took it back. Finally, the British won it again after a seven-year war, then returned it. The Brits gave them fishing rights as well. The islands are remnants of the old order and are under French control."

"We'll need to work with the local gendarmes."

"It seems that way. John told me a French Prefect is assisted by a privy council that governs the island. They oversee the police. We are to contact Lieutenant Colonel Boudon. John has spoken to them about our investigation, and they will cooperate," said William. He brushed up against a young man with a knapsack.

"It's getting busy up here. Let's go inside," suggested Patrick.

They left the deck and sat in a row of chairs away from the snack bar. "Where were we? Hong Kong Interpol sent John some additional info. Apparently, Qi Ping, a billionaire, was ransomed and his submarine stolen. During our warehouse raid, Tracy's kidnappers escaped in Qi Ping's submarine.

"They also sent pics of our suspects." He showed Patrick a slew of pictures on his phone. "I'm forwarding them to you." He sneered at the photos. "The brass of these impudent men."

"Got the pics."

"The first one is a Captain Ho Chan formally of the Chinese Navy. Quite dangerous and well trained. The next one is Tang Dao. We met him at the warehouse. Not a bad shot. He is Ru's number one," said William.

"So, we can add these two with Ru and Bush."

The ferry blasted its foghorn, the engines reversed speed as the vessel arrived at Saint-Pierre. William and Patrick departed with the passengers and tourists.

They presented their passports and badges at customs. The officer, a sergeant, no less, interrupted the protocol of handing over their sidearms.

"Lieutenant Boudon has allowed these visiting detectives to carry their firearms with a special permit." He wore a dark navy-blue uniform with gold epaulets and shiny boots. He took his job seriously.

That document was presented to Border Control for clarification. The customs officers affirmed the waiver and passed William and Patrick through.

"Bonjour, Monsieur Fox. Comment allez-vous?" said the Sergeant.

"Très bien," said William.

"Do you prefer English? Perhaps Mr. Reilly doesn't speak French."

"That would be good. Thanks," said Patrick, relieved he wasn't going to stumble over the language.

"Follow me," said the sergeant. William noticed a dark blue Citroen C3 with *Gendarmerie* affixed along the side and a red and white chevron on the hood. Not suitable for the highways of Montreal, but quite adept in the narrow streets of Saint-Pierre.

The flashing blue light on the Citroen cleared the streets of cars and shoppers. Ensuring they could arrive at the Saint-Pierre's police headquarters on time.

They found Lieutenant Boudon in the cafeteria having coffee and a croissant. The sergeant was anxious not to miss his coffee break. He poured a cup and sat down with the morning paper.

"Bonjour, messieurs Fox et Reilly. Bienvenue," said Lieutenant Boudon.

"Thank you. We appreciate your warm welcome and your cooperation," said William, slightly miffed at the easy and relaxed attitude of the officers.

Lieutenant Boudon was vested, displayed brown cropped hair, a trimmed beard, and a benevolent leader's confident posture. He raised his coffee cup firmly with an athletic muscled arm. "Care to join us before we get down to business?"

"Sure, why not," said William turning up the corner of his mouth. He glanced over at Patrick and saw him crunch a cream pastry. They wasted no time accepting the French hospitality.

William took a sip of his coffee, a type of espresso, and got right down to business. "Can you take a look at these photos and see if you recognize any of these men?" He handed his phone to Boudon, who looked at it, then passed it to the sergeant.

Boudon swallowed a bit of puff pastry and brushed flakes of crust from his tactical vest.

"No, I haven't seen these suspects. Our customs officers work closely with us. We can check with them."

The sergeant folded his newspaper and shook his head. "Non," he grunted.

"In that case, perhaps Patrick and I can investigate ourselves," said William.

"Yes, I will permit it, but we expect you to keep a low profile. One of my men will accompany you."

William had expected more freedom in his search through the city. So be it. He flashed his eyes at Patrick, implying they would ditch the gendarme the first opportunity. Patrick smiled and nodded his head in agreement. Their covert language forged in Hong Kong.

"Let's get started," said William.

***

Driving through the city, William noticed the buildings were painted bright, beautiful colors and were prevalent throughout the colony. Reds, bright yellows, blues, and violet were scattered in unrestrained creativity. The architecture was preindustrial, and possibly vernacular. Peugeots,

Renaults, and Citroens bordered the curbs, along with reliable Toyotas and Mazdas.

Beyond the city, the island was stark and barren. Leafy forest transitioning into rugged hills and rocky lowlands, with peat bogs, small lakes, and ponds. The island coast was varied with cliffs and irregular capes, including rocky inlets favored by puffins, kingfishers, and seals.

The topography and the area's climate struck William as somewhat odd. Familiar with China's terrain and weather, this island would be improbable for a settlement. It would make a poor home, particularly for growing staples like rice and fruit.

He knew Tracy wouldn't be here. Ru and his crew would also find that out. That meant he and Patrick had to find Ru and Bush soon.

"We don't have a lot of time here," William said to Patrick. "Let's lose the tagalong cop."

William asked the gendarme to park on Rue Boursaint, the main street and said, "Let's split up and cover both sides. Special Agent Reilly will be with me since he doesn't speak French." William turned to the gendarme. "You, start there and show the pictures of our suspects."

"Oui," he responded and entered the first hotel on his side.

William and Patrick started walking toward a few shops. They heard musicians playing in the music store. They stood in the doorway, enjoying the melody. One of the band members invited them in.

"Would you like to join us?" asked the guitar player.

William and Patrick shook their heads. The pianist clinked on the Steinway.

"That's Chuck. He's from New Orleans," said the baseman.

"That's a haunting piano riff," said Patrick.

"A Latin jazz theme," said Chuck. He stopped performing and swiveled around on the piano chair.

He was wearing a Navy Vietnam Veteran baseball cap frayed at the edges. He appeared around seventy, unshaven, bright-eyed with bony slender fingers. "It's called *Poinciana*, composed by Ahmad Jamal. And debuted at the Pershing Club," said Chuck.

"Hey, let's play *Take Five* guys," said the guitar player.

"We played that ten minutes ago," said the baseman kindly.

The band members looked concerned and hoped they would never get afflicted. The baseman spoke, "He has stage two dementia and there are some personality changes. He makes his living, entertaining seniors with old favorites. We wonder how long he can continue to do it."

William and Patrick nodded sympathetically.

"I was wondering fellas," William held up the phone images. "Have you seen these men?"

"I've seen that guy," said Chuck pointing to Ru's photo. "He's hard and light on his feet. I fought guys like that in Vietnam. He came out of the computer mart a few hours ago."

"What did he do?" asked the baseman.

"Can't discuss it. Thanks for your help," said William.

"Chuck, you play a cool piano," said Patrick.

They ambled along Rue Boursaint, onto Rue Marechal Foch, and arrived at the computer shop. William flashed his badge and Ru's image. The clerk confirmed it was him.

The gendarme came running up the street and said, "The car rental agent confirmed renting a Jeep to men fitting the description of Ru and Bush. I asked the agent to locate the vehicle. It's on the other side of the island on a dirt track."

"Let's go check it out," said Patrick. He was anxious to get underway.

"Not with this vehicle," William said. "It won't make it over the rough terrain."

The gendarme drove William and Patrick back to the station and escorted them to Lieutenant Boudon's office.

Seated in the lieutenant's office, William said, "Several shop owners recognized Ru. Your gendarme located the Jeep and it appears to be abandoned on the other side of the island."

"We will need to send our forensics team. We must follow protocol and report to the Prefect," said the lieutenant.

"You don't mind if we tag along?" asked William. "We know these killers quite well."

"The sergeant will take you there now." William and Patrick followed the officer to the SUV parked outside of the police station.

After traveling over an uneven track, the sergeant parked beside the abandoned rental. The forensics team examined the Jeep. William noticed boot scuffs in the sand. Rocks were recently disturbed. Further scrutiny indicated a boat had been pulled over the beach. William surmised that Ru and Bush had departed by a skiff and were picked up by the submarine.

"We're too late." William was livid.

Fifty-Six

To the Airport and Fast

JEFFREY WAS LOOKING forward to relaxing in his hotel room. He had left Tracy and the team at Gabarus Wilderness Area. The younger people would live on-site during the excavation, but at his age, he preferred a comfortable bed.

Yulin had joined him on the chopper to Sydney and was entrusted with Zheng He's jade journal. It was decided to secure it in the hotel safe to be available for translation into contemporary language.

Jeffrey pulled the Mustang in the valet parking area, beside a pillar in front of the hotel lobby entrance.

"Would you get the journal from the trunk and bring it to the safe?" asked Jeffrey, as he stepped out of the car to retrieve his iPad. Yulin went to the rear of the Mustang.

Jeffrey turned as the vehicle approached. He realized the white and blue ambulance driven by an Asian man was headed directly toward him. The ambulance didn't stop. Jeffrey was confused and hesitated. Longer than he should have. Then the emergency vehicle swerved. The rear doors flung open. Two hefty Asians vaulted out and restrained him. The tall one forced Jeffrey's head down and shoved him into the back of the van.

"What the hell are you guys doing?" shouted Jeffrey. He tried breaking free by thrusting his shoulder into the short guy. His attacker responded by directing a punishing elbow to Jeffrey's soft ribs. The pain left Jeffrey in tears. He stumbled, trying to regain his balance. Then the electrical shock of a taser rendered him unconscious. The abductors laid Jeffrey into a man-sized crate.

Yulin heard the panic in Jeffrey's outcry. He sprang into a sprint around the ambulance, recognized the danger, and jumped into a high-flying kick. His foot strike was about to connect when the hefty Asian sidestepped and snapped a front kick. The force slammed into Yulin's thigh, spinning him rearward. His torso banged into the ambulance, and he slid to the ground, knocking the back of his head. Yulin passed out. The doors slammed shut as the ambulance disappeared in a cloud of burned rubber. People in the lobby, hearing the commotion, found Yulin on his knees, rubbing his head and cursing in Mandarin.

"Are you all right? Can we help you?" asked the concierge.

"No, everything's okay. Just a fright from a bad driver. Yulin cleared his mind and decided to leave. He had just witnessed an abduction. He went to the front desk. I'm checking out of room 403. Call a cab for me," he said. He had to get out before they came back.

"Certainly, sir," said the concierge.

Yulin returned to the trunk of the Mustang and removed the jade journal. Bags packed, he sat in the lobby waiting for the cab to arrive. He knew this wouldn't look right to Tracy or the other scientists. Professor Jordan had been kidnapped, and Yulin had been beaten and bruised. But an opportunity like this didn't happen very often. The journal itself could be sold to a wealthy person. Only a few people knew of its existence, making it easy to smuggle out. Sold to a private collector, he could become wealthy and retire. Yulin got into the back of the cab.

"To the airport and fast," said Yulin. There was a long pause. Then he chuckled.

"Are you all right back there, sir?" asked the cab driver.

"Couldn't be better. Thanks for your concern."

***

The ambulance raced along the waterfront and maneuvered left on Highway 4. The emergency vehicle lights flashed all the way to J.A. Douglas McCurdy Sydney Airport. It stopped at hangar nine on Airport Road, where an Avicopter AC352 waited to whisk them away.

Ren Bo waited for his cronies to bring him his prize. He had convinced Canadian authorities his group, the Chinese Human League, was on a humanitarian mission and they were allowed to land and pick up medicines. His forged documents indicated the vaccines were for the United Nations Refugee Agency in Northern Africa.

"Put him in the back. Make sure his hands and feet are secured," said Ren Bo from the co-pilot seat. The stout one removed Jeffrey from the crate, effortlessly threw him over his shoulder like a sack of feed corn and set him down in the rear seat.

The helicopter swiftly left Canadian air space without a snag. Visibility was clear as the chopper flew over the Atlantic and landed on the helipad of the Xin Feng.

Landing at dusk, the light diminished into the darkness. Ren Bo's intelligence agents wedged Jeffrey between them. He winced. They propelled him along the deck to a cabin midpoint. There was a sense of urgency, as Jeffrey's presence was classified.

Jeffrey quit resisting and settled into the suite with no fight left. He had been tasered, bruised, sedated, and was exhausted from the ordeal.

Ren Bo spoke with the captain. He explained that the package had been secured and to set sail for Senegal. The captain explained their assignment hadn't been completed yet as they were waiting for the submersible to return from the ocean's depths after it collected vital information.

The delay concerned Ren Bo. The timing of his mission was critical. Ren Bo exhaled a couple of short breaths and rotated his neck muscles to relax. The gamble in kidnapping professor Jordan could unravel if Canadian authorities pieced together what had happened. He was concerned the captain's assignment meant delays that could compromise his mission.

Ren Bo sat in a stateroom and opened his laptop. He stared at the screen and searched for local news in Sydney. After ten minutes of searching, he was relieved that the kidnapping of Jeffrey Jordan was not yet public knowledge.

He couldn't help wondering whether something else would interfere with the operation. He closed his laptop and fell asleep, despite the lumpy, well-used mattress.

Fifty-Seven

Where is My Father?

THE FOLLOWING MORNING, the helicopter from Sydney had not yet arrived. Tracy wasn't concerned that her Dad and Yulin were late. While waiting for them, she assigned new duties to the exploration team.

Tracy and Kevin walked past the students and archaeologists working in their designated areas, chipping away at stones, brushing debris, and searching for relics.

She pushed the tarp away from the entrance of the tomb and invited Kevin to join her.

Once Kevin descended, he gasped. "Amazing to think these Asian explorers made first contact with my ancestors."

"I know it's hard to believe, but the evidence is here."

"Any idea of the value?"

"It's priceless. It will take time to ascertain the market value, and historical significance."

"I am going to spend some time here and then send an interim report to the grand chief."

***

The grand chief summoned the elders to the community center.

"Kevin Steptoe gave his report on the trove found at Gabarus Wilderness Area," said Grand Chief McDonald. He handed out copies of the preliminary report. The description included a list of the major pieces and photographs that were supplied by the site photographer, June Fields.

"So, are we rich?" asked René Doucette.

"I suppose we are. But we have another interesting discovery. Another burial mound was found. Ground-penetrating radar images confirm it's a First Nations final resting site."

The grand chief continued, "The images identified four adult skeletons wrapped in bark, surrounded by pots, beads, iron spearheads, and clamshells. Rather than disturbing the site, Kevin suggested placing a granite marker to honor the resting place of our ancestors."

"As a nation, we are always concerned about these finds. We know most authorities don't take them seriously," said Dr. Underwood.

"At a future date, we will assemble our people to perform a ritual that will signify its importance," said the grand chief.

"Shouldn't we notify the authorities or the coroner?" Olivia Francis asked.

"That won't be necessary, Olivia. Kevin didn't waste any time after they found the burial site. He has made sure it's protected under the Cemeteries Act. He also notified The Nova Scotia Museum that we will restore the area, clean it up, and erect a fence."

"I'm impressed. That will prevent the area from being desecrated, and our ancestors' graves are protected," said Dr. Underwood.

"While we are discussing the marker, may I suggest an inscription?" said Eva Prosper.

"Certainly, everyone is welcome to speak," said the grand chief.

"This is my suggestion: *Our ancestors' spirits will no longer wander and will live in eternal peace.*"

"A moving statement that defines our sentiment in an eloquent and befitting way," said René Doucette, normally an irascible and ill-tempered man.

"If we all agree on the passage, then I'll pass it on to Kevin to have it engraved. And with that in mind, I would like to close the meeting," said the grand chief.

***

A gust of salty sea air briefly made its presence felt over the excavation site. Tracy brushed her hair back across her ear and placed the orange wanderer hat over her tousled hair. She arranged the day's work schedule on the portable table. The breeze riffled the loose sheets across the work surface. A carefully placed coffee cup intercepted the migrating paperwork, enabling her to complete her task. Her makeshift office was covered by a canvas canopy tent, providing shade from the morning sun.

"Has anyone seen Professor Jordan or Mr. Yulin?" asked Tracy, now concerned about why her father and the historian were so late.

"The helicopter hasn't arrived yet. So, no," said Kian.

"All right, in that case, let's continue cataloging the tomb," said Tracy. "Deshan, Kian, Fields, Liao. I'll need your expertise; please come with me."

This was Tracy's core group of archaeologists who were the most capable of assisting in evaluating the contents. Historian Yulin would be missed.

Deshan said in Mandarin, "We're ready to proceed when you are!"

Tracy overlooked his rude behavior since she expected English to be spoken. She thought of her father and sighed. She was reluctant to proceed into the tomb without him but wanted to stay on schedule. She was becoming very worried. *Why hasn't my dad contacted me?*

"Everyone, please proceed to the tomb opening and wait for me," said Tracy as she stepped away. She called her father's cell, which went directly to messaging.

Next, she called the front desk of the Mira Suites Hotel and got the assistant day manager. She convinced him to check Jeffrey's room. Reluctant, since he was alone at the front desk, he agreed to call her back and let her know if he'd located her father.

A few minutes later her cell rang. "Tracy, this is Steve, assistant day manager. I entered your father's room, and he's not there. Could he be on his way to the airport?"

"Maybe. What about Yulin? He is also a member of the exploration team."

"It seems he checked out early yesterday evening after he was attacked in front of our hotel. Apparently, Mr. Yulin asked the valet to park Mr. Jordan's Mustang."

"Was he hurt?"

"Couldn't say. I was told little about the incident."

"Thank you, Steve," said Tracy, overwhelmed by sudden nausea. She knew what a kidnapping looked like. *Is that what happened to her father? And what about the jade-covered journal?* She told herself not to have these feelings. But it was hard to overcome. The trepidation was overwhelming. She reached for her inhaler. She had to do something and soon.

She found her contacts list and dialed Tom at the airport to see if her father had arrived by other means. She knew it was fruitless, but she had to try.

Tom responded. "I've been waiting all morning for them. The helicopter has been ready to go, but no one showed up," he stammered in frustration, feeling to blame for not reaching out to Tracy sooner.

"Okay, Tom, thank you. I'll take it from here and tell you if I find him. But be on standby if I need to fly back to Sydney."

Tracy called the Cape Breton Regional Police and asked for Sergeant Rideout.

"The sergeant is not here at the moment," said the officer on duty.

"My name is Tracy Jordan. My father is missing. Could you tell the sergeant to call me the moment he gets in?"

Tracy wondered why she hadn't asked Sergeant Rideout for his cell number at the demonstration outside the Membertou Heritage Park's cultural center.

"I'll let him know. But would you like to come in and make a missing person report?"

"Yes, I would. I can be there in a few hours."

Tracy knew it would take Tom at least an hour to fly to their location. She would have just enough time to examine the coffin discovered the previous day. Tracy went to the tomb, hoping her examination of the crypt would distract her from her emotions.

When she arrived, she paused and took audible breaths to clear her mind. Deshan and his group were lined up, ready to descend into the vault. Tracy took charge and entered first. The LED headlamp brightened the chamber. Her movements were brisk. Tracy stopped in front of the coffin and waited for her team. The coffin was a linear box with lacquered images along the surfaces. Time was not kind; the illustrations had faded.

"Everyone, please take a portion of the lid of the coffin and lift it," said Tracy. June got busy filming the proceedings.

Deshan, Kian, Liao, and Tracy removed the lid, and gently placed it on a cloth-covered wooden platform students had previously erected.

"The body is prepared in typical Muslim funeral tradition. It's wrapped in linens and bound with ropes to secure the shroud," said Deshan.

A crouching dragon carved in jade rested on the body's chest. Tracy slipped on cotton gloves to retrieve the statue. Turning it over, she discovered it was a seal.

"May I see it? I think my expertise is needed here," said Deshan.

Tracy sensed the professional tension building between Deshan and herself.

"In a minute," she said. "This powerful seal was used by the admiral to command the world's largest fleet."

She held the dragon aloft so everyone could see. Tracy saw Deshan wrinkle his forehead, quelling a scowl.

"The seal was his legitimate power for all his actions and policies on behalf of the emperor. I can translate if you like?" said Deshan.

"That's not necessary. I am well-versed on Ming dynasty linguistics," said Tracy.

Tracy ran her thumb over the inscriptions. Then brought the hefty object closer. In the old language, with perfect diction, she recited *"serenity, repose, strength of the sea."*

Deshan's eyes became stone-like and impenetrable. Tracy knew he had lost face. The other team members were rooted, awaiting a break in the tension.

The sound of a helicopter approaching penetrated the vault.

Tracy shouted, "I've got to go. My father may be in danger. Deshan, I'm leaving you in charge. Make sure the coffin gets taken to the university for further study."

Deshan softened. "We'll use traditional conservation methods. Also, we will document the research thoroughly."

She placed the jade dragon seal into a recovery bag and took it with her. She had a premonition to protect it. The jade journal was missing, along with her father and Yulin. She ran, then ducked her head, avoiding the propeller wash of the helicopter.

"Hi, Tom. Let's get out of here!" she said, buckling herself into the seat.

Tom engaged the cyclic bar and flew the craft back to Sydney.

Where is my father?

Fifty-Eight
We Could Lay a Trap

WILLIAM AND PATRICK watched as the Saint-Pierre forensics team tested the Jeep for fingerprints. The regional gendarmes compiled a report for their superiors. William and Patrick became weary, losing interest in the forensic process. It was a moot point since they knew who had driven the Jeep. The visiting officers felt obligated to be on good behavior in case it reflected poorly on their respective organizations.

"It won't take long for Ru to find out the real coordinates of the dig site," said William.

"We could lay a trap," said Patrick.

William shook his head. "We don't know how many men they have onboard the submarine."

"Then we need help. Will John give us any support?"

William was quiet for a moment as he considered the suggestion.

"Here's the deal. Let's find out where Tracy is because Ru will go there."

They stared at each other. The stakes were getting higher and higher, and both knew it.

"All right, I'll contact Deputy Minister Abbott," said William.

William explained how serious the situation was to John and requested assistance from the Ministry of National Defence. "The best way to fight a submarine is with a submarine."

John was taken by surprise. When he'd placed William Fox on special assignment, he did not expect this request.

"The submarines have been a nightmare to bring into service. Our Federal Government Procurement Department has been bargain-hunting. All four submarines are tied up for repairs and maintenance," he said, frustrated, as any public employee would be who had to justify this poor decision by their government.

"Is there any chance for at least one of them to get out to sea?"

"Unfortunately, no."

"Could you send a Canadian Navy destroyer with a task force to help us?" asked William, desperate for a positive answer.

"The corridors of Parliament Hill are fraught with pitfalls. If I do something like this, the Prime Minister's Office, the External Affairs Department, and my boss will not like it. I may be able to get the Joint Task Force 2. We can keep it extremely low-key and disguised as a military training exercise. For that, I need to call in a favor."

William felt relieved, even if the sensation only lasted for a few minutes. It gave him the strength to continue knowing that John would do everything possible to provide him backup.

William's satellite phone rang.

"Hi, Tracy. This is a surprise."

"William! My Dad's missing! He was supposed to show up at the dig site this morning but didn't. I called the police and made a report."

"Let me guess. The police are having a difficult time piecing it together."

"Could you please come and help?"

"Sure. Where are you? You may also be in danger."

Tracy told William the discovery site was in the Gabarus Wilderness Area. And that he should fly to Sydney and meet her at the Mira Suites Hotel. Since there were no immediate flights from Saint-Pierre airport to Sydney, Tracy arranged for Tom to fly the helicopter to Saint-Pierre and pick up William and Patrick.

***

In the taxi en route to the hotel, William phoned the Cape Breton Regional Police headquarters in Sydney and was patched through to Sergeant Rideout. He introduced himself and explained that he and FBI Agent Patrick Reilly were working on an ongoing case that may be related to the disappearance of Jeffrey Jordan.

"Patrick and I are meeting with Tracy Jordan at the Mira Suites and from there we will head over to the police station," said William.

As William and Patrick exited the taxi, Tracy ran over and threw her arms around him and started to cry. He held her tightly.

"It's going to be all right. We're going to find him," consoled William.

"I'm so glad you're here."

William lifted her chin, and their eyes connected in understanding. He held her close and stroked her hair. They walked into the lobby and seated themselves away from the reservation desk.

William gestured toward Patrick. "Tracy, you remember Patrick Reilly from Hong Kong?"

"Yes, I do. Thanks for coming, Patrick."

"Glad to be of help."

"What do the local police say?" asked William.

"Sergeant Rideout has a personal interest because he knows us. But he hasn't updated me on the investigation," said Tracy. "I think my father has been kidnapped."

"Why do you think that?" asked Patrick.

"It smacks of it."

"But who? Ru and the submarine vanished yesterday. They can't sail here that quickly," said William.

"Could it be related to something from my father's past?"

"Give me a minute," said William. He ambled to the hotel reception and spoke with the manager. He showed his credentials and requested the security video from the day before. The manager graciously provided the screen and the computer. William, Patrick, and Tracy watched the video unfold.

"The Cape Breton Regional Police have already seen the tape," said the manager.

"Here, look!" Tracy pointed to the ambulance. "Two men are grabbing my father!"

"Wow, Yulin tried to save him. That would have been a nice kick if he had completed it," said William. "Zoom in on the plates. There. We'll check, but they are probably bogus." He took a snapshot of the screen with his phone.

Patrick faced the manager and said, "We will need a list of the witnesses in the lobby who saw the altercation."

William added, "Also, we'd like to talk with the guy in the video who helped Yulin get up."

"Sergeant Rideout has all their statements," said the manager.

"The Mustang was removed by the Cape Breton Regional Police for their forensic investigation," said Tracy.

"The witness statements and the video footage can help us narrow down what happened," said Patrick.

"I am sure Sergeant Rideout will cooperate with you," said Tracy.

"He will. I spoke with him earlier," said William.

Tracy explained the police station was situated outside of the city and called an Uber to take them to the regional headquarters.

The police administrative building was boxy and fabricated in bright red brick. It had a cantilevered, hexagonal second floor shielded in white aluminum; it resembled a minimalist utilitarian structure designed for function over charm. The emergency services building was located across the street, and both projects had obviously been built by politicians on a fixed budget.

When they arrived, Tracy introduced Sergeant Rideout to William and Patrick.

"Glad to meet you," said William.

Rideout shook hands with the detectives. "Likewise."

William, not wasting any time, said, "Let's track the ambulance through its escape route."

Sergeant Rideout had the computer adeptness of a sixteen-year-old gamer. He plotted the route the ambulance had taken from the hotel to hanger nine on Airport Road.

"There it is. Abandoned," said Rideout.

"What's the time stamp on the video?" asked William.

"7:04 p.m."

"Contact air traffic control and find out what flew out around that time," suggested William.

Patrick gave Tracy a nod of reassurance. She was too despondent to react.

"Let me call since they know me," said Rideout, as he reached for his phone, spoke to his contact and hung up.

"Air traffic control checked the evening flight plans. An Avicopter AC352 with Chinese nationals had arrived and then departed later the same evening. Their visit had a special status as the group was on a humanitarian mission," said Rideout, conveying the distressing news.

Tracy choked on the bitter-tasting acid reflux.

"We have to get to the airport and speak with l'Agence des services frontaliers du Canada," said Rideout.

Patrick mouthed, "Agence des services what?" squinting his eyes in confusion.

"Mr. Reilly, that would be the Canada Border Services Agency," said Rideout.

Unfazed, Reilly stepped ahead and placed his hand on William's shoulder.

"You should go back to the hotel and take care of Tracy. Sergeant Rideout and I can get the necessary information. Besides, the Chinese nationals flew out to who knows where."

"He is right. We can be back later tonight and develop a game plan," said Rideout.

"Sounds good," said William as he slipped his arm around Tracy's waist and looked into her eyes. "It will be all right. They've got this," said William. Then he directed her away from the tactical room.

***

The cabbie drove them back to Mira Suites. Tracy invited William to her room.

"Is there a good place for dinner around here?" said William realizing he hadn't eaten since breakfast.

"There's an Irish pub around the corner," said Tracy.

She sat down on the bed's edge, put her head in her hands, and started to sob quietly. William opened the minibar, selected two Jack Daniel's miniatures, and poured them into a plastic cup. He sat beside Tracy, put his left arm around her, and hugged her. He handed her the cup. "Here, drink this."

She took a sip. "Thanks." Tracy gulped the rest and became steadier. She leaned tighter against William's muscular bicep, and he held her closer.

She knew William was kind and that he loved her. Tracy cared about him, too. That was her downfall. Her strong attachment to him increased her fragility. She was a career woman, and even though she'd fallen in love, she didn't need to settle down. But Tracy had fallen against her better judgment and ambitious nature.

William drew her to face him, surrounded her in his arms, then kissed her fiercely, achingly. Tracy kissed back, her tongue darting around his, their mouths crushing together, inseparable.

He pushed her down onto the bed, unbuttoned her blouse, and unzipped her cargo pants. Tracy released his belt, pushing down his trousers and pulled him onto her. Their bodies heaved through the ebb and flow of their movements. Finally, a pleasurable bellow from him, and from her, a satisfied gasp.

William slipped off Tracy and lay beside her, looking into her blue eyes. "Better?"

"Much better."

***

Tracy walked to the bathroom to take a shower. "I'm getting ready for dinner. You should clean up, too."

William got up and followed Tracy into the shower. She started to lather him up. The water was hot and comforting. They made love again. After the shower, they toweled each other off.

"We really need to get ready for dinner," she said.

Tracy applied makeup and fastened the silver dolphin earrings. She adjusted her plunge-cut backless green dress, sat on the bed, and donned suede green flats.

"Not only are you a great lover, but your fashion taste is equally unique," said William.

He stood beside her, dressed in a white button-down twill dress shirt, gray linen pants, and a black cashmere-silk blazer, which he had purchased from the hotel boutique.

"Don't you think we're a little overdressed for an Irish pub?" said Tracy.

"We're on a date. Just go with it. The distraction will be good for us both."

***

Tracy and William were escorted to a dark wooden table surrounded by captain's chairs. She remembered the scuffed flooring and the brass rail from her previous dinner with Kevin. William ordered drinks. A call interrupted before they could give the waiter their menu selection.

"Where are you two?" asked Patrick.

"We're having dinner at the Irish pub," said William. "Join us."

Patrick arrived fifteen minutes later and seated himself.

"What did you find out?"

"Air traffic control allowed me to view the security tapes. The Chinese nationals loaded a coffin-sized crate onto the chopper. 'Medical Vaccine' was stenciled across the box."

"That's it?" said Tracy.

"Canada Border Services agents didn't check," said Patrick.

"The box was a perfect size to hide a body," said William.

"Probably how they smuggled my dad out."

"Any idea of their current location?" said William.

"Satellite photos indicate a Chinese cable ship was their destination. Approximately a two-hour flight from the coast," said Patrick.

"I wonder how long we've got before they sail?" said Tracy.

"Probably not long. We need to delay that ship," said William.

William tossed back the remaining twelve-year-old Macallan single malt, then asked for the bill.

He turned to Tracy. "I'll walk you back to the hotel. Keep your cell on."

Fifty-Nine

Remember What the Prize Is

THE SUBMARINE SLIPPED covertly beneath the Atlantic and cruised away from Saint-Pierre Island. Ru and Captain Bush joined Captain Ho Chan in the control room. Ru took command. Both captains, used to being in authority, submitted power to the formidable triad boss. The overlord could kill them at any instant, given the slightest provocation.

"By now the French authorities have probably discovered the abandoned Jeep," said Bush. "They'll know we escaped by submarine."

"Captain Ho, sail her into international waters so we can evade the French and Canadian coast guards," said Ru. Chan ordered his crew to plot a course into the Atlantic.

"I'll be in my quarters," said Ru. "Call me when it's safe to resurface. I have an important call to make."

Chan turned to Bush and whispered, "What happened?"

Bush told Chan the events that led up to them being picked up by the submarine. He finished his account and said, "Ru is pissed because Tracy had misled us again."

Ru's misjudgment of Tracy was causing the crew to question their loyalty toward him. Even Dao, Bush, and Chan doubted his leadership. They knew he was neurotic and a brutal killer. What else could Ru offer now? They feared him, and because of Ru's frustration, he could become enraged with any one of them.

Ru returned to the control room and said, "Captain, bring the sub to the surface. I need to make that call now."

On top of the conning tower, the signal was strong, and Ru could hear Bojing clearly.

"I used my contacts in the government to trace the Jordans. Their credit card usage indicates they are in Sydney, Nova Scotia."

"Thanks. Now we know where they are. Tracy gave us the wrong coordinates."

"Really?"

The sarcasm did not escape Ru. "Once we get the treasure, I am going to kill her."

Ru descended the conning tower and directed Captain Ho Chan to sail the submarine to the coast of Nova Scotia, near Sydney. When they arrived, they waited in situ, just below the surface, unobserved by regular sea traffic.

Ru took the opportunity to discuss the plan with his men. "Dao will take a Zodiac watercraft to the coast and slip into the city of Sydney."

"Who do you want me to follow?"

"Tracy Jordan because you can recognize her. Watch her movements closely and follow her to the excavation site," said Ru. "Make sure she doesn't see you."

"Bush, you go with him. If there's trouble, watch his back."

"Meaning?"

"You're not a seaman now. Just do it," said Ru, his eyebrows coming together. He placed his hand on the butt of his gun for emphasis. Bush bristled. He didn't like being threatened. Ru handed Dao and Bush burner phones. Then, he gave them loaded firearms.

"Find the location, how many field workers, get a layout of the area. Don't get discovered. Call me when you find out and we'll take the appropriate steps."

Bush was impressed that, on balance, Ru could work a good plan. He started to feel better, even though he felt mistreated. Dao and Bush slipped on their kit bags packed with necessary clothes, documents, and phones. Their firearms tucked in their belts, both men climbed the conning tower onto the submarine's deck.

The coast was shrouded in darkness contrasted with the lights of downtown Sydney. The city's workers had departed as the night scene took over. The electric motor on the inflatable hummed. Its course varied against the tide. A profusion of buildings and streetlights provided a beacon and guided them ashore.

"Look, I know how you feel. Ru and I have been there before. But we are Foo Dog Triad brothers first," said Dao.

"He's pushy, and it gets to me."

"Remember what the prize is. You can put up with some crap."

"My time will come. Then we shall see."

"Take my advice. With Ru, his goals surpass any morals. He will do anything to achieve his objectives. That is the difference between you two. Bear that in mind next time you meet."

The Zodiac scraped along the beach as it landed. The Lingan Generating station loomed up in front of them. Stepping out of the watercraft, they bid the pilot goodbye. Dao and Bush crouched down, running from shadow to shadow. At last, they reached the employee parking lot. The night shift was in full swing. Dao and Bush approached an older Honda Civic. Dao picked it because it was nondescript.

"Keep an eye out while I shim the door," said Dao.

"How much time is this going to take?"

"Not long. In Hong Kong, this was my specialty."

Dao punched out the coiler mechanism on the steering column and used a screwdriver to start the car. "Jump in and let's get going."

He drove along Lingan Rd. and entered Sydney from the north. He found a professional building and ditched the car in the underground lot. He wiped down everything both he and Bush had touched.

They located the Mira Suites Hotel and set up surveillance across the street. Both took turns trying to spot Tracy. After hours of observation, the men were bored. Eventually, they saw her.

"That's her heading to the entrance. I recognize the guy with her," said Bush.

"He's a cop. Nearly killed Ru and me in Hong Kong."

"He was on the bridge of the Sofia's Odyssey, too. Let's be careful here."

"Time to improvise. I'm going to pick up electronic equipment and get a car rental. You find a room and get comfortable."

"Tomorrow, we can follow her. Hopefully, the cop has moved on, and if not, we can finish him off," said Bush.

"We shouldn't be presumptuous and provoke him. I've seen him in action. He's deadly."

"All right, we'll do it your way. Keeping in the shadows is not my style. But we have too much at stake."

***

In the morning, salespeople, tourists, and hotel guests kept the lobby busy as Tracy and William left the hotel. The guests were catching cabs or hailing rides that kept the doorman engaged and the vestibule crowded with milling people.

Tracy and William emerged, and she pecked him on the cheek before entering the cab. Dao and Bush were up at dawn and waiting nearby in the rental.

"Get ready," said Bush as he zoomed in the binoculars and got a close-up view.

Dao started the car. Tracy disappeared in the local cab and Dao got the nod from Bush to follow. As they went after the cab, Bush saw a Cape Breton Regional Police car arrive. He slouched down to avoid detection.

Patrick had borrowed a patrol car and picked up William. He was pulling out of the hotel driveway and directly faced Dao's rental. Dao drove slowly after the cab, looking forward, avoiding William's gaze. If he recognized him or Bush, he wouldn't hesitate to shoot. A ripple of concern passed across Dao's gruff features. Bush had never seen this side of him. He was relieved to see Dao was human.

"She is taking Regional Four," said Bush.

"The airport, just as predicted."

The cab dropped Tracy off, and she entered Tom's office to arrange a flight to Gabarus Wilderness Area. She was anxious to return to the site; knowing that William and Patrick were searching for her father gave her some comfort.

"You should've called ahead, Tracy. Someone else rented the helicopter for the next hour," said Tom.

"Oh, Tom, I'm really in a hurry today."

"Any word on your father yet?"

"Nothing yet, but I have a very close friend looking into it."

His phone rang. "Hang on a sec, Tracy."

Tom came back to the office and had a smile on his face.

"Good news, Tracy. The people changed their minds. I can take you; get ready."

The chopper lifted off revealing a tapestry below them of affluent ranch homes and inconspicuous apartment buildings. As the aircraft ascended into the azure sky, the buildings became small and insignificant.

***

"Did you get the GPS tracker attached to the helicopter?" asked Dao.

"Yes. Your diversionary tactic paid off," said Bush. "The tracker's tucked away where they won't be able to find it."

"Soon, we'll know the location."

Both men sat sedately. The rental car was across from the landing pad and behind chain-linked fencing. Dao opened his iPhone and chose the app for the tracking program. The men watched the helicopter disappear over the horizon. Dao was adept at these deceptive set-ups. Ru would praise them at this turn of events. An hour later, Dao raised his eyes from the phone and smirked. "Got the coordinates."

Sixty

Let's Go, Men

AFTER THE CALL to Ru with the coordinates, Dao and Bush retraced their steps back to Lingan Generation Station and waited till nightfall. When they reached the beach, Dao used the iPhone flashlight to signal the rubber raft to pick them up.

Ru was pleased that Tracy's location was uncovered and excited when he received the coordinates. Chan coerced everything from the propulsion system. The submarine arrived a short distance from their destination in Gabarus Bay.

The crew's mood was upbeat as the news traveled from bow to aft in the confined submarine. A wrench tapped water pipes in the engine room. Then, more sailors hammered at any exposed metal throughout the submarine until there was a cacophony of echoing acoustics. The leadership was loath to interrupt the roisterers, but soon the racket became unbearable. The captain picked up the microphone and asked for order. After a considerably long voyage, naval personnel and triad brothers were apparently united in solidarity, anxious to take the project to the next level. Ru and the top echelon realized the crew was once more motivated.

"I'm relying on your military background to quash and subdue the expedition team," said Bush directing the question to Chan but looking at Ru for approval. Ru said nothing.

"We'll surface and initiate drone surveillance to evaluate the terrain," said Chan.

***

The drone technician's joystick edged the aerial craft to the wilderness area across the bay. It swept over the empty beaches with its cameras displaying loose cobble, sand, and complex dunes. From the conning tower, Dao pointed at the lighthouse safeguarding the fishing village in the distance. "There could be curious fishermen if gunfire erupts."

Ru nodded but was focused on the progress of the radio-controlled aircraft. "Move it toward the meadow. There seems to be some activity and structures."

The drone diverted toward low cliffs of glacial till and drumlins in the distance.

"Take her up. Get a view of the whole area," said Ru to the technician, who dabbed perspiration from his forehead.

The miniature helicopter rounded the area, startling airborne cormorants and plovers. Satisfied there was enough footage to plan an assault the drone was guided back.

Chan ordered everyone from the observation platform and called for controlled descent of the sub, considering what Dao had said about the fishermen.

The submarine was positioned just below the waterline and out of view, while the team planned their invasion.

"The terrain is suitable for a direct assault," said Chan.

"The video shows remains of stone walls and building foundations. The area has fields and meadows intermingled with white spruce, providing good cover. Besides, workers are spaced out over the meadow," said Dao.

One of the naval officers asked what military strike they would employ.

"With enough combat-ready men we can overwhelm the group," said Chan.

"Excuse me, gentlemen. Forget a classical military strike. They only have a few security guards. I know this idea sounds too straightforward. But we can exploit the situation. Take out the guards and usher our men into position," said Ru.

"When do we commence operations?" Chan asked Ru.

"At lunch time. That's when."

"Send one of your men to reconnoiter the area. As the group assembles for their midday meal, we will deploy our team onshore," said Dao, who was on board with Ru now that the plan was clear.

Just before noon, Chan raised the sub to the waterline. Two of his trusted crew in a rubber raft traversed to the shore.

While in the Azores, Chan had arranged with a munitions dealer named Parabellum to deliver armor-piercing assault guns, previously stolen from the Russians. Before returning to Algeria, the gun dealer's parting words were, "watch out for the Jordanians, they think the guns are theirs."

The naval team picked up assault rifles and handguns and waited.

The triad spotter contacted Ru on the submarine and said it was a go. A few stragglers remained at the dig site, but most were seated for lunch. Ru rousted his team onto the inflatable boats, while Dao and Bush commandeered their teams as well.

The three boats arrived concurrently, carrying eight men each. The sound of boots hitting the gravel beach was faint. Ru smelled the wildflowers and grasses caught on the salty air. The spotter waved them up to the high ground. When the twenty-four men reached the cliff's pinnacle, the spotter pointed at the makeshift canvas canopy.

From the peak they could see a view of the bay and the old settlement. Staffers were milling about with plates in their hands. A buffet table laden with food and drinks was nearby.

"Let's go, men. Follow my lead," said Ru.

He dashed along a trail. His men fanned out and surrounded the lunch area. The assault force arrived before anyone realized the swiftness of the attack.

June dropped her plate. It smashed. Shards slashed the ground and edibles slopped everywhere. She thrust her hands on her head. "Oh, my God! Oh, my God!" she screamed.

The archaeologists and students showed alarm at the Chinese military strength.

Kevin Steptoe's two security men sprinted toward the infiltrators, pulled their Glocks, and aimed, but it was too late. Ru dashed behind a young student. Using her as a shield, he fired two rounds at the closest sentry. Blood and gray matter speckled the guard following him. But before the second guard could get a clear shot with his gun, Dao fired his Russian pistol. Two armor-piercing rounds penetrated the guard's vest and jolted him backward.

Dao approached the splayed-out guard who looked up at him, defeated. He clutched the pistol with both hands and pointed at the injured man.

"No, no, please, my family needs me," he begged.

Dao abhorred men who pleaded. He thought they were pathetic. Dao stepped over the man and pegged him above the eyes. A signature red dot froze the man's appeal for mercy mid-sentence. The man's body twitched.

"You Goddamn bastards. You have no shame," yelled Tracy.

"I've had enough of you. You're nothing but a fucking bitch. This time you will pay for your bullshit," said Ru, incensed by her independence and insolent attitude. He punched her in the mouth, splitting her lip, then tied her hands behind her back.

Tracy wheezed and gasped for air. "I need my inhaler!"

"You got to help her!" said Kian.

"Shut the hell up," said Dao.

Ru ordered his team to zip-tie the assembled hostages, and asked, "Is everyone here and accounted for?"

The captives looked at each other. Someone was missing but nothing was said.

"Bush, get your team and search the grounds, pick up any stragglers, and bring them here," said Dao.

***

Kevin was in the crypt, gathering information for the Mi'kmaq organization when he heard gunfire and screams. He made the final step on the ladder and poked his head out. He realized the area was overrun by a military force. Kevin pulled out his iPhone and scrolled until he found Sergeant Rideout's number.

Sixty-One

How Do We Keep the Ship from Sailing?

LITTLE WAS SAID as Patrick drove the squad car to Cape Breton Regional Police Headquarters and deposited the vehicle in the lot. By the time they entered the austere facility, William and Patrick were feeling the graveness of the situation. Sergeant Rideout greeted them and escorted them to a meeting room to discuss Jeffrey Jordan's apparent kidnapping.

"Let me know if you need anything," said Rideout.

"Last night, you said we need to delay the ship," said Patrick.

William searched the room with his eyes and then focused on the previous evening's conversation. "We know they're on a cable-laying ship. Is the ship there legitimately or as a front for the kidnapping?"

Patrick fidgeted in his seat and put his hand over his mouth while he contemplated William's remark. "You mean they aren't repairing cables."

"Talking about cable repairs, did you know about the town in western Canada that lost its internet service because a beaver had severed the fiber-optic cable?"

Patrick caught on quickly. "Was the beaver tapping it for free Wi-Fi service?"

"I don't think he liked the satellite bundling options."

Both men chuckled as their sense of humor returned.

"You know the beaver may have been searching for Sesame Street reruns," said Patrick.

Both men broke out in spontaneous laughter. William buckled over in a huge belly laugh, and Patrick slapped the table in unison.

The door opened, and Sergeant Rideout entered, baffled at the men. It seemed as if they had inhaled laughing gas. "Everything all right?"

"Letting off some steam," said Patrick.

The sergeant's entrance soured the mood. Rideout closed the door. William and Patrick returned to their discussion. Rideout wondered what kind of men he was entertaining in his station. Bemused, he walked back through the hum of the office.

"Back to work, William. How do we delay the ship?

"I'll get to that in a minute. When my father was ambassador in Korea, Jeffrey Jordan was stationed there. I remember him in and out of the American Embassy. We know that espionage agencies work through the embassies."

"Are you insinuating that Mr. Jordan worked for the CIA?"

"It could explain why he was kidnapped. Possibly by the Ministry of State agents. Maybe he pissed them off years ago and now they've located him."

"If it was Chinese agents, how would they play out this scenario?"

"Hypothetically, if it was me running this operation, we would be tapping cable for information while we kidnapped the asset. A classic example of Chinese efficiency in clandestine operations."

"Assuming your scenario makes sense. How do we keep the ship from sailing away with Jeffrey?"

"Flypaper. We manipulate the kidnappers to stay put, then trap them. Perhaps legitimately, perhaps not," said William.

"It was only a day ago he was kidnapped. Operations are working on getting some satellite photos. We'll know soon if the ship is still there," said Patrick.

Rideout entered the office. "I have a Kevin Steptoe on line four, he said. "There's been an incident at the dig site. I forwarded the call to your cell."

"This is Inspector Fox. How can I help?"

William put his phone on speaker so Patrick and Rideout could listen in.

"Inspector, this is Kevin Steptoe. I've been working with Tracy at the excavation site. We've been raided by a paramilitary force. Everyone else has been captured. What should I do?"

"Find out how many there are. I'll wait on the line."

Kevin stepped out of the crypt, and crouched down, trying to be as inconspicuous as possible. He hunched over and walked in the direction of the canopied lunchroom. He moved stealthily and slipped behind a porta potty.

"Are you still there?" asked William, concerned.

"Yeah, I'm still here, and I'm trying to get closer. I can make out over twenty men. They have semi-automatic rifles and guns. They're dressed in green military outfits. It's hard to see, but most of them look Asian."

"You! Stop there!" said the marine.

"They found me," whispered Kevin as the cell remained out of sight.

"Turn around. Give me your phone."

Kevin handed it over, the call still in progress. He was cuffed and led away.

William was not surprised at the turn of events. But he was concerned with the presence of an armed force. The mercenary didn't realize the phone was on. William listened, acknowledging how clever Kevin was. Any information overheard would be vital to planning a rescue.

"What are you going to do with us?" asked Kevin.

"Put you to work. You're going to carry the treasure out of the crypt."

"What about after?"

"That's up to the boss. Now get moving."

Kevin was pushed into the group of scientists. Tracy nodded at him.

The iron fist of the triad leader was about to fall on Tracy. Like many gang leaders, Ru was convinced all women were chattel, personal property to be bought, used, sold, or disposed of. He had fantasized about Tracy and wanted her after seeing her seminude on the *Lucky Star*. Now he had total control over her staff and could use them as leverage against her. Ru knew he could force his carnal lust on her. He reached out and tucked her blonde hair behind her ear affectionately.

"No! Stop it!" shouted Tracy.

"Don't touch her, you prick," said Kevin.

"Shut the fuck up," said Dao as he rammed his rifle butt into Kevin's head. Kevin fell to his knees, clutching his forehead to squelch the blood.

"The men are restless. Let's get going. You can fuck this bitch later," said Bush.

Dao was amazed Bush was still pushing his luck after his warning. Ru, on the other hand, was pissed off. But remained calm, knowing he and Bush would come to terms. *It would be a pleasure to off this fat pig.*

"Okay, get our team and the hostages together. Start a line of people passing the treasure and start loading the boats," said Ru.

"The sooner we can get everything into the submarine, the better," said Dao.

"Have you seen how much treasure is in the crypt?" said Liao.

"It will take a few days to do it carefully," said June.

"I'll send one of the men to take a look," said Dao.

"In that case, inform Captain Ho to submerge. We'll contact him tomorrow," said Ru. He looked at Bush, hoping he would mouth off. He imagined squeezing the trigger of the automatic pistol. Then watching Bush quiver and twitch with each bullet slamming into that overstuffed hog. Just thinking about it made him grow hard.

William caught snippets of conversation before the phone was turned off. He had learned enough. Everyone was in trouble. His earlier call to John about possibly needing military help was now a reality.

"I've got to go after Tracy and the science team."

"All right, leave Jeffrey to me," said Patrick.

"I'm taking Rideout's office for a private conversation with John," said William.

"I'll stay here and call the FBI director to organize a rescue plan."

"Let's keep each other up to date. These events could be linked."

"Agreed," answered Patrick.

"Say hi to Jeffrey when you see him," said William. He was out the door as his remark echoed in the hallway.

William strode through the office occupied by officers and detectives. Weighty conversations droned on from desks and cubicles. Rideout was gracious and understood the enormity of William's position. He stepped out of his office, allowing William to call John.

***

FBI Director Simmons picked up on the third ring. He hadn't heard from agent Patrick Reilly in quite some time. "Patrick, nice to hear from you. How are things going?"

The latest Democratic administration had placed Simmons in charge. Not because he was a liberal supporter but because of his experience. Before being shot in the line of duty, his years at the FBI had been exemplary, and his arrest record of the most notorious criminals was legendary. Now he relied on the use of a wheelchair, and its electronic functions were extensions of his brilliant mind. He liked Patrick's spunk and wished he could be part of his operation. Spending special attention to the Irishman and his missions was a secret pleasure.

"Jeffrey Jordan has been kidnapped by Chinese agents. He was flown out of Canada by helicopter, and it landed on a cable-laying ship in the Atlantic. Our concern is the vessel will leave before we can intervene," said Patrick.

"All right, here's what I'm prepared to do. I'll contact the US Navy for assistance, and the US Coast Guard, and have them send the closest ship."

"William suggested the Chinese are tapping the internet cable on the seafloor. That could be our excuse to board the ship."

"Stay where you are for the moment until I hear from the navy or the Coast Guard. Once we have a sea base of operation, we can formally board the ship."

Patrick put his cellphone away and scratched the back of his head. That part was easy. How long would he have to wait at the police station? Waiting was the hard part.

***

William settled into Sergeant Rideout's office, picked up the desk phone, and dialed Ottawa. John was in a meeting with a senator when his secretary interrupted them.

"Sorry to disturb your meeting. But I'm going to need that back up now," said William.

"I take it the discovery site has been located."

"Yes, they've been attacked, and hostages were taken."

"Just the way you predicted."

"That's right. One of Tracy's associates contacted me, and he explained what transpired. It's Ru's gang from Hong Kong."

"All right. I called in some favors, I'll have you know. First off, Joint Task Force 2 is on standby. This was not an easy thing to do."

"The team can meet me at Sydney airport. Once there, we can plan a rapid incursion. I'll make sure to have photos of the area."

"Lieutenant Colonel André Lévesque and his team will be there in a few hours."

William got up and ambled through the officers' bullpen. He leaned into the doorway of the meeting room. "My op is organized, and I'm heading to the airport," said William. Patrick looked up and covered the phone with his palm.

"Take care. I'll see you on the other side," said Patrick.

William left Patrick still on the phone with the director and walked out the front door of the police station, where he climbed in the back seat of an Uber.

"Where to?" said the driver.

"The airport."

William thought about Joint Task Force 2 and its stellar reputation, primarily its performance under demanding conditions. The team consisted of men and women with type A personalities, and like the US Navy's SEALs, they were taught to overcome the fear of failure. They were trained to capture strategic facilities in covert and brutal raids.

William had smashed numerous criminal organizations in the pursuit of justice during his career, but in this case, he couldn't just stroll in and arrest these mercenaries. Anticipating a gunfight where people could die, William knew he had to rely on the military specialists. He had been shot at by gangsters and criminals before, had trembled with fear, then overcome it. And for the first time, at the warehouse operation in Hong Kong, he had sustained a shot to the shoulder. Strong as he was, he had a hard time controlling his personal demons, now that the woman he loved was in jeopardy and could be caught up in the crossfire. William knew he needed every ounce of courage he could muster.

The distinctive clicks of the signal indicator interrupted William's thoughts. A crunch of gravel startled him. The car rolled onto the soft shoulder of the road.

"Is there's something wrong?"

The car came to a stop. The Uber driver turned to face him. The pistol was leveled at William's heart.

Sixty-Two

The Xin Feng

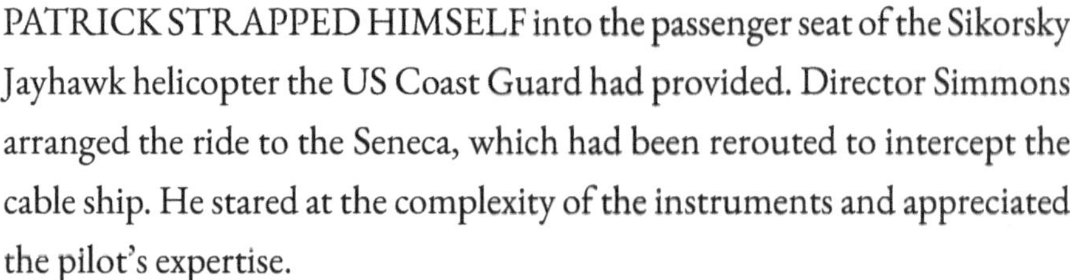

PATRICK STRAPPED HIMSELF into the passenger seat of the Sikorsky Jayhawk helicopter the US Coast Guard had provided. Director Simmons arranged the ride to the Seneca, which had been rerouted to intercept the cable ship. He stared at the complexity of the instruments and appreciated the pilot's expertise.

Patrick addressed the pilot, "How long before we arrive?"

"Couple hours should do it," said the pilot.

"Did you catch the game between the Boston Bruins and the New York Rangers?"

"Very colorful, sir. The Rangers gave the Bruins a lesson in civility."

"The Rangers play the Montreal Canadiens tonight."

"I think the Habs will keep the Rangers on their toes."

The pilot turned toward Patrick and tapped his headset's earphone to indicate a message was coming through. "Sir, FBI Director Simmons is on the radio."

Patrick nodded. "Hello, sir. What have you got for me?"

"Good news. The Seneca will be at the Chinese ship's location by the time you arrive."

"Any preliminary information before I get there?"

"Our team identified the Chinese cable ship as Xin Feng. It carries a deep-sea exploration submersible called Fendouzhe. They are at a sea depth of approximately two thousand meters. It would take an underwater robot about three hours to contact the sea bottom. Then a few hours to tap in and extract information from the cable, finally ascending back to the surface. The process takes twelve to thirteen hours."

"This will give us time to get our plan operational."

"You have the full force of the American justice system behind you."

"I'll keep you apprised." Patrick grimaced and folded his hands. He was on the verge of exhaustion. He closed his eyes. A slight rest was better than none. Drifting off, Patrick knew the countdown for Jeffrey's freedom was approaching.

"We're landing," said the pilot, waking Patrick from his snooze.

"Thanks for the lift. I'd put money on the Rangers."

The pilot gave him the thumbs up.

As soon as Patrick set foot on the *Seneca*, he was welcomed just like his previous visit.

"Welcome back, Patrick," said Captain Green.

"Glad to be back. Hope you don't mind me taking over the ship again?"

"No problems. We all work for the greater cause."

Patrick entered the bridge of the formidable gunship. Green told Patrick about the logistics involved in boarding the *Xin Feng* in international seas. With the *Seneca's* advanced technology, the search and rescue vessel was ready to flex its muscles. Her radar sensors and transceivers collected vital information to locate the cable ship.

"What reason should we give the captain of the *Xin Feng* for boarding his vessel?" asked Patrick.

"There are many reasons we can use. Fishing or pollution, implementation of international security standards, or one of my favorites, customs and smuggling," said a lieutenant. Captain Green gave his young officer, who had overstepped his authority, a stern look. The lieutenant flushed in embarrassment.

"Patrick, leave it to us to get you on board. I have a lot of experience dealing with captains from foreign countries. In this case, United States codes allow us to board any ship, make inquiries, inspect, and search if we feel they have violated United States laws. In this case, the submersible may be tampering with the international fiber-optic cable. That alone gives us all the authorization required," said Green.

"Not to mention hostage-taking is a federal criminal offense according to the Department of Justice code 18 USC 1203. It applies even outside of the US territory," said Patrick.

The lieutenant, still unable to curb his enthusiasm, offered more proof of his argument. "Last year, we stopped a Columbian fishing boat and searched for five days before we found 26,000 kilograms of cocaine hidden under the fish tanks."

"Yes, we can keep them tied up as long as there isn't any political intervention," said Green, shaking his head at the young man. "I feel the best approach is to investigate why the *Xin Feng* is positioned over cable lines," he added.

"Sounds good. I'm going to the mess hall. I haven't eaten yet," said Patrick.

***

A few hours later, Petty Officer Noah knocked on Patrick's cabin door and said, "We're here. Captain Green has informed Captain Gao of the Xin Feng for our reason to board."

Patrick stepped away from the cabin. "Does he suspect we are searching for Jeffrey?"

"If he does, then he is playing us because he offered no resistance," said Noah.

"I'd like Captain Green's impressions of Captain Gao," said Patrick.

Patrick followed the petty officer and trudged to the bridge. His heavy boots trundled on the metal stairwell. He noticed the Chinese ship from the landing as he entered the bridge.

"Captain Gao is not resisting?" asked Patrick.

"He insists that he has permission to examine the cable for damage. He has documents affirming the work order," said Green.

"Let's see the documents."

"Captain Gao said Chinwah Optics Electric was selected to upgrade the system."

"This falls under my purview. Homeland Security has mandated the FBI to intervene in US telecommunications security."

"The patrol boat is being lowered in the water. You better get down there, pronto," said Green.

Patrick hurried out of the wheelhouse, just in time to join Petty Officer Noah and the boarding team. Settling in between well-equipped personnel, he grabbed onto a rope and held on. When the patrol boat hit the water, the motor started up, and they were speeding across the short expanse to the Xin Feng.

"Follow my lead and stay within regulations. Got that?" said Noah.

The Coast Guard team members acknowledged the squad leader. Patrick didn't get perturbed when Noah took control. He knew better than to interfere with those who were there to help him. Patrick decided he would take charge, when necessary, in the interest of his country's national security and for the safe return of Jeffrey.

***

Ren Bo was distraught with the developing circumstances, especially after Captain Gao stated he was amenable to the American demands.

"Why are you cooperating?" asked Ren Bo.

"Don't worry. We have legitimate reasons to work on the cable. There are documents to support this," said Gao.

Ren Bo immediately radioed Guan to explain their dire situation. "Under no circumstances are you to turn over Jeffrey Jordan. Also, destroy any information you don't want to fall into American intelligence hands."

"I've made arrangements. The Americans will not find him."

"The president expects you to deliver him. My reputation and yours are at risk if we fail."

"I won't fail. But the death of General Po is also a high priority. Something about this entire incident is perplexing, and key facts are linking up. Nothing concrete, but I'm sure it will come to me."

"Hold your ground for now and contact me if the situation becomes untenable."

"I have to go. The patrol boat is approaching."

Ren Bo slipped the radio handset back in its cradle and turned toward the captain.

"What do you propose I do with our guest?" said Captain Gao

"Already taken care of."

***

Noah and Reilly, and the intervention team boarded Xin Feng. The Chinese marines stood down while the Coast Guard team scoured the vessel, searching for Jeffrey Jordan. Noah scrutinized the documents Captain Gao had provided. Hours of searching turned up nothing but frustration on the part of the investigation squad.

Patrick was losing hope that Jeffrey would be found alive. He pulled Ren Bo aside and prepared to debrief him. Patrick sat opposite him in the meeting room, adorned with communist propaganda posters and pictures of state navy officials.

"Let's not waste any time. We know you are a State Security agent of the Chinese government. And you have kidnapped an American citizen. This ship is not going to be released until we find Jeffrey," said Patrick.

"My captain assures me that we have reasonable grounds to be working on the cable. This man you speak of is not here," said Ren Bo tersely, placing both palms on the table, primed to rise up in anger.

Patrick matched his body posture, leaned in, and leered at him. "Sit down until I'm finished with you."

Ren Bo, a man of action and independence, reclined reluctantly. "This action is unwarranted and will be met with political sanctions from our government."

"So be it," said Patrick. He abruptly left, his chair spinning, as he stormed out of the room.

Patrick made his way to the bridge and met with Noah.

"I'm not making any progress with the state agent," said Patrick.

"Nor am I with the captain and crew," said Noah.

"I know he is here somewhere. Let's look a little harder and see if there is something out of place."

Noah contacted the squad via the Motorola handsets and dispatched his men around the ship once again.

A Coast Guard crewman approached Noah and Patrick with a peculiar dilemma a few hours later. "Sir, there is docking for two submersibles. The submersible servicing the cable returned hours ago. It should have been obvious one was missing. The Asian crew camouflaged the sea vessel's cradle, so we didn't notice the first time around," said the junior crew member.

"That son of a bitch. They have Jeffrey concealed in the submersible!" said Patrick.

The wheelhouse was becoming crowded with personnel as Noah and Patrick burst in, furious with the Chinese nationals' behavior.

"Bring up that submersible right now before you create an international incident. We are prepared to escort this ship to the nearest United States harbor," said Noah.

"All right, all right," replied Captain Gao and ordered the bathyscaph technician to recall the Yongshi to the surface.

The submersible was eventually lowered from the stern boom crane, upon opening the hatch, a pilot, a guard, and Jeffrey exited the vessel. The Chinese marines and six coast guard crewmen looked on. The Seneca drifted meters away with the bow cannon aimed at the bridge. The scene was tense, not unlike the Cold War days with Russia. Patrick was first to reach Jeffrey and escorted him portside.

Patrick was about to help Jeffrey down the ladder to the Coast Guard patrol boat when Ren Bo defiantly stepped in front of their way and trained his sidearm at them. Before Patrick could register surprise, seven marines surrounded them. Even Petty Officer Noah wasn't prepared for the hostile challenge.

"Everybody, return to the aft and be seated. The Chinese government will not allow American intervention in multinational seas," said Ren Bo.

"We have a great navy presence in the area and can take this vessel by force," said Noah.

"Yes, you can. How many lives will be lost over this man? Consider that," said Ren Bo, who had taken command, superseding Captain Gao.

"Everyone, stay calm. This is a political situation for our respective governments to rectify," said Patrick, who was coming to realize that this standoff was tenuous at best and explosive at worst. The time for diplomacy had arrived, and he knew he was out of his element. This was not a textbook hostage situation taught at the academy.

Sixty-Three

Do Something Before I Bleed Out!

WILLIAM STARED at the gun in his face and realized he had been too preoccupied to be on full alert. He appreciated the perfect stopping point—a remote, barren field with very little traffic and thick brushwood ideal for depositing a lifeless body.

"Get out slowly," said the burly man. With his left hand, he reached behind his back, opened the car door, and slid out. Then, he stood with the gun braced across the roof. William exited from the rear passenger side and stood beside the car, hands clasped on his head.

William took stock. The man resembled a beefy wrestler who had fought one too many rounds. His prominent features consisted of mangled ears, dull eyes, and a scar carved from the corner of his lower lip to his chin. A formidable triad killer, it would be a challenge to put him down, but not impossible.

The ambusher walked around the front of the Toyota Corolla until he stood firmly behind William.

"Spread your legs," ordered the triad gangster as he placed the muzzle of the Russian pistol at the base of William's skull. Then he proceeded to tap William's lean frame down from shoulder to ankle.

"Are you carrying?" He found the Smith & Wesson tucked under the front of William's black jacket. "Sure, you are." He removed the gun and lodged it under his belt.

His ambusher stepped around to face him. William glanced at him, looking for an opening that would allow a swift strike but found none. "You work with Ru. Am I right?"

"I'm your welcoming committee, you dumb cop."

"That's a yes. How did you find me?" William intended to keep his ambusher engaged as he formulated his scheme to free himself.

"We discovered a cell call was purposely left accessible by one of the captives. Then we traced the call back to you. Believing that you heard too much, we needed to make you disappear."

"It's too late. Our police forces are aware of the triad's plans."

"Start moving, now," said the assassin forcing the gun into William's back. The solemn walk to his death was through high vegetation and toward a copse of pine. The hard metal barrel made William wince with every step.

William and his instructor Mr. Kim had mastered a technique not shared with the taekwondo students in class because it was very dangerous with only half a chance of success.

"Keep going toward the pine trees," insisted the gangster.

William shuffled along submissively, then without wavering, abruptly bent his knees and twisted right like a corkscrew. The gun discharged; the noise ear-splitting as the heat of the bullet grazed the fabric on the right shoulder of his jacket, the projectile landing harmlessly in the thicket. By then, he had completely turned around and his left hand grabbed the assassin's bent elbow and wrapped his right hand and arm around the gun. William pushed down on the assassin's forearm in a burst of strength, forcing the triad man on his knees, simultaneously wrestling the pistol from the gangster.

William gripped the unfamiliar gun firmly, took aim, and shot the assassin in the thigh to disable him. Any information from him could be vital and killing him would prove nothing.

"Yeow," he cried as he fell onto his back. You, fucken prick!"

"Hand me my gun. I could kill you right now. Consider yourself lucky."

The gangster passed the gun to William with one hand and held the puncture with the other, attempting to stem the profusion of blood seeping through his slacks. Panic conveyed on his face as the ruby liquid created a broad motif, like a spilled glass of French claret.

"What's your name?" William asked.

"It's... it's Shrimp Boy, but I... I prefer Raymond," he said, grimacing in pain.

"Okay, Raymond. You know you're in deep shit."

"Do something before I bleed out!"

"You won't bleed out. The bullet missed your femoral artery. I'll call an ambulance but, first, some information."

"The brotherhood doesn't speak to cops."

William knew Joint Task Force 2 was in the air and would arrive at the rendezvous soon. He was out of time to conduct a by-the-book interrogation. He fired a round between Raymond's splayed legs. The slug kicked up dirt and dust. The prisoner hurled himself backward, disbelief and panic turning his legs to rubber. Raymond understood his bravado and arrogance weren't enough to save him.

"Next one will not miss."

"Ru sent me to kill you."

"Tell me something I don't know."

"I have to stop the bleeding!"

The assassin yanked his shoe off, grasped his sock, and wrapped it around his thigh to squelch the oozing. His eyes never left William and the Russian pistol aimed at his center mass.

"There is no time left. My only option is to finish you here and now."

"You can't! Even cops have morals."

"I have no morals for men like you. Not when innocent people are in danger," said William. "This is too grand a scheme for Ru. I need to know who is really responsible for this plan."

"If I tell you... You're not going to kill me, right?" he whined.

"Here's the deal, tell me who is responsible, and then you will get medical help."

"All right. The Chinese cultural minister organized the whole scheme. His name is Chu Bojing."

William looked for tells through neuro-linguistic behavior but saw none. The man was being truthful. Probably this was the most arduous transgression he had ever perpetrated against his triad brothers.

"How do you know about this?"

"It's a long trip in a submarine from Hong Kong to Canada. Men talk, and word gets around."

"Tell me how you tracked Tracy Jordan in Hong Kong."

"We had help from a military satellite."

"How does a common street gang get access like that?"

"Rumor is Chu Bojing bribed General Po from the Space Administration," said the gangster. He flinched in pain.

"That's it?"

"Yes. That's it. I need a doctor!"

"What happened to the general?"

"He was found dead. Suicide."

William had a nagging suspicion that all was not what it seemed. So, he persisted in his questioning. "Would you say Ru or Bojing could have been responsible for General Po's death?"

"I can't say, but anything is possible with those two."

William had heard enough.

"What happens now?"

He lifted him and cuffed his ambusher's wrists behind his back and placed him in the trunk of the Toyota.

"The airport is only a few kilometers away. There is medical staff to help you." He slammed the trunk door.

William slid in behind the steering wheel. He was anxious to arrive at his meeting with the commando team. The information he extracted from the gangster was important.

The Toyota was hardly a race car, but it managed to stay fixed on the asphalt even at the high speed William maintained. It weaved and sagged, its dampers and coils getting a racetrack workout. Eventually, reaching the airport, William brought the car to a screeching halt in the small parking lot northwest of the main terminal.

William hauled Raymond out of the trunk, lowered the passenger window, then cuffed Raymond to the door pillar. He phoned airport security and explained the situation. Minutes later, he heard the chuff, chuff, chuff of the Griffon helicopter blades chopping through the eddies of its wash. Joint Task Force 2 had arrived.

***

William waited for the blue-gray chopper to land on the triangular patch of grassy real estate. The field housed two hangers opposite each other on a service road leading to the northwest parking lot.

The smaller hanger would be used for organizing the hostage rescue. The lieutenant colonel jumped out first, followed by his ten-man team. William escorted them over to the hanger away from the noisy conditions, where they introduced each other.

"Hi. I'm Inspector William Fox with the RCMP."

"Good to meet you. Lieutenant Colonel André Lévesque from Joint Task Force 2."

William and André convened the squad around a makeshift table of steel fuel drums and planks scrounged from the hanger.

"Do you have the satellite images?" André asked.

William picked up his phone and selected a couple of buttons. "On their way," he said.

André and his team gathered around their linked-up computers. André pointed out how he expected the hostage rescue to unfold. William looked on, following the military strategy that linked weapons and troops into cohesive warfare.

"This area is the size of a major league football field." André pointed to the screen. "See here. Building foundations, white spruce here, and cedar trees bundled in pockets there."

"My source told me they are being held under that tent," said William, highlighting the structure south of the pond and west of the crypt.

"Once we land, the sniper team will proceed to the ridge. Brick One east side of the tent and Brick Two west. I'll be on the ridge with the sniper and his spotter. William, you are with me until we have the hostages secure," said André.

"Bricks?" said William expressing confusion over the terminology.

"Military-speak for teams."

"We should act when it's their dinnertime."

"That's the plan. Time on target will be limited to avoid casualties."

"As soon as you have the hostages secure, the Cape Breton Regional Police can take over. Your task force can get back to base."

"Roger that," said André.

The task force spent the afternoon resting and enjoying ready to eat prepackaged meals. The sandy-haired, brown-eyed sniper ravished a veggie omelet while his spotter joked about it being a "vomlet." The sniper smiled and offered up his omelet to the spotter, who turned up his nose. Many team members found the two men's interactions hilarious and broke out in laughter.

André had them refocus and go over the battlefield environment to review the course of action. Before the sun began to drift over the airport terminal, André mustered the team and boarded the Griffon helicopter. After flying south for an hour, the Griffon swooped in over the meadow as specialists dropped smoke grenades while the chopper was landing. The task force wasted no time hitting the ground.

Brick One ran entirely around the artifact storage area. With the drumlins and Gabarus Bay on their flank, they swooped the perimeter to the east of the tent and took positions in old building foundations.

Brick Two assaulters ran through the smoke toward the west end of the tent while André, William, and the sniper team scampered up the drumlin and took positions on the cliff, overlooking the meadow.

The spotter assigned the targets, and the sniper with the McMillan Tac-50 terminated two triad sentries consecutively. Assaulters forced themselves into the tent area, shooting noncompliant gang members. Brick One surrounded the captives and defended the area. As Brick Two secured the tent and set up an eastern flank, much of the triad gang dissipated and scampered toward the old stone foundations. Trapped in the crossfire, Brick One assaulters shot and killed many criminals. Within ten minutes, the task force had decimated the gangsters, the few remaining surrendering.

Ru, Dao, Bush, and a few gangsters ran toward the beach to regroup and counterattack.

William, André, the sniper, and the spotter focused on the breakaway group. André laid down a rain of machine-gun fire from a Heckler & Koch MP5. Dao took a chain of projectiles across his chest, nearly severing his torso. He fell back, his finger frozen on the Russian Vintorez, spewing rounds skyward as his body dropped. A gangster returned fire with his automatic pistol, penetrating the protective vest of the spotter who died instantly. Seeing his comrade fall, the sniper instinctively swooped around and fired a 50-caliber bullet. It removed the top part of the gangster's head.

When more gunfire erupted, the onslaught forced Ru and Bush toward the opposite side of the rock and sand dunes.

In a sweeping motion, William spun, raised up the Smith & Wesson, left hand supporting the gun hand. Sighting the gangsters, he emptied half a dozen rounds into a pattern no one could avoid. Bush took the majority and collapsed in a heap, twitching uncontrollably as his life drained away from him. Ru, who was beside him, dove to the ground. Shaken by the loss of so many triad members, Ru hid behind a rubber boat shrouded in dried underbrush. The few remaining gangsters scrambled further away, leaving Ru in a compromised position.

William took a spare magazine from his jacket, reloaded his gun, and ran in a stoop searching for his target, clenching his teeth together until his jaw muscles hurt. His concentration was intense. He found a cover position behind a sea battered stump washed up meters from a heap of dried brush. He could clearly make out the figure of Ru crouching there. William nodded at André and the sniper to provide cover fire, enabling William to execute an aggressive flanking maneuver to be in a more favorable firing position. Tracking left to right, William changed direction and joined the other task force team raining Ru with rounds.

While Ru was cowering under a shower of 9mm rounds, William sprinted like a Greek Olympian and covered the distance in mere seconds. André and his sniper ceased their onslaught, astonished as William ran and jumped up into a classic flying kick. With his right leg extended and left tucked under, his muscled torso soared like an airborne cheetah. William gripped the Smith & Wesson in his right hand, never wavering his aim. Ru rose from a prone position, elevating his Russian pistol and firing. Not used to the wide grip and powerful recoil, it was unwieldy to master for an average user. The more powerful ammunition bucked the gun upward and away. The bullet missed William as his right leg impacted Ru, who dropped the sidearm. The force of the impact lifted him up on his toes. The gangster had the breath driven out of him. William skidded to a halt, turned, and trained his sidearm on Ru.

Ru tried to recover by bending over and breathing heavily. He was humiliated. Again. His martial arts skills couldn't help him now.

"Finally, we meet again. Your time as a free man is up," said William.

André ran over to assist William and quickly zip-tied his quarry.

"Thanks for the assist," said William as he stood staring at Ru, inhaling deeply after his own exertion.

***

Captain Ho Chan put away his marine binoculars, resolved that the mission had failed. The glint from the sniper rifle telescope on the crest of the cliff and echoes of gunfire was ample confirmation. He lost hope as the team hadn't returned, and Ru ignored his phone calls.

Chan decided to save the submarine and his remaining crew. He knew the military sniper would alert his troops to the submarine's position. Curious fishermen from the village were aroused by heavy gunfire and took to their trawlers. Chan secured the conning tower compartment outer doors, then slid down the ladder and into the command center and ordered the submarine to dive. The helmsman set a course away from the turmoil. Chan couldn't help thinking that the mission failure was a result of Ru's overconfidence.

***

The task force sniper sweeping the cliff scoped the submarine just as it slipped away. With no time to react effectively, the sniper decided not to fire on the vessel. He notified André of the submarine's escape and the eager fisherman navigating into the bay.

"Nothing you can do. Just get yourself back here fast. We are ready to fly out," said André to the sniper. Headed to the tent, the sharpshooter lifted the dead spotter and used the firefighter's lift to carry him downhill, careful not to trip over the uneven ground.

André's team began assembling at the tent. The 427 Special Operations Squadron pilot engaged the Griffon's helicopters drivetrain, the aircraft propeller's vibration resonated across the meadow and beckoned the task force like a mythical piper.

André turned to William, "Do you want a job with my unit? That was some very nice shooting back there, and you can run like a gazelle. Good qualities for a task force member."

"Thanks for the praise but let me think about it."

Ru became restless and began straining at his bonds. "Fuck you two. I'm a Chinese citizen and demand to speak to my embassy." He was becoming belligerent and regaining his arrogant command style.

"In due course, in due course," said William, as he lifted up Ru's shackled arms and frogmarched him into the tent.

The task force carried their fallen comrade and entered the helicopter, soon to be airborne, on their way back to base.

The task force and Cape Breton Regional Police helicopters passed each other. The first group had finished their mission, and the second group was ready to begin theirs by processing the crime scene.

***

Watching the task force helicopter disappear, Tracy turned to her staff. "Everyone, I recommend we take some time off to recover from this ordeal. Also, you may know that my father has been kidnapped and I am very worried." Murmurs of support were heard among the group.

Tracy redirected her gaze toward Kevin. "I am so sorry for the loss of your security men. Please give my condolences to their families."

"It's a devastating loss to our community." Kevin looked exhausted. "I have arranged for off-duty police officers to guard the archeological site."

"Thank you, Kevin."

The scientists and students stood huddled in a group, as Tracy retrieved her cell to call Sydney Helicopter Service. "Tom, it's Tracy. Can you please fly out here? We need transportation for the entire team."

"Be there in a jiffy," he said.

While Tracy and the science group were waiting for the helicopter, she noticed William was busy speaking with Sergeant Rideout. She was anxious to see for herself if he was okay and sent him a text.

William saw Tracy's message flash across the screen.

Are you okay?

Yes, and you?

Okay. Really worried about my dad. Do Rideout or Patrick have any news?

Not yet. Will call you as soon as I know more.

Sixty-Four

Their Own Brand of Justice

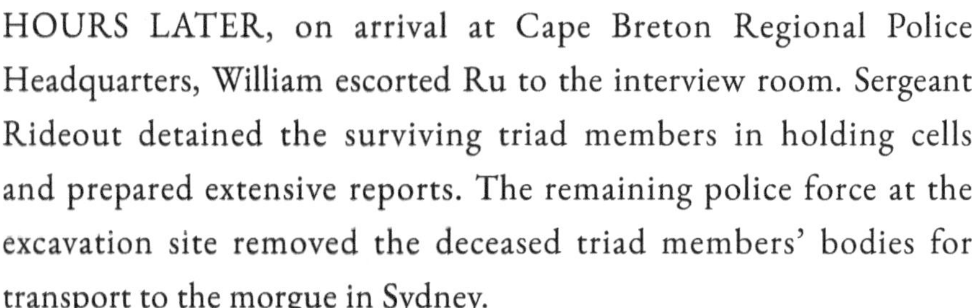

HOURS LATER, on arrival at Cape Breton Regional Police Headquarters, William escorted Ru to the interview room. Sergeant Rideout detained the surviving triad members in holding cells and prepared extensive reports. The remaining police force at the excavation site removed the deceased triad members' bodies for transport to the morgue in Sydney.

William found an empty detective's office and called John at the Department of National Defence in Ottawa."

"How did it go, William?"

"We got the ringleader, Ru. Unfortunately, there were casualties, including one of the members of the task force."

"How about the submarine?"

"Got away cleanly."

"Are Tracy and the site team safe?"

"Yes, they're safe. The task force was absolutely the best."

"I'll leave it to you to process everything."

"By the way, how is the scene on Parliament Hill?"

"So far, only the joint operations commander knows about our so-called military exercises. So, let's keep it that way. Ottawa has had its share of recent scandals."

"Okay, sir. Thank you for sticking your neck out. For all of us involved."

As soon as William finished speaking to John, he immediately got on his cellphone and contacted Patrick.

Patrick put the cellphone to his ear to avoid any verbal spillover. He looked at Ren Bo, expecting his disapproval. The scene on the aft section of the ship was still tense, but now all eyes were on Patrick as he answered the phone.

"Patrick, we managed to capture Ru."

"I wish I could get excited, but I'm under the gun. We located Jeffrey on the Xin Feng, but a Chinese state agent named Ren Bo has taken command and won't let us leave. We are in a bit of a stalemate with no resolve in sight. The Coast Guard cutter Seneca has its cannon trained on the ship. It's very tense, and we need some sort of diplomatic resolution."

Ren Bo became progressively agitated, as did Captain Green on the Seneca, who watched Patrick pacing back and forth through his binoculars.

Patrick alluded to Ren Bo that he needed some privacy while ambling toward the main superstructure. As he listened to William, he began to feel relieved as a plan was emerging from the nightmarish standoff. While hunched up against a lifeboat, he continued listening to William's idea.

"I propose a hostage exchange," said William. "Ru has information on the death of a General named Po. My preliminary investigation indicates that General Po commanded the Chinese Space Administration. He was blackmailed by Chu Bojing, the Chinese cultural minister. I have a third-party confession, which suggests Ru and Bojing are complicit."

Patrick's Motorola two-way radio buzzed. He asked William to hold and addressed Captain Green. "Yes, sir, something is happening. RCMP Inspector William Fox has a plan we are discussing right now. I'll get back to you when I know more," he said and signed off.

Ren Bo and some of the crew were getting restless as they watched Patrick speaking on his cell.

"Ru could be valuable to the Chinese. They will want to interrogate him about his involvement in General Po's death," said Patrick. "Besides, the Chinese administration would probably insist on their own brand of justice."

"Precisely. Start a dialogue with Ren Bo on the off chance they want Ru to testify. See if that sparks Ren Bo's interest. If it does, you can handle the rest."

"I'll tell FBI Director Simmons to hold back on the state department negotiators for now."

It had been a few hours since the standoff began, and the swells in the ocean were menacing as the wind picked up. A gray cloud mass was developing on the southern horizon and was racing toward both ships.

Patrick hung up the cellphone and approached Ren Bo, confident that a solution was imminent. "I have someone valuable for you to consider exchanging for Jeffrey Jordan."

Ren Bo squinted his eyebrows together, took a deep breath of exasperation, and asked the marines to lower their assault rifles.

"Who is this person you're speaking of?" asked Ren Bo.

Petty officer Noah stepped away from his squad to stand beside Patrick as he felt this turn of events needed backup.

"We have Ru Fa Zhong, a Hong Kong ringleader of the Foo Dog Triad in custody who can testify to General Po's death," said Patrick.

Ren Bo grabbed his ear and fiddled with the golden stud while contemplating the offer. "I have strict orders not to release Mr. Jordan."

"I'm offering you and your government a way to resolve the situation without anyone getting killed. Or, for that matter, causing an international incident. The last thing we need is for the media to accidentally discover and report this event."

"Give me a minute to speak with my superiors."

Ren Bo brushed by the marines, pulled out his phone, and dialed Beijing.

The wind picked up and blew his jacket open as he traversed across the open deck. The cloud band was closer now, the storm gradually advancing.

After concluding his call, Ren Bo stepped around Noah and Patrick and stopped in front of his marines. He had spoken with Yin who had expressed reservations about disappointing the president. This could prove dangerous for them both. If she offered an alternative solution, she could avoid political suicide.

Yin explained her reasoning to Ren Bo that vital information could shed light on General Po's death. And if it was suicide or made to look like suicide, a final resolution to the matter would put the Communist Party at ease and they would find out who was behind the affair.

A major international crisis between China and the United States could be averted by resolving this stalemate at sea. If the incident ever became public, all parties would deny it.

A drizzle filled the air as both ships noticeably began to rock back and forth, the white caps heaving aggressively.

***

Captain Green was extremely curious about the behavior on deck. He took the initiative and called Patrick a second time on the Motorola two-way radio. "What's your status over there, Patrick? Weather conditions are deteriorating fast. We need to consider moving off."

"Looks like a go for a hostage exchange, but I'm waiting for a firm answer," replied Patrick. "Gotta go. Ren Bo is waving me over."

"My superior concedes we have common ground and is agreeable to the exchange. We await the arrival of Ru Fa Zhong," said Ren Bo.

"Give me a few minutes to arrange that," said Patrick as he threw a thumbs up in the direction of the *Seneca's* bridge.

Captain Green shook his head in bewilderment and mumbled, "I'll be damned."

Patrick leaned on the railing for support as the approaching storm buffeted the *Xin Feng*. He called William at the police headquarters in Sydney.

William picked up in anticipation of Patrick's call.

"We have a deal. Get Ru out to the *Xin Feng* right away," said Patrick.

***

Anticipating that the hostage exchange would take place, with the support of several police officers, William had already escorted Ru to the airport. He had prearranged a Bell helicopter to be on standby. The helicopter service was owned by former Royal Canadian Air Force officers who had combat experience flying tours of duty in Afghanistan.

Getting Ru on board the ship was the highest priority. When William received the confirmation from Patrick, he initiated takeoff with the pilot, reaffirming the distance and coordinates to the boat. The former officer was concerned by the Doppler weather report, but William insisted they could pull it off.

"We are on our way. Our estimated time of arrival is one hour, thirty minutes," William said.

"Copy that," said Patrick.

Patrick kept his elated emotions in check. He turned toward Ren Bo, made stony eye contact with him, and said, "We should discuss the exchange details."

"Agreed," said Ren Bo.

"When my people set down, we will bring the prisoner along the aft deck and exchange midway," said Patrick, pointing to an area beneath the massive crane in front of the cable carousel.

Ren Bo was equally firm, authoritative, and nodded. "Let's make it quick. The weather is getting worse, and my captain estimates the main storm front will arrive in the next two hours."

***

When the helicopter with William and Ru reached the cable ship, the pilot was apprehensive about landing on the pitching deck. Again, William reassured him and impressed upon him the importance of the prisoner swap.

"Everyone is ready to expedite the exchange of the detainees. We should be in and out before the storm breaks," said William.

"I'll risk it. But it's a tricky job," said the gray-haired pilot who had flown similar sorties for NATO.

William and Ru exited the chopper, preparing for the roll and pitch by optimizing their stride and gait. With this awkward manner of walking, they descended from the top level to the main deck to meet Patrick.

"You can't hand me over to these communists," shouted Ru, knowing there was no Dao or gang to help. William and Patrick each supported an elbow as they whisked him bodily aftward.

"Bring him over," yelled Ren Bo, standing legs spread, battling the wind and spray while the marines stood stoically behind him.

Ren Bo looked at Jeffrey and said, "Go!"

Jeffrey staggered across the pitching deck. He looked worn and exhausted, and William could see the cuts and bruises on his face. Clearly, he had endured the typical Chinese torture methods of being beaten and kicked. As the detainees passed each other, the look of defiance and fury on Ru's face shook Jeffrey.

Ren Bo seized Ru under his cuffed hands and hustled him away.

Turning back, he said, "I suggest you all leave. Now!"

The wind whipped up a dizzying twister of sea spray and drizzle, showering all on deck with a heavy deluge, threatening to hinder their departure.

After the exchange, Petty Officer Noah gathered his Coast Guard squad together. They departed in the patrol boat and battled the rough sea back to the Seneca.

Captain Green, relieved that the exchange was a success, prepared his ship to sail away from the storm.

William turned to Patrick and shouted, "Let's get the hell away from here!"

Patrick grabbed Jeffrey and helped the bruised man off the helipad and into the chopper. William eased the battered professor gently into the seat and strapped him in.

The veteran pilot hastily swung the Bell aircraft away from the fierce weather and directly toward the coast of Canada.

"Thanks for the help, brother," said Patrick to William.

"Anytime, pal."

"How are you holding up, Jeffrey?" asked William, angry they would beat an older man.

"I'll be fine. You guys were terrific," said Jeffrey.

"What a relief to see you again," said William. He patted Jeffrey on his knee affectionately.

William placed a call with his satellite phone and said, "Yes, we have him." Smiling, he handed the phone to Jeffrey. "Someone wants to talk with you."

"Tracy! I can't wait to see you again and get back to work," said Jeffrey. "I love you, too." Jeffrey handed the phone back to William.

"Let's get you back to Sydney and cleaned up," said William.

"I sure could use a shower!"

"Then you can tell us what this kidnapping was about," said Patrick.

***

Captain Gao resumed command of his ship now that Ren Bo's operation was over. The submersibles were on board, and the hostages were exchanged. The approaching storm front was almost on top of them; it was time for the *Xin Feng* to get underway. There was no earthly reason to be pounded by an Atlantic nor'easter.

"First officer, chart a course around this weather pattern," said the captain.

Ren Bo took a deep breath and sighed, confident that Yin could explain the change in plan to the president. He would make sure the incident would be covered up, and the crew and Captain Gao would remain quiet or face severe consequences in Beijing.

He escorted Ru into the lower decks past the common rooms to find a makeshift brig.

"Make yourself comfortable. It's going to be a long trip to Beijing." He shoved the disheveled man into the cramped bosun's locker.

Ren Bo noticed a manilla envelope tucked in Ru's back pocket. It was addressed to him.

Sixty-Five

Coming to Grips

THE CAPE BRETON Regional Police Station was busy, and the officers were well organized in their division of labor. Most of them carried out procedures or processed administrative data or evidence of some sort, whether it was weapons cataloging or fingerprinting, examining shell casings, or managing prisoners. Specialists had been called up from the RCMP Halifax office to help with the overload.

In William's temporary office the morning sun's brightness filtered through the horizontal blinds, casting zebra-like shadows across his desk, where he was typing multiple reports.

During his coffee break, William wondered how Jeffrey and Tracy were dealing with their traumatic experiences. He knew they would need time to recover. Not everyone had nerves of steel. *Would they ever be the same? For that matter, would he?* He continued to prepare his statement of events reliving the stressful moments of the past few months. His biggest concern was that Ru might get away with murder. But that was out of his hands.

John would certainly follow up with him on the military operation results. Messages of thanks would be sent to the gendarmes on Saint-Pierre for their cooperation. The RCMP in Newfoundland would also require a report.

He lifted his cup for another sip and found it empty. How many was that now? Two or three? *Oh well, another coffee would help move this thankless exercise along.*

William pushed back the office chair and walked to the kitchen, passing through the busy and chaotic activity of the constables.

Sergeant Rideout saw William slicing through the office. He stood up and waited for him to arrive at the metal desk he was leaning on.

"How's the report going?"

"It's going to be lengthy, to say the least," William replied, his eyes weary.

Rideout evaluated William. He saw a trodden individual too tired to carry on. His team was there to help sift through the overwhelming material that William and the joint task force had accumulated.

"You have been at it for hours. Take a break," said Rideout.

"Good idea," replied William." I'm outta here." He stepped back into the office to retrieve his blue Harris Tweed sport coat and sunglasses.

William grimaced as he passed Sergeant Rideout on his way to the front door. "I can finish up later after I bring Tracy and Jeffrey to the meeting."

"Be back at 2:00 p.m. sharp for the Zoom conference with the top brass."

"Oh, with our illustrious government leaders and flunkies. Did I miss anybody?" said William realizing he sounded like a jerk.

"Hey, I get it. It was tough out there. But do you have to be so sarcastic?"

Patrick overheard the conversation and poked his head out of the office he was occupying. "I'm holding off completing my reports until the conference call. A lot of the information is sensitive."

"I'll see you at 2:00 p.m.," said William.

"Can you bring back a box of donuts? My treat."

"All right. But you should watch that waistline."

Patrick smiled. "I didn't know you cared!"

William clenched the arm of his sunglasses between his teeth, muttered something inaudible under his breath, turned, slipped on his sport coat, and headed to the parking lot.

"What's gotten into him?" said Patrick.

"Don't know. But he needs an attitude adjustment," replied Rideout. "Tracy will smooth out his wildcat nature."

"I hope you are right. Because we're going into a Zoom meeting with powerful and overly critical people."

"He'll be fine," said Patrick as he stepped back into the office.

***

Jeffrey and Tracy were at the Mira Suites Hotel in Sydney, recovering there until they could find permanent accommodation.

Jeffrey was resting his haggard body, attempting to gain back his strength and, most importantly, his composure. The medical staff at Cape Breton Regional Hospital had dressed and bandaged Jeffrey's wounds and then sent him away with a few Tylenols for the pain.

Tracy was emotionally drained from the dread of her father's kidnapping and then the traumatic abuse he suffered at the hands of the Chinese. At least he was here and not in Beijing being tortured, or worse sent to a prison to be lost forever.

She, too, was coming to grips with her own demons.

***

William arrived at the front of the hotel valet parking area and pulled the Explorer over to a concrete portico pillar. He locked the vehicle, left the flashers on, and entered the hotel as casually as a bishop entering his basilica for vespers.

Tracy answered the door on the third knock and allowed William to enter.

"How are you holding up?" asked William, hugging her.

"Shaky but getting better."

"How about you, Jeffrey? Still have some of that English mettle?"

"In spades," replied Jeffrey squinting through a bandaged eyebrow.

"Enough to entertain coming to the police station for an interview?" asked William trying to be friendly but not official.

Tracy and Jeffrey looked at each other

"Sure," said Tracy.

"Me too," said Jeffrey.

"Good," said William.

"Give us a few minutes to get ready," said Tracy.

Within fifteen minutes, the police vehicle was weaving through afternoon traffic. The mood was cheerful as William was delighted to be in Tracy's company. His disposition was no longer laconic, and he became lively. Tracy felt his warmth and telegraphed it back by touching his knee. There was that recognizable feeling of trust and compassion William longed for. He broke out in a broad grin, conveying with his eyes he loved her.

Jeffrey observed the private moment and broke the tacit communication between them. "Ahem, ahem," he coughed.

"Are you okay back there?" asked William.

"Never better. How are you two?"

Tracy turned around to her father, blushing a faint pink and revealing a disapproving frown. Her message was quite clear. Jeffrey sat back, stifled a smile, folded his arms across his chest, and distracted himself by looking out the window.

"We should be there soon," said William.

They arrived at the police station just before 2:00 p.m. and joined Patrick and Sergeant Rideout in front of the large monitor in the meeting room. A pitcher of water and half a dozen glasses sat in the middle of the extended, well-used table. Adjacent to the water tray, William placed an open box of fresh donuts and seated himself to the right of Tracy. Kevin Steptoe entered the room and seated himself on her left. Patrick and Jeffrey joined Sergeant Rideout on the opposite side. Patrick reached over and helped himself to a big chocolate frosted sinker and bit off a large chunk.

"Is there anything better than a chocolate glaze?" he asked rhetorically.

Everyone was focusing on the impressive flat screen in anticipation of the conference. Rideout clicked the cursor on the encapsulated message "Join Meeting" to start the zoom session. Video images of Deputy Minister John Abbott, FBI Director Simmons, the prime minister's chief of staff, and the group from the police station in Sydney appeared on the screen.

John shuffled a stack of dossiers in front of him, looked into the camera, and addressed the gathering.

"Since the kidnapping incident occurred on Canadian soil, I will chair this debriefing. I trust everyone knows each other except for Alexa Farouk, chief of staff from the Prime Minister's office. Any information deemed sensitive should be discussed with their own government officials later. Everything that pertains to this case can be shared as freedom of exchange between our two countries. Let's begin with a short summation from Jeffrey about his kidnapping."

Jeffrey reached over and filled a glass with water, then refreshed his dry mouth with a short sip. "In my earlier career as a professor of archaeology, the CIA was also my employer. As a federal agent, my job was to recruit top scientists from other countries. We were acquiring talent at scientific conferences around the world. My kidnapping may be tied to our assignment to recruit Dr. Chen Hao, a specialist in material physics and chemistry. I approached him at a conference, offering a position in the space shuttle program. His closest friend was Wei Lei, who was responsible for the Chinese delegation at the conference."

The chief of staff blurted out: "The president of the People's Republic of China?"

"The same. At the time he was just a representative. The extraction was foiled by Chinese state security agents. Later, I learned that Dr. Chen had been taken back to Beijing and hung for treason."

"So, you believe it's revenge playing out here," said Director Simmons, who was leaning closer, his white eyebrows furrowed.

"The more I've had time to think about it, yes." Jeffrey used the armrests of his chair to shift his aching body into a more comfortable position.

"Okay, Tracy," asked John, "What about your take on this? Primarily why so much interest from the triad about Admiral Zheng He's treasure?"

"A little history, Mr. Abbott," she replied. "It's about why there are so few great treasures of cultural significance in China now. During the Cultural Revolution under Mao Zedong's direction, his Red Guards destroyed literature, scrolls, and priceless antiques—"

Jeffrey interrupted with his notable "Ahem," his frequently annoying fatherly quirk. "The official campaign was called the Destruction of Olds."

Tracy shrugged his behavior off as if a fly had buzzed her and there was nothing to it. "Historically, the Communist Party's strategy for power was to mobilize the working class by destroying the middle class, their values, traditions, and beliefs. The Party then allowed a few select individuals economic control over the entire population.

"Today there is a new cultural hunger by the wealthy. It's a movement to reclaim their prized cultural heritage. They want to bring home the antiquities that were misappropriated over the centuries. China's flourishing economy has encouraged the rich to acquire Ming dynasty relics. That's why there is such an interest. Not to mention the high value placed on these types of treasures by Sotheby's."

"That explains the triad's interest," said FBI Director Simmons.

"What we discovered at Gabarus Wilderness Area is significant," said Tracy.

"Enough to kill for," said John.

"Yes, sir. The deaths of all those people are tragic."

"The Chinese ambassador has already approached our office with demands," said Alexa.

"Will the US be making inquiries?" asked John.

"No, not our domain. Agent Reilly, your thoughts?" said Director Simmons.

Before Patrick could reply, Kevin stood up abruptly, overturning a glass and spilling water. Everyone stopped talking.

"I'm sorry." He pulled a tissue from a box and wiped up the mess. "The Mi'kmaq have an interest as the discovery is on First Nations land," he said, tossing the wet wad in the wastebasket.

"Yes, that's true," said Tracy. "And we have a signed agreement attesting to a joint cooperation."

"Duly noted," said John.

"The federal government will honor the agreement," said Alexa.

"Over to you, Patrick," said Simmons, perturbed by Kevin's interruption.

Patrick spent ten minutes relaying his experiences so that everyone was clear on his participation.

"Thank you, Patrick. We need you on the next available flight to New York. We have a new assignment for you."

"I can catch the afternoon flight with Air Canada."

John turned the conversation toward William. "I expect your written report tomorrow. But what can you add now?"

William spent twenty minutes explaining the circumstances and the journey across the globe before finally closing in on Ru Fa Zhong, then exchanging him for Jeffrey.

Rideout reported next that all the evidence was being processed and presented to the Department of Justice and the attorney general. His department also released a story to the local media about a military training exercise.

"That should explain all the shooting and smoke," said Rideout.

Deputy Minister Abbott and FBI Director Simmons were satisfied by the verbal reports from everyone present.

"Let's wrap this meeting up," said John.

"Before we all go, I would like a private word with Inspector Fox and Deputy Minister Abbott," said Alexa Farouk. "Everyone, please give us the room."

Chairs scraped the floor as the group disbanded. Rideout clicked the door behind him. FBI Director Simmons signed off, and his screen went blank.

When Alexa was satisfied the room was free, she examined her laptop and looked up again.

"This should come as no surprise to you, John. The prime minister was very impressed with the positive results. William, your behavior was exemplary. The prime minister is creating a position that suits your special abilities. That is if the deputy director agrees," she said, nodding toward John.

John had been in Ottawa long enough to know when to bend with the wind. "My pleasure to serve," he replied.

"William, how do you feel about expanding your role in protecting Canada's interests?" said Alexa. "The PM's office wants you to work with the Canadian Security Intelligence Service, the Five Eyes Alliance, and the RCMP."

"May I think about it?"

"Don't think too long. We have a time-sensitive assignment."

"All right, I get it," said William. His shoulders sagged. "Will John be my contact?"

"Yes, for now," she said.

William didn't like Ottawa politics but knew his duty. "Can I take care of some personal matters first? It should only take a few days."

"That will be fine," she said. "Report to John next week."

"Oh, by the way we just received a report from the Hong Kong constabulary that should please you. They have captured Captain Ho Chan and the remnants of the Foo Dog Triad on their return to Hong Kong. The submarine will be returned to billionaire Qi Ping."

"What about Yulin, the guy who stole Admiral Zheng He's jade journal?"

"Through diplomatic channels, we have learned he was apprehended and incarcerated by the Chinese mainland police before he could find a buyer. The journal is being turned over to the minister of culture, who plans to put it in the National Museum of China, in Beijing."

"I am sure Tracy will be interested to know this," said William.

Sixty-Six

It Starts With You

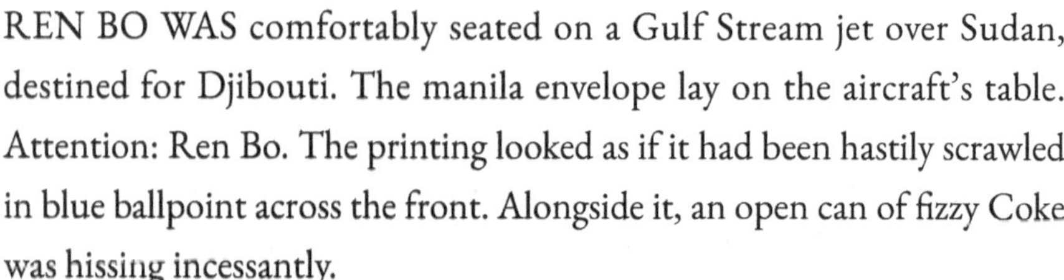

REN BO WAS comfortably seated on a Gulf Stream jet over Sudan, destined for Djibouti. The manila envelope lay on the aircraft's table. Attention: Ren Bo. The printing looked as if it had been hastily scrawled in blue ballpoint across the front. Alongside it, an open can of fizzy Coke was hissing incessantly.

He was tired, he took a swallow of sweet cola. The energy boost was welcome as the caffeine and sugar would fortify him for the next few hours.

Fingering the envelope, he wondered who had placed the enigmatic envelope in the back pocket of Ru's trousers. The mystery would be over soon as he reached for his pocketknife to open the taped-up flap. Quenching an insistent thirst, Ren Bo took another swallow of Coke; the carbon dioxide globules tickled his nose. He pinched the bridge between his thumb and index finger to relieve the irritation from the bubbles.

Ren Bo looked toward the rear of the cabin and set eyes on Ru, handcuffed in slumber with an IV drip in his arm. A fentanyl cocktail was subduing him until they would reach Beijing. He gazed through the porthole, mesmerized by billowing cloud formations. The moving terrain below it coursed along a trajectory where lush jungles met vast desert landscapes. Occasionally, his stare was drawn away by the glint of the sun on the aluminum wing.

Back to business, he flicked out the sharp blade from his pocketknife, slid it under the flap, and cut the tape in an even-handed stroke. He removed the glossy photograph and noticed a handsome man in uniform smiling and standing in front of a helicopter. Dark and swarthy and, in his estimation, Slavic-looking. Maybe of Russian descent. A Canadian Coast Guard emblem adorned the aircraft. Ren Bo turned the photo over and read.

This is Victor Stupendski, a Canadian murdered by Ru Fa Zhong. Multiple witnesses, including myself, were there. The Canadian government will want Mr. Zhong extradited to stand trial. I trust you can arrange that after he testifies. Any overture to an entente between our countries would be a significant step forward.

It starts with you.

Respectfully,

Inspector William Fox, RCMP

Ren Bo was astonished. He was unaware of an unspoken arrangement between himself and the RCMP officer. Puzzled, he knew it was not up to him to make this decision. A nagging sense of guilt came and passed in an instant. Perhaps there was a hint of camaraderie between the two men as they both did their jobs honestly, bringing bad actors to justice.

Out of a sense of professional courtesy to William Fox, he would approach Yin and see if there was a possibility to help the Canadians since he understood China and Canada were not doing well in the political arena. Ren Bo drained the can of pop, stretched out, and decided to get a few hours of sleep before arriving at Djibouti.

The layover was prompt and efficient, allowing a doctor to examine and clear Ru for further travel.

The last leg of the long flight to Beijing took more than twenty-one hours on the Y-20 military transport. Exhausted, Ren Bo made his way into the State Security Building from the airport. On arrival, he entered his director's well-appointed office, the manila envelope gripped firmly.

"You've arrived. Finally, we can get to the bottom of this," said Yin.

"Yes. Ru Fa Zhong is being held and remains to be questioned."

"Please be seated," she said.

Ren Bo moved closer and caught a trace of fragrance as Yin passed him. She glided to her desk like an ageless goddess and sat down. Yin was dressed in an elegant two-button pantsuit, complemented by her signature Gucci flats. She had selected dark gray pointed ones to match her ensemble. Yin always dressed well, setting an example for other accomplished women. Patriotic, she was partial to EP or Elegant Prosper, one of China's oldest fashion brands. Ren Bo envisioned her lithe body under the classic-fit suit, and it was electrifying. Shifting his weight, he felt riveted in place by her strength and beauty.

"You can begin," she said, her mouth turning up, creating elegant lines fringing her enchanting eyes.

His chinos started to become snug, so he crossed his leg over in an awkward shift. Did she see my desire, and does she feel the same?

Yin was amused by the effect she had on Ren Bo but stifled her smile.

His verbal report was a rehash of the interview with Captain Li of the Lucky Star, and the events leading up to the apprehension of Jeffrey Jordan and the final exchange for Ru Fa Zhong.

Ren Bo felt anxious as his mission had not gone as planned. "At least we managed to salvage the operation with Ru as a witness to General Po's death."

"Your report is satisfactory," she said, as she rummaged through the dossiers embossed with red stars. "President Wei Lei may have a dimmer view of the outcome."

Ren Bo slid the picture across the table.

"What's this?"

"The RCMP officer who arrested Ru addressed it to me."

"How does that affect our case?"

"It's a photo of a Canadian Coast Guard pilot killed by Ru. They want him back for trial."

"We shouldn't promise them anything until we question Ru. Also, President Wei Lei will have a word to say about it," she said. "Definitely not an easy solution. You question Ru, and I will speak with the president."

The phone intercom rang, and Yin pressed the button to listen. "Send her in."

The female officer dressed in a Red Army uniform entered after a solid knock on the door. "Madam Minister, we have found Professor Peng Lixin dead in a remote northern village." The officer handed the director a report describing how Peng Lixin was murdered.

Yin waved her away.

"Is that pertinent?" asked Ren Bo.

"The professor was in contact with Minister of Culture Chu Bojing."

"Oh, is that a coincidence?"

"Too much of one, I suspect. We will know more after questioning Ru," she said. "You are dismissed.

He rose and left the room.

***

Ren Bo was in his office preparing his written report to be sent by encrypted email to Wei Lei and Guan Yin.

A heavy pounding on his door had an urgency that he could not ignore.

"Come," he shouted.

"Colonel, the prisoner Ru Fa Zhong is dead," said the corporal.

"What?" Ren Bo swore under his breath.

The corporal stiffened at the fierce expression on Ren Bo's features.

"Take me there now!"

He pushed out his chair, and it tumbled to the floor. Racing after the prison guard, they were in the lower levels of the security building within minutes. The frightened corporal opened the door to the high-tech cell. Ru was hanging from the upper bunk bed with a tightly coiled blanket around his neck. Ren Bo grabbed Ru's wrist and checked for a pulse. There was none.

"What the hell kind of security do you have here? You stupid shits!" yelled Ren Bo staring at the prison guards. "Search the building and find the killer."

Ren Bo ordered the entire complex to be shut down and a thorough search was initiated. The alarm rang throughout the compound.

***

Hours later, the interrogator approached Ren Bo. "I got a confession. You won't believe it!"

"What is it?"

"Chu Bojing bribed guards to let the assassins into the prison. He was behind the murders of not only Ru, but Professor Peng Lixin and was complicit in the death of General Po."

Ren Bo waited for the interrogator to leave his office and placed a call to Yin. "Chu Bojing is the man responsible for the murders. I am assembling a team to arrest him."

***

Ren Bo and the state security agents entered the National Museum of China, where Bojing was overseeing the installation of a new display featuring Admiral Zheng He's jade journal.

Surprised, Bojing said, "What are you doing here?"

"You are under arrest for severe disciplinary and legal violations. In other words, corruption, blackmail, and murder."

"This is outrageous!"

"Using the triad to do your dirty work is outrageous."

"I was doing this for our country."

"Men, take him into custody."

Ren Bo and his team left the museum and brought Chu Bojing to the Central Commission for Discipline Inspection where he was placed in a holding cell.

Speaking to the prosecutor, Ren Bo said, "Under the guise of repatriating Chinese artifacts, this man ordered the murders of three people."

"Do you have evidence to support this?" asked the prosecutor.

"Yes, we have a confession attesting that Chu Bojing and the triad were working together."

"Damn him. He was the mastermind of the whole affair," said the prosecutor. "With a charge like this, the Beijing High Court will sentence him to death by hanging. His organs will be harvested and used for medical or scientific experiments.

"Not a total loss," said Ren Bo.

***

Yin and Ren Bo could no longer deny their attraction and were consumed in a blinding fury of lust.

They embraced in her office, kissing passionately, forgetting all the troubles around them. Yin's intense desire had devoured and exhausted Ren Bo, who was sprawled on the couch like a spent stallion. His breaths became less labored. He was satisfied, like the greedy fox that devoured the chicken. Yin buttoned up her top and brushed her hair in place.

Ren Bo regained his composure and zipped up his pants. "He really thinks the government is his to run as he pleases," he said, speaking of President Wei Lei.

"Let him believe what he wants. Finding General Po's murderer and removing Chu Bojing from the Party was more important than a personal vendetta against the American professor."

***

President Wei Lei had watched the pair embracing and listened to them discussing him. Staring at his computer screen two buildings away, he smiled. During Yin's office restorations, his team placed hidden cameras and microphones into the lighting system. This deception allowed him audio and visual of her entire office. There would be no secrets in his administration.

President Wei Lei pretended to be pleased with the apprehension of Chu Bojing. For now, he had to focus on more pressing international matters which consumed his daily agenda. He was still mourning the loss of his old friend Hao and vowed to continue his vendetta to apprehend Jeffrey Jordan and exact his revenge.

Sixty-Seven

Hold On!

TRACY AND HER father were poking through debris under the sifter screen, searching for First Nations artifacts. The cool breeze from the bay moderated the intensity of the black flies, a sign that warmer weather had arrived.

"Is Brenda Tadler coming from the Smithsonian?" asked Tracy.

"Yes. She is collecting Mi'kmaq artifacts for the museum."

"I hope you two are going to enjoy each other's company."

"Most definitely," he said. "How are you and William doing?"

"Great. We have been talking and texting almost every day. "He's had a lot to deal with, but he is finally accepting that what happened in Seoul was not his fault."

"The two of you are good for each other."

"Yes. He's been very supportive of me, too. I'll never forget the feeling of helplessness being kidnapped, but... having William to talk with about it, and you too, Dad, really helps."

Jeffrey smiled at his daughter. "When does your flight for Montreal leave?"

"Very early tomorrow morning." Tracy looked up at her father and smiled. "I can't wait to see him."

***

Tracy's Air Canada flight from Sydney arrived at Montréal-Pierre Elliott Trudeau International Airport on time. She was surprised at the ease of departing the aircraft and soon found herself outside the arrival area. Standing among passengers waiting for taxis or limos or family, the warmth and radiance of the sun provided a comfortable moment. She adjusted her knapsack to shift the weight. William had suggested she travel light because they were taking the Triumph Rocket on their trip to Toronto.

After a few minutes of watching travelers heading home, she heard the rumble of the motorcycle. Leaning out over the curb, she could see William approaching the taxi stop. He stopped, boots touching the ground as he supported the heavy bike. William removed his helmet.

As Tracy stepped off the curb, a gust of wind playfully blew her blond hair about, she tucked a strand behind her ear and smiled at him.

"You look great," he said.

Tracy leaned in and pressed her lips to his. "You are the best part of my day."

William's eyes took her in, and he smiled. "You're so distracting. It's going to be hard to keep my mind on the road."

"I'll squeeze you if you ever waver."

"Now, that I can appreciate," he said, as he started to hand her the spare helmet.

"Hold on a sec," Tracy said. She rolled her long hair into a bun, and tied a red kerchief around it, took the helmet from William and put it on.

William looked over at the irate passengers at the taxi stand, restless with the delay he and Tracy were causing. He raised his hand and said, "A couple more minutes, please."

"Can't wait to see your mom and brother after all these years."

"They were so excited when I told them we're back together. They can't wait to see you either."

Tracy swung her leg over the seat and settled in behind William embracing him tightly.

"Hold on," was all she heard before the Triumph accelerated away, its departure echoing against the acoustic glass panels of the airport terminal.

Acknowledgements

My first novel was the combination of input from many generous people. I am deeply thankful to my wife Angela van Breemen for her encouragement that grounded me during the many years it took for the first draft. Her support and eagerness to read and help edit the final drafts were immeasurable and her experience in website design created a conduit for readers to find me.

Next is Christopher Bird who is by far the pinnacle of all this by way of his gift of a Gavin Menzies book called 1421 which outlines the voyages of Admiral Zheng He. Gavin's book contains mountains of research that sparked the story.

Also, my sister Elizabeth Pontsa-Mueller and my brother-in-law Dieter Mueller have my deep respect for their candid remarks on the various book covers they reviewed for me.

My sincere appreciation goes out to the Wordsmiths writing group who listened to my readings and provided their input to the book cover design.

Also, I'd like to mention my membership in the Crime Writers of Canada. Their mentorship program, the zoom meetings I attended, and the kind words and review of the story summary inspired my deep conviction to finish my manuscript.

I'd also like to mention Richard Scarsbrook and Judi Penz-Sheluk both great authors for their writing workshops that pointed me in the right direction.

Furthermore, I had much help from a lot of the staff at Friesen Press who organized the book's development. And I would like to thank my friends and a host of wonderful people who guided me through my journey and if I've missed you my thanks to you as well.

And finally, I'd like to explain that any fault or inaccurate facts are solely my own and I take full responsibility bearing in mind the book is a work of fiction.

It was a great pleasure writing this book and I hope you enjoyed it! Reviews are very important to authors, so I would be grateful if you would leave a review wherever you purchased the book or if you bought the book at an in person event, please leave a review on Goodreads at:

https://www.goodreads.com/author/show/27863014.Peter_Thomas_Pontsa

Thank you,
Peter Thomas Pontsa

About the author

Outfoxed is Peter Thomas Pontsa's first book in the Inspector William Fox Series. He is a member of the Crime Writers of Canada and the Wordsmiths based out of Alliston, Ontario. An avid British sports car enthusiast, he has raced with Jagged Edge Motorsports, is a former president of the Headwaters British Car Club and a student of taekwondo with a second-degree blackbelt. A retired businessman, he lives in Loretto, Ontario, Canada, with his author wife Angela van Breemen, and their orange tabby, Mr. Tee.

***

You can connect with Peter on his website and social media:
https://peterthomaspontsa.com/
https://www.facebook.com/InspectorWilliamFoxAdventureSeries
https://www.instagram.com/peterthomaspontsa/
https://www.goodreads.com/author/show/27863014.Peter_Thomas_P
ontsa

SANCTITY OF FREEDOM

AN INSPECTOR WILLIAM FOX SERIES

PETER THOMAS PONTSA

Iconic Scribes Press Inc.

Excerpt from Sanctity of Freedom: The Note
May 2019

The ship's shadow shimmered against the sun-bleached skyline of the distant city. For once, Do Yun Cho had made the right choice. The price he would pay could very well be his life. He took a drag of the cigarette, exhaled and flicked the remainder over the stern. Little did he know it would be the last one he ever smoked.

He turned toward the approaching footsteps and stared into the face of trouble. After thirteen days at sea, the North Korean agent demanded his answer. "Are you coming back?"

"No, I made a promise never to go back."

"You, stupid man," he said. "You must return!" he yelled shaking with fury.

"Never!" said the other.

"This was your last warning," he shouted. He stomped and grabbed Cho's windbreaker. Cho struggled, pushing away from the aggressor.

"No," he repeated as the glint of polished steel, followed by searing pain, felled him to his knees. He grabbed at his gut, now perforated with multiple stab wounds. The blade's final slash severed the trachea. The killer threw the body over the aft rail, the splash imperceptible, lost in the turbulence that washed it away. The activity drew seagulls and cormorants soaring toward the void that disappeared as fast as it had appeared. The killer wiped the blade and his blood-splattered hands with his bandana, then replaced the knife back in its sheath. He released the bandana into the light wind and watched it flutter to the river. His eyes swept along the deck. It was empty. Relieved, he placed both hands on the aft rail and peered into the propeller wash. Reassured, he found his phone and cupped the device as a gust tousled his hair.

"Is it done?" asked the grit-laden voice.

"It was quick. He refused to obey," the killer uttered in harsh Korean.

He retreated from the stern and paced to the galley for his shift. His assignment, set by his superiors in North Korea, had been completed to the letter.

He had anticipated a small degree of remorse from the defector and made provisions to bring him back. This awkward execution was right on Canada's doorstep. He tried reasoning with the stubborn man to no avail. His orders were clear: bring him back or dispatch the traitor. The Reconnaissance General Bureau (RGB), North Korea's Intelligence Organization, had trained him to be an artful killer. He had performed his duty. There was nothing else he could have done.

The ship carrying Japanese manufactured electrical machinery would be delivered at De Port-de-Montréal this afternoon at Terminal Tremont Fifty-Two. He planned to disembark and meet an accomplice, be driven to the airport and flown out of Canada before the authorities pieced it together.

His mission and escape route were planned with little leeway for mistakes. There was a high probability of being apprehended if his associate missed their rendezvous. It was essential he cut and run to the safety of North Korea.

✳✳✳

The spring weather's ice melt cleared the St. Lawrence River. Freighters and cargo ships moved freely along the seaway. Much-needed materials arrived and resupplied the country, because of its explosive economy.

Blessed with a balmy day in May, William Fox and Tracy Jordon arrived at the marina for the pre-opening of boating season.

William took a weekend off. As an inspector at RCMP Montréal's C Division his busy schedule allowed little time for fun, so he was looking forward to some downtime with Tracy.

A few enthusiastic boaters primed for a glorious Sunday morning milled about the docks. The marina owner making his rounds waved to William who towered above the rest.

"Make sure you bring your vest," he said, nudging his friend beside him.

"Got it," said William holding up his life jacket gripped in his well-developed arm.

"Not that one, the bulletproof one," he replied as both men chuckled.

William extended his middle finger hiding it along his thigh.

"I saw that," said Tracy. "Just smile and wave back."

"He's an asshole," said William waggling his hand.

"I know. Just ignore him," Tracy said, tossing a microfiber cloth at William. "Let's get started."

Last year while on patrol, William and officer Philip White were ambushed, on the seaway. The gangsters shot up and damaged his cruiser the *Midnight Fox*. A near death experience William would like to forget.

Tracy stood mid-height with blonde hair and steel-blue eyes and resembled Scarlett Johansson. An outspoken and strong-willed woman, she had led an expedition for Chinese artifacts. She reunited with William after he rescued her from Triad kidnappers intent on stealing the treasure. Like today, she often kept him in line when he got antsy.

William wore torn jeans and a beat-up sweatshirt with McGill embossed on the front. Tracy dressed in dingy leggings and a perforated t-shirt. They spent the better part of the morning cleaning the vessel for a shakedown run. The marina had dry-docked the boat for the winter and now it required attention.

William's brown eyes swept across the sleek sharp bow. His soft circular pressure with Carnauba wax made its surface glisten. A lax river breeze tussled Tracy's blonde hair. She rubbed her microfiber cloth over the *Midnight Fox's* hand painted cursive. Overlaid beside it a red stripe split the length of the stealthy hull. William strode ten paces to the stern and removed the engine cover. He checked the fluids and assessed the boat's running gear.

In preseason, an opportunity opened for boaters to carry out early safety maintenance. William, an experienced skipper, expected to be on the water sooner by taking precautions. Most issues could be remedied during pre-inspection and a shakedown run.

William started the twin Mercury Engines and released the bow while Tracy freed the aft lines. They leaped into the cockpit as the boat drifted away. William slid the throttles forward and the cruiser's bow lifted. He guided the boat out of the marina, headed into the channel and coxswained toward the Jacque Cartier bridge. Tracy shook her head in the gust, and it tangled her lustrous locks. She smiled face-first into the breeze, enjoying the cool crispness of freedom. William braced himself as he shoved the twin levers forward in the gate.

"Let's see what this baby can do," said William, grinning.

William freewheeled across the channel, checking his gauges while listening to the sterndrive for issues. The police scanner crackled. Frowning, he reduced the engine speed and slowed to a crawl, listening to the dispatch. The Longueuil Agglomeration Police Services

(SPAL) was attending a homicide scene at Parc de l'Ile Charron near Terrasse-Charbonneau. The Coast Guard was on location along with the investigating officers. A body had been discovered on the municipal beach on Charron Island and the media was already on scene. Grasping the severity of the situation curiosity got the best of him.

"Tracy, we're not far. I'd like to check it out."

"Oh, my God. When are you going to stop? This was supposed to be our day together!"

"Just for a few minutes, Tracy. I need to see what's going on. They may need my help."

"All right. But we have to get back, and soon," she said, rolling her eyes.

William knew the better idea was to forget the call rather than get entangled. But a dead body on a public beach concerned all police departments. His curiosity already had annoyed Tracy, and it might get worse the more he immersed himself.

His main concern dealt with national security. If the deceased had an international connection, part of his mandate, set down by the Ministry of Public Safety, and the Federal Police Commissioner, included connecting homicides with terrorist activities.

He arrived at the scene only to be waved off. William extended his badge, and the officer gestured him back to the dock. Two uniformed police officers helped secure his cruiser.

"Bonjour gentlemen. I'm Inspector William Fox."

"Bonjour Inspector. What brings you here?" said the officer.

"Just professional interest. Perhaps the RCMP can help."

"We have a homicide investigator on the scene," said the officer pointing toward the orange security tape.

"Tracy, wait here. I'll be back in a minute."

Tracy slapped the vinyl seat, scowling. Her date with William had taken a turn for the worse. She nearly exploded in fury, bouncing in the seat.

William walked past the large mobile command center; a high-tech vehicle capable of data processing. He lifted the perimeter tape, glanced over at the still body under the protective canopy. William saw an officer near the crime scene, appearing to be the person in charge, and waved at him to get his attention.

Montréal Gazette journalists rushed the orange tape in anticipation of a statement from the new arrival while constables held them off.

The investigator rubbed his forehead and stepped forward in comfortable rubber-soled boots. A snug, grayish windbreaker hugged his solid frame, along with his slim fit charcoal chinos, his grizzled hair and his beard neatly trimmed. He turned to William, holding a clipboard and wearing blue micro flex gloves. A pen in his left hand publicized his south paw, a liability to unsuspecting challengers. William approached and exposed his belt badge to him.

"Bonjour, je suis l'inspecteur Fox."

"Ton français est rouillé. Peut-être que l'anglais sera meilleur. I'm Detective Guy Allard by the way," he said, launching an automated smile.

"Pleased to meet you," said William.

"Inspector Fox, your French ... a bit rusty, yes? Perhaps you'd prefer English?"

"English would be preferred. May I speak with you about this homicide?"

Guy handed over the pen and said, "Sign in."

William's eyes darted along the sheet as he signed.

"How may I help the Inspector?"

"I'd like to take a look at the body."

Investigator Allard looked up from his sign-in sheet, wrinkling his brow.

William caught the annoyance and realized Guy Allard was formidable. As tough cops went, he resembled a pillar of hardened flint. The kind of guy who went by the book and dished it out as good as he got. The sort of professional William respected.

"Why?" asked Guy.

"This is not protocol, but the victim may be of interest to my department. I'd like to take a few photographs," said William. "We'll run them through our system."

Guy removed his shades, gave William a cold disapproving glare, and slapped his clipboard on his thigh.

"Okay, your database may be useful."

The coroner paused and waved over the gurney that would transport the body to the pathology lab.

"Pardon, Monsieur. I am with the RCMP. Detective Allard gave me permission for a peek," said William.

Guy said to the coroner, "It's okay. He can take a look."

The coroner unzipped the bag. William took a facial photograph first. The slash through the neck was grave. William noticed scrapes and bruises indicative of a desperate struggle.

William retrieved his cell and located his Mobile Biometric Check, a digital fingerprinting application. He asked the coroner to rotate the arm and focused the camera lens at the digits of the sodden hand, then repeated the process with the other hand. Satisfied with the image results he hoisted himself up and stood beside Detective Allard and shook his head.

"His prints are not in the system."

"He may be a foreign national," said Guy. "It's amazing how fast the Biometric system check works. Far cry from the old days."

"True."

Guy brought the clipboard to his chest.

"We discovered a temporary Canadian passport. His name was Do Yun Cho." Guy held up an evidence bag containing a white official document. "As well as this," Allard added. He held up another baggie with waterlogged note paper.

The address was bleeding but readable. William's eyes twitched and his stomach lurched as he recognized the location.

"Thank you ... Detective Allard."

"Are you feeling well, sir?"

William did his utmost to compose himself and said, "Yeah, I'm okay. Who found the body?"

"Over there. The young boy."

William heaved a sigh, turned, and ambled over to the boy who appeared to be in his mid-teens. A police officer was consoling the young man as William approached.

"Excuse me, officer, may I speak to the witness?" said William.

The officer moved away as William smiled at the young man. The boy's face was ashen, and his eyes blinked frequently. William registered the signs of shock, something he saw all too frequently.

"Hello, my name is William. I'm an RCMP inspector. I heard you're the one who found the body?"

"Yes. I ... I found it," he replied.

"The policeman told me you are Anthony Fabergé," said William.

"Yes," said Anthony.

"Can you tell me what you saw?"

"I was fishing, and I hooked a massive fish. I pulled it over to the shore. Except it wasn't a fish," his adam's apple bobbed up and down. "The man didn't move, and I wasn't sure what to do," said Anthony. "So, I ran over to the bait shop."

"And he's the one who called the police?" asked William.

"Yes, the guy at the bait shop did."

Tracy slipped out of the boat and made her way over to them.

"Hi, I'm Tracy,"

"This is Anthony, our witness," said William.

"How are you feeling?" said Tracy.

"I never saw a dead body before," he said.

"You have been brave. Is someone coming to get you?"

"Yeah, my parents will be here soon. We live nearby." He swallowed, "They say we have to go to the station first for a statement. My mom and dad have to come with me."

"They will have someone there for you to talk to," said William.

"Why would someone kill him?" said Anthony, his nostrils flaring.

"That's an interesting question. I don't know the answer. But Detective Allard will find out. Here, take my card. Call me if you remember anything," said William.

"He's too traumatized right now," said Tracy, whispering in his ear. William placed his hand on her shoulder.

"Can I go for a ride in your boat someday?" said Anthony. "I saw you come to shore in it."

William smiled and took a sideways glance at his cruiser.

"Why not? But get your parent's permission. Okay?"

"Okay," said Anthony.

William's chest tightened as he exhaled. Stepping onto the cigarette boat, a sense of dread lingered. He sensed the address on the note was about to change his life.

Tracy and William waved goodbye to Anthony and powered up the boat. Traveling back to the marina, it was a Sunday that neither had envisioned.

On Monday, he planned to liaison with the Canadian Security Intelligence Service (CSIS) in case they could provide further intelligence data. Their vast database updated information every second. Alongside his department's resources, the combination would furnish leads necessary to help the police in Longueuil.

William's response to the note's washed-out address upset his stomach. He chewed a couple of antacids to relieve the distress. The familiar address belonged to Mr. Kim's Taekwondo Dojang. If the dead man was a student, William had never seen him. Had he studied taekwondo in South Korea? If so, Mr. Kim had never introduced him. Could it be someone from Mr. Kim's past? A policeman or a military man? Did he come for help or for some other nefarious reason?

Just who was Do Yun Cho? And, would this homicide case test his friendship with his mentor, Mr. Kim?

Many questions and dubious explanations led to nothing. Perplexed, his mind was automatically engaging in this exercise of deduction before the issues became difficulties. In normal circumstances the sequence would follow a logical progression of thought. Not now, not today. He knew it was already too late the moment he realized whose address was smeared across the note.

"Tracy. I apologize for today," said William.

"I know. You just can't help yourself. That's why I love you," said Tracy. "But I was still disappointed."

"At least we know the cruiser is seaworthy," said William raising his voice against the wind speed.

"Yeah, I guess that's one thing." Tracy brushed back her hair while William slipped the boat around. "I'll make dinner and you're washing dishes," she said in a coquettish manner.

William made an evasive expression, his eyes rolling and wandering away. He had to see Mr. Kim about that note.

***

Sanctity of Freedom will be available on March 18th, 2025.
https://www.amazon.ca/Sanctity-Freedom-Inspector-William-Fox-eboo
k/dp/B0DPJM3D1D